MW00781659

Damsel with a Dulcimer

K.R. Feather

Book Two of the Friends of Dragons Trilogy

To Dempsey Rae
March 12, 1939 - October 13, 2020
&
To Michelle Jahn
October 9, 1962 - May 13, 2021

Till I see you both again, this one's for you.

A Special Thank You to…

Lauren King
You have been my biggest supporter,
and remind me everyday the value of literature.

Prelude

Ethan

I didn't mean to get into this life. To be honest, I hadn't planned on having a life for very long.

I just wanted to live until those I cared for found fulfilment, and then I would be done.

Why did she have to come back into my life? And why did she have to bring a whole new world with her?

I had watched her from afar during our childhood, then Adam met her in the forest when we were fifteen and confessed some outrageous obsession he thought was love, so I taught myself to give up any thoughts of her. But when Erika dropped the ring in Adam's hands three years ago, I felt the pull again.

I had always felt like Erika was gravity, pulling me back into existence.

Staying far away from her was an effective way to avoid that hold and continue to exist in my world washed in death, aggression, and well painted-over depression.

Then I watched her kill a man and give my best friend a piece of jewellery, and before I knew it, her force had pulled me under, drowning me in a lifestyle and world that challenged everything I believed in.

God, how I fucking loved a challenge.

And when she died, I found my religion again. Not because I needed to pray that she got to heaven - if anyone was going to heaven it was going to be her: the girl who believed in and feared a higher power, and sacrificed herself for the entirety of two worlds.

No, I found my religion again because I wanted to battle God. I wanted to fight to the death and prove that I could display more wrath.

But God won. He defused me by sending her back, thus answering my prayer. All the anger and rage drained from my body. She may not have been tangible to me, but it didn't matter, she was back in my universe even if I wasn't allowed to be in her orbit.

Nonetheless, I shamefully admit I made other prayers after that. God answered them too.

So, to you, *my friend*, I am so sorry for what I've asked.

Prologue

Erika

"Can death be sleep, when life is but a dream,
And scenes of bliss pass as a phantom by?
The transient pleasures as a vision seem,
And yet we think the greatest pain's to die.

"How strange it is that man on earth should roam,
And lead a life of woe, but not forsake
His rugged path; nor dare he view alone
His future doom which is but to awake."
- John Keats "On Death"

Life is the acknowledgement of Death. One does not start living until they live like they know they are dying. Even immortals can die, if they stop pursuing life as if they will not see the next day. Joy, forgiveness and peace are only found in those who know that one day Death will find them, and they will only be allowed to leave regret or happiness in their departure.

3

In my dying, I pray I leave love in my wake.

Adam

"Nature's first green is gold,
Her hardest hue to hold.
Her early leaf's a flower;
But only so an hour.
Then leaf subsides to leaf.
So Eden sank to grief,
So dawn goes down to day.
Nothing gold can stay."
-     Robert Frost "Nothing Gold Can Stay"

I have found my joy and purpose in life. The gaping plot hole in my mind was filled, sown together when I found a world no human was meant to know existed. There's magick in this world; haunted rings, spiritual waters, and blesséd creatures with jagged jade stones set into flames for eyes. I've watched green go to gold, burning flames hotter than magma. I've laid with the jade and the flames and found that both feel like heaven.

Now I am ready for eternity, wherever that may be.

Ethan

"Ere the birth of my life, if I wished it or no

No question was asked me--it could not be so!
If the life was the question, a thing sent to try
And to live on be YES; what can NO be? to die."

NATURE'S ANSWER
"Is't returned, as 'twas sent? Is't no worse for the wear?
Think first, what you ARE! Call to mind what you
WERE!
I gave you innocence, I gave you hope,
Gave health, and genius, and an ample scope,
Return you me guilt, lethargy, despair?
Make out the invent'ry; inspect, compare!
Then die—if die you dare!"
- S.T. Coleridge "Suicide's Arguement"

There's not a person in my life I haven't lost. My brother and father are dead, my mother disappeared into a bottle and never came back, my friends have left me behind to pursue their own love, and the one I thought could understand me, seems hellbent on sacrificing herself for anyone but me. So why should I not flirt with Death? Slipping away alone, to dance with the shadow of the only being I still have an intimate relationship with seems fitting when everyone else has slipped from me to do the same.

But now I've tasted the love from her eyes, I've licked the spare drops of devotion from her spirit and I know, I have sampled the flavour of the Tree of Life.

1

Adam

"An appearance changing spell? Are you even sure that's going to work?" I asked, one hundred percent *not* convinced.

Erika turned back from the spell circle she was currently kneeling in, stark naked. We were in Darbie's basement so early in the morning that the sun hadn't even come up. Not that we would be able to see the sun anyway. Darbie's plants had grown up and over the small slits that the basement had for windows.

"It's just like the spell that Darbie uses to cover up his blueness and make him look more human," she explained, then leaned back over to finish lighting her candles.

I took in the bright white sight before me. "First off," I started. "Nice butt. Second, Darbie is a two thousand year old sorcerer who makes a living off of creating spells, potions, curses, incantations and whatever else there is. You are an unpracticed druid who beats up magick-using criminals who are outside their parole. On top of that, Darbs's spell is not foolproof, sometimes if he sneezes you get a flash of blue. It's actually really funny to watch when he walks past the flowers in the supermarket."

I recalled a few weeks ago when I was accompanying the blue elder elf to the store. I hadn't known he was allergic to daisies and shoved them right in his face. Old man Oreland had to be escorted out of the store as he went raving about the blue man with the potatoes.

He's back at the treatment centre for his PTSD, now.

I still feel bad.

"Adam!" My eyes wandered back down to the pale Erika who was snapping her fingers at me, "I need the Powder of a Thousand Chameleons please."

I looked down at the jar of powder in my hands. It was constantly cycling through various colours and appearances. Currently it was a faint purple and its consistency resembled something like the pollen out of a flower.

I leaned down and handed it to her. She popped the mason lid off and poured a minor layer into her brass bowl before resealing it. She twisted back to hand it to me again.

"Thank you, Love." She gave me a rather unconvincing cheeky grin.

"We need to work on your smile," I teased.

She gasped. "I thought you like it when I smile? You always tell me I look cute and innocent."

I shook my head. "When you're not trying. Right now you look like you just killed my cat and don't want to be blamed for it."

"You don't have a cat."

"I know, I was just making a comparison."

"Do you want a cat?"

I furrowed my brows, "Not really, I have you."

She rolled her eyes and went back to her task at hand. "I'm just saying," she continued nonetheless. "You know, your parents know you're dating me, err, well, a fake name and backstory version of me. They know we're going to be moving in together. We're really moving on with our lives and becoming a normal couple."

"If normal people pretend to be students studying history, while they're actually hunting old magick artefacts and creatures with their professor, who is actually their friend who's over a thousand years old and a blue elf? Then sure, yeah, normal couple," I agreed, sarcastically.

"I'm just saying it's normal for a new couple who moves in together and who have been dating for a couple years to get a pet together," she finished her thought, completely disregarding my side thoughts on the matter.

I shook my head, "Why do I need a pet when I have all of your little dragon spawnlings to look after?"

She looked back at me and shrugged, "The spawnlings are a part of the orphanage. They're like our job, not our pets," she leaned to her left, flipping open an ancient spellbook. "A cat would be for our enjoyment."

I huffed, "Are you a cat person?"

"I'm an animal person. And I'm just saying the house has a lot of land so we can start raising animals."

"We're not getting a cat."

Erika raised her hands as I finished. At the same time the stairs leading down into the basement creaked. I leaned over and down to look up at the doorway. A leather clad Ethan was descending. A rather large bowl balanced in his rough hands, a spoon no doubt designed to serve with instead of feed from was nestled between his fingers.

"What's this I hear about cats?" He asked as he took the steps in stride. He pointed the milk dripping spoon at Erika, "And why is the dragon lady naked?"

"Chameleon Spell," Erika and I said in unison.

"My parents are having a big dinner in her honour tonight so she's finally being forced to meet them," I explained further.

Ethan nodded, crunching loudly on a new load of cereal he had shoved into his mouth. "Using a classic appearance altering spell? Nice." He smiled and milk dripped down his chin, pulling some half chewed bits of oats with it.

I rolled my eyes.

"A professor at the college is publishing her essay in a famous history magazine," I went on. "Everyone is demanding that they meet the student brilliant enough to present a new theory on why humans believed in more than one god."

"Kind of hard to have a picture to go with the article if the student who wrote it is only an online scholar," Ethan vocalised. "I'm surprised she went back to school to begin with. Considering she knows literally everything there is to know about anything. I mean she actually lived it."

I leaned in to try and whisper to him. "I think she likes making the Professors sound like uneducated idiots."

"You know I can still hear you right?" she called over her shoulder.

"Shh," I waved her off. "Go back to your spells and thinking about cats."

I looked Ethan over. He was dressed in cargo pants and light-weight combat boots. On top of that, under his nice leather jacket was just a standard t-shirt, one that - if I were him - I'd be okay getting covered in blood.

"You on mercenary work today?" I inquired.

He shook his head. "No, just got back from one yesterday. Had to bring a Greek god the head of some Greek vampire thing. Sucks on the blood of living creatures to stay alive, but on the magick of magick users to stay looking pretty. I killed the head of the party like the god wanted, but the coven is still roaming," he nodded in Erika's direction. "Better keep her close, with how much magick she has, whatever it is will probably be looking like *America's Next Top Model* model if it gets ahold of E."

"Pretty sure she can handle herself, but thanks for the heads up."

Another set of pounds on the wooden stairs made both Ethan and I look this time. We watched as Jack came down, a very lively spring in his step like there was most mornings.

"Good morning lords, lads and ladies, I thought I heard voices down here." He slipped in next to Ethan. "Why is Erika naked on the floor?"

"Chameleon Spell," Ethan joined Erika's and my chorus now.

"Ohhh, for the dinner party?" Jack asked.

I nodded in approval.

"Ahh," Jack sounded. "Are we all invited to that or are your parents being picky again?"

I laughed. "They're always picky. But please come. There's going to be more food than we know what to do with, and enough awkward space for the entire town to fit in."

"Do you want me to bring my new banjo thing I got?" Ethan piped, nearly blowing out every last bit of oats and milk from his mouth onto my face.

I wiped my cheek with my fingers, "Banjo thing?"

He nodded violently. "It's like a super narrow, figure eight shaped banjo-like thing. I have no idea how to play it, but it's old and cool."

"Figure eight banjo thing?" I echoed, looking to Jack.

He shrugged and raised his hands in surrender. He backed away from the man in black, who had now diverged onto a rambling path about how he came into possession of his figure eight banjo thing. While Ethan rambled on, half with cereal in his mouth, half with air, Jack wandered around the spell casting circle, inspecting the process by which Erika was conducting the spell.

After we all had become acquainted, Darbie had taken Jack under his wing and begun to train him, so he was no stranger to whether or not Erika was doing the spell right. Jack, while human, had taken a very quick understanding to spell casting, but excelled in alchemy in a way that nearly rivalled the elder, blue sorcerer. I always thought it stemmed from Jack's irritatingly well rounded knowledge of chemistry.

The door to the basement bursted open.

"Howdy ya'll!" Darbie was called before any of us had even turned around. "How are we all doing today?"

He was slid up into the grey space between Ethan and Jack. He took a glance at Erika, then right back to us, completely unfazed.

Ethan quirked an eyebrow. "You don't find E being naked in the middle of your basement weird?"

He shrugged, "Eh, I've seen it a thousand times."

Ethan looked at me, eyes wide and eyebrows high.

"If you weren't into men I would be sincerely concerned that you're trying to move in on my girlfriend," I confessed.

"With all due respect, young apprentice, I have known your lover for a thousand years. She lived with me for nearly one hundred during which I conducted several experiments on her," Darbie explained. "I think I still have one of her cut off breasts in a jar somewhere. Luckily for you we were able to get it to grow back, huh?"

Ethan's eyes widened even more. His lips rose on his face and curled in against his teeth at the same time in an obvious grimace. He suddenly was not holding his breakfast close to him like it was a precious child, but rather holding it down and away from him as if it was rather a child who had just taken a foul bathroom break in its nappy.

"And on that note…" he said, still mid grimace, and shoved his bowl into Darbie's hands. He spun on his heels, eyes still wide but mouth slowly beginning to settle as he put distance between the awkward tension and him.

"Come on, Ethan!" Darbie called, as the leather wearing man reached the first step up to the house. "Severed breasts can be harvested and used for several fertility or love potions."

"That's Nice!" Ethan called back, but his voice was muffled as he ascended up past where the basement ceiling blocked the view of the stairs.

Darbie turned and looked to me, "Really, the milk duds are excellent for -"

"I really don't need to know, Darbs," I shook my head violently.

"But it's so interesting," Darbie lit up and I sucked in a breath, "You see, you just have to first distinguish the fatty tissue that lays over the blood vessels, then -"

"Shush!!" Erika was, once again, my saving grace as she yelled for silence. "I have prepared it. Now I must cast the incantation."

"What language are you using?" Jack asked.

"English," she answered. "Besides gaelic, it's the only language I won't botch. Even gaelic I'm out of practice with.

Better to play it safe and say it in a language that I won't mess up."

Darbie laughed, "Yes, let's not have any mistakes like last time."

I didn't want to know what happened last time.

Erika took a deep breath. "What I look like now, let me look it not. What I am now, let me be it not. Take me as I am, and make me something new. My hair a little lighter, my eyes a brighter hue. This figure does not fit me, so make it slimmer too. I call upon Lord Ogmios, god of eloquence; my face - to make - be his. I call upon god Cernunnos, the keeper of wild things that live; my strength - to build - I give. And to my lovely lady Brigid, the queens three who heal, mend my skin to your liking, each feature at your will."

"'Queens three?'" I questioned, looking to Darbie.

"She's called the triple goddess of healing," he explained. "She has three different aspects of herself that incorporate different things."

I nodded, mostly just pretending to grasp the content, but also partially understanding the general idea of the thing.

The main conclusion I always continued to come to was that the knowledge that came with this life was complicated. It was a massive puzzle of constant new discoveries and information that needed to be sorted and sifted through in order to be understood.

And I loved it.

I looked at Erika. She was curling over wrenching her guts out. Her skin was bubbling, her hair twisting as if it were burning and shrivelling off. I watched as her spine slithered up against her skin. It moved upwards, stretching her torso so it was longer, just enough so that her skin could tighten over her, pulling in her waist a few centimetres. Her skin was boiling and pulling

13

itself inwards, smalling her out. The strength I could normally blatantly see in her shoulders dwindling down to smooth marble. The lovely pink of her porcelain skin faded to chilly pearl granite. The deep chocolate curls of her hair fell to less than curved tumbles of red.

I was both mesmerised and not impressed. The look was fair and beautiful, in a very soft and light look, but the shield-maiden I knew now laid before me as a princess to be rescued from a tower.

When she turned to look up at us I nearly cursed the gods. The forest floor in her eyes? Algae now, as if a swamp had invaded my lovely woods and washed out the beauty of the trees.

"Well?" She asked. "How do I look?"

"Different," I didn't hesitate. "Your lips are the same, but your nose is a bit shorter and upturned. You're fairer. Your hair's a damn fiery sheet on your head, and the spells gone and cursed your eyes to be a ugly beautiful shade of green."

She nodded. "I take it you don't like it."

"I'd rather get a damn cat."

Darbie laughed beside me. "Hey, the good thing is it's not permanent. It only lasts until she casts the spell to remove it."

"Yeah, but this look is going to come back isn't it?" I was disgruntled.

"Anytime I say the spell, now that I've done the casting and taken on the form, I can resummon it," Erika explained. "Just have to keep from getting ill while casting the spell."

"Why does that matter?" I asked.

"The spell is connected to Erika's lifeforce," Jack jumped in. "Therefore, it's in direct relationship with her immune system. If she suddenly feels sick, gets the flu, food poisoning or even something as common as a common cold, it'll start taking a lot

14

of focus to divert the energy from fighting her sickness to holding the spell."

"Got it, white blood cells make my girlfriend look different. Makes sense."

Jack shrugged, "I guess that's sort of a connection that could be made, but not exactly it."

"It's more attached to her will and energy force," Darbie explained simply.

"It doesn't matter *how* it works," Erika interrupted. "All that matters is *that* it works. Now I can go out, and be with you guys without worrying about anyone freaking out when they see me. Most importantly, it means I can meet with my professor today and go to Adam's parent's celebration."

"Well then," I shook off my frustration. "I guess I should go get your clothes."

Erika

I hadn't been in a classroom for close to two years. But I had been in classrooms, academies, colleges, and any other type of teaching institution in existence since around four hundred B.C.E.

I was *old*.

Teaching was just as ancient as I was. Though when I was young, being taught was mostly a gift for the higher class or those gifted with abilities that warranted them to have more attention given to them.

I was only one of those categories, my sister, though… my sister was both. A daughter of an ex-dragonrider and a

15

councilman of a king. She was a high-born with a gentle hand and a natural talent to paint, *and* draw, *and* sing, *and* dance, *and* speak. She was a true lady.

I stared down at my hands, thickly covered in charcoal. My self-portrait looked more like an advertisement for a new horror film.

"Art used to be for bards," I whispered to myself.

"Well bards aren't around anymore." I whipped around to my art teacher scowling down through his thick but narrow glasses. "And you need an art elective to graduate, so start trying or I'll fail you."

His hunched over stature took short strides away from me. His tan moccasin shoes picked up more dust than the janitor's broom.

I shook my head, I liked this class better online.

"Young people are so rude these days," I said under my breath, trying to think of the fraction that my professor's life was to mine.

I looked at the girl sitting in front of me. Her black coarse hair was drawn away from her face in a braid. Exposing her long, dark neck that was craned to look back at me in confusion.

"What?" I asked.

"You're like a quarter his age."

I let out a huff, but made no comment.

I ripped out my grey stained sheet.

Start fresh, Erika. Gentle hands, Erika. Art is not like swordplay, I don't care what your father says. I could hear my mom's voice in my head.

She was always trying to make a lady out of me, as if she wasn't, at one point, a knight, clad in beaten and bloodied armour. Even having her own ice dragon to ride into battle on. If anyone should have encouraged sword play over art it should have been her.

I remembered the painting hidden away in her chest. After my family had died, I had gone through their things, deciding what to take with me to the wars. I had found a painting that had been done for my mother years before I was born. Painted after a battle by some nameless bard. My mother had stood covered in blood, blade dripping in it. The most intricately engraved iron on her chest and thighs, with hardened leather linking the places in between. Her helmet had gone as was her dragon considering she was on the ground, sword limply angled down. The dead and fire surrounded her, giant eagles flew in the sky instead of dragons. This would have been the battle when they all fled, on the verge of extinction, because they chose to fight instead of sit idly by.

Before I knew it, my fingers had sketched a sad excuse for a replica of my mother on her battlefield.

My art professor was slowly dragging himself towards me. My eyes looked up to catch the time. Six minutes left on the clock. While the old man moved slowly, I doubted class would be let out before he reached me. I could, technically, just leave, but I hated failing.

"Well come on child," he motioned with his hand, rotating it inwards summoning my work. "Let's have a look."

I sucked in my breath. "Well, you told me to start trying." I turned it around.

He pulled down his glasses and moved closer. He nodded in approval.

"Hmm," he pushed the glasses back up, "Perhaps sitting portraits are not your niche. This active one is not horrible, we can work with this."

The time.

Three minutes.

"Tell me," He inquired, "Where did you learn this technique, I have not taught it yet?"

My shoulders relaxed, I need not lie now. "My sister was an amazing artist, my mum pushed me to try to be like her."

"I see, well your mother is a smart woman. We can all use a bit of the arts in our studies."

I laughed bitterly. "My entire family is dead. Lot of good studying art did them."

He looked down, this time removing his glasses completely. For the first time, I truly saw how old he was. His life light at the very end of its wick. Blue eyes so light they reflected all the rays around it. They were deeply sunk into his face, one that was delicately marked with brown patches of skin. His skin looked like a bed spread well slept in, wrinkled and folded on itself. His hands shook when he used them.

"I didn't know," he said, and I could hear the graveness in his voice. "I am sorry my dear."

I reached for his hand, grasping it in mind. I had lived far too long to start insulting the elderly now. I understood what it was like to outlive all your loved ones, and so did they.

"Sir." I held his hand as tightly as I could without fearing I would break it. "Honestly, it doesn't hurt anymore. And I should be the one apologising for rudely announcing that."

"Professor," a middle-aged and less witted man called from the front door. "Some of us have other classes so we gotta head out."

I took my chance, I let my hands slip from the old man's and snatched up my belongings. I rushed out with my art pad still folded over to the drawing of my mother. The charcoal stick was no doubt staining my shirt, and my backpack revealing all within to those around and I rushed out into the hall.

18

Over two thousand years and I still couldn't take people saying "sorry for your loss."

Over two thousand years and I still missed my family.

Immortality is death, and loss is the coffin you lay in.

Adam

My first class was in ancient medicines. We had been on blood letting for the last week and I was contemplating bloodletting myself to death if we didn't move on from such a well known topic.

I had come from dropping Erika off at art class, and she looked like she was about to bloodlet herself too. It brought me some comfort knowing I wasn't the only one between the two of us desperate to move onto our next course.

I moved towards the backend of the middle of the room. Raising my bag over my shoulder, I slipped it off in order to set it down on a desk along the wall. This was the perfect spot to be lost amongst the other students, completely unrecognised in the professor's attention.

I cracked open my grimoire. It was filled with various poisonous plants and possible mixtures that could be brewed together to cause different types of harm. I was currently working on paralysis that could be delayed by a few hours. In case we had to poison someone in a public affair and wait until later in the evening to collect them.

"That's a very detailed personal grimoire."

I slammed it closed. I looked up to purple eyes and lots of leather.

"Umm, oh, yeah…" I fumbled. I was panicking a lot less once I realised she was a classic goth girl in black with bright coloured contact lenses. Most of the ones I had met typically had grimoires of their own. Theirs', of course, were useless. Nonetheless, I felt exposed over the fact that she had seen it.

She reached into her worn satchel. The bag looked ancient, like something that an old farmer boy would have from the early 1900's. It was worn leather, designed in a retro style with two belt straps to secure the bag closed.

She pulled out a leather-bound book. The pages were thick, like cloth, I could tell before she opened it. A massive moonstone was weaved into the centre of the cover with several small plates of silver above and below it. The metal and stone came together to depict the phases of the moon as they shifted from new moon to new moon.

She displayed it in both hands for me. "I won't tell anyone about yours, if you don't tell anyone about mine."

She gave me a smile from her peach brown lips, and I made a note of how she was pretty in a golden way.

2
Erika

After taking the time to collect myself and my belongings, I headed off to find Adam. We had a brief break together before we each had to head off in different directions again. It wouldn't be until after our next class that we would see each other again in Darbie's course.

Adam would be in his ancient medicines and remedies class if I remember correctly. I manoeuvred through the halls of the school of art towards the exit that led to the courtyard.

Our university was small, each school had their own individual building that consisted of no more than maybe a dozen or so classrooms. The only exception to that rule being the school of sciences, which held every science class possible from physics to psychology to biology to other natural and earth sciences. That building was three stories tall and the size of half a football field in terms of length and width. It held all our lab rooms and plenty of storage facilities for various plants, rocks, studiable bacteria and a few rodents that were no doubt bound to glow in the dark if they lived passed some of the experiments that the weirder classes performed.

I took my leave from the art school.

Even though we had very few art majors themselves, the art school was not the smallest of the schools here. This was due to the fact that our art school also sponsored writers and photographers as well as those who paint, draw or otherwise something else artistic.

Instead the smallest of schools was held by the school of law, with the school of business close second.

The schools moved out in order of smallest to largest from the offices of the university. School of business to the right of the office, beginning the first turn in a seven sided shape staring inward to the 2 story library that oddly mirrored eight sides instead of seven. Next the school of law, then the school of art making another turn of face into the significantly larger school of history. It nearly touched the School of Science as the school of science was big enough to extend well past the back of the school of history and reach all the way to the octagonal building of the food court which then folded back towards the office, completing the encampment of the campus.

I made my way between the parallel walls of the library and the school of history, up towards the stairs leading to the school of science. The stairs were a story tall and part of the school of history had to be built into them.

There was a rumour that the school of science had a basement where mad scientists had conducted experiments trying to create super soldiers during the World Wars. I had lived long enough to know that the only old secret the building held was that there *was* in fact a basement, but that it was only the living quarters for old catholic monks who would come to the college to study and meditate. On the rare occasion an exorcism may have taken place, but that would have been early on in the school's founding near the late 1880s.

The only thing strange or supernatural about St. Ailbe's University was the history of the saint it was named after, and the fact that it had a dragon and a sorcerer in its attendance.

I climbed the steps to where it flattened out into a small study patio. There were a few tables with umbrellas held into place in the centre of them. I found an empty one as students poured out and headed to their next course. I didn't sit, I didn't have time, so I leaned on one of the fixed benches and waited for Adam. When he finally exited the building, he was with a sun-kissed golden girl. Her hair was as black as ink, but as glossy as polished volcanic glass.

She was gorgeous. If it weren't for her beady purple eyes.

Well, that was a lie.

They were also gorgeous, and not beady at all. In fact they were rather like sparking balls of amethyst in her head.

It was the fact that I knew what they meant. If I cut her, she would bleed blue. Ichor, the blood of the gods, was in her veins. Had she been born mortal, she likely would have had brown eyes.

I stood watching them.

Adam saw me and walked over, bringing the god-bastard with him. She smiled at me, indicating she was either very smart or very dumb. Smart if she knew what I was and chose to be friendly, dumb if she had no clue.

"Hey," Adam chirped as he leaned down to kiss my cheek. "This is Reika," he introduced, and the purple eyes smiled into mine.

I stared back with intensity.

"Does she know?" I was staring at her, though the question was pointed. If Adam answered that she didn't then she was dumb and I pitied her. If she answered then she was smart, but a possible enemy.

Adam shook his head. "I didn't say any-"

"Don't answer her," Reika said. "You don't understand her question."

Adam stood there, looking back and forth between us. "Yeah... apparently not. Did I miss something?"

Reika looked me up and down. "This is the one you said I have a class with next?"

Adam nodded. "Yeah, this is my girlfriend..." He paused at my name.

"People are calling me Michelle when I'm in this form. But my real name is Erika," I said, opting not to lie to her. She could probably sense the appearance changing spell.

"You're of incredibly old magick, I've never sensed anything like it," she mumbled and extended her hand. "I'm Reika Lupin, a priestess of Artemis. My goddess has sensed an evil soon to erupt here and has sent me to investigate what it could possibly be."

"The gods and other immortals are not permitted to meddle in mortal affairs anymore," I deadpanned. "So unless this evil is magick or-"

"The evil my Lady saw was of immortal stature," she stated.

I nodded.

If she was here to help fight evil, then we would be smart to be her ally and not her enemy. Besides, Artemis was always one of the better gods. She was extreme, but at least she sought to protect the innocent for the most part.

"We should get to class," I said and looked to Adam, hoping to communicate with my eyes that I promised not to kill her. "We don't want to be late."

Adam smiled, stooped down for one more kiss, then headed off.

I nodded back to the school of science building. "If you're in the Carbon Based Dating class it's going to be back in this building."

She offered me another polite smile. "I'm pretending to pursue a degree in ancient civilizations in order to attend here and investigate my Lady's visions."

"Then you had Darbie as a professor?" I asked as we started wandering off in our heading.

"Yes, Adam was telling me that all three of us will be in that class together after my next course in ancient architecture."

"Darbie teaches the class on ancient myths and beliefs,' I explained. "He's like us, he has magick, so you can trust him and hide out in his office if you ever need to."

Keep your enemies where you can see them Erika, my father had told me when I was first learning to sword fight. *If your enemy is out of your sight, then you cannot see what they are preparing in regards to you. If they stay in your sights, you can see the directions that they plan to move in.*

I doubted this green, purple girl was our enemy, but best to keep her where we could see what she wanted, rather than let her find counsel in someone or something that wasn't on our side.

"Thank you. Your offer of refuge is admirable and appreciated," she said. "But I can handle myself just fine."

I laughed. "I used to say the same thing. I found it to be quite… tiring."

We walked down the near empty halls of the science building. We only had a few minutes to reach our lab room, but it was only just around the corner.

"To fight all alone takes a lot of energy," I explained. "Fighting beside even one person means you expel half the energy. Our group is currently at five who are able to help. Not including our friends or those we're teaching-"

25

"You teach magick?"

I thought of the other little dragons we were training to control their powers. All the little green, gold and blue kiddos with wood, fire and water dragons in them. Fat, grey kids with rock dragons to match their half stoney weight. Others that harboured air dragons in their centres between their tiny light frames. The last of a species surviving in another. There would never be any other beings more rare.

"We teach unique creatures how to control their gifts," I said simply as we reached the doorway to our class.

Reika stopped before we entered. I halted as well.

She leaned in to whisper, "Does that include Demigod witches?"

I looked away and searched my thoughts. "Haven't tried teaching one of those yet." My eyes flitted back to her. "But I don't see why we couldn't."

And with that, I stepped across the threshold, my hand reaching out and pulling her with me by her arm.

"Come on, let's sit together near the back." I nodded to the empty lab table in the far rear corner by the window. I had come to find that as the light dragon I didn't feel content unless I was under the rays of the sun.

Maybe I could never tan because Fintan was always too busy soaking up the UV rays as a sort of power recharger? I doubted it, but it was fun to think of myself as a walking solar panel with wings.

Each station normally housed two students, lab partners of sorts. So it was convenient that she and I were coming into the actual classroom together on the same day.

Immediate partners it would seem.

We set our stuff down and the professor began.

He apologised to Reika and I, claiming that we may be a bit lost since we've missed the first month of the in-person labs. He was surprised when we were the first to accurately date a tool from the bronze age. It was from before I was born, but not by much.

"So you're from the bronze age?" Reika whispered as we worked on writing our report on our findings.

I shook my head. "I was born in Ireland during their Iron Age." I looked up at her. "Do you know anything about Gaul?"

"A little, mostly just the area it comprised and the little writings that Caesar had written about the region," she admitted.

I leaned over and in a hushed tone said, "I was alive to see Caesar conquer the area. He killed many of my friends, much like some of the Greeks before him." I locked eyes with the purple. "But I will say I'd defend the Greeks who killed my friends before I defend the Romans. We fought the Greeks and invaded them just as much as they invaded us. We had respect and sympathy for each other. We never brutally wiped the other out like the Romans did. I guess, to some degree, you and I can find some solace in the fact that we understand one another."

Reika smiled, but shook her head. "I'm not from the time of Olympus. My mother met my father during World War Two. I'm sorry, I don't share your pain."

"Did your father die during the war?" I asked.

She nodded hesitantly. "Yes, I never met him, and my mum sent me away to live with Artemis since her husband would have killed me."

"Then, you at least understand my pain of losing someone because of another kingdom's brutality. It may have been a different year, but the attempt to destroy and take over land is something that many rulers tried at and in the process killed many loved ones. Loss still burns the same, regardless of when it happened." I nudged her and gave her a smile.

27

A World War Two baby was definitely young for someone like us, and it explained why she couldn't tell what I was. She likely had only experienced the other Priestesses of Artemis, and probably never left her temple in the Otherworld. She could sense magick, but couldn't yet sort out anything beyond its age.

When the class was completed I instructed Erika as to how to get to her Ancient Architecture course.

I also told her where Darbie's class would be after her class.

"If he's not hosting it outside like the weird guy that he is, it'll be two doors down from your architecture class," I explained. "Just listen for the super loud professor standing at his door, welcoming students in like they're kindergarteners about to go on a fieldtrip."

"What's a kindergartener? And a field trip?" she asked.

I shook my head. "Nevermind, just look for the super excited professor at his door, he'll also be the youngest professor you have."

"Got it!" She headed off towards the history building. "See you in class!" she called over her shoulder before being lost in the crowd of humans.

I wandered into the library before trying to go find Adam. I browsed through the mythology section before heading to the check out with three books.

"Doing some research on the Greeks huh?" the librarian asked.

I nodded. "Figured I should dip my toe into a subject I don't specialise in."

I actually wanted to figure out who's daughter Reika was. She was willing to talk about her past, but she hadn't mentioned who her mother was, it dawned on me she may never confess her lineage.

I gathered my now on-loan books into my bag and left.

If Adam wasn't studying in the library, which he hadn't been, or working at the table outside the library, which he wasn't, he would be in the dining hall, eating and studying. I headed that way. I could use some food myself.

As I entered the long polygon building, I looked at the names of each food vendor, trying to decide what sounded best. I settled on Italian and ordered two meals, one for myself and one to burn as an offering for the friends I had had in Italy who died during World War One and Two.

I carried the meals and slipped into the janitor's closet. I said a prayer and burned the hot pasta and salmon dish in my hands. Praying that it be multiplied and given to my lost loved ones who missed the tastes of their home.

Once the smoke had faded and the pasta ash was gone, I slipped back out. I wandered back to the main hall of the food court.

Adam was in the far corner. His nose so far in his book, his fish and chips still untouched.

"Maybe you should stop reading and start eating," I said as I sat down across from him.

I set my bag and to go plate down. I removed the lid and smiled at the scent of tomatoes, olive oil and grilled chicken. It brought back good memories of Tuscany.

Adam set his book down.

"Did you kill Reika?" he asked before saying hello.

I laughed. "No, doubting Thomas, we actually bonded quite well and I told her how to get to her class."

"Hmm, I thought you were late getting here because you were hiding her body."

I rolled my eyes and pulled out the books I had checked out. "I wanted to get these, I also burnt an offering before coming to find you."

He tilted his head. "Burnt an offering?"

"For friends lost in World War One and Two. Reika reminded me of them today."

I took a bite and chewed slowly.

"Do you ever wish you were never immortal?" he had asked the question before and it was always the same answer.

"If it weren't for you, I'd rather be laying with my loved ones," I answered.

"But?" He asked.

"But you're my loved one now, so that's the only reason I stick around instead of finding a tall cliff and-"

"Stop," Adam said strictly. "You bring so much good to this world, don't ever take yourself out of it if you can help it okay? Even if I'm gone, do right by me by continuing to help people."

I sucked in a long breath. "Fine. Only because you asked me."

A dragon and a human fall in love... sounded like the makings of a horrible joke or a most tragic fairytale. I should have prayed that it was neither.

We ate in silence after that. Each of us leaning over food half the time, and over our research the other.

There were many immortal witches in Greek mythology, but there weren't many who were married. Most witches were like Circe, they took lovers, but ultimately spited men and, since they weren't dependent on men for their protection, didn't take husbands.

"Maybe she's the daughter of Hera," I thought out loud. "Although Hera has always been loyal to Zues…"

Adam looked up at me. "Is Hera a witch?"

"Not a witch per say, but she practised magick and wielded it like many gods. It could also be Medea, but I doubt her husband Aegeus would really care if she had a kid with someone else."

"Wasn't Aegeus mortal, he'd be dead right?"

I shook my head. "He's cursed to live until he and Medea's son becomes a king, but that's not a commonly known story."

Adam smiled. "Sometimes the fact that you know unknown or forgotten pieces of history is really amazing."

"Wait until I tell you how the pyramids were *really* built, that's gonna blow your mind."

"Was it aliens?"

I laughed and looked back at my book. The smile on my face began to hurt after a long while of Adam begging for me to reveal how the pyramids were made.

"Come on," I said, finishing my page and closing my book. "We should head to class, it'd be for the best if we warn Darbie of Reika before she just wanders into his class."

Adam whined, "But I'm reading up on how to use the stars and the season to determine where I am in the world."

I put my book away as I looked at him with a judgemental stare. He let out a huff and began packing up. I shovelled the last couple of bites into my mouth before picking up the empty package.

We disposed of our trash, exited to our left, rounded around the back of the library, and walked right past the school of science.

I looked up at the aged red brick. With its grand but scaled windows and its sharp pointed roof the school of science could almost pass for some sort of miniature castle. It was the oldest

31

building on campus, that couldn't be argued, but it was young enough that the gothic style was obviously not from that era.

"I don't know whether to be creeped out or in awe of that building," Adam commented, noticing me staring.

"Five buildings on campus," I said. "This one is the only one that looks like it has too many secrets."

"Does it have secrets?"

"None that I'm aware of. Just a basement where monks would meditate. It may have been reinforced and used as a bomb shelter when the World Wars were going on, but I don't know for sure."

"Wow, the ancient sage Erika Gavina doesn't know something?" Adam mocked. "What is the world coming to?"

I shoved him lightly. "Oh shut up. If it wasn't historically important or vital for me to know for some other reason, I didn't go digging."

"And here I was beginning to think you knew everything about everything."

"I only know things about special things. I can confirm there is nothing special about St. Ailbe's University."

Darbie was drawing old runes on the chalk board when we walked into the dingy old room, small dust particles floating off the board and through the air.

Darbie nearly broke his neck looking over at us so quickly.

"Erika!" he yelled. "I need your help writing the last of these runes before the class gets in."

"Call me Michelle, that's what all my professors know me as," I said, dropping my bookbag onto the front row of desks.

"Cool, Michelle, whatever. You remember how to write in ancient nordic right?" he waved me off.

"Yeah, let me see what we're writing."

32

He handed me the sheet with the list of nordic rituals he wanted to cover. I knew how to do most of them, but a few were more difficult and foreign to me.

"I'll take the bottom two and draw them on this side board." I motioned upwards towards the chalkboard on the wall by the door. Adam sat down next to me and watched as I started scrawling on the wall. His nose wasn't in his books, or writing in a notepad. He didn't even crack his computer. He just sat down, propped his head up on his hand, and watched me draw.

"You know, you're painfully cliche," I told him when I had finished the first ritual of Darbie's list.

He laughed. "I'm sorry that I think you're amazing."

"Even in this form?"

There was a small smile on his face. "Even in that form."

I went back to finishing the task at hand. As boring as writing on a chalkboard was, learning about various cultures now, meant being able to understand members from that group later, including gods. Each of these rituals we would be learning about today were designed to give some sort of praise to the ancient norse gods.

I was preferable to my Celtic gods, they were the only ones who had ever come to my aid when I called. But I knew that the other gods were just as real and just as powerful. They were also just as willing to give out quests to have their dirt work for them. Especially others like Adam or magick users who knew of the Otherworld and could still interact with this world without violating any laws placed after the man vs god wars.

God how I wanted a quest.

Nearly three years and nothing *good* had come our way. Every contract we took was so boring.

Fetch a golden necklace for some goddess - who accidentally left it at her lover's house - before her husband-god found out. Go collect six big toes from giants for this useless potion that will do nothing to change the world. Kill off some nymphs terrorising the local population's single farm-boys.

I wanted some world-saving, life changing, all around gruesome action.

I finished the runes.

The classroom filled with students.

Darbie talked about gods everyone in the class thought were myths.

I sat there thinking about my mum's journal that had gone up in flames and magick river water three years ago.

That journal was full of information about dragons. It also held information about my dragon, Fintan; the dragon soul who chose me as his host. He never explained why either, that unhelpful little turd.

He hadn't spoken to me in almost a year too. No matter how much I meditated and reached out to him, he remained silent. I had no idea what I was capable of, all I knew was that I was powerful enough to help create all of existence itself, and the two beings who could help me unlock this power were either trapped in a piece of jewellery or ghosting me inside of my own head.

I looked at the clock, if my ability to read time was correct, it would be over soon. Both the class and my wait. I could feel it in my soul.

Adam

Erika wasn't tuned in the entire class session. Her eyes were glazed over as she stared at the runes on the walls.

It was times like this where I couldn't guess what was on her mind.

A psychology student back before I knew about Erika's true past, had said when Erika was like this, her face looked like a post traumatic stress patient that they had worked with for an internship. Like she had post traumatic stress and was coping with it from deep inside.

Knowing what I knew then, I had wondered if that was what this was.

She had opened up once and described everything she had seen. All the wars, all the blood shed. I read up on soldiers who returned from all the famous wars and what they described seeing. They were scarred for life, and they had only fought in one war, most of them. Erika had been in at least a dozen, not including all the killing and fighting that she had participated in in-between wars.

Two thousand and four hundred years of being surrounded by death. I'd say that's more than enough trauma to be stressed about.

"Alright class," Darbie called. "And since we are almost out of time, I think we will call it there. We'll pick up the next class on the religious and cultural significance of orgies and how they connected to the gods."

A small group of guys in the front laughed as they packed up their belongings. Typical. Reika was sitting next to them. She had gotten lost and could only find a seat right next to the students taking this course to satisfy their cultural awareness requirement. She looked at them with a very heated stare.

She crossed her arms and spat, "Do you have any shred of maturity in you, or will you always be stuck in the mindset of a toddler born to a religious cult in the 1950's?" She scrunched up her nose. "Your tiny brains may not be able to comprehend this, but the act of sex was considered to be a very powerful ritual in many ancient religions. Of course, I understand that you wouldn't get the idea of powerful sex, because you can probably barely comprehend balls in holes and not true earth altering passion."

"Ha!" Erika yelled from next to me. "I have no idea what's been going on, but I am so glad I tuned back in to hear that. Tell him he has a tiny dick next."

"Well thank you Miss Michelle," Darbie yelled over the chaos that was slowly building, bringing the levels back down slowly. "For confessing that you were not paying attention on your very first day."

Erika flashed him a flat look. He was trying not to show favouritism, no doubt to keep the facade that we were just his students.

I watched Erika chew the inside of her cheek. She wanted to fire back so badly, but she didn't. Darbie, Erika and I all knew Erika already understood everything she was being taught in her classes, but a normal student her age most certainly would not, and she needed to keep people believing that.

She nodded. "Sorry Professor, I'm just not incredibly interested in Nordic mythologies. I prefer Celtic myths."

"Well either learn to like it, or get out of my class and stop taking up space that another student could fill." The class went silent, no one moved and no one dared leave. "I'm just kidding. We'll get to the celtics soon. They too had religious based orgies," Darbie finished in his normal peppy tone.

He spun around and threw the nub of chalk into the tray. When he turned around he scanned the room with a confused look on his face.

"Well get out of here you children, I didn't bring any candy to hand out today!" he exclaimed and began literally shooing people out the door.

36

Reika and I hung back, packing up slowly. Erika on the other hand rushed to put away her belongings.

"I have to go speak to my professor about publishing me," she said into her bag.

"Okay," I responded for the bag. "Have fun, don't kill any humans."

She finished and slid the bag off the table. "Thanks. Don't die by any non-humans."

"Noted. Human serial killers only," I said with a smile.

She gave me a kiss as she ran out the room, along with a faded "Bye Darbie" as she went.

As she flew out the door, Jack was slipping in. He walked around with a cane now. Well, not really a cane. It was actually a magick staff, but that would be incredibly hard to explain to people.

The old knotted ash wood was hand carved by Darbie. A dense and sharp looking green gem was set in the handle, the wood wrapping around it like the roots of a tree.

Humans held magick in their souls, and soulrendering - where a wielder syphons off their own soul, was the most potent form. It was also the easiest to do. Darbie didn't want that for Jack, but learning how to get it out of the world around him took years, so the green gem was apparently designed as a channel for Jack. Until he could conjure magick of his own volition instead of sucking magick out of himself, he'd walk around with the rock.

The idea of accidentally soul-syphoning was why I would always be more of a potions guy.

"Hey Dabrs," Jack said, completely ignoring the existence of Reika and I for his boyfriend.

"Howdy," Darbie spritely grinned back. He basically skipped over to Jack to give the faded red head a kiss on his cheek.

I rolled my eyes.

"By the way guys, the new girl's name is Reika," I interrupted their pet naming session as I walked closer to the front of the class.

Reika was standing off to the side. Her silent presence seemed to be awkward for anyone but herself as she stood there just watching and listening. Her vivid lavender eyes were filled with one hundred sharp daggers, whether she meant to pierce your soul with them or not, it seemed like that was all they could do. I shook as a shiver ran down my spine.

Jack looked over at Reika who was literally standing on the other side of a desk from him.

She smiled.

He pulled away from Darbie to look her up and down suspiciously. When he was satisfied he stuck his hand out to greet her like this was some sort of business interview.

"Pleasure to meet you," he said stiffly. "My name is Jack McGregory."

Reika bowed her head. "Reika, high priestess of the goddess Artemis. Forgive me, but I'm not really meant to touch men. Talking to them is forbidden even, but exceptions had to be made."

"Made for what exactly?" Jack crossed his arms.

He was judging her with his stare that screamed he thinks she's trouble. He hates trouble. Even now, after a few years and so many adventures, he's still a coward. I shook my head.

"Artemis had a vision or something and sent her to help prevent the end of times," I answered for Reika. "Erika and I figured it'd be better to help her then get in her way."

Jack glared at me. "And do the rest of us have a say?"

I shrugged. "You don't have to participate in saving the world. You can just sit back and die if you want," I deadpanned.

Jack uncrossed his arms. His guarded exterior was mellowed now and an enlightened expression rolled across this face.

Darbie smiled and reached up to Jack's face. His delicate hands cupped Jack's cheeks where his freckles ended, and he smooshed them together so that Jack's lips were wrinkled and puckered out.

"Awww." Darbie moved his hands out and in with each syllable, causing Jack's cheeks to squish and unsquish. "Did someone wake up on the wrong side of the bed this morning? Is little Jackie-poo a wittle grumpy?"

Jack smacked Darbie's hands away. "Don't show weakness in front of the new girl."

Reika laughed, her hand quickly covering her mouth.

"If it's any consolation, I would have thought you were weak regardless of the face squishing. At least now I think you're most likely weak, but with a sweetheart somewhere in there," she explained. "It's also some comfort to know you're gay, Priestesses are sworn from any romantic relationships with males so I already feel more comfortable with you."

"They don't teach you social skills in your cult do they?" Jack snarked. "Most people don't just casually talk about *another* person's sexual orientation and how it makes you more comfortable."

Reika's lips tightened into a flat line. "In the Priestesshood, we only have each other. There's no thought or feelings we don't share."

Jack laughed. "You should really get out more." Jack looked between Darbie and I. "Adam is having a party at his house for him and his new girlfriend. You should come… if you're really one of us."

3
Erika

"In all my Years as an educator and scholar I have never read a work that gives even remotely similar insites as yours does," Professor WhatHisNuts was ranting on about the work he was having published for me.

I hated that he was publishing my thesis essay on the interaction between early celtic peoples and the ideas of their gods. It wasn't really a thesis so much as a toned down recollection into how my people and I would pay homage and communicate with our gods, and how we thought it worked.

I was mostly frustrated that this professor would begin the process of publishing it without my permission. It wasn't until the publishing company accepted it that he informed me and summoned me in to help him in the process.

I didn't need the culture of my extinct people being reviewed by the new york times anytime soon.

He carried on with his discussions of needing an author photo, a statement of purpose, something else I didn't care about and a few more things I *also* did not care about.

I leaned back in my chair, the cold leather pressing hard against my back as I looked out the window.

The sun would be setting in a few hours, even though it was becoming spring the amount of light in the day was only around 13 hours worth.

Tonight was a full moon, a peaceful time for Druids, as it was a power source for all magick beings. Unfortunately, tonight the full moon did not put me at ease for several reasons.

For one, I hadn't been in tune with my druidic powers since I cleansed the ring and the cave collapsed onto me. And secondly, because magick spells and powers would be stronger tonight. While I hadn't sensed anything dark about Reika, I still didn't know her. The full moon could potentially open an opportunity for her.

Then there was the issue of Adam's parents and the party to think about.

They were truly lovely people, but they had never liked me even before I was thought to be a killer and a fugitive. Even now, when I was concealed to be someone else, I was still me; untamed and volatile as the day I was born.

Adam was raised in such a controlled household, there was no way in any heaven or hell that they would approve of me. Even worse, I was going to have to put on a nice dress and convince all of the guests at the party, as well as them, that I was okay.

"I'm sorry I wasn't more of a lady, mum," I whispered to myself.

"What was that?" my professor snapped.

I looked to him, I had truly forgotten he was there. I shifted uncomfortably in my seat, trying to remember the last words I had heard him say as I was allowing my mind to wander.

"I said I'm sorry I'm not more ladylike." I smiled. "I was thinking about the interviews with the publishers you want me to have. You see, I am not very sociable, or friendly for that matter.

42

If we really want this to be published, we should probably keep the talking to just you. Also, I was very much so hoping to remain anonymous if you don't mind."

The professor sighed. "There really needs to be a name on this if we want it to get published."

I smiled and stood up. "Perfect, I think your name would look great under the title, and you can just say it was co-authored by an anonymous scholar."

I began to walk out.

"I don't understand why you are so dead set on making sure no one knows you exist." It was phrased as a statement, but I recognized the question.

"Can I ask you a question, sir?" I asked and he crossed his arms and nodded in response. "Why should I worry about the world knowing who I am and what I think? What kind of power does it give me in the long run to make money off of an opinion that will mean nothing to me when I die?"

He opened his mouth to speak, no doubt hoping to give me some sort of long winded advice from someone who claims to have lived more of a life than you. But that was just the problem. I had lived more of a life than any great sage who had ever offered me advice.

"You may value a life of experiences, one filled with more people who claim they love you than you can count, but I don't." I sent him a pointed glare. "The only thing of value to me is to love and be loved by those who will seek me out in the afterlife. Eternity means nothing if you are alone, even if your crypt is made of solid gold. So if you'll excuse me, professor, I would rather spend time with the little family I have left instead of wasting my time trying to publish an essay that does not bring me closer to those who take the time to actually know me."

I left before the man could put in another word. *How unladylike*.

I stretched as I walked. I paid no attention to what was going on around me as I moved down the hall to the stairwell. I took the first two steps down with a bounce, thinking about getting to Darbie's house and taking a long hot shower. As my left foot hit the carpeted shelf beneath me, a chilling jolt went through my body. I looked up from the plaid carpet.

There was not a sound in the hall.

I walked back up to the top of the stairs in order to peer down the hall in both directions.

Nothing.

Not even the whisper of a soul was in the area. Yet I still sensed darkness. Like an endless void disguised as a pit that truly held no end to its blackness.

I shoved the thoughts down. The paranoia. There hadn't been anything catastrophic in my life since I died fighting Cailleach. I turned and took a step down the stairs only for another shiver to roll down my spine and a creak in the floorboards to accompany it.

I stopped and leaned back to look down the hall. Nothing. But I could feel *something*.

I huffed, then turned and moved back into the hall. I plunged headfirst back down without a single thought as to what I was looking for and what I would do if I found it.

I am one of the most powerful beings in existence. I said to myself. *Why should I care what's lingering around the corner? Odds are, whatever it is doesn't stand a chance.*

I wandered the empty hallway. I made it all the way to the end where the other stairwell was, leaned forward and looked down the steps, then craned my neck to look up. Nothing was there, not even another student. So I walked back down to the other end of the hall where I had come from.

My professor was in his office with the door closed. I could see him through the distorted glass, sitting at his desk. I reached out to turn the door handle. I pushed the door open slowly and looked around his room. His old eyes looked at me quizzically.

I could smell something in his office, but saw no signs of anything other than my professor.

"I'm sorry sir," I began, continuing to look for signs of anything. "Did you see anyone since I've left?"

He scoffed, "You hardly left a minute ago, surely you would have seen if anyone came into my office."

I nodded. "Yeah, right, sorry professor. I'll leave you now. And if you're going to put my name on the book, will you use the pen name Caoimhe O'Aodhan."

The professor blinked twice, "Those are some old names. How on earth did you come up with that?"

He reached forward and grabbed a pen, moving to write the name down.

"Those are my parents' names." I said honestly, "They're both dead so I figure they won't be offended."

"I'll let the publisher know immediately." He sounded excited. He finally had a name to put at the bottom of the book. A rather pointless notion, but at least it made him a little happy. "I am so excited that you're letting me put a name to the book," he continued. "I really didn't want my other professors thinking I wrote it and lied about a student of mine writing it."

I looked from the air conditioning vent towards the top of the wall behind him, and down to his age spotted face. He reached around his chaotic desk in an attempt to get through the high stacks of work and to his phone.

I let my shoulders relax. "Hey professor?" I spoke to gain his attention, "Thank you for giving my work special attention.

45

You're an incredibly intelligent instructor, and I appreciate all of your efforts to show my thoughts to the world." I gave him a smile, hoping to make up for being so rude earlier, "I have to go, my boyfriend's family is throwing a celebration party, but I look forward to discussing the publication more with you."

He gave me a smile and I began turning back towards the hallway. Before I could fully exit into the empty straightness of the corridor, I turned back to him.

"I'm being quite serious about your name being under mine, I hope that's clear to you sir." I gave him a pointed look.

"Of course, Ms. Lily." He arose and gave me a very kind bow. "I would be honoured to be on a book cover with you. I hope you have a wonderful time at your party this evening."

"Thank you." And with that I slipped out, shutting his door behind me and thus the thought of danger with it.

I speedily walked down the hall and rounded the corner only to have my nose tip to tip with a pale, slender face encased in black hair. It was a face I recognized, but still shocked me enough to result in my punching the Morrigan straight in her jaw.

Not to my surprise, the goddess of war and fate didn't flinch.

"Jesus H. Christ! What do you want?" I gasped before looking her up and down. Based on her attire, which was a lightweight leather armour vest and a shield resting against her lower half, blocking what looked to be the skirt of a black toga from my sight, she was here as Macha.

She peered into my eyes, moving her already close face closer to mine.

"I had a vision of you mourning and then another of you surrounded by death in a great battle," she leaned back and explained. "I came to see if it was time to collect your soul."

46

I pushed around her shield and began heading down the stairs. "Well, Ms. Morrigan, as you can see, I am very much alive and very much not in a fight," I said looking up at her. "So you can go now."

I turned around only to slam right into the other triplet in the morrigan trio, Nemain. Of the three, she was the least stable, and most definitely my least favourite,

I grumbled, "And we're here with the crazy one too." I looked back up to the other sister. "Since she's here should I still call you Morrigan or should I single you out as Macha?"

The cold goddess looked down at me calmly and collected. "Either is correct, but for simplicity Macha may be more helpful."

As she spoke, Nemain leaned forward to sniff my hair. Her dead white eyes looked down as she drew a rusted dagger from her blood stained belt. She slowly dragged the blade from one of my collarbones to the other, a movement that stung, but didn't break skin.

"I can smell it," she said, practically drooling. "Fresh blood."

I took a deep breath, still looking up at Macha. "This is why you're my favourite, I don't like any of you three really, but if I had to choose you'd be it."

A loud cawing brought my attention up to the windowsill about four feet above me. There sat a large and glossy looking crow, staring down at me with beady black eyes.

I pointed at it. "Don't like you either, Badh, you distracting little bird brain." I looked around to all three, huffing, "Fuck off, the lot of you."

I slapped away the hand holding the dagger to my chest, only to have Nemain hiss at me.

"Are you sure you haven't been slain?" Macha asked.

47

"No," I snapped at her.

"And you're not mourning the death of a loved one who has fallen in battle?" she followed up.

I shook my head, but stopped mid-shake. I last left Adam and my best friends in a room alone with a magick-wielding stranger. The panic set in on the top of my chest and the base of my lungs. It squeezed together until I felt like I couldn't breathe.

"Move," I demanded and pushed the goddess of war havoc out of my way, not fearing the consequence.

I jumped clear over the final descent of stairs, and while it was only a story tall, the impact caused a painful repetitive clicking in my knees. Despite the pain, I ran. All the way through the courtyard, across the way to the building where I had last seen my family. I burst through the door and charged down the recently polished floors of the hallway. I slid into the doorframe, jamming my shoulder against the hard wood as I came to a screeching halt.

My eyes peered over my confused looking friends. Darbie was leaning against his podium, with Jack sitting on the table behind him, his feet resting on either side of the camoflogued blue elf. Reika sat at the desk right in front of the pair and Adam, who's alarmed eyes washed over me as soon as I met them, had pulled up a chair and rested his feet on Reika's desk, his body stretched out in a relaxed manner.

At the sight of me he stood up and hurried over. I leaned in the doorway, holding my right shoulder with my left hand, and bent over slightly to clutch my aching knee with my right.

"Are you alright, mate?" Jack was the first to ask. "You look like you've seen a ghost."

Dabbie turned his body towards me. "Which god or demon visited you this time?"

Adam held his arms open for me to collapse into.

"The Morrigan," I said, leaning on Adam for support. He began leading me to a chair.

"Which one?" Darbie asked.

"All three," I said simply.

Darbie's face dropped and he sucked a breath in sharply through his teeth.

"Who is The Marry-gan?" Reika asked.

Jack leaned over so his head could be seen around Darbie's body. "The *Morrigan* is the three headed goddess of war and fate. One represents the chaos and bloodshed of war, one is a crow who foreshadows death and also influences battles, and the other represents the nobler sides of war."

"There are noble sides of war?" Reika scoffed.

Adam, having then helped me into a chair and was massaging my knee, chimed in, "That's Macha, she typically represents the spoils of war and victory. Land, kingship, wealth. That's all her area. It's typically why she appears to give heroes missions, because she has seen who the victor is."

"Not always," Macha spoke, appearing in the front of the classroom, right beside Darbie. The sudden appearance shocked us all, resulting in a collective scream of fright and Darb reaching out to slap the goddess.

A smile curled on my face at the thought of us both having struck the goddess of war within a few minutes of each other.

"I am so sorry," Darbie immediately stated. "Please great Phantom Queen forgive me, you startled me and I struck you, I did not mean you any harm."

"Screw that, come here crow-lady, I'll slap you again," I called out from my seat position.

I received a collection of looks from that comment, ranging from confused- Adam and Reika- to awestruck- Darbie- and on the verge of irritation, which of course, was Macha.

She looked down at Darbie with graceful eyes and smiled. "Thank you my knight, for your sincerest apologies, I forgive your misdeed and appreciate your fighting spirit."

Darbie gave the goddess a thumbs up and immediately backed away, revealing a frozen-scared Jack behind him.

Macha smoothly turned her attention over to me. Her eyes ran over Adam before meeting mine.

"I meant what I said, Erika. I have seen your fate, you need to protect yourself and your loved ones these coming days," she explained.

Out of habit I wanted to say something snarky in response, but I bit my tongue. Macha's message was clearly meant to be a friendly warning and a smart person would take it as such.

I gave the goddess a respectful nod. As quickly as she had appeared, she was gone.

I rested my head against Adam's forehead.

"Erika," Jack's shaky voice called out, I looked up at him so he could speak directly, "You're spell collapse, you're back to your regular self."

"Damn," I cursed under my breath. "It's probably because I sustained an injury. Give me a few minutes and I'll be healed. I can summon the facade back."

"You're very beautiful in this form," Reika said softly from her seat.

I offered her a smile, but no response. I could see Adam's concerned expression from the corner of my eyes and I wanted to look away as quickly as possible. I didn't have a poker face, but I didn't want him to see the worry beginning to swirl behind my eyes. Three of us were mortal and the other three were immortal, death is an even more bitter topic when it leaves eternal lonliness in it's wake.

"What did the goddess see?" Darbie asked.

I sighed. "Me in mourning, and then in battle."

"So we should be preparing for war?" Adam asked.

I locked eyes with him. "We're always ready for war. What we should be preparing for is grief. If Macha is right, one of us is going to die. Getting over the loss of a loved one is far more difficult than fighting a battle."

Darbie moved to his satchel. He folded the well worn leather flap over before slipping onto his shoulder. He moved sluggishly. Each movement was drawn out. He scanned our faces before motioning to the door.

"We should leave," he said. "I have more teaching to give to the young dragons back home. Most of those younglings aren't even remotely ready for a fight, let alone a war. Cover Erika's face and let's go."

At Darbie's house, I sat in meditation in an attempt to communicate with Fintan. Unfortunately the old dragon must have made a reptile retirement home somewhere in my subconscious and buried himself in games of bingo because he wasn't coming out no matter what I did.

Propping my elbow onto my knee, I leaned into my fingers, pinching the bridge of my nose in frustration. I let my head roll down so that it was hanging down, allowing my hand to drop back to my lap. I sighed and opened my eyes. I could see the sun beginning to set through the open window.

I was in the middle of Darbie's attic. We had cleared it out to be used as a meditation or prayer room, but right now the silence was unsettling to me.

The space had four walls, two were triangular but perfectly vertical, while the other two slanted towards each other to make up the angle of the roof. Each triangular wall housed massive, polished wood shutter windows. And on the slanting roof were two impressive blankets of glass as well. All in all, a total of six windows and many plants helped make the space a peaceful zone that was excellent for meditation and spells that required concentration.

I took the sky darkening as my warning sign to get up and get ready for the celebration tonight. I rocked back once then forward in order to use the momentum to help myself up quicker. As soon as I was on my feet the room started to spin.

Am I low on Iron? I thought jokingly. Before I could laugh at my own thoughts, though, I was falling back to the ground.

I braced for impact by closing my eyes and putting my forearms up to protect my face. As I collided with the ice and snow-

...Snow?

I opened my eyes only to stare into fresh powdery snow. I pushed myself to my knees and looked around me. Birches went on for miles to my right. In front of me, curving through snowy banks and tall thin trees of white, was a crystal clear river of teal. Large chunks of grey granite sat upright in the water with gorgeous curling druid symbols and knots engraved into them.

"It's time we met face to face, child," I recognized the voice calling me to my right, but when my eyes peeled from the stones to the elderly man, I didn't recognize him.

Over a short piled snow mound, sat a white haired nobleman by a fire, stoking it with a long stick. The red flames flickered against his face, washing over his white hair, making his moustache and beard appear as if they were burning, while the white atop his head looked like a fresh layer of snow powder. His chin was pointed, and his cheekbones sharp, combined with his orange eyes, he was a rather grand looking elderly man.

He opened his cape to me and said, "Come sit, young one, you will find yourself cold here soon. Your mind has not yet caught up with the transition from one reality to the next."

"You mean I am not just in a vision inside my mind right now?" I asked, moving up and over the snow. As my feet sunk into the fresh flakes, I was beginning to become aware of the pain of the cold in my bare skin. I looked down in confusion then up at the man, "How did you do that? I can actually feel the ice."

"Come sit and get warm, I will explain what I can in this short time we have."

I studied the cape before moving in. Thick white wool boasted golden suns with gorgeous golden loops spreading out from each of the small stars. The edges of the cloak were red, and ivory beads were sewn in with thick golden thread.

I sat down into the warm fabric and he wrapped me tightly into it. Immediately, familiar warmth spread over my whole body, even my feet, which still sat on the ice, uncovered.

"Fintan," I breathed out, taken aback.

The man smiled at me. "Yes. We finally meet when I am in my true form."

My brows furrowed before I asked, "I thought your dragon was your true form?"

He shook his head. "No, at least not for myself and Muireann. We have a dragon form, but it is simply one of many powers. Our children, on the other hand, were either born with their dragon form or with their mortal form. The mortals were

53

simply just that, mortals, and the dragons were simply just dragons."

"And then you gave some of your power to the mortals, therefore creating the first gods and goddesses?" I concluded.

Fintan gave me a nod of approval. "You are very clever to be able to figure that out on your own."

"You have told me that you and the dark dragon were the ones who created the gods," I said. "It wasn't that hard to put two and two together. But tell me, why am I here?"

"A time is coming where you are going to need to be able to control all my powers."

My facial expression dropped. I could feel irritation snaking through every muscle and limb I had.

"Really?" I deadpanned. "You decided to teach me now?"

Fintan pulled the charred stick he was using to poke the fire out of the flames and hit me square in the centre of the top of my head. Ash and embers flicked everywhere, raining down on my shoulders and into my hair.

"Hey!" I shouted. "What the hell?"

He put the tip of the stick back into the flames. "Be grateful I am teaching you at all. I could leave you to flounder on your own like the rest of my children are. Now listen closely, before I explain these powers to you, you need to understand how it is possible in the first place."

"It's possible because you put your dragon soul in me as I died," I said.

"Wrong," he responded. "And if you cut me off again, I'll hit you for a second time. Muireann and I didn't simply give our powers to our hosts. Our existence and therefore our souls exist on two planes, the higher, or celestial existence, which is what you are in now; and the second being your plane. If we die in one we still exist in the other, but we can no longer access the one in which our bodies died in.

"Similarly, when we bonded with each of you, we created a third realm within you to live and to grow strong. This was because merging our souls was not about hiding or giving power to other's, it was about saving species, both the hosts and our own, and therefore maintaining balance. We knew that the druids and the dark elves would eventually die off, so we each made a choice of whom we'd want to take when their time came. You are the last of the druids, picked before they were truly threatened. And Condan is the last of the dark elves. You both are beings with natural dispositions to darkness and light. You stay alive, Muireann and I stay alive. Balance."

He took a moment to turn to his side. Reaching down he pulled a sizable log into his hands before casting it into the fire. I leaned back to look at the pile of logs beside him. I realised then that the one we were sitting on was a fallen tree, brown like oak. The pile of wood next to Fintan appeared to be what was left of our seat with several curling logs matching the same colour and texture as the one beneath us.

"So you chose me because you knew the druids were going to go extinct?" I asked.

"My child, you are not just a druid, but also a dragonrider by blood like many other druids. Dragonriding druids were the first bloodline of druids. Since they were the sons and daughters of my close friend Dagda, they grew up amongst my children and thus were the first to be gifted and to master the power of dragon riding. They were already a dwindling breed, but as the rest of your people were to be decimated also, I chose to find one of your kind to bond with. In order to have a stronger host sure, but mostly to provide an opportunity to save two types of peoples."

I nodded in understanding before asking, "What about the dark dragon? Why did she pick her host specifically, instead of just any dark elf? And what is he like?"

Fintan looked out into the cold. "She picked the dark elf because he was of a long line of militant royalty." he looked back at me. "After the wars and after years of being hunted and our children being killed, Muireann changed. Originally, her natural affinity for water and the earth made her constant and steady, never wavering no matter what someone threw at her. I was the one who was volatile and explosive. After all the loss, she felt that two strong and battle ready leaders were what we needed.

"She was the first to take a host and she chose Condan. With him she controlled armies of magick wielding dark elves and dragons. She destroyed any village, town or kingdom that worshipped Cailleach. She fought against any and all gods, fearing they'd eventually turn on us.. It's why Dagda and The Morrigan decided to trick them in the ring." He looked down at me with his burning ember eyes.

I shook my head in confusion. "Wait, I thought he wanted the ring to be made as a way to help the youngling dragons."

Fintan shook his head softly. "No, it was most certainly a trick. They convinced him to put his magick in the ring combined with the All-Father's and The Morrigan's in order to help hone magick. I imagine they told him it would only be some of his magick and it would make him out to be a hero. He fell for the bait, and they were able to put him in completely, trapped under the thumb of two gods' magicks."

"Question," I said and raised my hand. To which the ancient dragon leaned back and looked at me in disbelief.

He pointed at me. "Yes, Erika, what is your question? I point so as to distinguish you from every other student in this classroom."

I put my hand down. "Wow that's a lot of sarcasm for an old guy," I started. "Anyway, so then, is it your magick or the dark dragon's magick that makes Adam immortal so long as he wears the ring?"

He smiled, "And that is where we come to our first lesson. Dragon Riding and The Bond of The Dragonrider.

"The Bond of The Dragonrider has been misinterpreted as a spell or a curse that ties a Dragonrider to a Dragon's life force, but in fact the bond is not a spell or curse, but rather a contract. Like how all non-magick creatures must have a contract or bond with a magick creature in order to pass between your world and the Otherworld, a bond between dragonrider allows the dragon to give a small portion of its power to the rider."

"Is that why they can also summon Dragon aspects?" I asked excitedly.

"Yes. Now the ring is like a temporary Dragonrider bond, when McLeon takes the ring off, the bond is broken and therefore he can die and age. If Condan were to ever break free of the ring, it would break the enchantment that keeps our magick there -"

"And therefore break the temporary rider's bond or whatever," I finished.

"Precisely. That is why the first spell you should learn is how to conjure the bond and create the magickal contract," Fintan said. "Shall we begin?"

I sucked in a breath through my teeth.

"I would love to," I started. "but you see, I have a party I need to go to…"

His facial expression dropped. His lips pursed together into a tight line.

"A party?"

"Yeah."

He rubbed his temple with his middle finger as he spoke, "And you think a party is more important than learning Magick directly related to your Dragon Abilities?"

I shrugged and fiddled with my fingers. "I mean," I trailed sheepishly. "The party is for me."

Fintan shook his head and raised one hand motioning for me to stop.

"Fine." He said. "We shall pick this up again tomorrow. I expect you to come back bright and early."

I squinted my eyes and tilted my head in confusion. I looked around me, half expecting to see a door or a ladder somewhere that would take me in and out of this realm. Not too much to my surprise, there was nothing but snowy forests.

"Yeah.. about that…" I looked at the old dragon. "How did I get here and how do I leave?"

Fintan rolled his eyes, lifted his half burnt stick and once again slammed it down onto my head.

I closed my eyes as it came down, preparing for the impact. Instead of the feeling of being hit with a stick, my face was met with the feeling of slamming into a wooden floor.

I rolled onto my back, holding my now bleeding nose. My eyes watering to the brim.

"Son of a-" I started to say, but the door bursting open run louder than my last word.

"What the hell E?" It was Ethan yelling at me from the door frame.

I could hear his footsteps pounding closer when I didn't answer. Involuntary tears were streaming down my face and blood was pouring into my hand, leaking out between my fingers. I leaned onto my side, using my elbow and shoulder to push myself up so that I could stand.

"Are you good?" Ethan asked, I could see his blurry figure through the tears, standing next to me and reaching out to inspect me. "You don't look like you've been in a fight or anything, how the hell did you hurt your nose?"

I blinked the tears away to look at him. "I apparently fell," I said and moved towards the door, blood trailing behind me.

"Okay?" Ethan's tone sounded unsure.

He followed me into the stairwell down from the attic. The narrow and turning stairs lead into a closet disguised as a bookcase.

Opening the door opened into the second story of the house's library. Slipping out of the bookcase door, we stood on the top walkway, overlooking the library floor where young dragons sat in silence reading.

Following the walk away around to the back of the library were the stairs to the first floor. Along every wall were floor to ceiling bookcases only broken by arching glass windows. Wooden grids lined the windows before stretching out at the top into a cathedral arch.

The library inside was lit by a massive chandelier hanging in the centre, four smaller ones hung down around it, illuminating almost every inch of the square space. While the library was tall with its two story stature, it was not incredibly large. From wall to wall, only four men could lay foot to head across the ground. Maybe five if they were unusually small men.

I followed the path past the books to the stairs. The sun seemed to still be in the same place it was before I hit the ground, which was good. It meant I still had time to get ready.

"Hey Ethan?" I asked, spinning around to look at the man while still walking backwards, "What time is it?"

He looked down at his gorgeous silver watch, and, for the first time since he ran up to find me, noticed he was dressed sharply in a black three piece suit. A deep toned purple tie and pocket square sticking out.

"It's only nine past seven," he said. "You have plenty of time to get ready, assuming your nose heals in time."

I scrunch my eyebrows at the sight of the purple clothing. Pointing to it I asked, "You chose to wear a purple tie?"

"Yeah, it's majestic," he responded.

His answer left me even more confused.

"I didn't take you for the kind of guy who liked purple, let alone thought it was majestic," I said.

He shook his head. "No, no. Majestic purple, as in the shade of purple," he explained.

"Oh," I sighed after speaking. "Did you meet Reika yet?"

He cocked his head to the side, and hesitated to ask, "Like the third reich?"

"No," I managed to get out before I laughed out loud, finally letting go of my nose. I wiped away blood from my top lip before saying, "Reika. Not reich-ah. She's the priestess of Artemis who we ran into. She's coming tonight. She has purple eyes so I just assumed you chose purple because you liked her eye colour or something."

Ethan looked down at his tie. He ran his hand across the matte fabric. Then he looked back up at me. His ice blue eyes set firmly on mine.

"No," he said. "But the goddess I ran the job for was Artemis. I dealt with her problem. If this priestess is here for the same reason then she should be gone by now."

I clenched my jaw. I turned around and waved it off over my shoulder. "A problem for later tonight. Right now I need to figure out what to wear."

I began descending down the stairs.

60

"Should I bring weapons just in case?" Ethan called down to me from the second story.

I looked up, taking in his tall and broad stance.

He had become a gloriously strong man since I had met him. Looking up at him, light from the chandelier reflecting off his crystal blue eyes, one large, rough hand resting on the wooden railing of the second story walkway, he looked like a beautiful domineering man from a romance novel.

There was no doubt in my mind that Ethan Lios was a loyal friend, fierce protector and an impressive fighter all rolled into the body of a gorgeous man. Looks and strength like him were both very helpful to our team.

I smiled up at him a devious smile. "You should always bring weapons just in case. But do me a favour will you?" I asked, and he nodded, motioning for me to continue. "Use those good looks of yours to try and coax out what she wants."

Ethan smirked. "Is there anything off limits?"

I rolled my eyes. "Please don't try to make any more demi-gods. There are already enough people who use magick."

4

Adam

I sat by the kitchen bar in my parents house, looking out over the dining table set with hors d'oeuvres and cupcakes with little magazines frosted onto them. Beyond the food was the sunken living room, about three feet down with a grey L-shaped couch facing towards the floor to ceiling fireplace. A wood and glass coffee table sat between the couch and the fireplace with various different volumes of the magazine Erika was to be published in on it.

The walls were a bright shade of white that was just barely in the zone of "tolerable to look at". Grey trim lined the large windows that overlooked the dining table, as well as the sliding glass doors that spanned almost all of the walls down in the living room. To the right, against the wall, was a matching grey arm chair angled in to face the couch. An end table matching that of the coffee table sat next to it. In the corner, between the wall and the couch was a weaved basket full of freshly washed throw blankets.

Built into the fireplace bricks were two open shelves. On the bottom was a pile of larger longs, and above it, on the higher shelf, were smaller sticks that we typically used to start the fire.

Because my mum hated vacuuming up bits of wood, she and my dad had paid someone to tear up the carpet down in the living room a long time ago. Instead they had the concrete sealed and painted to look like black and white marble.

Thrown down on top of it was a faux black fur rug. The coffee table sat as close to the centre of the rug as it could get, considering the faux fur was cut with round edges that protruded to make it look like it truly came from a bear or some other animal.

The fire was crackling and popping, but it blended in with the sounds of people talking. I rubbed my eyes with the back of my fingers before looking around again. My mum had invited some of my extended family whom she stood talking to just outside one of the sliding glass doors. There, she stood on the patio overlooking the small backyard that opened into a set of woods we shared with our neighbours. She was talking rather animatedly with her sister and her sister's eldest daughter, my cousin. My cousin stood there bouncing as she held her young baby in her arms. Inside, her husband was sitting on the couch with my father. I could vaguely here the premise of their conversation. They were discussing their degrees and comparing it with my choice to study history with a focus on ancient societies.

"At least his girlfriend is successful," my cousin's husband said. "If they get married one of them will be able to afford to put food on the table."

I rolled my eyes and looked over at the professors who were talking with my brother. Three old guys in expensive, but well worn, suits stood around my brother who sat stiffly in the arm chair. They were very loud as they encouraged him to apply to each of their specific programs.

I recognised Dr. Platepeccia, the anthropology professor who specialised in ancient human remains. He had worked on dating the remains of several mummies found in egypt, as well as the occasional consult for crimes in which bodies were found after they have decomposed. He was one of my favourite professors, but his constant talk about how fascinating dead bodies were was obviously doing nothing but making my brother extremely uncomfortable.

Over my shoulder, down the hall on the other side of the kitchen, I could hear the front door opening into the foyer. Laughter was already erupting as the group made their way through the doorway and down the hall to me. Looking over my shoulder I watched my friends as they approached. Jack in a simple pair of khaki pants and a white sweater which Darbie wore a matching one of. I looked down at his pants half expecting to see a whole matching outfit from the two of them, but was pleasantly surprised when I saw black slacks instead.

I was then unpleasantly not surprised when I noticed he had no shoes on.

"Darbs, where are your shoes?"

"I came without them," he explained, hand wrapped around Jack's waist. "So much better to go all-natural. Ooo, cupcakes!" With an excited coo he pulled Jack over to the other side of the table where they could better reach the white frosted pastry.

I looked back to Ethan who now stood next to me with Reika nervously shying behind him. She was in a form fitting, but covering black dress. The sleeves went all the way down to her wrists and the bottom hem all the way to her mid-calf. Besides the small slit that showed just past her knee, there was practically no skin showing, as the collar rose all the way to her neck and her long black hair spilling down to her lower back helped to conceal any skin that could have shown beyond her face and fingers. I looked down to her feet.

64

"Black leather heels?" I looked up at the priestess. "Aren't you supposed to be more conservative?"

She crossed her arms over her chest. "They were the only thing in your wife's closet that fit me," she explained. "I apparently am a size smaller than her in shoes."

"Sorry about that," I said before motioning between the two of them. "So I see you two have met, but maybe you should go meet some other people instead of hiding behind Ethan."

Reika opened her mouth to talk, but was cut off by Ethan.

"She's staying behind me for the course of the night," he said. "E and I don't trust her."

I scrunched my eyebrows before asking, "I thought Erika trusted her, for the most part?"

Ethan's jaw was tight as he talked, "Yeah she did, but considering I just finished up a job for her goddess-" he jammed his thumb over his shoulder at the purple eyed girl- "and she's not gone yet, we're not one hundred percent positive that she's not lying to us."

"My goddess sent me here on a different mission," Reika said through gritted teeth. "I wasn't on a mission to kill a Dhampir. You were. We were tasked with completely different things."

I could see one of her hands gripped tight into a fist at her side, the other hidden behind Ethan who was talking to her without the decency of turning around to look at her.

"Listen sweetheart," he said. "You haven't even told us your mission yet so why should we-"

"I did tell you," she seethed. "I am here to monitor and report back to my goddess anything that indicates a coming darkness."

"Great," Ethan said sarcastically. "That super vague mission is exactly why we don't trust you."

"You're an asshole," she actually spat into his back.

He turned to glared down at her and I swear I heard his breath catch.

Her purple eyes were almost glowing. She was staring at him so aggressively. Even though she was a smaller girl, only standing just past the middle of Ethan's chest, she had stood up to him. Her jaw was set, her fist clenched and those intimidating purple eyes of her's bared into his like she was trying to burn him with them.

And what was Ethan doing? In any other situation like this he would have leaned forward and done something cocky like twirl her hair around his finger or boop her nose before saying something along the lines of, "Awe, did you get your panties in a twist?" But this time? This time he stood there for a second, hand still in his pockets, looked her down and up once then turned around without a word.

He rolled his eyes. "Just keep an eye on her with us will you?" he asked, but was already walking away before I could get a "sure thing" in.

He moved around the table and down into the living room, where he was undoubtedly heading to talk to my attractive blond neighbour. She was Mr. and Mrs. Day's niece who had moved in with them after getting a job as the local elementary school teacher. She was cute, in a petite, giggly blond sort of way. Reika moved to the other side of me, where she slid onto one of the stools. We both sat there silently for a moment watching him blatantly hit on the poor girl.

The worst part though? She obviously liked it. She was already leaning a bit closer, resting her lips against the rim of her chardonnay glass, and reaching out to grab his bicep when he told a stupid joke.

"Is he always this rude?" Reika asked.

I cracked a smile before responding. "Ethan is a very defensive guy. He's also a very hot guy, and he knows it. So, yeah. I guess you can say he's always this rude." I looked down at her and offered her sympathetic eyes.

I shifted my weight so that instead of leaning away from her, towards the hallway, I leaned in her direction. I figured it was a more inviting position, one that showed I was interested in her company and her thoughts. As a newcomer to our little band of merry men, it was likely she felt out of the loop and awkward. Anything that we could do to mitigate that meant increasing the likelihood that she would trust us and therefore be honest with us.

She looked me over and then looked him over before turning back to me. "You are all attractive in your own regards," she said. "You're wife and you are a lovely couple, equally matched in beauty and intelligence."

I laughed, looking to the ground to hide the blush the was creeping its way up my neck to my cheeks. I shook my head before looking back at her to speak, "Erika and I aren't married. We've just been together for nearly four years now."

"That's quite a long time. Most engagements I am familiar with are less than a year in length," she explained, her tone full of ups and downs, signalling her confusion.

I chewed on my cheek for a moment. "I don't disagree. But I'm barely getting close to twenty five. She's quite literally ten times my age. Four years is to her what four months is to me."

She reached out to gently rest her hand on my shoulder, her voice just as soft. Her viciously purple eyes soften into a sweet royal colour. "Four months in this kind of life is a long time to be in love with nothing to show for it but a ring."

I looked down at the ring that started it all, wrapped around my finger like a golden embrace. I crossed my arms as I thought.

67

"I guess that's true," I agreed. "But, at the same time, marriage was originally a way of uniting two people into one in front of capital G, God. If all the lowercase gods exist, I'm not sure if I even know if uppercase God exists."

"I definitely think He exists."

I jumped slightly, but turned to see an unsurprised Erika talking.

My breath caught in my throat.

She had left her eyes as their usual colour this time. The beautiful pine green with flecks of brown around the pupil was amplified by the pale tone of her spelled skin.

Her small nose bended into rosey, freckled cheeks framed in by long brilliant red locks. Each strand curled down like a waterfall that splashed down into a whirlpool. The apple red curls tumbled onto white chiffon that seemed to plume like clouds over Erika's shoulders. Dulled-copper toned leaves wrapped around the neckline that just barely clung to her chest, showing an amazing, but tasteful, view of her cleavage. The leaves grew around the corset bodice and down the back of the dress.

As she walked to the front of me, I could have sworn I saw the copper leaves tumble off like they were falling from an oak tree in November.

I reached out and placed my hand on her hip. The milk white material looked like chiffon, but felt like warm butter at my fingertips. I sunk them into the fabric. Then pulled her close to me, never once taking my eyes off those beautiful eyes.

"Erika, I-," I began, trailing off to stare into her eyes.

"Michelle!" my mother called out. "The guest of honour!"

Reika, Erika and I all turned to look at my mum. She had stepped into the living room and now stood in front of the fireplace with her hand stretched out. She motioned for us to

68

come down with her outstretched hand since the other one was clutching a large glass of wine closely. The yellowish toned liquid sloshed in her cup as her beaconing became more and more dramatic as they went.

The three of us got up to move, I looked back at Jack and Darbie who had been hovering over the hors d'oeuvres. They turned to look out over the railing and down into the living room. My father got up and followed Erika and I, whose waist I held tightly and pulled her into my side.

Reika slid into the spot my dad had been sitting at previously. She picked up the glass of brandy he had left behind on the coffee table, sniffed it, violently recoiled, and set it back down. I let a smile out, but suppressed the chuckles that tickled along with it. A demigod over seventy years old as experienced as a five year old was humorous to me.

Once my entire family was standing up in front of the fire, two of us on each side of Erika, and all our guests were circling in front of us, my mum began to talk.

I loved my mother, she was a very caring and thoughtful woman, but she loved to feel important. Which is why she took it upon herself to throw this party.

"I can't believe that my son and his successful girlfriend are flying the nest already," she said about five or ten minutes into her speech. "It seems like only yesterday I was wiping his butt."

There was an eruption of chuckling in the room. I, meanwhile, subtly turned to look at the fireplace so that I wouldn't have to make eye contact with anyone.

While the room was still not completely silent and while I was looking away, Erika leaned over and whispered in my ear, "Where's the ring?"

I looked at my left hand's middle finger that was pulled up against my torso so that my elbow could be in a crook for

Erika to gently hold on to. Where I had just seen a golden ring was now nothing but a pale tan line.

I shot my gaze over to the couch where Reika had been sitting. She was gone.

I leaned in to kiss Erika's temple in order to disguise my whisper, "Reika was asking about it."

Erika looked up at me and gave me a forced loving look.

"She's gone," she whispered through a stiff smile, making the look all the more awkward for me, but I'm sure adorable for the cameras that only caught her side profile.

"Mhmm," I mumbled.

I could hear Erika's long and sharp sigh. My mum, who was on the other side of Erika, casted a glance our way. Erika was glaring up at Darbie, no doubt try to communicate either via some sort of telepathy or really intense eye contact… definitely the eye contact.

I was left to briefly lock eyes with my mum before she turned back to the crowd.

"But let's not ruin the night with stories and endless talk," she said, clearly wrapping her speech up early. "This night is for all of us to share memories one last time before our kids move on to the rest of their lives. To Michelle and Adam, may their futures continue to be bright." She raised her glass and everyone followed.

"Slàinte!" Everyone toasted.

As soon as the drinks had been downed and the music sprang up again, Erika walked quickly towards the stairs. Professors and friends were coming up to talk with her, but she ignored them as she practically ran up to the kitchen, down the hallway to the foyer which looked straight up into the stairway.

"Sorry everyone," I said to those who were looking at me confused and concerned. "She had to pee terribly when she got here but didn't have time before the speech started. She's only now able to go."

Look of understanding or acceptance immediately washed over their faces. I offered nonchalant smiles to everyone as I scanned upwards to the kitchen.

Darbie was trapped talking to a professor who had arrived late, but Jack and Ethan were free and already on the move. I waited for them to disappear upstairs unnoticed before turning to my mum.

"I'm going to go check on her," I explained, already beginning to step away. "Make sure she's not just being shy and hiding."

My mum gave an amused smile. "It's sweet you know her so well. Bring her back as soon as she's done alright? This night is for her after all."

I nodded, "Yeah, alright mum."

I hurried to make my way to the stairs, but was stopped by just about every person possible on the way just to the dining table. Everyone I had known consistently since childhood or at least within the past five years was here, hugging me with each step and wishing me well. I was slowly making progress with each "thank you" but it still must has taken at last a full two or three minutes before I was stepping into Darbie's conversation and declaring he was the best friend of the guest of honour and he was needed upstairs.

"Oh, right, of course," Professor Germain agreed politely and stepped away so that the two of us could leave.

We turned around and began heading towards the stairwell.

"Reika swiped the ring and disappeared with it." I said, trying to explain the situation as quickly as possible.

Darbie's eyes widened. "Oh, Unicorn turds."

5

Erika

My stomach felt like it was being squeezed. Cold sweat pooled only on my lower back. The base of my skull throbbed like there was a bruise someone decided to try to drain with a precisely poked needle. The skin at the crook of my neck twitched as my pulse threatened to push through my skin. I had flung my white heels off once I got to the foyer and proceeded to charge up the stairs.

At the top, the stairs levelled out into a large open space with an office desk built over the stairs and foyer, a large window illuminating the mahogany structure. Two large black chairs sat at either end, each half of the desk was cluttered with slightly different organised messes.

To the left of the desk, was the doorway to Mr. and Mrs. McLeon's room, the door was wide open and very empty beyond just the painfully grey furniture.

Immediately in front of the stairs was Adam's younger brother's door. Then, just next to that and angled inwards was the navy blue door that led to Adam's room. Between Adam's room and his parents are the double doors that lead into a suite style bathroom. They were also open, revealing nothing but marble and soap. So I took the three steps and tried to open Adam's brother's door first. Not much to my surprise the door was locked. I moved on to Adam's door.

I reached out and gripped the brass doorknob tight but ultimately hesitated.

I hadn't been in Adam's room since the first time three years ago, when he had hid the ring for me. He didn't like being home, and he didn't like having me around his family even more, so, since that night, I had never really been further than the front door and the kitchen once. Now, I felt like I was invading a part of him he didn't want me to be in.

I rolled my eyes at myself and twisted the knob. I used my whole body to shove the door open only to see Reika sitting at Adam's desk. Her reflection was dancing off the window, holding the ring above a lit candle chanting.

"What are you doing?" I snapped as I rushed in to pull her away.

She dropped the ring into a candle below as I gripped her by the shoulder. I bawled the material of her top into my hand to get a better grip, twisting as I yanked her up and back. I slammed her against the wall shared with the bathroom.

"I was trying to study it," she begged.

I let go of her shoulder, using both hands to fish for her wrists as she talked. Once I had a grip I raised them to where I could see them then pinned them against the wall, just on either side of her ears.

"Bull shit," I spat.

Her eyes were panicked, but I still saw no signs of malice as she swore to me, "I promise Erika, I was just curious. I wanted to know what kind of magick it was and if it was why he loved you."

I gritted my teeth. "You think I'd fucking spell Adam to love me."

She shook her head. "No, I just wanted to be sure."

I opened my mouth to curse some more, but couldn't. Feet quickly shuffling in, forced me to bite my lip. I didn't know who it was or what they would think if they heard anything.

"What's going on, E?" Ethan's voice sounded off just behind me.

I looked over my shoulder at the two sharp dressed gentlemen moving into the scene. Ethan looked between Reika and I, while Jack moved over to the candle that was popping in the corner.

I nodded over my shoulder at Reika while still looking at Ethan.

"She stole the ring right off Adam's finger and was in here chanting with it," I said.

Ethan immediately began glaring at Reika. He only needed to take one large step towards us before he was on line with me. He reached out and gripped Reika by the jaw, forcing her to look at him. Her olive skin paled out in small patches around his finger tips. Her eyes creased together tightly as he jerked her head over to parallel his.

"What were you doing with it?" he asked.

She clenched her jaw, so he gripped tighter.

"I'm only going to ask one more time," he stooped down so he was in her face as he threatened her. "What were you doing?"

"Studying its enchantments," she said.

"I think she's telling the truth," I spoke before Ethan could harm her any more.

While I didn't like what she did, and I definitely didn't trust her after what happened, I also don't believe that

74

maliciously hurting someone was right. It's one thing to tackle someone to the ground or pin them to a wall, but to harshly touch or move them around in a way that is blatantly for the intent of pain is not in my preferred approach.

That's not to say I wouldn't, nor haven't, done it, though, just so we're clear.

Ethan looked at me. I watched the centre of his eyes flick back between each of mine before he let go of her jaw.

"Guys," Jack called both of us.

We looked over.

"The ring melted," he said, leaning over the candle on the desk.

I looked to Ethan. "Hold her," I commanded before letting her go and moving straight to the candle.

Sure enough, as soon as I looked into the pool of white wax I saw thick gold floating through the liquid. I was no longer interested in the why. By then, I was just seething.

Not only was that piece of jewellery the thing that kept Adam safe. But it also kept the dark dragon and its host locked away.

"You used a candle that was blessed by the Morrigan to get a closer look at the ring?" I bellowed. Still looking down into the floating gold.

"I needed better light," Reika responded, sounding so innocent.

I almost felt bad as I turned and violently grabbed her, pushing her to the floor with me on top of her. I grabbed at her collar. The neckline already rose so high that it was only an inch away from becoming a turtleneck, yet as I pulled her up by that fabric, the collar stretched out so that- if I had wanted- I could have fit two of her heads through the hole without even having to unbutton it.

"Then you flick on a light switch, Reika," I snapped at her.

Jack and Ethan were both at a shoulder, trying to pull me off her. Unfortunately, the fear of loss fueled a rage that even them combined weren't strong enough to break. Now, the once collected and refined girl was shaking beneath me.

"I didn't know how to," she cried.

I pulled the collar higher, pulling her closer. I could hear the fibres of the cloth popping. "That's why you take one of us with you. We're a team. We communicate, we help each other. We don't steal from one another!" I yelled down at her through the inch gap between our faces. "You have no idea what you just destroyed."

A chilling laugh rolled over the room. Ethan's hands let go of me to pull a knife out of the inside of his coat. He was spinning to face the unknown laugh and throwing the knife as I let go of Reika and twisted around to look behind me where the laugh came from. I saw just in time for the dagger to stop midair, crystalize with ice and shatter within moments.

One yellow eye rolled towards Ethan. "Cute try little boy, but it takes more to kill a dragon." The eye then flicked to me. "I've missed seeing the fury of the Light Dragon in person."

I let go of Reika and she dropped with a thud. I stood and took in the sight before me.

Maroon scars carved in the shape of magickal glyphs looked significantly less coloured on ash grey skin. White hair fell down in soft, straight strands over his bare chest and biceps. He had perched himself on Adam's desk, one foot placed on the chair, propping his knee up so that he could lean against it while the other leg swung softly off the ledge. In his leaning position, his hair draped all the way down to his undressed lap, where it pooled and ultimately covered his nakedness.

76

He had one dead eye, only a shade lighter than the blueish-grey that was his skin. A deep entrenched scar cut down from above his eyebrow, through his eye and down over his nose. Another even deeper scar stretched from the corner of his eye by the bridge of his nose, to where his cheek bone met his ear. The other eye was bright yellow- not quite as rich as gold, and not as pale as a rose. More like honey, or butterscotch candy.

I stepped over Reika so that I was no longer straddling her and could fully turn my attention to the metaphorical and possibly literal Greek god in front of me.

"Who the hell are you, lazy eye?" Ethan quipped from behind me.

I heard two more sets of feet clamouring up the stairs, but my eyes were trapped on the stranger's one golden one. He leaned to look behind me for a moment, before staring me down again.

"Do we know you?" I asked.

There was a pit in my stomach that moved at the sight of him. Part of it curiosity, part of it familiarity, and a lot of it another feeling I couldn't quite place. But it all crawled up to my chest and tightened there, making my heart beat faster like it was trying to run out of me towards him. Or away, I didn't know for sure.

He gave me a lazy smile as he dragged his eyes over my body.

"A part of you may know a part of me from our shared past," he said.

He lifted himself off the desk with his arms and stepped down fluidly. His exceptionally toned body moved in such effortless ways that I couldn't stop staring.

Even when he stood tall, his hair lifting from its protective place by his groyne, I didn't stop looking in amazement.

77

Jack's eyes flickered down to the stranger's waistline, where they nearly bulged out of his head. He was standing just next to the naked man only one or two steps from me and only an arm length away from the new guy's naked body.

The naked stranger took a step for me, but was quickly shut down. "Alright," Ethan said. Suddenly his arm was snaking in front of me, pulling me back then pushing me behind him. "That's close enough sunshine orb," he warned.

The stranger must have been only a few inches shorter than the height of a door. As he loomed over us, I tried to breathe evenly while looking up at him, but the knot in my chest held firmly in place. As if my lungs too were as tied up as my mind, all whilst my heart was racing.

His intimidating statured only stopped catching my attention when I realised Ethan was nearly touching noses with him.

I could feel the stranger's power radiating off him, seeping into my bones. Almost like they were corrupting me, they were so infectiously strong. His flawless build and violent gaze didn't make him any less terrifying or gorgeous.

But Ethan was a wall.

The stranger may have had darker skin and a menacing stare, but Ethan was the only mortal I knew who created invincibility for himself. He stared down this newcomer at the same height, with a wider and stronger build and eyes so icy they could freeze the dark dragon himself in his place.

Cold sweat cropped up on my cheek bones. The same ominous cold from this morning.

"Holy shit," I whispered, my face dropping and the fascination officially burned out of me. I reached out and grabbed Ethan's wrist. "He's Condan," I said, loud enough for the room to hear. "He's the Dark Dragon. Out of the ring."

Out of the corner of my eye, I could see Jack's eyes grow wide again and he took one large step away from Condan, pressing himself against the wall.

There were a few moments of awkward silence as we all scanned the room. Darbie and Adam both stood in the doorway, ready to attack, but with hesitant looks on their faces. Jack was clearly just nervous - he was the only one separated from us by the individual who's alignment we didn't know yet. Reika was crouching on the ground behind me, her eyes literally pulsating purple, a dagger already drawn.

"So is he friendly or not?" Ethan asked over his shoulder nonchalantly and with no hint of a whisper. "What are we doing with the stray, people? Let's make a decision."

Condan chuckled, an eerie smirk casting across his face.

"Ethan," Darbie whimpered from the doorway. "He's a ridiculously powerful prince with an even more powerful and old dragon soul in him. You can't just act like he's a feral cat we found outside."

Ethan turned around to give him a look consisting of a creased forehead and bored eyes.

"Why not?" he asked, "He has the same amount of hair as one."

"Why you insolent…" Condan trailed off as rage consumed him.

A blue hue illuminated from his hand with wintry steam trendling from it as he raised it towards Ethan face.

His dead eye illuminated white, like the light from the sun through an icicle.

Without a second to think, I balled Ethan's shirt fabric into my fist and threw him back with one hand and stepped forward into his place. With my other hand I summoned fire and brought it to Condan's face.

79

Both of our magick mere centimetres from each other's heads. The orange from my hand danced in his yellow eye like it belonged there. In his other one, blue rotated like souls circling a watery grave.

He was the one who stopped first, I followed suit, both of us letting the light from our power fade.

I held my fist up for a few moments, waiting for him to move and finish backing down. He cocked his head a little closer to my hand and scrunched his nose as his lips curled into a twisted smile.

"My-my Fintan," his voice was melodic to my ears. "You picked a fiery one."

"My name is Erika Gavina," I said and the flames in my hand lit up once again with my irritation. "And for the record, this power is mine." The flames licked his face and I watched as some of the ash coloured skin curled and boiled close to the magick. A stream of red blood streamed down from his cheek and dripped off his chin.

He sucked a breath in through his teeth and pulled away, but his expression didn't change, almost as if there was no real pain that followed the burn.

"How about we drop our weapons, dear?" he asked. "I wouldn't want to hurt you without you asking me to."

"I drop mine once you promise not to harm my friends," I bargained.

"Deal," he accepted immediately.

I was almost shocked at the speed in which he agreed. Slowly, I lowered my hand.

"What are we gonna do with him, Erika?" Adam asked.

I sighed. "Get him dressed and get him looking human." I turned around to look at Adam. "We still have a party we have

80

to attend," I further explained. "Tell everyone he's Darbie's brother who surprised us with a visit."

I looked over at Ethan who apparently had been caught by Reika as he was still half in her grasp with one of her arms wrapped around his back. His arms were holding a sword I didn't know he had stowed, and her other hand was still holding a dagger out.

"You can put the skewers away now, ladies," I said to them.

Adam stepped forward. He rested both his hands on my shoulders and kissed my forehead. He leaned back to speak, "I'll give him some clothes from my closet, if I can find anything that fits. Then we'll meet you downstairs, but you should get down there before my mum comes looking."

I nodded once. "Keep Darbie and Jack with you, just in case."

"Good it's not me," Ethan said. "Because I need a cigarette."

I laughed bitterly. "I don't smoke, but-" I looked up to Adam hoping my apology would be conveyed in my look- "I think I'll join you for one before rejoining the party."

Ethan, who had now sheathed his sword, slipped an arm around Reika's waist. He gripped her tight.

"And you're coming with us," he said. "Because now I really don't trust you."

He basically hoisted her off the ground as he started walking out of the room. She had to stay on her tiptoes to follow him out.

I leaned on my toes to give Adam one last kiss before slipping after them. I passed Darbie with a squeeze to his shoulder, him moving into the room as I moved out. In the doorway, I turned to look at those I was leaving behind.

Condan was a dark elf with a dragon soul inside him. Elves, even if they were naturally drawn to evil like dark elves, were bound by their words. Just like the rest of the magick community, contracts we agreed to bound us with our lives. He couldn't hurt my friends even if he wanted to. So I trusted my friends to manage him, and I left.

Outside it was raining. Water pitter pattered off the roof and down onto the vegetation around the house. I stepped off the patio that wrapped around the house and followed the worn path around the side that sloped down to the detached garage. Ethan sat on the stone wall the separated the grass from the gravel drive. He was trying to light a cigarette with a lighter in the rain.

Reika was underneath the small overhang of the roof. She sat with her knees tucked up to her chest. Her arms wrapped around her legs and her chin rested on her knees. Despite being close to seventy years old, she looks small and young. It was a reminder that years had nothing to do with experience. Reika had been hidden away in the Otherworld her entire life, deprived of a life and experience that would have given her years their due worth.

By the time I reached the pair, I was well wet and dripping. With a snap of my fingers Ethan's cigarette lit.

He flicked his lighter closed and saluted me with the burning stick.

"You know those things will kill you, right?" I asked.

Ethan laughed bitterly, his face was down watching the gravel as he kicked it with his black dress shoe.

"This might be hard for you to understand," he started, stopping only to take in a long drag of the cigarette. "But not all mortals wanna live forever."

He looked at me, his blue eyes clear like water.

"This might be hard for you to understand," I mimicked, reaching my hand out asking for a cigarette. "But not all immortals want to live forever."

He fished a fresh one out of his box and put it between my fingers.

"Touché," he offered.

I lit the paper as I put it to my lips. I chewed on the end whilst I kept breathing in through my nose, barely tasting the smoke as it burned.

6

Erika

Adam's mum was, of course, very confused. She did, after all, have no idea that Darbie had a brother. Nor that I had known Darbie and his brother beyond just school. We explained that I had grown up with Connor, who was actually Condan, and gone to school with him in the States. Which led to even more confusion. We reached a point where we all realised layering on intentional confusion was more effective in getting her to stop asking questions than to try and explain any of this rationally.

After the ordeal and a few hours of socialising, I found myself outside once again. This time with a cup of tea instead of a cigarette. I leaned against the wood board attached to the iron railing of the patio deck. Everyone else was inside due to the rain, and the McLeons had shut the sliding glass doors to try to keep it dry and warm inside. Almost all of the guests I knew were gone, the majority left were either my specific friend group or neighbours who were simply invited out of respect and had no attachment to my writing or myself.

Rain ran off my nose and into the reddish brown hue of my tea cup until it spilled over the china sides. I watched as it poured down towards the soft mossy grass beneath the patio.

Behind me the sliding door opened and shut. I didn't hear the feet approach me, but a subtle shadow ever so slightly loomed over my tea cup through the rain.

"You would think that the dragon of fire, air and light would avoid the rain," Condan said, now right next to me. "Yet here you are."

"I'm still a druid by nature," I said. "The rain, the ground, the sky and anything else on this planet are still my elements. Still things that I love and find peace in."

His hand reached out and pulled the wet hair from my face. I slapped his hand away as I rotated my whole body to face him.

"Don't touch me," I commanded. "We're not friends yet."

He smiled and reached for my hip, "More like lovers."

I set my cup down on the railing, reached across myself and flicked his wrist away.

"No, we are not," I snapped. "Maybe the two souls inside us were at one point in time. But you and I are strangers, and I have someone who is more than just a lover."

"Oh yes, the mortal," He laughed.

And we stood there. Facing off in silence. Nothing but the sound of water splattering on wet grass as it poured from the gutters around us.

"You know we're the keepers of this world and the otherworld, as well as the worlds beyond these," he said.

"I don't understand what you mean."

"We hold the power over the trinity," he explained in a consistently vague manner.

"Still not getting it," I said harshly.

Condan sucked in a breath, his mouth beginning to open-

"Hey Erika," Adam slid the glass door open and announced. "We're all heading home, are you and him ready?"

"Absolutely," I announced, and headed towards him. Leaving the tea cup behind.

"So now that we're home, can we have a family chat about what to do with the feral cat we've apparently adopted?" Ethan asked.

"Be careful, human, despite the promises I made to your owner, I will still kill you where you stand," Condan warned.

I looked around the very green kitchen. It was supposed to be a gentle sage, but right now it looked how I felt - like sick.

Jack raised his finger. "Actually, since you made the deal with Erika, you can't hurt us under magick contract," he pointed out.

Condan laughed. "Magick binds don't apply to the light dragon and I, we are the sources of the original magick. We chose what it can and cannot do."

Immediately everyone turned to me. The green cabinetry pressed inwards towards me, until I feel like I couldn't breath.

I took a sharp breath to try and catch what was slowly being squeezed out of me.

"Okay don't fucking look at me like that," I argued. "I've only known about what I am for like five years okay? He's literally been in communication with actual dragons and gods for like three thousand. Of course he knows shit I don't know."

"Actually, I have been a dragon for twenty-seven thousand, three hundred and forty-four years," Condan said casually. "The last time I spoke with a dragon that was not myself was three thousand, four hundred years ago."

The green paled even more. I had to give myself a quick second to process exactly what I had just heard.

This being was almost thirty *millennia.*

There were bones in museums to creatures that had been long forgotten younger than him.

I pointed at him. "See," I said, then motioned to him like he was evidence. "Way more time than me. I'm two thousand years old."

I said it trying to sound funny, but to me it sounded like I was trying to justify his age by comparing it to my own.

30,000? That's nothing. I'm 2,000. Totally normal to live through every age known to man. Is what it sounded like.

"And I thought we were old," Darbie whispered to himself, gawking at the dark elf.

His comment brought an ease to my chest. It was nice to know I wasn't the only one thinking Condan's age was absolutely insane.

"Just to clear this up," Adam spoke up. "So you became a dragon around the same time as the last human ice age?"

Condan smiled. "I was the ice age."

Ethan's gaze snapped to me as he raised his hands in the air. "Yeah, hell no, this psycho has to go."

Arguments ensued between our group, Darbie and I arguing that Condan could be a great support as we try to train more of the youngling dragons. Ethan and Adam practically screaming that the elder was a raging lunatic. Reika and Jack were still arguing about her releasing him in general.

All in all, chaos was erupting quickly in the kitchen of Darbie's antique home.

"Enough!" Condan yelled.

Immediately we all quieted down and looked at him, only for Ethan to say, "Shut up grandpa, the kids are talking."

Condan's dead eye began to churn again, his nostrils flaring with anger.

"What were you going to say Con?" I asked, pulling his attention away from my friend.

He sniffed, as if his anger came from his nose and he had just breathed it back in.

"I was going to say," he began and leaned against his elbows on the kitchen island. "This conversation should only be held between yourself, the other elf and I considering we're the only ones here with any age or power."

"Um, excuse me," Reika spoke up for herself. "I am seventy years old and the daughter of a witch goddess."

"Seventy years old is no more than a crying baby," Condan hissed.

"Hey, we don't age discriminate here," Jack said.

"Yeah," Ethan agreed. "Besides, no existence in society for three thousand years, no opinion."

Condan's eye flared again.

"Ethan!" I yelled at him. "Are you trying to get yourself killed?" I finished in a hush.

He shrugged at me. "I mean yeah, a little bit."

"I can grant that wish for you," Condan promised.

Adam reached out and pulled Ethan so that the dense boy was behind him.

"Yeah, he was just kidding," Adam said to Condan. "He kids a lot. You can just ignore him."

Condan stood up straight, looming over Adam by a few inches.

"He insults me every time he opens his mouth," Condan fumed.

Adam smiled. "He does that to everyone, it means he likes you."

"No," Ethan said behind Adam. "It does not." To which Adam elbowed him in the gut.

Condan raised the eyebrow over his good eye, clearly waiting for another blatant lie from the group explaining why Ethan was a dumbass and a dickhead all at the same time.

"We're keeping the cat and that's final," I announced. "So everyone is going to play nice and if you can't, I will deal out the punishment, does everyone understand?"

"I believe you, and I should take the other dragons and leave," Condan said. "That is my opinion."

"I brought the dragons here." I crossed my arms. "My opinion is law here, not yours."

"I am the mother of these younglings," he argued.

"Then I am the king of everything. I command everything, including you."

I could feel strength I knew wasn't coming from me. Somewhere in the back of my mind, Fintan was screaming, reminding me that while the dark dragon and I were equals, I was still the king and she the queen. As archaic as it was, kings always held higher control than the queens, and I had no issue reminding Condan of that.

He gritted his teeth as we glared at one another.

Even though he was the queen, he was still a former prince and a dark elf at that. Dark elves were militaristic and egotistical. They had conquered large parts of the world and the otherworld before they were overthrown by the young gods like the egyptians and the greeks. Now the dark elves are nearly extinct, and the few that remain are no more than mercenaries and assassins. But Condan didn't live through their extinction. The last time he was alive, dark elves still held a significant amount of power over the otherworld. He still held to the ego that told him he was the strongest and most powerful being on this planet.

My mum always commented on how druids and dark elves were natural born enemies. Druids - who believed we were all one united by nature and life - and dark elves, who believed they could conquer and destroy everything in their wake.

"Understood," Condan said. He turned to Darbie, who was now blue, sitting on the counter, and eating a slice of pound cake. "Sea elf, show me to my lodging if you please."

Darbie stopped mid bite, mouth wide open, to stare at the other elf in confusion. Darbie casted a glance over to me as he pulled his mouth away from the cake.

"Umm," Darbie hesitated. "All the dragons sleep together in a big group out in my barn. I have a spare bed upstairs if you would rather sleep on a bed."

"Is the bed made from bones?" Condan asked.

All of us immediately laughed uncomfortably. Condan, on the other hand, did not. He looked over at me, his dead eye seeming to look too, baring into my soul like it was looking for Fintan somewhere inside of my eye.

"You're joking right?" Darbie asked.

Condan turned to him. "Us dark elves were slayers of all, kings and queens of the world, we constructed beds from the bones of the kings we killed, and tanned their skin to be used as padding and blankets. Why would I joke about such a conquest?"

Ethan let out a loud sigh, bringing his hand up to rub his forehead before dropping it down, palm up, fingers pointing at Condan. "Are we sure we wanna sleep under the same roof as this guy?"

Adam and I locked eye contact. His jaw was tight, I could see the muscle clenching as he looked at me. He was angry about something, unfortunately I was unable to put my finger on exactly what it was that he was angry about.

"I'm going home," he finally said, looking to the ground and beginning to walk away. "Erika, our bed frame and mattress were delivered to the house. I set it up while you were here getting ready. I'm going to go sleep there, you can come join if you want or you can sleep with your new pet, its up to you."

Condan looked to me with what almost looked like excitement in his eyes. "The mortal has a good idea. We can retire to your private accommodation so that you and I can rest together."

Adam laughed. "Yeah I don't think so, my house, my rules. No dark dragon elf people allowed."

Adam shot a look at me before walking out of the kitchen. I watched him turn to slip past Condan, between the grey man and the pistachio walls, he appeared almost blue.

"You should stay here Condan, let the other dragons know you're back," I said. "Reika, you should either come stay with Adam and I, although we have nowhere for you to sleep… So you should probably stay here."

I moved around the kitchen island, opposite of Ethan, and met Condan at the door frame. Condan turned his body as I moved, watching me with more than just his eye. The hair on my arms rose as I walked past him. The breath that left my nose blew out like steam as if the temperature dropped several centigrade. I was suddenly very aware of the power literally radiating off of him. Even though we were supposedly matched in power, a crushing feeling of dread washed over me as I felt and thought for a moment that there was no way my magick and my strength could ever go head to head with his.

I stared into that dead eye. Just so I could memorise the layout of his scars in hopes of figuring out how he lost it.

If he was a prince who commanded some great army, as well as a dragon who fought in countless battles, then he had to have been stronger and more cunning than me. How could two thousand equate to twenty thousand? Who the hell managed to be strong enough to gouge out that eye?

"Is there something you wanted?" Condan asked sweetly.

I shook my head. Behind him Ethan was watching us intently. The rest of the group was slowly moving, beginning to prepare to move to their various sleeping arrangements. But not Ethan. His eyes were wide, bright, and practically contained crackling lightning. He was energised off of suspicion, and now that my original intoxication from Condan's power had worn off, I was slowly beginning to board the Ethan boat to full blown paranoia.

Any time a god or some other powerful being fell into our laps we ended up having a problem on our hands. Right now we had the Morrigan with her prophecies, a demigoddess with her mission, and a dragon who was just released from what was beginning to sound like captivity. What could go wrong, right?

"I'll make sure he's all tucked in, E," Ethan said to me, meeting my eyes. "He'll be comfortable and get a good rest. I promise."

He chewed on the inside of his lower lip, making it wiggle. He was lying. And that was his way of telling me.

"Thanks Ethan." I gave him a smile, hoping that Condan wouldn't be able to tell I was also lying. "Thanks for trying to be cool with this. I would appreciate it if we could really make Con a part of the family."

I walked away while Condan was distracted, throwing a smug looking towards Ethan.

Adam was already at the front door, his hand on the old copperknob. It had long since rusted to a teal-green, standing out magnificently against the espresso wood door. Black iron was

92

curled in the centre, holding in exquisite antique stained glass. The stairway leading up stairs to the second floor was painted a pistachio green which I always hated, but Darbie claimed it was soothing to him.

Green, to druids and nature based elves, was a colour symbolising peace and comfort. The colour of nature's home.

Adam opened the door before looking back at me. His emerald green eyes staring into mine.

Emerald was so much more beautiful than pistachio.

At home, our house was barren.

The older cottage was on a lush hillside that spanned all the way down to the coast which could be seen some many kilometres off in the distance during the day. During the night, as it was then, you could hardly even see your neighbours beyond just a tiny blip of light. The driveway was long from the road and made of loose gravel pebbles. I could hear them crunching under the car as Adam drove. The grass had grown tall leading up to the house, no one had bothered trimming it while the house was up for sale. When we pulled up just to the left of the cottage, the motion sensor light out front struggled to flicker on.

"Remind me to replace that," Adam said, unbuckling himself and getting out.

His head was turned towards the front yard, away from me so I couldn't see his expression. The drive home had seemed long as we sat in silence.

Even though I had been with him for the past three years, he still was hard for me to read. After spending two millennia learning every expression in the world, you would've thought I could read anybody. But there were still times where Adam was an unread page to me and I would have to sit down and ask him what he was thinking. It was, I believe, one of the primary reasons why I wanted to be with him so badly. He was excitement where the rest of the world had become dull.

"I can also replace it," I said as I got out and rounded the front of the car.

Adam stood in the middle of the yard. A three foot high rock wall was stacked around the house, marking where the tame garden was separated from the wild grass and weeds beyond. A gravel path led to the front door where a small concrete patio no bigger than a car sat at the base of the front door. Stepping stones walked out directly in front of the door from the patio, leading around to a raised vegetable garden that was currently empty, but would eventually be Adam's herb garden.

A bird bath was set in the empty grass just beyond the stepping stones, a ring of thistles and primrose lay around it. In the far corner of the garden, where the rock wall squared off was a tall rowan tree.

Both the primrose and the rowan tree were natural wards of evil, one of the many reasons we chose this house.

"I think you're about to be too busy *handling* Condan to do anything around here," Adam spoke, hissing out the word handling like it was some sort of curse word.

He walked over to the front door and drew out his keys, struggling to get them into the keyhole in order to unlock the front door.

The light was flickering angrily now.

I walked up to Adam and rested my hand over his, gently grabbing his fingers and the keys.

"Adam," I said soothingly. "You, and making a home with you, are all I have ever wanted," I said, leaning down to try

94

and meet his eyes. "I have been around a long time, and I've never wanted to spend the rest of my life with anyone until I met you."

"He's quite literally made for you, Erika," he said, finally meeting my eye. "How can I compete with someone that was created by a higher power to complete you."

I shook my head. Leaving one hand on his, I brought the other up to cup his cheek. "Oh love, he wasn't made for me. If he was, I would feel it. The more I see and experience this life, the more I know that God is real, and if he wanted me with Condan, we would be. Instead, I am here with you, about to go into *our* home." I stressed the word *our*, because it was true. This life, my life, belonged equally to Adam as it did to me. None of me belonged to anyone else. I knew that without a doubt in my mind.

"I'm going to die one day," Adam said, barely above a whisper. So quietly that I almost didn't hear it over the sound of my own silent breath.

I brought my hand back down to his, and leaned my head into his chest.

I whispered back, "Not if I can help it."

7

Ethan

I was sitting in a chair against the house messing around with my figure-eight banjo thing. The barn was a good half a football field away from the house.

Darbie had bought the property specifically because it had a lot of space, was super far away from any civilization while also being surrounded in a forest for privacy, and because it had a three story house and barn that could house the dragons that Erika had brought back with her.

I had spent the six months after she returned helping to refurbish both structures so that we could use the space as a school and orphanage for all the wayward magick borns of the world.

Now we had a threat living amongst us. And I wasn't talking about the equal parts mysterious, equal part airhead demi-goddess with eerie purple eyes. I was talking about the grey, shirtless, scarred up, old, bitter, elf guy that couldn't stop hitting on Erika. The same one who was currently teaching the baby dragos to sword fight by brutally kicking their ass in the open field between me and the barn.

"Despite all your years alive and training you're still this pathetic?" he yelled at Xavier who was leaning on his elbows flat on the ground, blood dripping from his eyebrow and the corner of his lip.

Xavier was one of the older dragons, both in physical appearance and in actual age. He was one of the strongest of them, despite having no magick of his own or any knowledge of magick before he accepted his dragon's soul. Because of his strength, he had always been like a captain in our hierarchy of leaders. Erika was always at the top with Darbie and Adam as her left and right hand men. Jack and I were then just beneath them as their sources of information and strategy. Xavier was not remotely close to being as in charge as our closely knitted group, but he was always included in our conversations, and any decisions that needed to be made that would impact the dragons, he was there and his opinion was worth gold.

He had taken care of them for over a millennia before Erika showed up. He kept the dragons safe and trained them while also protecting the ring, something I now understood was an immense responsibility.

And Condan, the ashy asshole, had just dropped him on his ass and called him pathetic.

In conclusion: I didn't care how old he was. I hated him.

Around the same time Xavier was getting up and walking away with a limp, and Condan was looking for his next victim, Erika showed up with Adam. They came out of the mudroom door, heading down the stairs, both with a coffee in their hand. Adam was chewing on a piece of toast from the looks of it.

"Hey," Erika said first.

"Hey," I said back, looking up at her.

The sun illuminated behind her like a halo and for a second I almost believed she was letting off golden hues

"Good morning," she added.

I didn't say anything back, but I did take an extra second to look at her. She was intimidating in her true form. Hardened eyes and skin, yet they were both so light and easy to look at. Her dark hair stood out against her paleness, even when it was pulled back in a tight and high ponytail like today. She had on an incredibly light grey sweater, so light it was almost white, which was abnormal for her. She normally stuck to black.

She looked so. Fucking. Gorgeous.

She always did, but in white? I had to bite my tongue to keep myself from falling into a daze.

Adam, who stood behind her, had on a burgundy version of the same sweater.

"Did you steal that sweater from Adam?" I asked.

They both looked down at her choice in clothing as if they hadn't noticed.

Adam cracked a smile. "Yeah it is. I laid it out last night to wear today and when I woke up she had taken it."

Erika's pale face tinted pink ever so slightly before she shrugged. "It looked warm and our room was cold when I woke up."

Adam pointed at her with his coffee still in his hand. "She also stole my warm wool socks. I had to fish out another pair from one of the boxes."

"Still a lot of unpacking to do then, I take it?" I surmised.

Erika crossed her arms and settled her attention on the scene before her.

"Lots," Adam said. "We only have our bed in the room and some basic things in the bathroom. We have a lot of furniture laying around either still packaged or wrapped in plastic wrap waiting to be used."

I took a glance at the field to watch Condan backhand a small dragon with the pommel of his blade. I clenched my jaw for only a split second before turning back to Adam.

"I don't have any contracts right now," I said. "So when you both head back home, I'll come with you, and help you unpack."

"Thanks mate," Adam offered. "We really appreciate that."

Once we had gone quiet, we were left with only the uncomfortable scene in front of us to watch.

"What's going on here?" Erika asked, breaking the silence without looking away.

At first I didn't answer, I just looked out over the same display she was watching. Condan was advancing on the fallen kid as if he was a genuine enemy.

"The douche-canoe has been teaching our kiddos how to be tough, apparently," I explained.

Erika looked down at me. "They're not really kiddos to you."

"They look like kiddos, and that's what you call them."

Erika laughed and looked out at the sea of defeated faces sitting on the grass. "That's because my Dragon is a couple hundred thousand years older than theirs'. Most of them were born as humans only a couple hundred years ago. Which, for the record, is a couple hundred years older than you, ya child."

"Hey hey hey," I laughed. "If I'm a child, then you are a raging paedo because Adam is a month and a half younger than me."

"Actually that reminds me," Adam chimed in. "When exactly is your birth date? I know it's the equivalent to July twenty-third, but what year."

"Four hundred and twenty-seven B.C.," she said without hesitating and I nearly choked on air.

"And when are you again Adam?" I asked snarkily.

"Ninth of November, nineteen ninety-nine," he smirked. "I'm just a baby."

"How do you feel about that, eh, E?" I sassed her and watched her roll her eyes without looking at me. "You're practically having sex with a newborn."

The door opened again, this time revealing the mysterious, air-headed purple eyed demigoddess. She was dressed like she was about to go on a hunting trip in the renaissance. Her faded black cape had the hood down showing off her long, braided black hair. The cloak was pinned across her chest, opening up to a red long-sleeve, fitted down over her hips and drawn tight by a black corset that scooped snuggly under her chest. Warm-looking black tights were tucked into calf high leather boots.

I eyed the hunting bow slung over her shoulder and the collection of arrows that were peeking out from her back as well. I didn't say anything. I had come to the conclusion that she meant no harm, even when she acted on edge around Condan.

Despite releasing him, she clearly wanted nothing to do with him.

She saw the three of us at the base of the stairs and stopped on the first step. Instead of descending and joining us, she stayed and watched from there, leaning on the railing to get a closer look.

"Who's next?" Condan yelled again. "Have you all grown weak since I've been gone?"

"I really want to put this guy in his place," I whispered to Erika and Adam.

100

Erika sighed. "Don't. We don't know what he's capable of and you're still mortal."

I tapped my thumb on my banjo thingy. When no one volunteered to be on the receiving end of his abuse, he stepped over the sword laying on the floor, leaving it behind and began taking long strides towards the congregation of young dragons. Despite Erika's words and everything I had witnessed, I rose to my feet. I left the unknown instrument in the seat behind me.

"Ethan…" Erika started in a warning tone, but trailed off without saying another word.

I didn't look back at her. I kept striding towards the threat, moving quicker than him. I picked up the sword he left behind when I was only three paces off. A few more large steps and I was there. He raised his sword up from his side, threateningly pointing it in the direction of a fire dragon no older looking than sixteen. He had red hair, red freckles on his face, and pale red eyelashes. I could see the fear in his brown eyes as he looked at Condan.

"Use your power," he seethed. "Defend yourself you little-"

I slipped in beside the white haired cunt and swung my sword upwards, colliding with his and sending the blade arching upwards, towards the sky. Condan hung on for dear life, stumbling backwards with the sword. As he stumbled back three steps, I rounded in front of him, putting myself in between him and the kids.

I pointed my sword out in front of me, looking directly down the metal at the angry elf. It only took him a second before he was back standing and composed. And boy did he seem angry. The gold in his eye glowed, and this dead eye spun like the bottom of a well. He left his sword by his side as he eyed me.

"I think they've had enough, mate," I warned.

He smiled. "And you? You would like to fight now?"

101

I spared a glance over to Erika and Adam. I watched Adam running up the stairs past Reika who stood with her bow drawn. Erika was still at the base of the stairs, standing ready.

I appreciated that she trusted me enough not to come break us up immediately, but my pride had hoped she'd be right behind me. I thought of myself as a strong fighter, but not against an older than dirt warrior dragon prince and since Erika and I always fought well together, I would have liked to have had her right behind me in this.

I shrugged nonetheless. "Why not? Kicking your ass sounds like a good warm up."

His eyes narrowed. "I don't believe in letting humans live."

Without warning, he arched his sword back down across him, slapping my blade to one side before he brought his foot up and kicked me square in the chest. I tumbled back into the crowd that parted like I had some deadly disease.

I tried to rise to my feet, but Condan was faster. He kicked me so hard in the ribs that I was lifted into the air a few inches and sent landing hard on my back.

I once again tried to roll over and push myself up quickly, but instead had to stop to block his advance. He swung his sword like it was a golf club and my head was a massive golf ball. I panicked and turned my metal up, colliding with his perpendicularly. I held it at an awkward angle with only one hand, resulting in the flat side of the sword being pushed into my face as he slowly applied more force.

He kept pushing, so I let myself fall back onto my back. I brought my other hand up to wrap around my sword.

With one hand on the hilt, and now one towards the top of the blade, I was able to stabilise the weapon with one hand on either side of Condan's. I attempted to force my sword away from

102

my own face. He pushed onward, fording into his sword so that he could thrust harder into mine.

Before I knew it my whole body was being shoved backwards, dragging along the ground.

I tried to keep my hand flat at first to keep from cutting it, but as I was pushed along the ground, I found myself having to hold on tightly to keep it from slipping.

Condan's sword was only held away from my head by my own failing strength as he picked up pace and practically ran me into the barn. At first I dragged across grass, then, as we entered the structure, my body, led by my head, slammed into the doors, breaking the wood and the hinge, pushing it in. I was then sandpapered across the hardwood floor. And even with the painful friction, we were still picking up speed.

I dropped my head back to see the hard wall at the other end of the barn approaching quickly. I looked up to Condan, he was looking right down at me, teeth gritted. I began to let out a curse as the wall became inevitably close when a silent wave of flame came careening into the back of his head. It slammed into him, raining down his neck and lighting his shirt on fire.

It pushed him forward and he tripped over me, right into the wall. I shot to my feet rapidly. Rushing forward, I slid in behind Erika, who's hands and eyes were still hot with fire. Once I was safe behind her, I turned to look at Condan.

He was still on the ground, kneeling against the wall. His back was turned towards us, his shorts burning away and floating to the ground gently. Burn marks singed into his back were healing almost as soon as they had shown up. His hair had burned to his scalp, but even that grew back out like nothing had ever happened. The rapidness of his healing left me confused as I drew out the lines of scars in my head.

Once he looked back to normal, he stood up, rolling his shoulders like nothing more than an arm wrestle had taken place.

103

"That could have seriously hurt me, you know," he huffed, and turned to us. He had let go of the sword during his tumble, and now stood unarmed and unaggressive.

Erika rolled her eyes at his comment. Unlike him, however, she kept her hands at the ready. I could smell her fire, it always smelled sweet, like she was burning maple wood despite her flames being completely woodless.

"Even if I had somehow miraculously killed you," she scolded. "It's not like you wouldn't have just popped back up a few hours or weeks later."

He furrowed his brows and took a step closer. He leaned in as if he hadn't heard her correctly.

"I'm sorry," He said, "Pop back up? After dying? I don't understand your meaning."

"You're a celestial dragon," she responded. "We die, we reincarnate later on down the line, depending on how bad it was."

He looked at her. His mouth was parted by a hair, his eyes, both living and dead, were looking at her like he was still waiting for a punchline.

"That's not how it works. We're still only immortal," he said. "Immortal means hard to kill, mortal means easy to die. Immortals do not come back after death."

I watched as Erika shifted. Her back flexed visibly even under her sweater, like the room had just grown hotter all of a sudden.

"What do you mean? Yes we do," she argued.

Condan laughed bitterly. "No love, we don't. All those gods you killed are still dead, are they not?" I watched her hesitate as he asked, so he kept right on talking, "All those dragon slayers with their twisted souls, and those immortally cursed creatures like the wendigo never came back. You and I, while we may be hard to keep down, we can still die, love. And if I die,

104

you do too. Darkness cannot exist without light. Just like light cannot exist without me."

Erika *paled*. Any blood that was in her body grew cold to the point that I could feel it radiating off of her.

She shook her head. "I've come back," she whispered and Condan's face fell.

"You what?" He checked.

I thought her fear was from the guilt of having killed so many. But she could do something that no one, not even Condan could do; live forever, alone. That was much more petrifying.

Erika cleared her throat, strained her back. Adam was jogging into the barn by this point, a sword in hand. Reika was right there as well. Her arrow still knocked and her bow drawn back to her cheek.

"I come back," Erika said with her chest. "I have died more times than I can count. And I always come back."

Erika

After the ordeal, I sat in the dining room. Adam had brewed a cup of tea for me and I sat at the far end of the grandiose table unable to drink it.

Behind me was a window that looked out over the front yard where Jack was teaching a class on how to summon elementals. At the other end of the room, another window looked out towards the barn. The yard was empty now, besides Xavier, who stood on a ladder attempting to fix the broken barn door.

Next to the window, a doorway led into the kitchen. I could hear Adam and Ethan talking in hushed voices. Somewhere in the house, a shower was running and I could hear the hot water rushing through the pipes in the walls too. Then, all at once, the voices and the water stopped.

I watched Ethan step into the dining room from the doorway. He had his hands in the pockets of his jeans. He walked over to me with his hands still stuffed deep down, as if his wrists were cold even in the warmth of the house.

He pulled one hand out to point at the chair next to me.

"Mind if I sit?" he asked.

I nodded and he pulled it out and sat down.

He put one hand into the other and placed them both on top of the table where I could see them. A bloody bandage was wrapped around his right hand.

I hadn't noticed he was injured until then. I reached out and put my hand over his. Without needing to think about it, I focused on the feeling in the pit of my stomach, the one that crept up any time someone I cared about was hurt. By the time I pulled my hand away, the feeling was gone.

Ethan pulled his hand up and examined it as he unwrapped the gauze to reveal a freshly healed hand. Two bright pink lines were the only thing left of his injury, one across the pad of his thumb and palm, and one stretching across the middle digit of his fingers .

"Huh," he sounded. "That's handy." He set his hand back into the other on the table, then looked to me. "Do you think your ability to heal has anything to do with you coming back from the dead?"

I shrugged and looked down at my tea. I stuck my finger in it and stirred, it was still boiling hot, but like normal, heat didn't seem to affect me.

"Maybe he thinks that because he's never been killed before?" I said, but my hesitation made it come out like a question.

Ethan's eyes softened, something they rarely did, and I could tell immediately that it was pity on his face. He looked behind him towards the door, then down at his hands. He rubbed the healed palm with his opposite thumb.

"I was raised Catholic, you know?" he asked, but with his eyes still on his hands, I got the feeling he wasn't talking to me.

"My mum, didn't believe," he added with a slow sigh. "She brought me to offset the judgement she got for her drinking. I never complained about going though because I completely believed that there had to be a Father out there who loved me." He looked up. "My mum is still alive, but you and Adam, and Jack and Darbie, you lot are the only family I've ever had. I've always believed that God gave me this family. Despite everything we've seen, every god we've dealt with, I still believe big G God is the one true, all powerful God. Maybe he has plans for you. Maybe that's why you're still here."

I rubbed my face into my palms roughly.

I dropped one hand to stir my tea again and left my forehead in the other. A headache was beginning to pulse at the base of my skull.

"I lived through Jesus, heard the stories of him dying and rising again," I told the tea. "Even though I always believed in a higher power, like an idiot I assumed Jesus was just a god pulling a prank on mortals. I feel like an idiot for never knowing that being immortal just means harder to kill."

"I think you were just in denial," he said simply. "If you admitted to yourself that Darbie or any immortal you loved could be gone forever like your family-"

"I wouldn't have ever been able to leave them behind," I nodded in agreement, finally sipping from the teacup.

107

"Death is inevitable," he said. Unlike every other mortal, when Ethan talked about death, it was almost like there was nothing but peace in the concept. No fear, no pain, just this stable end that we should have all looked forward to.

Adam leaned into the room, holding himself in the doorway. "We have a mission request, are we taking it?"

I breathed in, happily accepting the end to the conversation. "Depends. What's the mission?"

"Artemis wants her priestess back," he said. "Reika apparently needs an armed escort through the Otherworld."

"Why?" Ethan asked as if the thought of spending more time with her made him sick.

Adam let go of the doorway, and stood fully in the room. He shoved his hands in his pockets as he shrugged his shoulders.

That used to be how he'd shrug when he was a teenager. I remembered seeing him do it in the hallways of our school. I hadn't seen him do it in at least a year. I guess I forgot that he was still young.

"Something about her mom's husband killing her because of her mom's infidelity, ya-day ya-dah ya-day," he said so casually.

"Nice. Okay," I said, not really wanting to add someone else's trauma to my list of things I needed to process. "Sure, I'll get my pack ready. It should still be upstairs."

"Are we gonna bring You-Know-Who?" Adam asked.

"We'll put it to a vote," Ethan said.

"Mm-mm," I mumbled, "There's no way we can leave him alone with the dragons. We're gonna come back and he'll have killed them all. He has to come."

"Great." Ethan rolled his eyes. "Sounds like a fun family bonding trip. What could go wrong?"

Adam

Ethan was the first one ready and waiting. At first, when I approached the hidden door built under the stairway, I assumed I was going to be the first. The door was sealed tightly, like it hadn't been used in at least a day. To open it, I had to push hard once then even harder a second time before it would pop open. Because of the wetter weather in Scotland, if the hinges weren't used, the first attempt to open it would typically be stiff as it had been for me.

The doorway was heavy enough to release a high pitched squeak. But the sound of the ancient iron hinge couldn't cover up the horrible noises below, and as I descended I saw it was none other than my blue eyed best friend. He was playing - or attempting to play, I should say - his dulcimer.

"What the hell are you doing?" I asked.

His head popped up, eyes wide and looking up at me.

"I'm trying to find an ounce of serotonin in this hopefully brief life," he said jokingly.

Or at least I hoped he was joking.

"I can't believe you accepted that thing as payment not knowing what it was," I mocked him.

He shrugged at me and set it aside. "It was either this or a fairy wife and I really don't want a wife."

I walked up to stand next to him and nudged him in the shoulder with mine.

"Oh, come on," I dogged him. "You mean to tell me that you don't want to come home to someone everyday? Have someone to spend time and life with?"

Ethan laughed. "Hell no, having to explain my life to someone? All my traumas and personal shit, and trust that they're going to stick around throughout all of my darkness?" he asked grimly. "With all do respect man, there is no fucking way you can talk me into the misery that is a relationship."

I gave him a disappointed stare.

"Erika and I are happy," I said simply. "And she has two thousand years of trauma."

Ethan moved his eyes back and forth between mine like he was reading the same line in a book over and over again, looking for something. He clenched his jaw and I saw the muscles tick.

He sighed through his nose, jaw still tight. He looked to the ground and his jaw went slack. He nodded slowly, softly, which was unusual for Ethan. Nothing he did was ever soft.

"Yeah…" he said quietly to the floor. "I would be with someone if it was what you and E have."

I reached forward to rest my hand on his shoulder, but before I could touch my friend, the loud hinge of the hidden door let out another scream. I recoiled my hand back into my chest and looked to the stairwell.

Erika was walking down, eyes watching her feet, in a pair of cargo pants and a grey long sleeve. Her hair was pulled up into a braid, but small strands of hair still hung around her face like the thin connection of a spider web. She had her leather pack on her back and her old hatchet and dagger hidden into her tall boots.

She looked ready to kill.

She looked marvellous.

When she made it down the stairs, she looked up from her shoes, the first place she looked was Ethan. I followed her gaze, turning to look up at my friend. I hadn't really seen him much in the last year, and standing next to him now in this moment of stillness, I realised he had grown much taller than me. Three years ago, when we were twenty, he and I were the same height at around 183 centimetres. Now, he easily had another six centimetres on me and could nearly look over the top of my head at Erika.

He had also gotten stronger. While the rest of us had gone back to school to try to build a life here on Earth, Ethan had chosen to focus most of his attention on making money from the Otherworld. He had become an excellent mercenary, picking up jobs that the rest of us didn't want and that were easy enough to handle alone.

Erika had told me something about Ethan having Darbie install a portal to the Otherworld in his flat, just like the one we had here in the basement.

I roamed my best friend's face and noticed small scars I hadn't seen before. There was one that followed along the top of his eyebrow, another just across the bridge of his nose. A large one was hidden away in hair before popping out from the top of his sideburns and curving down to where his jaw met the bottom of his ear. His thick scruff covered it well.

Subconsciously I reached up and rubbed my neck and chin. I had shaved yesterday for the party, and although I could feel it, my hair was still very short. I doubted anyone could even see a shadow of it growing back.

I turned back to Erika. She had shed her pack and knelt down with it about a metre away from us, adjusting the magick scroll and quill she always brought with her on missions. The magick equipment could be written on and the message would

111

immediately appear on its sister parchment which was in Darbie's possession.

She stood up again, slinging the bag back over her shoulder.

I gave her a smile and opened one arm up to her so that she could slide into it and lean against me. She took one step and stopped as the stair door once again let out a horrendous noise.

"I swear to fuck," I hissed. "I'm just not allowed to touch any of my friends am I?"

Erika gave me a concerned look as she reared back, obviously shocked by my outburst. Ethan just chuckled beside me.

Darbie and Jack wandered in, with Reika taking up the line in front of them and Condan wandering in at the rear. The young Xavier came down just behind them a few moments later, shutting the door with a satisfying seal.

"How's the face, kiddo?" Ethan called out to him.

The young looking dragon's face had been left darkly bruised from the morning's events. The bridge of his nose was split and purple, and he had one black eye. The corner of his lip was still swollen and red. He tried to give Ethan a smile, but only half of it turned up.

I looked down at Erika who was watching Condan closely. If we had more time to get to know Reika or Condan, I would have voted to leave some of the group behind with the dark dragon. But, we didn't know what either of the newcomers were capable of, and we weren't about to take the risk that only sending half the team with the witch would be a safe bet. We all already knew that leaving Condan behind would be disastrous if he turned out to have less than honourable intentions. Noone in our group, besides Erika, had the potential to match him powerwise. And even Erika had only been aware of her powers for the last three years. She still had a lot to learn.

112

Condan on the other hand…

Not only was Condan apparently older than the Ice Age, he had possessed the dark dragon's soul for more than twenty-thousand years. He knew his powers as well as he knew himself. On top of that, he was a dark elf, a species naturally inclined to war and winning battles. If he showed any signs of being against us, we would need everyone in order to just subdue him.

All in all, we were stuck going on our little family road trip with the psychopath in the backseat.

I sighed and looked up at the wall in front of us.

The portal to the otherworld was strategically connected to a priceless painting by Darbie. *The Death of Socrates* painting was hanging on the wall, one of Darbie's most precious possessions. He claimed it was the original and that the one the Metropolitan Museum of Art had was a magickal recreation. I wasn't sure if he was telling the truth, or just using it as an excuse to keep it behind a locked glass case and therefore from the Otherworld, one that would have to be closed after us.

After we passed through into the Otherworld, Xavier would have to then lock the painting back up. Just in case the other Dragons stumbled across it. The door to the basement may have been hidden into the wall of the stairway, but that didn't mean the mischievous smoke dragons wouldn't somehow manage to find this place while we were gone.

"Once we're through, we'll close it on the other side," Darbie informed Xavier. "Obviously, keep it open on this side so we can get back through, but shut and lock the case. We'll just break through the glass when we come back."

"I still don't understand why you're so worried about keeping the dragons from the Otherworld," Condan scoffed. "That is literally our world. Dragons should be the rulers of it."

Erika crossed her arms. "Dragons aren't the rulers of any world. We maintain the balance, that's it. And we're keeping the dragons away from the Otherworld so that people continue to think they're dead. Even though the majority of the dragonslayers are gone there are still a few out there, and more can always rise up. Until all the dragons have a handle on their powers, all of them stay here, hidden."

"Let's stop arguing and just get a move on," Ethan snapped. "We're burning daylight, both Earth's and the Otherworld's."

Darbie summoned his staff and pressed the gem of it against the glass. I watched the glass crinkle back like pulling back cling wrap. The frame of the painting started to glow blue instead of shimmering gold, and the colours on the canvas churned together until nothing but a grey, thick void was spinning in the centre.

"Who goes first?" I asked.

Ethan looked to Erika and motioned towards the portal.

"Ladies first," he said.

She motioned towards it as well, mimicking him.

"Well get going then," she sassed.

He dropped his hands and looked at her with an insulted and disappointed expression.

"Age before beauty," he piped back.

She rolled her eyes, "Then you should still go first because your fucking ugly."

He walked towards the painting, flicking her on the forehead as he went. He smiled back at her before he stepped through the frame. She followed immediately after him, only turning back to reach her hand out to me. I took it and stepped in with her.

Stepping through Otherworld portals are all different. There are ice and ash portals in the dark districts that push you through layers of magickal ice and snow before you come out on

114

the other side. Fire portals in the light districts that cannot be used by anyone who's not a resilient immortal. The forest district has some of the most peaceful portals, but they often leave you dehydrated or sick with a serious illness.

No matter which portal you used, it always took energy and magick out of you - that was the cost of using it.

The ice gets into your bones and leaves you feeling painfully cold for days. Those are the worst for Erika, I've seen her go through two and she comes out blue and deathly sick with something that leaves her useless for almost a week.

The painting portal reminded me of a mud gate we came through in the forest district once. It was like the thick pastels leached into our bodies and began to harden. Your breathing became laboured, your limbs felt heavy, every pore in your body felt clogged, and your vision was always in black and white for at least the first hour.

When my head emerged on the other side, we were stepping out of a brick wall, painted in a very poor rendition of the sidewalk overlooking the river Thames and Big Ben, and into a narrow alleyway. Erika stumbled out first, all but catching me as I slumped out, needing to catch myself on the adjacent wall for support. My vision was completely discoloured, and the wet ground beneath me looked like it was soaked in blood as what I hoped was water darkened patches of the concrete.

"You okay?" Erika asked me as she pulled me forward, away from the painting.

I nodded and rubbed my eyes, hoping that when I opened them again, I would be able to see in colour again. I was, sadly, not surprised when I pulled my hands away and could still only see greys.

Erika had gently pulled me along towards the mouth of the alleyway. There, Ethan stood tall, still tucked in the shadows, but with his head high and his eyes wide and alert like he hadn't just been sucked of all his energy and colour.

"How are you both so okay?" I asked.

Even after using gates and portals about a dozen or so times, I still couldn't handle the transport. Meanwhile, Ethan, who was just a human, and Erika, who had only travelled to the Otherworld two or three times since she died three years ago, both were able to stand tall and move without any lethargy.

Ethan casted a glance back at me. He looked me up and down as I leaned into Erika for support. A flash of judgement struck over his face before quickly receding as he looked back out over the bustling, steaming city streets.

"We've both done this a lot more than you have," Erika said.

Ethan looked back over my head as more tumbling ensued behind us.

"It's like giving birth," he said. "Each time is still the same process, still the same amount of blood loss, only it starts to feel easier because you get used to it."

Erika scowled at him. "I'm sorry, are you an expert on giving birth now? I wasn't aware that you've pushed a child out of your-"

"I wasn't aware that you have either," Ethan cut her off.

Erika rolled her eyes. She adjusted my weight on her shoulders, then casted a glance over to see the newcomer approaching. I looked back as well, wanting to know who the next in line had been.

Condan was on his hands and knees, vomiting his guts out onto the alley floor.

"Right," Erika mumbled. "He existed before the Otherworld was closed. He's never experienced a gateway before."

She turned to look at Ethan then reached up and pulled my arms off of her. She tugged me a half step forward so that she could hand me off to my friend. Without hesitating, Ethan tucked under me, his hard shoulder meeting my chest at first before sliding into the crook of my shoulder.

"You take him-" Erika said then jabbed her thumb over her shoulder - "and I'll take *him*."

Ethan nodded once.

"Be careful," I whispered.

Erika walked over to Condan and crouched down.

"What is this?" Condan raged, and I got the feeling that, had he been more energised, he would have blasted a hole right through the building beside him.

"You just experienced what we call gate-lag," she explained. "The Otherworld has been closed off from Earth for a while. The cost to travel is energy and magick. You're gonna feel like shit for a while."

Condan's head snapped up so he could look at her. His long white hair was wild, falling down around his face like torn curtains. His eyes were both glowing again, his one golden eyes hot enough to char the arctic, and his dead one cold enough to freeze hell.

"Let me help you up." She reached out to him.

He bared his teeth, gritted tight in frustration. He had been useless for the years he was in the ring, now, after just getting his body and magick back, he was useless again. I could only imagine how infuriating it must have felt.

He raised a foot up, tucking it underneath himself as he tried to stand on his own. He pushed up, but immediately began to shake and collapsed against the wall. He sat there for a moment, kneeling and leaning against the brick just to keep from falling more.

"I will support you, if you let me," Erika said.

She urged her hand forward again. Condan looked at it, studying it like it was a divorce contract. He clicked his tongue, and his shoulders fell in surrender.

Ethan's grip on me tightened, his breathing stopped. We both watched as Condan slowly reached out. This would be the first time that Erika and him had touched.

Then Darbie, Jack and Reika came tumbling out of the portal all at once. They tumbled out in a pile, slamming into Erika. She firmed it for the most part, but still stumbled over, her shoulder ramming into the brick wall. Reika had come out first and was shoved forward, right into Condan, by Jack, who had fallen backwards with Darbie flying into his arms.

Darbie and Jack landed on the ground with a painful sounding thud. Darbie was laying on top and the poor mortal-lad clearly had the wind knocked out of him. Darbie scrambled to get off, but his staff flying through next and bopping him square in the back of the head had him ducking back down into his lover's chest.

I looked over at Reika and the two dragons against the wall.

Erika had gathered herself again. She was back to being composed. With a quick brush along her shoulder to get the brick dust off she was completely good to go and was moving to help her friend and Jack back to their feet.

Condan and Reika were not so readily moving. The two were still pressed against one another. Reika had trapped Condan against the bricks, her body pressing flushly against his. His grey arms were wrapped around her upper back, curling around her shoulders, holding her steady against him. Her hood had been down, falling in line with her collar bone, leaving her upper bicep, up, exposed.

118

His fingers were dug into her skin, his veins trailed black from the point of contact all the way up to his eyes. Both his and hers were glowing like they were locked in a trance.

"E!" Ethan yelled and Erika's attention snapped over to him.

She locked onto his gaze, then spun back around to see what he was looking at. When she saw the position Condan and Reika were in, she reached out. She grabbed at Condan's hands, no doubt aiming to rip his grip off of her, but instead, was sucked into the trance-like state as well.

Only one of her eyes glowed white, the other stayed her normal colour. She was able to blink and gasp, unlike Condan and Reika who seemed to have become statues.

Ethan let go of me and I slumped against the wall. He sprinted forward, not hesitating to tackle Reika and Erika away from Condan. The three tumbled forward, ripping away from the dark dragon, who collapsed back down, broken out of whatever hypnotism he was in.

He gasped, desperately trying to regain the breaths he hadn't been taking when Reika was against him.

Darbie was on his feet now, and he stretched his staff out, the gem just under Condan's chin pointing towards the dark elf's throat. Darbie grabbed Jack and tucked the younger male behind him protectively.

Ethan spun on his knee, blocking the two powerful women with his body. He drew his sword slowly so that Condan could hear the singing of the magickal steel against his sheath. And when Ethan rose to his feet, towering over every person in our party, for a moment I thought I was looking at a god once again.

"You have a death wish, asshole?" Ethan shouted. "What the hell was that?"

Reika sat up quickly, so that she could grasp Ethan's ankle, gaining his attention not only for touching him, but also because of her lack of fatigue. She shook her head up at him as he looked down at her with ice in his eyes.

"He didn't do it," she said. "My mother is the goddess of witchcraft and sorcery. I inherited her ability to syphon magick naturally."

"What do you mean?" Darbie asked, lowering his staff.

Reika opened her palms so that we could see her skin, glowing mostly grey in my colour deprived sight, but with the slightest tint of fuchsia.

"When he touched me, my body began to take his magick in order to restore what I had lost going through the portal," she explained. "Same with Erika, when her skin touched mine, I began taking her's as well. I have no control over it. It's why I try to keep my skin covered."

Erika was still laying on the ground, struggling to stay propped up on one of her elbows so that she could watch the demi-goddess explain herself. She let out a loud, exasperated sigh, before she flopped back onto the ground. She threw her arm over her eyes, sighing once again, just for good measure.

"And *this*-" she began shouting into the sky- "is why we *don't* keep important shit *secret* from those trying to *protect us*!"

She grumbled some more, but rolled over and began pushing herself to her feet. She had to pause with each motion, catching her breath when she got to a knee, then again when she was on her feet and leaning against the wall. She cleared her throat and took a deep breath before she was able to step forward. Even then, it was a weak step, and Ethan sheathed his sword just to put his hands out, ready to catch her.

"Fucking magick-vampire-bitch," Erika mumbled one last time before she shook her shoulders one last time and was able to hold her head high, stably.

120

"I'm sorry," Reika said quietly as she drew her hood up, covering both her shoulder and head again. "In unrelated news, I have a request before you return me to the temple of Artemis."

Ethan glared down at her, clearing not feeling like we owed her any favours.

"What is it?" Darbie asked.

Jack slipped in front of him and offered Condan a hand up. The elder slapped Jack's hand away, so he retreated back behind Darbie.

Reika stepped in front of Ethan so that she could speak without being blocked by the tall man.

"There is a witch, who was a priestess at one point, and lives here in the industrial district, amongst the greek section of the gaslamp corridor," Reika said. "There is something I'd like to retrieve from her before we return to my goddess's temple."

Ethan scoffed. "You want to go shopping for souvenirs before you go home for another seventy years, is that it?"

"Reika," Erika called out to the girl before a fight could ensue. "It's dangerous for Condan and I to be here. I've been thought to be dead for the last three years, and Condan for the last two thousand or so. Not to mention, we're both dragons and DeathMarkers still exist."

"It will be a quick trip," Reika promised.

"I need to see Glemba about a payment anyway," Ethan added on, surprisingly resigning to the request before anyone else did. "Darbie, Jack and I can take Legolas over here to the general goods store and you and Adam can take the *magick-vampire-bitch*, as you called her, to her witchy friend."

I pushed off the wall, feeling better enough to stand steadily on my feet without support.

"Ethan." I shook my head subtly. "Can Erika and I talk to you?"

He stepped forward immediately. His feet splashed through the water on the concrete that had regained enough colour to assure me it was not blood. He wrapped his arm around Erika's waist, holding her up so that she could be closer during our conversation rather than alternating between leaning against the wall and standing hunched over like she was currently doing.

"I don't think it's a good idea to leave Condan without Erika to potentially fight him," I whispered. "I also don't think that Reika should travel with anyone she could suck magick off of."

Ethan furrowed his brows. "Okay, so what groups are you proposing?"

I motioned between him and I. "You and I escort Reika, everyone else takes Condan and goes see Glemba for you."

Ethan shook his head. "No, it's my business. I'm the one who knows Glemba."

"You're talking about Glemba Czarnota, right?" Erika checked. "The doolog who acts as a handler and miscellaneous store owner?"

"That's the one," Ethan confirmed.

"Darbie and I both know him," she said. "We'll handle your business for you. He owes me a debt too, so I'm sure I can get your paycheck in full with a good work bonus."

"He owes me one and a half million drachma," Ethan said. "Make sure he gives it to you in human currency."

"So about seven thousand U.S. Dollars?" Erika asked.

I shook my head. "No, the exchange rate has gone up again. It's just under ten thousand now."

"Okay, I'll make sure you get ten grand on the dot," Erika assured him. "You make sure Reika doesn't do anything stupid, okay? I don't think she means us harm, and she doesn't seem like she wants to run away from the priesshood, but she does seem pretty reckless."

"Reminds me of someone else I know," Ethan said and gave her a pointed glare.

He stepped away from us and turned to face the rest of the group. Darbie had given in to his kindness and moved to help Condan to his feet. Jack stood against the wall opposite them, his arms crossed and his eyes narrowed on the condescending immortal.

"Alright team," Ethan announced, taking control like he was the leader or something. "Adam and I will escort Reika. The rest of your will go to Glemba's for me."

"Oh, Czarnota?" Darbie asked happily. "How exciting. He and I have been friends for ages. He still owes me two sets of giants' toes."

"He owes me a couple grand," Ethan said bitterly. "So you can dispute both of our payments for me."

"He knows Erika too," Darbie said hesitantly. "Are we sure she should be going with us? He'll recognize her for sure, and his shop is runed against deception spells so she can't use an appearance changing spell."

Erika sighed next to me. I nudged her with my shoulder, encouragingly. Ethan looked over his shoulder at her and raised his eyebrows. I could practically hear his expression yelling at us that he thought this was a bad idea.

"Why don't you just kill this Glemba character and take what is rightfully yours?" Condan scoffed.

Ethan looked back at him. Jack piped up before Ethan could.

"Great idea!" Jack sassed. "Hey, while we're at it, why don't we just walk up to the Council of Magick and shit in their oatmeal and announce that we're taking over."

123

Darbie leaned back into his boyfriend. "I don't think they eat oatmeal, baby."

"I know, hun," Jack said to Darbie, softly. "It was just the first thing I thought of."

Condan scoffed. "Why shouldn't you?"

Darbie's head snapped to Condan, his eyes open wide with confusion.

"Why shouldn't we shit in their oatmeal?" he asked.

"No," Condan grumbled. "Why shouldn't we take over? We are the two most powerful beings," he said, motioning between he and Erika. "And we are backed by an army of dragons and you, a sea elf who has mastered their magick and harnessed enough power to become immortal. The light dragon and I will take the gods and you can take out the rest of lesser magick-born."

Darbie slowly turned his head to us. His eyes were even wider now, fear-induced concern pulling at the skin under his eye, causing it to twitch.

"And then what?" Erika said simply.

All eyes turned to her. She stepped to the side so that everyone could have an unobstructed view of her as she stood. She was so small in stature, but when she held her back erect like that, she could have been ten feet tall. Actual height meant nothing if you had enough strength and confidence to stack up and stand on, raising you several feet.

Condan and her had locked their eyes onto one another. Erika was cool, despite being a dragon whose power creates flames and heat. Condan's eyes were hot with irritation, but he balled his hand into a fist and I watched as the creases cracked with crystals of ice.

The sound of the freeze caught Darbie's attention as well, and he drew away from the elf. His grip tightened on his staff.

Condan's eyes flicked over to Darbie, eyeing the way our friend held the magick-enhancing rod.

Reika stepped beside Darbie as well, providing another body in front of Jack - who had drawn out the short wand he had created. Reika had slipped out of her bow and held it in front of her - while she hadn't notched an arrow, the crackling blue-energy beginning to snap off the riser gave me the impression that the weapon could also be used as a bludgeoning tool.

Even I gripped the dagger on my belt.

But Erika made no moves towards hostility.

Neither did Ethan, instead he leaned against the wall beside him, appearing bored with the current situation.

"Listen, mate," Ethan said, shaking his head. "It's been a while since you were kicking about in the otherworld or on earth. The way shit is running is fine, we'd like to leave it as is, if you don't fucking mind."

"And I'd like my children to be able to roam free," Condan retorted.

"And they will," Erika promised. "The only reason they don't now is because we want them to be able to understand and use their abilities effectively enough to defend themselves."

Condan hissed. He slapped the bricks beside him without much effort, yet the quick, powerless strike left a dent in the wall, with one brick completely shattered, and five or six surrounding ones cracked.

"We shouldn't have to defend ourselves," he growled. "If the dragons were just in control, we would be feared and-"

"And then people would rise up and try to overthrow us just like you are thinking of doing to the Council now," Reika spat, and I made a mental note that she said *us* instead of *you*. "Why create conflict just to get the same issues but bigger, when you could foster peace and keep your problems to a minimum?"

125

Condan chuckled. "You lack vision."

"You lack chill," Ethan snarked.

Condan smirked. "No, mortal. I am chill."

The ice began to move up his hand, but didn't make it to his wrist.

"Do we need to rehash what was said before we crossed over the portal?" Erika asked.

Condan opened his hand and the ice fell to the floor as water.

"No," he submitted.

The air itself relaxed after that. A gentle, warm breeze began to blow down the corridor. Excited voices hummed up and down the street behind me as magick- and non-magick-born citizens of the otherworld went about their daily lives.

In another life, I would have been born here. Erika was famous in this world for helping win wars over the last two thousand years and not dying. She was also known for being one of the last druids still alive. Of course, not many people know that all true druids are dead now. The ones left alive no longer have pure druid powers, but rather corrupted or changed forms of them.

For Erika, her ability to use any druid magick died when she did in order to defeat Cailleach. Luckily for us, she had a dragon's soul, which apparently is much tougher than other magick and could bring her back - something we were still trying to figure out.

"Alright," Erika sighed.

She casted a glance behind her, past me, watching the civilians walking up and down the streets. She slipped her pack off and reached inside, pulling out a large shawl to wrap around her head.

As far as everyone knew, she died when she killed Cailleach. That way, no gods or other immortals would come looking for her help. We had wanted a life under the radar, taking quests for our enjoyment and monetary gain. We figured the gods could handle their own bullshit for once.

Ethan moved around Erika, stepping in next to me so that we could both look down the street.

"Do you know where we need to go, Reika?" I asked her.

She nodded and began shuffling over towards us. She moved carefully, making sure not to bump into anyone even though her skin was covered again. She was uncomfortable, and felt guilty. I could see it in the way she kept her eyes no higher than everyone's waistline. She didn't want to meet the gaze of our magick-born friends. She had put them in danger by not telling them, and she knew it.

"I can lead us out, if you'd like me to?" she offered.

I glanced to Ethan who gave me a silent nod.

I looked down to the demi-goddess. "Sounds good. We'll follow you. Try not to get separated, okay?"

She gave me an awkward smile. "I need you both for protection, remember? I'll stick close."

I looked to Erika. Her eyes were warm as they took me in. I could tell she didn't want to be apart from me just as much as I didn't want to leave her. But both of us had enough faith in the other that we trusted we'd see each other again. A few errands wouldn't ruin us, even if they did, somehow, manage to go wrong.

"Be safe," she said.

"You too," I replied.

"We'll meet on the outskirts of the Flourishing District, just before the forrest starts," she announced.

Ethan cleared his throat and the two of them looked at each other. Ethan raised his eyebrows, communicating to her without speaking.

"Right, needs to be more specific," she muttered to herself, before she looked back up and spoke loudly again. "There's a garden with various shrines and statues to the nature goddesses there as well as a separate one for the nature gods. We'll meet you guys in the temple between the two."

"Try not to kill anyone," Jack shouted over at us. "Specifically you, Ethan. And Adam? Try not to make anymore friends. We don't need to add anyone else to this group."

I saluted him before stepping out of the alleyway into the busy public walkway. Ethan reached out and grasped Reika, pulling her forward and all but pressed her tightly between the two of us as we moved through the bustling, moving crowds. Within two steps, I could no longer look over my shoulder and see my girlfriend. I reached behind me and grasped Reika's hand, holding her close to me in case we were accidentally separated.

This errand was going to turn an easy mission into one long ass day.

8
Erika

"I know immortality can get lonely, but seriously Glemba, you can't avoid dusting and call the dust mites your friend," Darbie complained as he moved through Glemba's dark, dank and dusty shop.

The shop was just how I remembered it. Even hundreds of years ago, this place still looked the same. The ceiling was worn down wood panels that had dried out to be thin enough to see through the cracks all the way up to the floor above. The walls of the shop weren't much better, with the first layer of wood being covered with a second newer set so as to cover up the growing gaps.

Wood shelves, reaching just a foot below the ceiling, were piled high with random shit. From teddy bears, to magick amulets to… *fuck, I really hope thats not a box of anal beads…* Glemba had everything in his shop, and he'd sell it to you really cheap and completely under the radar. Especially if you had goods from the human world. He was like a crack whore for that shit.

"I would dust," Glemba's rolling, high toned voice sounded like someone constantly blasted on painkillers. "Of course, that would require more time, and since time is money, I'd rather spend it on selling things to fine adventurers like yourself."

Glemba rounded around his desk, Darbie and Jack right on his tail as they slid up next to it. Jack leaned against the wood that was so worn down it had faded from brown to grey somehow. He then immediately wiped a finger across the four thousand year old layers of dust and pulled his arms off of it.

Darbie stood behind him, his hands crossed, over the other, and laid on top of his staff as he rested it in front of him.

"What can I do for you and your friends, Darbithar?" Glemba asked, his tone as wary as his eyes .

The toad looking man casted a glance back towards Condan and I, who hung out several feet behind them, hidden amongst the shadows the crowded shelves provided. My face was covered, but that didn't mean my scent, magick aura, and body weren't recognizable. I'd rather not get too close and risk the doolog realising who I was unless I absolutely had to.

Doologs were passive beings, normally resigned to either river banks or damp city centres. In both locations they were always doing the same thing; looking for treasure by accumulating trash. They were slimy, and not just because they were related to earth's frogs, but because they would do whatever it took to get their hands on something that might have been of value. Of course, they didn't have teeth, so their croaks were worse than their bite.

If a doolog was ever trying to scam you, all you had to do was show them you had a knife and suddenly they were throwing in a free pair of well worn shoes for the higher price.

"We're here to settle a few debts," Darbie said. "My partner, Ethan Lios, the mercenary, he says you owe him half a million drachma. You also need to get me those giants' toes."

Glemba sucked air in through his slimy green gums.

130

"I only have around one hundred thousand drachma on hand," he said. "As for the giants toes, I don't have a full two sets, but I do have some thumbs I can give you to balance it out?"

Darbie nodded once. "The thumbs and toes will settle our debt. As for the Drachma, we both know you're lying. I need the half million, make it human."

Glemba shook his head and waved his hands through the air, crossing them over his chest like a big X several times. "No can do, I do not have enough cash."

"Fine," Darbie said peacefully, but I could hear the irritation already ebbing at the edges of his words. "We'll take whatever cash and drachma you have and we can settle the rest of the amount in other currency. The total will be around ten thousand."

"I have just under a thousand in mesopotamian shekels," Glemba said thoughtfully and pulled out a magickal chalk board. "So, the drachma will equal two thousand U.S. dollars, and the shekels are another thousand." he wrote the numbers on the board which immediately did the calculations for him like a dusty, enchanted calculator. "I have another two and a half thousand in gold coins from the egyptian district," he mumbled and wrote on the board some more. "So I can give you five and a half thousand now, which would be just five thousand or so shy from our mark. How about I give that to you now and then Ethan can come back and collect the rest later?"

Jack shook his head at Darbie. Both of them sighed audibly.

"We need it now," Jack said. "We're not coming back to the Otherworld for a long time after this trip and Ethan won't be able to make it to your shop soon."

Glemba waved them off. "Well don't worry, I'm not going anywhere. He can always collect it in a few years when you come back to town."

Jack scoffed. "He's mortal. He doesn't have a few years to waste on five grand. Stop beating around the bush and give us the bloody drachma."

"I don't have enough," Glemba insisted.

"Seriously Czarnota," Jack pressed. "Don't push us. Pay up or we'll go up to your office upstairs and take what he's due plus interest for the hassle you're giving us."

"I really don't have it," the froggy toadman shook his head.

I sighed, exasperated. Jack and Darbie were stubborn, but not violent. They would stand here and argue with the little man for hours without ever getting anywhere because they were too nice to press a knife to his throat.

I wandered up and down the shelves while they haggled with one another. I followed Condan loosely as he took in the contents on the shelves. Some of the items were newer, like a flickering gameboy or a nokia phone that somehow had a crack on the screen. Condan had taken to the world so well that I easily forgot just how long he was in the ring, and while he had still seen it by being on Adam's finger for the last three years, there were still a lot of things he had yet to experience.

I took a few larger, faster strides until I was next to him while he flipped a copy of Jane Austen's *Emma* between his hands.

"Tell me," I whispered up at him. "How long were you in the ring? Xavier said that time moved differently in Haven so what was two hundred years for them wasn't the same for me."

Condan set the book back down, making sure to alive the edges with the rectangular dust-free spot in front of him. He then looked over at me, flicking his gaze over my face. His grey eye moved with his golden one, and for a moment I could have sworn I saw the pupil dilate in its dead state. But then I blinked and realised it was only my imagination.

"Haven was a world I created in order to keep Cailleach and the dragon slayers confused," he spoked, his voice low and rough, almost husky as he whispered down at me. "The movement of time had to occur, as is the rule of the universe, but I could force it to speed up and slow down at various points in order for Cailleach to potentially miss it in relation to its creation had she ever discovered its existence in the first place. Even now, the world is real, but if we were to travel there, it may not yet be formed based on what time we arrive."

He reached underneath my shawl and brushed some hair out of my face. I didn't stop him. In fact, I had to resist turning my cheek into his cold palm. My body always felt like it was overheating, and his fingertips, small in surface against my temple, cooled down the small bits of skin they touched.

"I placed myself into the ring with the help of the Morrigan and Dagda five hundred years after we arrived in haven, but the time that passed in your world was merely twenty or so years," he said. "Our total time spent in Haven was close to five hundred and three haven years. Equivalent to two thousand six hundred and some years here."

"So you only spent what felt like three or so years in the ring?" I clarified.

He took up my hand in his, and brought it to his lips.

"That is correct," he said and then blew onto my fingers.

Ice crystals danced over my flesh and I sighed, feeling like I was stepping out of scorching heat and into air conditioning for the first time.

Of course, the moment he stopped blowing, the heat from my body melted the ice, and I was overrun with overwhelming warmth once more.

I peered up at him curiously. "Are you in a constant state of feeling cold?"

133

"Yes," he said. And I made a mental note to myself that he never bothered with nodding or shaking his head.

"I'm constantly hot," I confessed.

He blew once more.

"I know," he said when his breath ran out, and we both watched as his ice melted, some of it evaporating off in steam, and the rest rolling off my hand in droplets. "You and I have been both blessed and cursed. Blessed with power, but cursed to suffer with the discomfort of that power consuming us slowly from the inside out."

I cocked my head to the side. "What do you mean?"

His eyes stared down at me harshly. "We are merely hiding places. Our bodies were never meant to contain the power of dragons. Eventually it will consume us, unless we soul syphon them out or split our power with a dragonrider."

I shrugged. "That doesn't seem so bad. Just find someone you love and share your power with them. Then you get someone who can be by your side for eternity."

Condan flared his nose in disgust.

"I would rather soul syphon the power out," he hissed. "If you split yourself, you can still possess some power in this body and have created another form with the power in another."

I shook my head. "You're talking about combining a creation spell with a transmutation spell. That's probably the dumbest and riskiest thing you can do."

"Ah, but you admit that it can be done." He smirked as he lightly tapped his finger on the tip of my nose before he began walking off.

I shuffled after him.

"You want to create a new creature," I hissed over his shoulder. "Then soul syphon your dragon magick out, placing it in the new creature, and then also syphon part of your own

134

consciousness out and also place it into the creation? You're implying that, not only do you want to play God, but that you have enough mental, physical and magickal strength to split yourself in two and put part of you into something that you summoned and therefore relies off your magickal well?"

He spun around.

"That's exactly what I'm going to do," he declared in a hushed tone. "Dragon magick is nearly infinite. I would bet that I could run around with two powerful forms successfully until the end of times and potentially even after. It all depends on when this *God* you speak of decides to come back and challenge me."

A slow, amused and revolted smile spread across my face.

"You think you can face God and not be smited immediately?" I laughed bitterly. "You are fucking crazy."

To be clear, I wasn't totally sure if capital-g God existed. I had met several gods in my life, almost all of them insisting on being called king, lord, almighty, king of kings, and all that good shit. But like I had said before, none of the gods I had ever met were able to claim all of creation. And none of them insisted on being called the Father of everyone; loving every person no matter their life choices or fuck-ups. To be honest, that alone was worth a capital-g to me.

I don't think I would ever be capable of loving everyone.

Condan right now was acting pretty un-fucking-lovable if I'm honest. The little shit couldn't say more than two sentences without spewing some bullshit about taking over the world or fighting God.

…

Probably should have been a warning sign for the content of the next two books, but we'll get there eventually.

…

"If you think we can't consume God together, then you are the one who's crazy," he hummed, leaning down so that his cool face was close enough to mine that I could feel the cold draft of his skin. "You and I could wipe this universe clean and build a new one if we wanted to."

By this point, the haggling at the desk had turned into what was borderlining on a screaming match between a fired-up Jack and a stubborn Glemba. Only Darbie holding the boy back was keeping Jack from punching the toad man in the throat.

I was steaming with annoyance towards Condan, so the chaos was not helping the headache slowly beginning to pound at the base of my skull and behind my eyebrows.

I rolled my eyes.

"Oh, for fucks sake," I muttered and charged forward, slipping away from Condan and yanking my shawl off so that Glemba could get one good, long look at my fiery orange eyes and the face of someone he thought was dead charging at him.

Flames licked from one of my hands and I reached across the desk and yanked him close with the non-burning one.

"Recognize me, little frog man?" I seethed and he nodded frightfully. "Get the ten grand that I know you have, put it in a bag, then get Darbie's toes, put those in a separate bag, and hand it all over. If you don't, I get to show the Otherworld was deep-fried frog legs taste like, understand?"

"Yes, Erika," he whimpered. "I understand."

I let him go and turned off the fire show so that he could scamper off to get the goods. I turned around to stare at my two friends who were looking at me in mild astonishment. Darbie was still gripping Jack close to his chest, the boy's long shaggy hair was growing more and more red by the day, his cheeks flushed the same strawberry blond tones as his bangs, no doubt embarrassed that someone had to step in for them.

136

"Doologs respond better to violence," I said. "You should know this."

Darbie let go of Jack.

"Sorry Eri," Jack offered.

Darbie gently smacked his chest. "Don't apologise to her. We had almost worn him down, she just wanted an excuse to show off."

Condan strolled up behind me.

"Impressive intimidation tactics," he said. "But if you know he has what you want plus more, I would've just killed him and taken it all."

"Yeah, we know," Darbie snapped. "The whole smiting of the weak and overpowering the strong thing, you've made it clear you got a couple of domination kinks going on."

"Kinks?" Condan asked.

"It's, like, something that you do or someone else does that makes you hard," Jack explained.

"Hard?"

Jack opened his mouth, his hands motioning down around his crotch.

I pointed at him. "No," I snapped quickly before he could start to explain. "We are so not having this conversation. Especially not in this shop. Especially not with Mr. Fifty Shades of Grey over here."

"Awe," Darbie whined. "But it's so fun to fuck with him."

Condan stepped forward. "Careful, brother, you and I may both be of the same blood, but I will still watch you bleed out."

Darbie's hand gripped his staff so tight his hand turned white despite his dark blue skin. His storm grey eyes hummed turquoise like the stone at the top of his staff.

He was ready to unleash his full magickal force on this narcissistic bastard, and part of me wanted to let him do it, just to see what would happen.

Darbie was probably the most powerful elf I knew. If he dropped his pacifism and went to war against Condan, in Condan's weakened state, Darbie might've stood a chance. Throw Jack's growing abilities and my power into the mix, we could have subdued the dragon. We would have been injured and drained, but we could have done it.

"Alright, elf-boys," I said, stepping between the two. "Let's pipe down. No need to blow a hole in Glemba's shop. Besides, Darbie, we both know Condan won't actually do any killing, right Condan?"

I looked at the white haired man. He looked at me closely. Moving his head enough to take in both sides of my jaw, the corners of my eyes, the bend of my nose. He was looking for something, but I couldn't tell you what.

"So long as you and I are on the same team and you tell me not to," he said, then paused. "I will not kill anyone. Unless I have to or you ask me to."

"Noted," I said.

And we left it at that.

We all casted glances at one another, waiting for someone to break the newfound tension that had risen, but the return of Glemba with one massive sack of money and an even larger one of toes, meant our moment had passed. Whatever developing concerns that were hanging in the air around us would need to be buried in our pockets and packs for the duration of this mission.

Darbie reached out with his staff, tapping the cashbag at first, and I watched it curl up in a flurry of teal magick, no doubt whistling away to be stored in Darbie's magick until he needed to retrieve it. He did the same with the giant's toes. I watched as it swirled, like the white foam on the top of a cappuccino, but quicker and more blue, before disappearing completely.

The Darbie pressed the stone to Gelmba's cheek and the sliming green man freezed.

"And if you tell anyone about Erika," Darbie growled, still reeling with anger. "I will come back and take what you *will* owe us. Do you understand?"

The black, gorging eyes in Glemba's wide face flicked between me and Darbie. I flashed my orange eyes just to prove the point and he nodded aggressively.

"Roger, sir," he said. "Aye, aye, captain. Whatever you say chief. My lips are sealed."

We slipped out of the shop and into the dark, steaming, empty alleyway that Glemba's place was settled in. My shawl was pulled back up over my head, blending me in with the rest of the lowlifes that stalked up and down this side of the industrial district.

"Alright," Darbie said, taking up the rear with Condan and Jack stepping down the shop stairs in front of him. "We need to get through the flourishing district and into the forest zone in order to get to the shrines of the nature gods. Erika, any ideas on the best route?"

I casted a glance up the alleyway and then down it.

We had come from the top, which led out towards the main street. The main street was the shortest route distance wise, but was over-crowded. We would spend extra time just trying to push through bodies and keep my identity concealed. It was a struggle just to get here, I couldn't imagine trying to get all the way through the industrial district and into the flourishing on that road.

Meanwhile, if we went down the alleyway, we could get to the rail tracks which used to carry nymphs and sirens from the forest zone down into the dark part of the industrial district to be drained of their magick, blood and other valuable assets their body provided. Luckily, that kind of industry was outlawed long ago, and the council had such a hard lock on it that it was quite literally impossible to successfully traffic magick without being caught.

Someone could potentially do so on earth, where the council had little to no influence, but there was almost no market for it on earth, meaning it wasn't done there, either.

The tracks would be abandoned and barren besides the small congregations of homeless that wouldn't pay us any mind. It would be a longer walk, but we could move unnoticed and make up for time lost in distance by not having to shove through crowds.

I looked back to Darbie and raised my head in the direction of the bottom of the alley.

"We can follow the old rail tracks right into the forest zone," I offered. "It'll be more of a hike, but we won't have to shove through anyone like we did on the way here."

"Sounds good to me," Jack said.

Darbie, on the other hand, shifted uncomfortably. He and I both knew the dark history of the railway. In the past, passive elves like him would have been prime real estate. Elves recharged their magick if they were in contact with their element. Get some water and stick Darbie in it, you could syphon magick off him in almost an infinitesimal quantity.

Similarly, druid magick was rare, even back when I was mortal. Druids had the same lifespan as humans, making us a short lived peoples. Unlike elves or goblins or doologs, who could naturally live several hundred years, I would have been lucky to make it to ninety. That was a lot less time to have kids and grow our population. Getting your hands on a druid to syphon magick from was like stumbling upon a rare gemstone vein; it'd be depleted quickly, but the little I had would be worth a lot.

Stepping onto those tracks was a reminder that, at one point, our people were hunted, tortured, and killed just because of what we were and what we could give.

"I see you, Darbs," I said, letting my friend know I was in this boat with him. "It'll be quicker though. Plus, we shouldn't be afraid of the past."

With each step, my tan combat boots grew more and more black as charcoal dust wafted up from the ground and clung to my feet. The buildings off to our right were no more than charred husks of what they used to be, the only evidence left of the old storage houses for magick-born that would have been rounded up before being transported to various locations in order to be drained.

In front of me, and just to the left, the backside of abandoned shops provided a solid wall for homeless to build their temporary shelters against. I pitied a few of them, but I also knew a large handful were only here because they had lost their source of income when magick trafficking was outlawed.

Because it had been legal at first, when the council outlawed the trafficking and syphoning of magick, anyone who was involved in the business wasn't arrested or punished. In fact, the council pretty much just warned them that if they didn't stop they would be killed, but ultimately let them get away with it. It was the citizens of the Otherworld that dealt the real damage. After it was outlawed, and traffickers went looking for work elsewhere, no one would hire them or give them any sort of sympathy.

Traffickers were left shunned by society and out of work. But as immortals, we don't have to eat or drink to stay alive, just to keep ourselves from feeling the constant pain of hunger. So the shunned immortals were left to walk through their existence suffering until Death finally came to claim them. And honestly? I think that's better than killing them.

Unfortunately, it also made me very wary of the path we had chosen. With dozens of unknown beings just a handful of yards away from us and one unknown variable known as Condan, I felt like I had to be on high alert with each passing step.

"Why are there so many transients?" Condan asked.

He was striding along behind me, with Jack and Darbie taking up the rear. Jack was leisurely walking along, his eyes scanning the world around us, taking in the yellowish-grey skies and the black abyssal ground. But ultimately, he was unfazed. Darbie on the other hand, moved stiffly.

"Most of them are beings who have been rejected by society for their criminal acts," I explained to Condan, slowing down so that I could walk next to him.

He looked down at me, his features were relaxed now - gentle looking - making his attractiveness shine through the eerily cold aura he had.

"What was their crime?" He asked.

I clenched my jaw. "They would kidnap people like you and I, and they would drain us of our magick and sell it to the highest bidder."

"Hmm," Condan looked over at the rising and falling of tents and people. "Are you afraid that the dragons will become victims of this?"

I drew in a deep breath. The honest answer was yes. Magick-syphoning may be illegal, but the reason why traffickers rolled over so easily was because the majority of the magick they harvested wasn't enough to entice impressively high bidders. They had to kidnap and drain hundreds just to sell enough of it to feel like they were making an impressive income. But dragons had been the centre of attention for aeons. Dragons had something that everyone wanted. A heart, an eye, a scale, a claw, everything was valuable.

But a dragon's magick?

Priceless.

There was no other power like it. Dragon magick was pure, only ever perfectly light, or perfectly dark. Even DeathMarkers, back when they were dragonslayers, would admit that they developed a taste for certain dragons over others. Water dragons and air dragons could overwhelm the slayer with feelings of blissful euphoria, and Fire and earth dragons could consume them with intense bouts of feeling strong and powerful.

"No," I answered. "Not exactly, at least. I'm worried about the world finding out about them and taking advantage of the fact that many of them don't know the first thing about their powers. Whether that be magick trafficking coming back or simply people taking advantage of our kiddos, I don't know and I don't care. I just know I'd rather not give fate the opportunity."

"I tried to train them, you know," Condan said, and his tone almost sounded like he was ashamed. "As a dark elf though, I never had to be taught how to use magick or powers. As you may know, we have the ability to sense magick and feel its characteristics."

I laughed bitterly. "I'm well aware. You people use it as a way to understand your enemies and slaughter entire people groups. Including, but not limited to, my people."

He shrugged. "Druids were weak, it was easy to kill them and take over their land."

"You killed my ancestors, dickhead," I hissed. "Your people are the reason that the druids fled the Otherworld and moved to Earth."

He chuckled. "Not my ancestors, princess. Me. I was alive and prince when we ruled over large parts of this world and of earth. I oversaw my father's orders to push the druids out of the forest and run them through the desert and into the frozen lands. And I reaped the benefits of all the Druid sapphires and flourishing spells that your people placed in those lands."

"You son of a-"

"I am sorry," he said, shocking me into stillness. "Power, wealth and land. They are wonderful things. And I can't promise that I wouldn't do it all over again to enjoy the wonderful world the druids left behind. What I can say is that after living in the home the druids created, and seeing its beauty first hand and watching my brethren slowly destroy it, I was sad. I can admit that druids were the second most wonderful beings I had ever witnessed."

I stood silently, pondering his words and my thoughts carefully.

Finally, "And the first would be what? Your own species?" I asked bitterly.

He shook his head. "No. My heart will always be partial to the dragons. Pure darkness is a capability known only to them, and I always wanted to know what it tasted like."

"And now that you see how bitterly cold it is, do you feel otherwise?"

"Absolutely not," he confessed, a grin tugging at his lips. "The cold will always be worth it for this much power. Like I said, power, wealth and land are wonderful things."

"Erika!" Darbie shouted out.

Both Condan and I stopped to look back at the sea elf. He was sweating profusely, his staff out and humming. His eyes were narrowed like slits off to the left.

We followed his gaze, Condan spinning around in a half-circle so that he could follow Darb's line of sight.

A long, thin figure was approaching. One leg was all but dragging behind it, its other leg pulling it forward in a combination step/hop form. Its frail arms were nearly as thin as my fingers, letting me know that it hadn't eaten in a long while. His arms had curled in towards his chest from atrophy. I could see the mangled bones of his dragging leg in his shredded pants. But his cowl must have been newer, it lacked too much wear and tear, and therefore covered him completely beyond his elbows. No facial features could be seen in the darkness of his covering and the environment around us.

Condan reached out behind him and stepped back, blocking me in behind his dense body. I would be lying if I didn't say that it was a sweet sentiment. Unfortunately, all it did was make me feel like he was a condescending prick.

He and I had the same level of power, but he blocked *me* in like I was the one who needed shielding.

Fucking annoying.

I rolled my eyes, and grabbed him by the back of his shirt with one hand, and by his belt with the other. Then I picked him up and threw him aside. I let myself hum with light, casting rays onto the unknown approacher. My hands, raised, ready to turn the person into nothing but a scorch mark on the already charcoal covered ground.

The white beams illuminated the figure enough to reveal to me his human-like skin and his vivid, lime eyes. In another life, he would have had soft porcelain skin and the most gorgeous array of freckles, almost like stars in the night sky. But now - after what must have been two thousand years, a corrupted soul,

145

and hundreds of years of starving away - he was nothing more than the husk of what a druid would have been.

My hands dropped to my sides, and I let the creature reach out and touch my cheek. Condan stepped forward, his hand stretching out right next to my ear so that he could push the cowl away from the being's face.

It's hair was completely gone, save a few sad wisps of what would have been flaming red curls. His skin sagged so much with no fat or muscle to fill it out that I could see more of his pink meaty flesh under his eyes than the actual green irises themselves.

"A druid?" Condan whispered into my ear.

The shell of the druid fell to his knees, still grasping at me like I was the life he was clinging to. He was moaning now, and making some other noises that maybe would have been words had he not been left to waste away for so long.

I shook my head.

Jack strided right up to it. He knelt down so that he could take a better look at it's face and eyes. Then he looked up at me and cocked his head.

"He looks human," Jack said. "If it wasn't for the glowing green eyes, I would say he was mortal like us."

"He *was* mortal like you," Darbie said, hesitantly shuffling closer, staff still raised. "He's a druid magick-siphoner. Probably a trafficker too. He's got someone else's magick in him, it's why he's lived so long instead of dying."

I stared down into his green eyes.

I used to see eyes like that every day. When my mum would get mad at my father her eyes would glow almost turquoise, the leftover magick from her dragon riding days would bleed in with her green druid magick and she would glow the most wonderful blend of the river blue and moss green. My dad,

146

on the other hand, was like me, a pure mossy green glow showing our pure druid blood. When he would laugh too hard he would show their hue and plants in the house would start to grow.

We were just like every other druid.

Green burning eyes. Our nature was to help things prosper, to grow. We didn't take any more than we needed to, and if we took, we would try to pay back ten times over.

I didn't recognize these eyes.

"He's not a druid," I said barely above a whisper.

Condan was the only one who heard. He looked down at me, I could see it from the corner of my eye. While he stood there studying, I stood staring at the monster in front of me.

I had spent the last two thousand years wishing there was another druid out there with those glowing green eyes who had managed to live this long. I had been so desperate for the idea of family and for the feeling of my people that I hadn't thought of what the cost would be for a druid to stay alive this long.

It wasn't a druid. It wasn't even a man anymore. Just a vile insult to the people I loved and lost.

I heard the crystallisation of the ice before I saw it.

Condan had created a single spike of ice from the ground between the creature's legs, and I watched as it shot up, penetrating through its ribs into its chest cavity and then through the front of its throat, up through its jaw into the skull. It happened almost as fast as a bullet, and was a quick and merciful death considering how many people the thing had probably tortured and drained throughout its life.

Unfortunately, Darbie didn't see it that way. He spun around quicker than a fucking dreidel during Hanukkah and sent one blast of fiery teal magick right at the dark elf. I turned my body and open my right arm, taking the blow right to my chest. It hit with a satisfying *thund*, but didn't cause any pain.

147

"Erika get away from him, he just killed the druid!" Darbie was shouting in a desperate fear.

I put my hand up, silencing him and stopping Jack from taking another shot at Condan from his better position.

"It wasn't a druid anymore," I said. "A druid wouldn't have drained another being for more power. Condan killing him as quickly as he did was a mercy for my sake and for its. I can sleep peacefully tonight knowing that someone from my race isn't a monster, and now that thing doesn't have to live another two thousand years in pain, wasting away with no food. I'm sorry Darbs, but I support the brutality this time."

"We don't kill unless we have to, that's our way," Darbie argued. "It's keeps us separated from people like him who want to kill just to get ahead in life."

I motioned to the lifeless being who was slowly being encapsulated in ice, in front of me.

"Killing him doesn't get us ahead in life! That wasn't the point! It simply and rids the world of a creature that likely kidnapped, tortured and killed your ancestors for their power," I snapped. "In fact, with how green it's eyes were, I would bet it probably harvested my peoples, its own people-"

"You're calling him an it like he's not a person," Jack cried, his face twisted in utter mortification.

"It's not a person, not anymore. Look at it!" I stepped closer, jerking my fingers in its direction a few more times for reference. "It couldn't even fucking speak! Druids died off two thousand years ago. Either this motherfucker is the undead or he sold his own fucking soul. Either way, he's not one of my people anymore."

Jack stepped closer, sharp nose nearly poking mine.

"You're not a druid anymore either, Erika," he hissed, and it stung.

I closed my mouth. My arms relaxed at my side. I was *humbled*.

There is nothing more sobering than loneliness.

I didn't hesitate when I began walking on. I just stepped to the side, away from Jack and the frozen body, away from Condan and his watchful eyes, and away from Darbie and his judgments. And when I had them all to my back, I corrected my footing and walked down the railroad tracks alone.

After a few seconds I felt the quiet scuffing of footsteps following behind me. But whether they were my party's or that of another unknown figure, I didn't know, and frankly I didn't care.

I just needed to be alone for a while.

9

Reika

In the downtown of the Greek corridor in the Industrial District, somewhere deep where the sacrificed victims of Pompeii and Julius Caesar resided, there was a witch. An old witch, who had learned to love being in the middle of anything immoral that gained her more power or money.

She was no different now. The owner of a club, selling drugs and alcohol to minors and capturing souls in the VIP room.

I could feel the old magick as soon as I walked into the vibrating den of sin. There was new magick there too, and as I made my way through the classic looking dance floor I noticed that every masked stripper within their eccentric cages eyed me as they moved. They were young witches, modern sirens perhaps, enchantresses who gained their magick from collecting the magick within mortal life.

We were walking inside an old magick mill.

The cages the masked strippers were dancing in hung from the massive thick-chained hooks that dangled from the ceiling, where magick used to be syphoned by witches like me in the past. The dance floor was down in a squared basin, and I could see the etches of an old containment spell along the wood accent around it. It now had railings mounted into it so that patrons walking around the outside of the dance floor couldn't fall in.

A black, crystal chandelier hung above the dance floor, the cages circled around it so that the dancers could be seen the best in the red light that rained off of it. On the far back wall, was a bar that served blood for blood drinking customers. Across from us, next to the blood bar, was a regular alcoholic bar, and next to us, before the stairs that brought us up to another level, there was a bar that was handing out golden liquid known to the Greeks as nectar. It had also been called the elixir of life, amrita in hindu myths, liquid gold according to the Egyptians, and many other things.

In the Otherworld we knew it as potus or potion, a magickal drink that could heal injuries, or make someone high if they're already in a healthy condition. Of course, if they were fine, only a minimal amount could be consumed before the consumer would die.

As we walked past the potus bar, and came closer to the stairwell leading up, I reached back and grasped the boys' wrists to pull them closer to me. We were about to get closer to the sirens, and potentially come into physical contact with one or more.

Although I was under the impression that Adam was Erika's possible soulmate, I wasn't about to risk his safety on an old myth that stated men who had met their soulmates couldn't be charmed by sirens.

And in any case, no matter what, Ethan was absolutely a high risk target.

I looked back at him, his fair eyes flashing with the red light in the room. They stared down at me like flares, hot.

"Stay close, I think this is an enchantress den," I commanded.

151

I looked to Adam who looked between the two of us and nodded.

I continued on, aiming for the stairs that no doubt led up to VIP rooms.

I wasn't aiming for a VIP room though.

Venus Lupin was the witch we were looking for, and her office was on the other side of the halls.

Venus and her sister, Athena, were once Priestesses of Artemis. They had lived in darkness only knowing each other for centuries before they wandered into the territory and attention of Zues. Being both naturally powerful witches, the two were sought after by him as potential lovers. Artemis found them before he could get his hands on them and provided them sanctuary. They learned everything about the world from Artimess and the other priestesses, including how to speak. They even chose their names from ones they read in the history books kept in the temple archives.

Venus chose hers because she was vain and thought she could rival the goddess's beauty. Athena named herself after the goddess of intelligence and strategy because she wanted to learn and be better.

Eventually, the two sisters outgrew the priesthood and left. Athena moved to the mortal world to learn more about humans, she ended up staying to use her abilities to help. Venus went with her at first, and taught herself how to soul-syphon healthy human souls out of their bodies to be stored and eventually sold. A business she was still in, today. Only she had upgraded now, she was strong enough to soul-syphon magick-born

Souls were pesky buggards. If given the opportunity, all souls will try to continue to be free, meaning she had to learned how to work quickly and precisely or else the soul would be lost or she would have to venture into Perdition or Felicity to get it back.

Of course, going and getting it was never worth the hassle when she could just syphon another.

Having a private office just beyond the secure space made getting the magick maintained efficiently. No roaming souls lost.

She had gotten into trouble with her sister a few years back for wasting too many souls. Athena was a witch of Justice, a classic Sorcerer like Darbie, only she had wandered the edges of creation when it was first coming to terms with what it was. A fate perhaps was more accurate - but she always preferred Sorceress. She tried to maintain the balance of good and bad, but in a much more subtle way. Because of this, she recognized that if she stopped her sister, another soul-siphoner would rise up in her place and likely steal more souls than her sister did. So Athena turned a blind eye so long as Venus didn't steal too many lives.

I had met her once in the temple of Artemis, and when they called her Athena I almost believed she was the Goddess Athena herself, her beauty could easily rival Aphrodite.

But Athena Lupin was not a god.

Just like her sister, she was actually mortal, but like with every other mortal witch, necromancer, sorcerer or enchanter alive, Death was always willing to make deals.

It was why I had a feeling Venus was going to be valuable to us. Venus got away with taking lives before they were due, and both her and her sister had lived this long, meaning they were either playing Death, which was unlikely, or she had struck a deal with him.

Death does not like to be played, it was why he was friends with Fate, Life and Time. They all worked hard to keep the realms and world flowing correctly.

Well, as correctly as four deities can keep it considering an entire species of gods and goddesses messed it up to begin with.

If I had to guess, Death had probably collected plenty of souls from Venus over the years, meaning she could have the power to request one back if she wanted to.

"Reika." Adam leaned over my shoulder to draw my attention. "Who are we looking for again?"

"The owner of this club, she's an ancient witch," I tossed back.

His arm crossed my face, finger extended and pointing up to our right where an elevated railing overlooked the dance floor.

"Does she look like that?" he asked and I followed his finger to where he was pointing.

Staring down from the rails, stood Venus in all her glory.

Her hands were concealed in long elbow length leather gloves. The pair was clearly designed to go with the black leather cocktail dress she wore. The collar pressed flush against her throat, and the sleeves ended just past her shoulder. It was like a battle of class and mystery on her body. Her skin, like warm toffee, just added to the dark mystery that surrounded her - and her glistening midnight hair could entice even the straightest of women.

I nodded back to Adam, my eyes still tied to Venus's.

"She's definitely an enchantress," Adam mumbled. "I can feel her spell trying to pull me in from here."

I breathed in deep. "I feel it too."

My thoughts were clouding. Whether it was a potion in the air, or an enchantment placed specifically on her, there was definitely something going on that was pulling me towards her. The room was loud and the lights distracting, but all I could focus on was her. I wanted to feel the softness of her skin, smell the

154

fibres of her hair, and kiss the warmth of her lips. I could imagine they tasted like coffee and caramel. Just warm and sweet.

I was so entranced I hadn't realised that I had made it through all the bodies in the club, to the stairs, and begun to climb until after Ethan shoved me into the nearest wall. My head slammed so hard into the wood that it shook me from the spell.

It also shook me with a concussion, but I suppose it was necessary considering the strength of the trance.

He grabbed my cheeks in one hand, squishing my skin gently between his forefinger and thumb. My eyes zoned in on his. In the red light they looked like midnight, but then a strobe of blue would flash across them and I would see the lovely hue of sapphire.

In the haze of Venus, I was enthralled by his magnificence. An absolutely gorgeous man of bravery and heroism. Any other girl would get drunk off of his attention, all it did was make me sick with worry. I couldn't deny how attractive he was, but I needed to deny my intrigue. I could not lose Artemis's protection.

"Reika," he growled. "Don't go getting yourself cursed like that on me, alright?"

I looked behind him at Adam, whose shirt was clenched in the tight grasp of Ethan's other hand.

Between the two boys, it was Ethan who wasn't affected by her spell at all.

Adam, I could've understood, there were rumours that he was Erika's soulmate and therefore wouldn't be able to be seduced by anyone else. Ethan, on the other hand, was normal. He wasn't protected by a bond of fate like Adam and Erika were supposed to be, meaning he either was immune to a witch's enchantments or he was the most mentally strong man I knew.

Or he was someone's soulmate and he had already met them, a confusing circumstance for a man who was alone.

I cocked my head. "Why aren't you trapped in her spell?" I grabbed his arms and patted him down all the way up to his face.

He swatted me away, but remained close, keeping me pinned tightly against the wall. "From what I've read, in order for a siren's call to work correctly, there has to at least be some sort of attraction within the target. Whether it be something as simple as feeling lonely, unrequited love, or as far as the person actually finding the caster attractive, there needs to be a base."

"I know that," I enunciated. "I'm saying why didn't it work on you?"

"Because I don't need anyone in my life. I choose to keep people around because I care about them. Everyone I love loves me back, and I don't need anymore."

Ethan's words hung in the air with such finality, I didn't need to waste my time replying.

Adam's eyes were clearing and he reached out and gripped Ethan's shoulder.

When Adam finally finished processing the situation, he slowly began to pull the dark man away.

"Maybe we shouldn't be fighting in front of the powerful witch," Adam cautioned. "You know, don't let her know our weakness and all that."

I sighed, "The biggest weakness here is me."

The two boys instantly furrowed their brows in confusion.

I pushed away from the wall, eyes glued to the floor. I shifted from one foot to the other while reaching down and tugging on the end of my longsleeve. I probably looked like the poster child of teenage guilt, but it was true, I was guilty. Guilty about not caring for them, which made me lonely. Incredibly, cripplingly lonely.

"If Venus is going to be able to enchant anyone, it's me," I muttered. "I may be a witch, but I have more weaknesses than you two. I'm also going in not fully trusting either of you. She can use that as a weak spot."

Ethan shrugged. "Then get over your little insecurity fest and put some faith in us."

"Ethan," Adam hissed.

"It's not that easy-" I tried to fire back.

Ethan interrupted, "It is that easy. You just have to stop thinking about yourself so goddamn much, start looking around and realise that we're the only ones on this planet who actually give a damn about what happens to others. You know our track records, we save people. The only two people you seem to trust are yourself and your goddess Artemis, but who's here? Who are the three people who have had your back?

"Erika walked into the OtherWorld, risking exposing herself for you. I saved you from your weird magick attack when you touched Erika and Condan. Adam and I both voluntarily came with you to have a meet and greet with your not-so-pal witch-cousin knowing full well we're the only two mortals in the situation.

"So look around," Ethan paused to gesture over the area around us. "Your goddess isn't here, we are. We're going to have your back just like we have this whole time even if you're not gonna have ours. But I don't exactly want to be chopped up and put in a potion. So, if you can get over yourself and get on our side it would be greatly appreciated."

"My my," a voice like velvet pulled us from our feud. "Handsome and aggressive? I wonder what he is like in bed?"

157

"Venus Lupin," I acknowledged. "One of the first witches to leave the priestesshood."

I stepped out in front of Ethan, physically putting the argument behind me for now, and continued climbing the stairs.

Ethan had some valid points, but a few days of reliability doesn't equate to a couple decades worth of loyalty.

Venus laughed like a line from a symphonic orchestra. "I'm surprised a baby witch like you is even aware I was a priestess of Artemis."

I turned to face her, still making my ascent, until I was looking deep into her grey eyes. "You and your sister were one of the first non-god-born witches, human witches in fact, and the first to leave in order to master your magick. That's why you hate each other isn't it? Because you know that if you two are ever near each other you can both become more powerful, but disagree on how to use the power."

Venus smiled a crooked smile, her teeth as white as pearls.

"Twice as powerful to be exact. I'm surprised another witch wouldn't make that distinction," she said as she stared me down. "We hate each other because she wants to give that power away while I want to build it up. I hate her because she deprives me of my right."

"Um excuse me," Adam chimed in. "How would you two *each* become twice as powerful?"

Venus looked Adam up and down and chuckled. "Nothing your druid self would understand. But the Dragon that left its essence all over you might be able to explain it. Now come on, I'm assuming you three aren't here to chit chat, come into my office and maybe we can make a deal."

Ethan's thick arm encircled my chest. In one stern motion he pulled me back behind his solid body.

158

"Only if you swear on the river Styx that you won't betray us and sell us off to some other witch." He was growling at Venus.

A rottweiler in a fight with a green anaconda.

She could wrap her slippery body around him and squeeze until he couldn't breath or his ribs cracked - it would be easy for her. I'm sure the snake had done it a thousand times to a thousand different dogs, but this canine might have been different.

He might have been one of the few hounds that was lucky enough to get a solid bite on the serpent's throat and with one violent thrash that would be the end of things.

The serpent knew it.

The dog knew it.

I knew it.

But witches and mercenaries don't risk their lives on mights or maybes.

"I swear on the river Styx and the god who it was named after that I will not let harm come to you in my club." Venus's eyes pulsed purple with power as she smirked. "Death is bad for business."

Venus threw her leg to the side, stepping wide before dragging her other foot out to follow her. She headed away from us, down the wide start of a corridor that I could have sworn wasn't there before she started walking.

Ethan looked down at me and back at Adam before following after. I was hot on his trail, not bothering to check if Adam was alright with blindly following her or not.

The hallway grew out in front of her, like she was the light that was slowly illuminating the space as we walked further down.

Glass cages with mirrored sides were built into the walls. Each one held beautiful silk stream dancers, tumbling from the ceiling like turquoise waterfalls. Dark dressed security guards stood tall by cherry wood doors that separated each glass enclosure.

The ground beneath our feet was slowly fading from the crimson to a violent royal purple the farther down the hall we got. And after what felt like a few minutes of walking, I could see one mahogany door at the very end.

I almost felt like I was being led to a sex dungeon where a woman dressed in all leather with a riding crop would be waiting for me. I almost laughed at the thought, but then I took in how many doors there were with private guards outside. I doubted those guards were protecting offices.

"Each door is a sex dungeon isn't it?" I blurted out.

Ethan, who was still in front of me, glanced back, smirking. Although I couldn't see Adam, I heard a quick stumble and recovering of feet behind me, hinting to me that perhaps the boy hadn't been prepared to walk head first into a prostitution scandal.

Venus laughed. Her elegant fingers flicked into the air as if she was literally brushing the issue off of her shoulder.

"I have many clients come to use my specialty rooms for various reasons," she dismissed, "What they do behind closed doors is only my business if they don't pay me."

"Well that's low," Adam muttered.

Venus stopped and spun around to glare down the boy in the back. "*That* is *business*. In case you haven't noticed, the life of an Otherworldly being isn't like a human's. We don't fight to live comfortably, we fight to live, period. There is no shortage of beings in this world that feed off blood and life."

160

With a huff she twirled back, head held high and chest puffed out like she was about to start some sort of classical ballet.

When we reached the end of the hall Venus turned her hand so that it was vertical, palm facing the door jam. In the centre of her flat skin, a green orb the size of a marble began to form. It churned and spun itself like a spider's egg as she closed her eyes, uttering an incantation of some sort.

Once the orb was big enough to be about the size of a golf ball she opened her eyes and breathed, "*Resertenebris*."

The green faded to a soft yellow. It moulded down into a key made of pure magick, sliding perfectly into the lock. Venus twisted her palm, and without touching the key at all, it turned inside the lock. As it clicked into place the knob turned with it until the familiar sound of hinges creaking rang out.

As the door opened, a great chill rolled from the pitch place. The golden glow of the magick key disappeared along with the object itself.

"That word…" I started in awe. "You came up with your own spell."

Venus laughed. "Child, I came up with my own universe, that word wasn't a spell, it was a summons. Any true witch with bloodborne magick in her veins can do that. It is simply a matter of their mental strength. Now please, step into my office, we can discuss what you need and what I want."

She stood off to the side, waiting for us to enter first. Ethan stopped at the doorway. He looked at the frame, examining it for traps. After a minute, still not satisfied, he extended his hand to me. I looked down at it, but did not move.

Finally he demanded a reaction. "If one person goes in and it's trapped we're not leaving them alone. Between the three of us, you and I are more likely to be able to find a way out on our own, so take my hand, and let's go in first."

I relented, letting my shoulders roll back while I placed my fingers on top of his. He turned and slid into the darkness. It swallowed him like someone submerging beneath the density of dark waves. Although it was slow at first, it didn't take long before I was harshly pulled in. Out of instinct, I held my breath as I was slowly swallowed by cold. It felt like I was falling into freezing oceans and I did not want to go under with no air in my lungs. But just as I held it and my vision was swallowed by black, it was reopened to a spacious room.

A well lit ceiling held three chandeliers, one the size of a sofa chair deep within the room, right over a silky oak desk, and two others only as big as backpacks to balance out the empty space between the doorway and the desk.

To my left a series of book shelves with classics and grimoires ran from the wall adjacent to the door to the one in the far back. To my right there were two book cases of grimoires, and between them was a small sitting place and table/ With a floor to ceiling display of kettles behind it, I assumed it was where she took tea.

In front of the grand desk were two Victorian style chairs awaiting their hearing.

Everything in the room was Victorian style. A symbol of the grandeur and class that Venus Lupin held herself too. A little bit of gothic, a little bit of lust, a mixture of eccentric, and all of it power.

"Ethan," I hissed.

The boy had distracted himself amongst the grimoires. He may have been a dumb mortal, but at least he knew a powerful spell book when he saw one. His hand was still in mine, though stretched out far, and at the sound of my hoarse voice he snapped around.

"I need you to follow my lead," I explained quickly, praying I could finish before Venus and Adam came through the door. "I am going to make a deal with her that will benefit Erika."

"What?" He queried.

"I'm going to have to trade Co-"

"Welcome to my office," Venus sang as she and Adam padded into the room. The door shut on its own behind her. "Now that door will lead to the rest of my house unless I use a spell to open it into the Otherworld again, so just in case you were thinking of trying anything, you need me to get back."

Ethan gave me a quick concerned glare. His warm hand slid from mine and in its place there was only the coldness of this world.

Adam and Ethan followed Venus over to the desk, ready to sit down and settle business.

I hovered behind, taking down grimoires and trying to read them. They were all encoded in Venus's own made up language. A smart tactic to keep potential buyers from stealing it. Encode the spell and by doing so keep every other magick user from being able to read and memorise it.

I put the books back. All the spells I knew were in Greek anyway, and they weren't spells really, more so begs for blessings from the gods. These spells were in a different language and called for real casting. Chants and potions and stuff.

I pulled down one last book, it was small and thin - a travel spell book perhaps. The front had a moon burned into the leather. It was encircled by six dragon breath opals.

I opened the worn leather expecting to see more made up languages. Instead, I was surprised to see it was in Greek. It looked like it was the oldest book, and the smallest out of the collection. It also had the worst handwriting and was elementary

- it looked like Venus's first grimoire. Inside, pages were filled with spells on how to raise the dead and call upon undead armies.

A book of necromancy. Probably where the darkness first began setting in.

"Don't bother with that," Venus called over to me. "It's my sister's only dark book. She mastered necromancy to compete with me, gave me that as a gift to recompense. It's boring, every real witch can summon the dead with ease."

I guess I wasn't a real witch after all.

I closed the book and reached up to set it back with the rest. The stones stared back at me, they glowed like Erika's fire. I pulled the book back down. Something inside moved me and I turned to the last page.

There, in more messy handwriting, a note from Athena Lupin to her sister was written:

Sister, you are the witch. You summon. I am the sorcerer. I see. I have seen you will need an army. This is my gift. Summon your army.

~ Athena Lupin

P.S. Remember, it is okay to use darkness if there is no light to pull from.

I looked over to Venus who was brewing tea in a kettle in midair. She was pouring milk into four china cups, completely distracted. I picked up a book from a pile by the seating area and shoved it where Athena's grimoire used to be. I rolled the book of enchantments up and shoved it down into my quiver where it would be hidden amongst my arrows.

"Did your sister always give you gifts?" I tried to be casual as I approached the desk. I was curious about the book and the note, but I didn't want Venus to use that against me.

Venus eyed me briefly. "My sister hardly believed that someone as dark as me could be related to her. That grimoire was nothing more than her trying to manipulate me. I'm sure she thought that if she played with darkness, perhaps I would play with light to even the score, but no."

I hesitated. "The note in the back made it seem like she really cared."

"Athena talks in riddles. Although I am an expert in all spells, my enchantments mostly revolve around seduction, not summoning, so her words are no more than guessing games she wanted me to play into."

"So there's nothing significant about your sister giving you a book of her own spells?" I pried, knowing that act was incredibly rare even among sister witches.

"I doubt it, though there may have been. She sees the future and since speaking of the future directly causes it to fall into chaos, she uses vagueness to hide her motives. Now sit."

With the flick of her hand a seat was flying under my legs, scooping me into it and throwing me next to the boys in front of her.

She poured the steaming pink tea into the cups before settling down behind the desk.

"First order of business," she began as she leaned forward. "Putting value to things. You tell me what you want, and I tell you what it's worth."

"We need a soul back from Death," I said.

Adam's eyes grew wide and he looked over at me. When he found me unfazed, he looked over to Ethan. Ethan shrugged, keeping his expression neutral, but interested.

Venus leaned back into her chair.

"Getting a soul back will be incredibly expensive," she said. "Even more expensive if the soul is a rare one."

I crossed my arms and leaned back as well, making sure she knew that price wasn't a concern for me.

"We need a druid soul back," I said, bodly.

Venus scoffed. "Don't be absurd. No Druids are alive anymore, you can't fool me. You'd need a druid to put a druid soul into, otherwise it's just worthless."

"You leave those details to us," Ethan said. "We have our motives for needing the soul, you don't need to know the logistics of our situation. Can you get it for us or not?"

Venus rolled her eyes. "Of course I can get you Erika Gavina's soul. But she's dead so it won't matter. You can't bring back the dead if there isn't a fresh body. And respectfully, putting the soul into a new body doesn't bring the dead back, it just creates two consciousnesses in one person, resulting in a split personality and inconsistent powers."

I uncrossed my arms so I could reach out and tap my fingers onto her desk. "We can trade a dragon's soul for the druid soul. We give you information on where to find a dragon and you give us Erika."

Adam and Ethan both stiffened next to me.

"Dragon?" Venus hummed happily. "Show me a taste, little goddess."

"If I give you a taste it means you can track him," I sneered. "You either agree to the deal of a dragon for a druid, or you can send us back right now. No taste included."

Her eyes narrowed on me. "Deal. Now give me a taste or I take all of your souls as payment for wasting my time."

I pressed the back of my hand onto her desk and opened my palm so that I could let a small ball of Condan's magick rise from it. A ball of black spun around above my skin like dust rising off of a bit of charcoal. It spun and spun, picking up speed with each rotation and growing closer to itself until it finally solidified into one hard, glossy black stone.

Venus reached out and took the pebble between her fingers before popping it into her mouth. She swirled the magick around like it was candy. She closed her eyes and moaned in delight at the taste of Condan's power.

When she was satisfied, she snapped her eyes back open and looked at the three of us.

"Give me three days and I shall have the druid soul for you," Venus said.

"I won't be with them," I said. "So you will have to give it to these two without me."

Venus looked over at them, paying special attention to Ethan, the most attractive of the two.

"We may take longer than three days to return to you," Ethan said.

Venus waved her hand in the air. "Reika and I struck a deal. We are bound to our words now. She gave me a means to find a dragon soul. Now I have to give Erika Gavina's druid soul. Whether you get it in exactly three days time or three years time, I will have it waiting for you."

I stood up then. "Since we're square, you can let us go back."

Venus snapped her fingers and the door behind us glowed red, the club's lights returning behind it.

"Safe travels," Venus said. "I look forward to dealing with you again, little goddess." She then turned to Ethan. "As for you, human, you are very wrong. There doesn't need to be any sort of attraction within a siren's target. A being incapable of romantic feelings can still be trapped in a siren's call."

She paused, blinking repeatedly down at her desk, lost in thoughtful hesitation.

"No, dear, only someone truly, completely, irrevocably, and consumingly in love with one person and one person only is immune. It's because siren's are creatures of destiny, and all beings are destined for tragedy when it comes to love. Sirens provide that tragedy for those who have yet to find it.

"The fact that you were immune simply means that you have already found the man or woman who will be your all-consuming sorrow."

Ethan

Something was wrong. I could feel it. But a part of me also knew that it was nothing that I needed to be panicked about. It was more like a "damn I left the milk out" feeling instead of a "I left the stove on."

Nonetheless, it left me bouncing my leg like an ADHD kid who took too much adderall. I wanted to be back with my friends. Back with my family. Back to the dickweed Condan with his fancy ashy skin and his flowing white hair. I wanted to make sure he wasn't pulling any fast ones on Erika. He was, afterall, her supposed "other half." His dark dragon and her light dragon were destined to be according to the stars or some shit like that.

I didn't buy it, nor did I like it. But if I said anything that would be me stepping into Adam's relationship with Erika, and I vowed a long time ago that I would keep my nose out of anything involving her love life.

Adam called dibs after meeting her out in the forest when we were fifteen, and even though I'm a grown ass man now and recognize the stupidity that is calling dibs on a woman, it doesn't change the fact that they did end up together. No matter how I felt or what I thought, I would keep all matters Erika and the heart at a distance.

"Dude, if you keep that up we're going to end up crashing from you shaking us off the tracks," Adam complained.

I looked over at him. We were sitting in a jam packed trolley that moved around the four districts in the same circular formation they were laid out in. It would stop in the middle of each district where we could then board another trolley that would haul us out towards the forest zone or all the way in towards the centre of the Otherworld where the Council of Magick had their massive headquarters.

"I'm fine," I said. "I just have this weird feeling."

"Define weird feeling?" Reika whispered, leaning closer to me like she was trying to sniff my thoughts out of me.

I leaned back, all but crawling into Adam's lap to get away from the purple eyed witch.

"Just like a nervous buzzing in my shoulders," I said. "Not like a pit in my stomach or anything like that, but there's definitely something weird."

"Hmm," she turned her head to the side, eyeing me sideways as if it was going to help her decipher invisible words on my forehead.

I settled back down into my seat as she pulled away, suddenly much more comfortable without smelling her cinnamon and citrus perfume. I looked back at Adam and raised my eyebrows, trying to tell him how crazy I found this woman to be. But he just curled his lips into an awkward smile and opened his hands up to the sky, surrendering before the battle had even begun.

I was all for getting Erika's druid soul back, but I also recognized how entirely unrealistic that was. A soul ended up in Heaven or Hell if it was mortal. Here, in the Otherworld, people believed that souls went to Perdition or Felicity.

I would have liked to argue that no being had ever ventured into Perdition or Felicity and successfully come back; also that the idea of Heaven and Hell being on the other side of the ground we walked on made no sense and therefore it had to have been all bullshit; but I'd come to the conclusion that Heaven and Hell did exist, as does God, and that would mean immortals and magick-borne aren't that powerful, and Perdition and Felicity were the result of them being in denial and coming up with a whole new concept of the afterlife.

But better to keep my arguments to myself rather than be smited down by thousands of insecure, magick-psychos.

Plus, it was also possible I was just projecting my bitterness onto immortals.

I hated that there were people who got to live for thousands of years who squandered it.

If I knew I could live for so long I would have mastered painting, broken into the Sistine Chapel and painted over all the nude little boys. Or at the very least covered them enough that it wasn't so damn creepy. Then I would have mastered sculpting and metal working, or I'd take my drawings and I'd make the canvases bigger, like the side of a whole twenty story building big.

But since life didn't deal me those cards, and I had to work in order to eat and pay rent, I'd be happy if I spent the next five or so years watching my friends be happy and then died.

There's not enough time in my mortal life for me to accomplish everything I'd want to, and I have no desire to corrupt myself in order to live long enough to achieve it. I'd rather just be a decent person for a few more years and then let the angels take me away.

I pulled back the sleeve of my leather jacket so I could look at my watch. We'd been separated from the group for a few hours now. No smoke signals were sent up, there was no

170

commotion in the streets or any reports of an epic battle ensuing, which meant that Erika and Jack were keeping the two elves in line. Nothing bad had happened with them, obviously.

So then why was I feeling so damn weird?

I reached into my breast pocket and pulled out my phone, thinking I'd call Jack and ask, only to immediately remember that there were no cell towers in the Otherworld.

I groaned and shoved it back.

"Forgot about the cell service thing?" Adam whispered.

I nodded. "I normally come here alone, so I don't even bring my phone with me."

"How has the mercenary work been?" Adam asked.

I looked down at him. It had been so long since he and I had talked properly. He was always with Erika and I was always… avoiding her… I was a bad friend. In the last three years, the last time I had been with him for over an hour like we were today was on his twenty-first birthday two years ago. Seeing him and Erika all cuddled up that night was the nail in the coffin for me. I didn't go to his twenty-second or third because the thought of it still stung.

"It's been good," I said. "I pick up several jobs so I can get them all done in one trip and cash them out. It's good money."

He offered a visibly forced smile. "Yeah, Darbie told me you have your own flat down in Leurbost?"

"Yeah, I bought a house a little before you and E did," I told him. "It looks right over the loch. Maybe when we get home you can come take a look at it? I'm gutting one of the bedrooms to turn it into a library with hidden weapons behind the bookshelves."

His grin was genuine now. "Aye, I'd like that. I've missed you."

171

I threw my arm over his head and wrapped them around his shoulder.

"I missed you too, lad. I'm sorry I've been such a shite friend," I apologised.

"I've been a piss poor friend too. I spend all the time with my girlfriend."

I pulled my arm back and shrugged. "Ah, it's to be expected. You love her."

"I think I'm going to make her not my girlfriend."

I quirked a brow and looked down at him. My heart rate was picking up in my chest. The next words out of his mouth could have been the best thing I had ever heard in my life or the worst and I didn't know what to expect.

"I'd like to marry her, Ethan," he said and I had to remind myself not to let my shoulders drop with my heart. "If she says yes, I'd want you to be the best man."

And just like that, I knew why I was feeling so damn weird…

If only fate had given me a tingling feeling earlier. I could have hardened my heart and been prepared for my best friend to ask me to be the best man when he married the girl I was also in love with.

"You'd want me instead of Jack?" I laughed to mask whatever else might slip through the cracks. "Jack has a way better eye for details. I might forget to even write a speech or put on a tie."

"Jack is also my best friend, but Erika already claimed both him and Darbie to be on her side helping her plan things," he said. "Plus…" He looked down into his lap, his thumbs rolled around each other and he watched them closely. I imagined that was what the cogs in his mind looked like right now. Spinning. And spinning. And spinning.

172

"Don't close up just because you think I'll judge you for it," I said. "You've done that our whole lives. I don't judge you for feeling and expressing your emotions, dude. I just don't like to show mine."

He met my gaze and I could see the gratitude in his eyes.

"You did a great job of shutting everyone out when we were kids," he said. "You never let us in, but you were always there, reaching out and holding everyone else up. I think that's a real shame."

I sighed. "I don't think a lot of people could handle what I look like inside, but I've always wanted to help. I think that's why you and I are so damn close. We have that same instinct. I'd love to be your best man, Adam."

He outstretched his hand. "You'll be my best man, and I'll be yours? Watching each other's back in every walk of life?"

I slapped my palmed around his forearm and gripped it. His fingers tightened around my arm and we sat clasped like that in our viking's embrace long enough for the memory of his green eyes confidently staring into mine to burn into my brain.

When he finally let me go, he reached down into his travel pack and pulled out a flask.

"Slàinte," he said and took a swig of the drink.

I rolled my eyes and smiled. "I'll have to have a shot of orange juice for you when we get home."

He laughed. "One of these days we'll wear you down enough to get one beer in you."

"Until then, I'll stick to orange juice and IRN BRU."

The trolley came to a stop in less than a second. I had been sitting stiffly with my nervousness and only bumped into Adam a bit, still being able to grab him and hold him onto his seat. Meanwhile, Reika had clearly never ridden on an Otherworld trolly before and went flying into my lap. Her knees draped over

173

my leg, her buttcheeks on my thigh. She fell back so that her shoulders were in Adam's hands and her black locks were tumbling down over the side of the bench chair we had been sitting on.

She reached out in a hurry and grabbed me by the lips of my jacket so that she could tug herself off of Adam. When she drew up, her face was mere inches from mine.

It should have been romantic.

She was gorgeous. And strong. We were both single, even if her's was in a nun sort of way.

But instead it was just annoying.

The smell of her spicy scented skin gave me a headache, and her lack of poise, or confidence, or stability - whatever it was that was missing - irritated me. Maybe she wasn't bullheaded or intense enough. I couldn't quite tell what it was that I wanted in a woman, all I knew was that she, and every other woman I had met besides one, didn't have it.

I stood up, her small frame gripped in my large hands. I lifted her up and plopped her down onto her feet. I stepped into her, my foot stepping in between her legs and reaching past her, forcing her to step back with me. With the one step, we were standing in the centre of the car. I grasped her wrists and lifted them up until her fingers could grip the rails running up and down the vehicle.

She didn't hesitate to grab them. I could see the nervousness in her eyes. She was scared of me. Not enough to be in fear, but enough that she was on edge and ready to fight.

"Why don't you stand and hold onto this so your light body doesn't go flying, yeah?" I asked.

My jaw was tight as I talked, and I felt bad that I was so annoyed. If she had fallen into my lap like that four or five years ago, I would have pulled her lips to mine and kissed the shit out of her. Probably offer to take her out somewhere and hook-up with her.

But now?

I'd rather be alone.

Maybe I was getting old. Crotchety did not look good on me either.

I stepped back and plopped down into my seat just as the trolley took off again with a jolt. This time, we were all more prepared and no one went flying into anyone.

"That was a bit rude man," Adam whispered to me when we were well underway again. "Plus, that could have been a great opportunity to find love. Maybe she's the one Venus was talking about."

I rolled my eyes.

"If she's the woman who's going to be the recipe to my destruction then I definitely do *not* want her," I said.

The rest of the ride went by rather silently. The occasional magick-born with an impeccable nose would get a whiff of our human scent and either look at us with hungry eyes or grumble in our general direction.

Humans were supposed to report to the Council of Magick to get approval to be here, but they weren't technically the rulers of the Otherworld, so it was more of a formality. Nonetheless, die-hard supporters who wanted the council to have complete and utter control weren't the biggest fans of humans like us being around without the glowing magick badge that declared us as registered.

When we reached the intersection of the internal-to-external line and the round-about line, we exited the trolly. We were now in the middle of the flourishing sector. The sector was barren of people for the most part. There weren't very many jobs in this part of the Otherworld. Instead, people came here for religious and healing purposes.

There was a glowing blue hut a few metres away from the trolley doors where riders could buy another ticket or ambrosia - a healing drink that could also get the consumer high. The entirety of the ground was a lush and fluffy green moss, despite the foot traffic.

We walked around the small thatched hut to the left of the car. Just on the other side of the it, there were two more cars side-by-side. One was facing towards the centre of the Otherworld, and the other was facing out - getting ready to move towards the end of the flourishing sector, where the forest zone started.

A few nymphs were getting off the trolly going out and changing onto the trolly going in, leaving the outer facing car empty.

I was the first of my group to duck into the outer cart. Moss and flowers had begun to take over the inside of the cabin, making the seats very padded and comfortable to sit on. I headed to the back where I could sit and have a bench to myself, as well as look over the entirety of the space.

It wasn't an incredibly large cabin. It was no larger than maybe three metres long by two wide, and the ceiling barely hit two metres, making standing the entire journey comfortably impossible for guys like Adam and I.

Adam slid onto the bench across from the door and immediately laid down onto the plush overgrowth. Reika took a seat by the door, where she could lace her arms through the rail next to it and hold on tight.

"We'll probably get there before the rest of the group, considering they can't take public transport with Erika," Adam said.

I shook my head. "It took us a long while to get to the club, and even longer to talk with Venus. The rest of the group will probably beat us, assuming they don't kill each other or run into anything too concerning."

He was looking directly at me and just sort of staring, watching the way my shoulders shook with the car as it moved. It was uncomfortable, but there wasn't much of anywhere else to look. The plants had grown up around the limited windows the vehicle had, blocking us from seeing anything other than what was inside with us.

The only light came from the glowing purple and pink flowers scattered amongst the fuzzy grass, and the long stripe of blue magickal light rolling up and down the floating rails at the top of the car.

The first time I had seen the inside of a trolly here in the flourishing sector, I thought I had accidentally consumed acid, LSD or some other type of hallucinogen. The colours and movements of light and objects were just so unnatural to earthlings.

Magick as beautiful as this was everywhere in this part of the Otherworld, though. It was originally cultivated and kept by druids, who had brought plants and animals from Earth to grow and adapt here so that the Otherworld could have its own access to the rare sources of magick that Earth had.

But, of course, people are greedy, and eventually the druids were murdered and everything they maintained, everything that was peaceful and beautiful slowly was killed off and pushed back until only this small sector existed.

The Council of Magick and many other activists who wanted to be able to keep the rare elements had made it illegal to use or destroy any of the material in the flourishing sector. It didn't stop the stealing that occurred on occasions, but with how hardcore the council went on punishments, for the most part citizens stayed clear.

Now, the nymphs - who mostly lived just past the flourishing sector in the forest zone - tried to keep the flourishing zone as tended as they could. Without the same powers as the druids, though, it was hard to keep all the life in this part alive. Earth's wildlife was never meant to exist in this world. It would take someone with serious restorative powers to keep everything alive and, well, flourishing.

I scratched the back of my neck and shimmied down deeper in my seat.

"So Reika," I said, now comfortable enough for a conversation. "I'm very curious why you're in so much danger that you need a magickal entourage to escort you through the Otherworld. Care to enlighten me."

Her eyes narrowed like slits and she held that icy gaze on me until I almost became uncomfortable. *Almost*. Luckily, I was a man of intense staring, and she had nothing on me.

"My mother is a goddess, she's married to a king who is very powerful like her," she said through gritted teeth. "My mother went to earth during World War Two to help heal injured soldiers. She fell in love with someone, had sex, got pregnant with me, which pissed off her husband. She hid away with Artemis until I was born and then left me with the goddess. My mother's husband doesn't know who I am or where I was hid, but is still hunting me hoping to kill me because he's bitter that his wife has a kid and won't give him one. Does that answer the question?"

"So who's your step daddy?" I asked.

She rolled her eyes. "You don't need to know."

I crossed my arms. "Alright then, who's mummy?"

"If I say her name out loud both she and her husband will be able to hear it and he will find me," she explained. "The reason I have stayed safe and hidden this long is because I didn't even

178

know who my mother was until I was fifty and my powers started coming in."

"So you're telling me you've never said your mum's name out loud?" Adam asked.

"No, never," she answered.

I sat there in silence.

I hadn't uttered my dad's or brother's names since they died. It was easier, sometimes, to let the memory of loved ones fade. Remembering, for me, was what kept me holding onto the pain of losing half my family.

I wasn't attracted to Reika, but I respected her then, knowing that she also had a family she could never know or speak about.

You have found the man or woman who will be your all-consuming sorrow, Venus had said. But did that mean that I still had sorrow to endure? Or was my brother and father enough?

Who else did I have to suffer for because I loved them?

10

Erika

When Ethan and Adam finally arrived outside the shrine, I was ready to run to them, throw my arms around them and collapse into their strength.

It had been a long and emotionally draining day and we weren't even done yet.

When I saw the pair, however, I found myself taken aback.

Ethan, who normally walked with his chest out like he was trying to make his pecs look bigger than they were, had nearly curled up into his jacket. He still looked straight ahead, but he didn't meet anyone's eye. With his hands in his coat pockets, pushing it forward, the leather consumed his impressive frame, making him appear small.

Adam slid up next to me, planting a kiss against my temple. I cocked my head to the side as he did it, still trying to look over his shoulder to assess Ethan, while at the same time accepting my boyfriend's love. The strained position left a rather annoying kink in my neck.

Ethan strided passed all of us, heading right into the garden separating us from the forest zone where we'd find Artemis.

I leaned back to look at Adam. He pursed his lips and gave me a disappointed look, clearly not liking the fact that I had cut his display of affection short.

"What's goin' on with Ethan?" I asked, ignoring the look.

Adam's expression softened and he looked up to gaze after his best friend. He frowned.

"There was an unfortunate conversation about absent parents right before we arrived," he said, giving me back his attention. "Sort of put a damper in the air."

It was my turn to frown as I leaned my forehead into his neck, planting a sweet kiss on his collar before I pulled away.

"We'll have to remember to check in with him when we get home," I said, running my hand over Adam's firm chest.

He had truly grown into a wonderful man these last few years. I was lucky to have found him in this long life. Because of him I now could die or live feeling completely happy. I loved my family.

I dropped my hands to my side so that I could lean down and pick up my bag.

Darbie and Jack were standing just off to my left, whispering in the shade of the garden's headwalls. Their eyes watched Condan closely, until Darbie caught my movement out of the corner of his eye. He patted Jack on his shoulder, and motioned for him to pick up their travel bags. Jack handed Darbie his satchel while he dragged his melon green back pack over his shoulders.

Darbie riffled through the normal sized pack to pull out his six foot staff, before banishing the bag away to his ever-within-reach storage realm.

Knowing that my best friend had enough magick to have created his own pocket of time and space just to store things, and constantly consume the energy needed to keep it in existence every second of every day, still bamboozled me. Of course, manifestation and creation spells were easy for him even when we were younger, now that he had a thousand and some years to master it, it was probably light work for him.

"Condan," Darbie called out to the dark elf who was sitting on the other side of the garden entrance, meditating. "We're heading out."

The dark elf didn't move. He continued to sit there, his chest rising and falling with each strong breath that he took. Just like the prayer room, I found the silence to be unsettling.

Reika, who had been hanging back near the pathway leading from the transit centre to here, began striding towards Condan at the same time I did. We locked eye contact and both stopped. My stomach churned and a cold sweat began to bead down my back.

Adam moved around me and I caught the colour of his eyes in a sideways glance. Adam squatted down in front of Condan so that he could peer closer at the relic's grey face. He reached out and waved his hand in front of his face, and when the elf still didn't move, Adam looked back at me and shrugged.

"I'm beginning to realise that you've been outgrown by your counterparts," Condan said, his eyes still closed.

Adam snapped his attention back to the now speaking man.

"Excuse me?" Adam replied. "What do you mean?"

I could hear the justified offence in Adam's words, and the aggression that was building back up because of Condan filled the air like a spoiled cologne.

I took a few steps closer, ready to slap the first person who tried to pick a fight.

"Of this band, Erika is the most experienced in combat and the strongest, therefore she is the natural leader," Condan began. "Darbie is the most experienced in magick and therefore plays a critical role, and while Jack is not as skilled or impressive as him, he has an innate ability to act as a conduit it seems. He also helps to reduce the intensity of Darbie's pacifism. The other human is clearly an excellent mercenary and adventurer as he's a primary source of income for the supporting of mine and Erika's children. Therefore, everyone has some sort of special role except you."

Condan opened his eyes and stared on at Adam. He cocked his head to the side like a dog waiting for someone to drop food off the table.

"Tell me, *Adam*," Condan spat his name like a curse. "What makes you so special that you have been blessed with the opportunity to remain here?"

Adam stood up, hand balled up at his sides.

"Erika and I are together," he snapped down towards Condan, who was still sitting peacefully on the ground.

Condan chuckled. "Like a mortal consumed with dreadful loneliness takes to a pet, I think you misunderstand how far you are from being together."

In two large strides, I was next to Adam. I slipped my hand into his and moved him back behind me.

"I think you misunderstand," I said firmly. "Adam is a mortal I'm going to marry both on Earth and here in the Otherworld."

183

Condan laughed even more, still staring up at us from the grass.

"Forgive me," he said. "But your plan of getting a human to live for eternity with you by entering into a lifelong magickal contract is just as foolish of a plan as mine. He will still die before you. His flesh is weak compared to a true immortal's."

"Hey!" Ethan shouted from the archway into the gardens. "Can you three sort out your romantic triangle bullshit after we get the princess of magick back to her temple? I really don't feel like being in the Otherworld for longer than need be; it's bad for my complexion and means we have to shit in the woods."

I rolled my eyes. Condan grinned boldly and rose to his feet. I glared at his chest, his height a visible representation of where he and I were in regard to power and capabilities... I was doomed to fall short compared to him.

He looked over his shoulder at Ethan. "I think you're mistaken. It's a square that has four points."

Immediately, I furrowed my brows.

I motioned between Adam, Condan and I. "You can count, right? That's something they still taught twenty thousand or whatever years ago?" I sassed.

He looked back to me.

"Trust me, love," he said. "I know exactly what I've counted."

I waved both hands into the air, dismissing this conversation like it was mist in the air.

"Let's just move on, we need to get through the garden shrine and into the forest before nightfall," I announced, moving around Condan, towards Ethan.

Ethan had taken his weapons out of his pack and secured them to his body for easier access. Now, with his sword on his hip and a great axe on his back, not to mention the several small

184

knives tucked into his boot and in small sheaths along his belt, I was hit hard with the realisation that I may have been the one to unleash his darkness.

He had always been a little bit of a bad boy, but since the pub back when all this first started, when he stared down a slaugh and I saw in his eyes that he could face hell without fear, he had just continued to plummet into this world of brutality. I introduced him to a world where he could be at war with real demons instead of the ones in his head. Now I was afraid the demons inside were consuming him. Why else would a mortal be so willing to run into battle. He was only twenty-four, quarter of his life done, and he looked into the eyes of ancient deities like Condan with nothing more than iron.

He should have been afraid. He shouldn't have wanted to live this life. But I brought him in, and now he was nothing short of addicted to it.

Adam

Erika took up the lead with Reika by her side. Darbie and Jack wandered behind them but off to the side of the trail, their noses facing the ground while they gathered magickal ingredients to bring back with them.

Behind me, Ethan was taking up the rear. Originally, he had told me it was to stay as far away from Condan and all his creepy commentary. But Condan clearly had a target set on Ethan.

The old man started off between Erika and Darbie. Then Darbie wandered off with Jack, so Condan fell back to me. I tried to keep him entertained by asking him questions about his life and what it was like during his time, but all I got was the silent treatment and an occasional side eye. It didn't take but a few minutes before he suddenly just halted and waited for Ethan to catch up to him.

The pair walked in silence for the first few kilometres, then, as the light went down, Condan began to come alive. He breathed in the scent of the setting suns. He followed the path of the first sun as it fell beyond the horizon. Then the second fell. Now the third was beginning to touch down where the greenish sky met the end of the Otherworld. Once the third sun set, only the fourth and dimmest of the four would remain.

"You love the darkness don't you?" Condan asked, his voice low.

Ethan remained silent.

"It's cooler here," Condan continued. "Quieter. Calmer. There is a peace in the dead of the night, almost like it's a sample of what death will sound like. It's our own little sample of oblivion."

Then nothing but the sound of footsteps was behind me. The pushing of leaves, and the soft wet squishing of moss-like grass as their heavy feet moved.

"I can smell it on you, you know?" Condan whispered like a growl.

Even though I couldn't see them, I could imagine how they looked just from his tone. Condan was leaning close to Ethan's ear, a satisfied smile barely shadowed on his lips. And Ethan would be gripping his sword, a spirit strong enough to go toe-to-toe with Condan burning in my mortal friend's body.

Had Ethan lived the same amount of years as Condan, and trained in magick and warfare like the elf had, I would have bet that Ethan could have beat him. Even with his dragon soul, the content of Condan's heart would never rival my best friend's.

186

Passion is the true measure of the soul. Ethan was more passionate than Erika, only his was controlled. Stored up like reserve grain, prepared to feed an entire nation for years should they need it.

"You reek of death," Condan told Ethan even though the latter had shown no interest in the conversation. "It smells like a perfume of a lover, rubbed all over your skin after you've rolled around with them in a fit of passion."

Twigs snapped and moss smashed into an intense slap as feet pounded to an abrupt stop.

I hesitated to turn around, afraid of what I might see. But curiosity got the best of me.

I slowly shuffled on and looked over my shoulder as I did.

Ethan was looming over Condan. His features were relaxed as he spoke quietly down towards the dragon. I couldn't make out what he was saying, but Condan's face looked up at the human and puffed out his chest like a proud father.

The blue fourth sun met with the horizon, sparking a flash of blue light to streak across the sky. It met with Ethan and rippled over his jet black hair and crystal clear eyes then down to his finger tips before being cut off by the mounds of forest around us. The movement of the light running from his head to his hands reminded me of lightning shooting down from the sky.

"Alright," Erika called from behind me. "Last light, we should start setting up camp for the night."

My eyes were still fixed on Ethan and Condan, who remained holding each other's gaze.

Ethan was the first to break it. He stepped out, stared deeper into Condan's eyes for a second longer, then turned away. As he moved, he caught my eye, looked me down then up, and offered me a stark expression. Whatever he said to Condan, there was nothing but truth in his words. I could see it in his eyes.

187

Ethan turned and headed off deeper into the forest. He drew out of axe and disappeared over a mount of soft moss and into the depth of the forest's shadows.

I looked back over to Condan. The dragon walked closer to me, an almost friendly smile on his face.

"I don't respect many humans," he said gently. "No mortals at all, really. But I have respect for your friend. You must have an above average intelligence to know to choose such powerful allies."

"Thanks," I said, trying not to sound disappointed. "That was almost a compliment."

"Adam!" Erika shouted. "Condan! Either get firewood, food or freshwater. Those are your options. Not stand around hosting a tea party."

Condan rolled his eyes then flicked me back with his finger tips.

"Step back human," he grumbled.

"My name's Adam," I whispered under my breath, but took a few steps back nonetheless.

I watched as Condan closed his eyes and rested his hands behind his back. He took a breath and the ground around us stopped humming with life. The lush green ground dimmed from lime to olive. The blue-ish brown wood of the tall, thin trees faded until they almost looked airbrushed with black. The rolling bumps of the floor were suddenly scattered with shadows instead of softness.

The area between Condan and I let out a whine, the same sound chalk makes against a chalkboard but deeper, like the chalk was bigger and the whiteboard thicker.

With the sound, the gap between us began to descend down. Moving and popping as it settled into a soft basin. Then, the depression grew out in a thinner dry aqueduct away from us.

It followed up the small hill to my left, then the hill began to grow up and back, pushing trees aside so that it could rise into a subtle-declining cliff face that was lost into the cloud above the treeline.

A few moments after the geography morphed, water clearer than tears began to run down from the cliffs via the mossy aqueduct. It gathered into the pool that was between Condan and I running not faster than a trickle at first. But then Condan began to step back, his eyes still closed, and the pond followed after him, growing bigger and the water growing faster, filling the space beautifully.

The ground behind Condan flattened as he walked back too, creating more of a clearing in the lumping forest.

He stopped and the pool stopped growing with him. Instead, a small stream split off from the pond and ran off into the forest behind the dragon.

He stood there longer as the ground around the rest of the group gently began to flatten beneath our feet, bringing us all down into a soft floored, level clearing.

We each looked around, watching each other in disbelief. The grand, grey rocks began to emerge out of the ground closer to the edges of the clearing, like ramparts. Smaller boulders formed in a circle of seven in the centre of the clearing with a depression between, just large enough to be perfect for a fire.

Then the ground was silent. Only the continuous flow of water and our disbelieving breaths filled the magnificent looking space.

I looked over to Condan who was shaking his shoulders out now, his eyes back open. He stepped forward, stepping onto the water, and rocks rose up to meet him, making a perfect path through the small river.

"There," he said. "Freshwater."

"Did you do that just by thinking it?" Reika asked.

Condan nodded once. "Yes. It's just a small example of what the celestial dragons are capable of."

"You just created an entirely different geography," Darbie gapped.

Condan laughed richly now.

"How quant," he threw out. "My brethren, I have created an entirely different world that ran on a completely different concept of time. Why are you shocked that I can flatten earth and summon water? Celestial dragons were the right hands of God in the beginning, we can create anything he can."

"You know Lucifer was the right hand of God too," Ethan said, emerging from the forest with a small hoard of cut logs in his arms. "He was cast out of Heaven and doomed to end up in a cage under a lake of fire for all eternity once God decides to come back."

"That's merely a prophecy," Condan mocked. "Prophecies are not guaranteed."

"No, but the word of God is," Ethan said and dropped the logs into the divot between the centre rocks. "Personally, I think God is not only guaranteed, but I think He's so indefinite that the existence you've had that you consider long and grand is so insignificant to Him that He wouldn't even need to sneeze to watch you roll off His chess board."

"You would face Death and and tell him you appreciate his cologne, I would face God and tell Him I could do better," Condan jeered. "We are not the same."

"No, you fear Death and I don't, which I'll make sure to tell that to The Big Man when I get there first," Ethan's words were smooth.

Condan grinned, "So you confess that you know you'll meet Him first?"

190

"I want to," Ethan stated. "That way I can wait at the gates and be the one to chuck you into Hell."

"You and I were destined to be friends in another life," Condan said and licked his lips.

Ethan knelt down next to the fire pit, shaking his head.

He stacked logs into the pit two at a time. Four logs at the bottom, then two, leaving the centre open so that he could place dried leaves and smaller sticks there. Then he crossed two more logs across the top going in the opposite direction, before adding one on top, completing the triangle.

He didn't say a word while he worked. Neither did Darbie and Jack as they went into the woods to find more wood or food. Erika approached the pit, her eyes trained on Condan, but the elf continued to simply watch Ethan.

Erika knelt down next to Ethan, who stood up as she went down, like they were trading off roles; one keeping an eye on our fragile friendship and the other providing us warmth.

Erika gave a little flick of her fingers and the fire roared to life.

"Adam," she called to me over her shoulder. "Will you and Reika go find some food?"

"Sure," I said. "You okay with us leaving you and Ethan behind?"

She looked over at me and smiled. I could see the natural light in her eyes and my heart skipped a beat. Even in tense circumstances, she was still so wonderfully bright.

"Don't worry, Adam, Ethan and I will watch each other's backs," she insisted.

I turned on my heels and walked over to Reika. She had prepped her bow already, notching an arrow in the string, but kept it low and undrawn.

"I'll hunt if you gather?" she offered.

"There's a joke somewhere in that statement, but I'm pretty sure it'd be sexist, so let's just leave that."

"Sexist?" she cocked her head to the side.

I opened my mouth, preparing to explain the concept of sexism to a seventy year old woman who had never interacted with a man until she met us.

"You know what? Don't worry," I waved it off. "They don't have men where you're going so it's irrelevant."

Our feet scuffed against the ground as we headed deeper into the growing darkness. As the light around us faded, I realised that Reika's eyes were not just bright purple, but they actually let off small amounts of light, glowing through the shadows.

"You're eyes glow?" I said in wonder, but I was so confused that it came out as a question.

She looked over at me and nodded once before returning her eyes to the horizon.

"Yes," she whispered. "I absorb magick from anything and everything I touch, including the small amounts of it in the air around us. As I absorb it, my eyes glow. The more magick, the brighter."

"So if you were to touch a patch of magick mushrooms would you absorb the whole system it's connected to or just the small patch?" I asked.

"If it's one organism, I'd absorb from one organism."

We were approaching a collection of glowing mushrooms. Their soft pink edges pulsated each time our feet met the ground. They were simple magick elements, their only purpose being to act as an early warning system. They could be brewed into a potion that temporarily allows the consumer to have heightened senses. Nonetheless, they had magick and were connected in systems that covered kilometres of forest.

"Can you touch them for me?" I pleaded. "I just want to see how bright your eyes can shine."

She sighed. I could see as she rolled her eyes, yet she still walked over, took a glove off, and touched her fingers against the fungus. The pink edges of the organism began to dim while Reika's eyes began to light up like car headlights.

She let go of the plant when the purple light off of her eyes could cast more than an arms length away.

She stood up and rested her bare hand on her hip.

"Happy now?" she snapped, a scowl deeply etched into her face.

I nodded excitedly. "You are incredibly interesting."

The irritation in her face was overtaken with a smile.

"Thank you," she bashfully whispered. "I think all of you are interesting as well. I wish I could have spent more time with you all."

"Why don't you?" I asked.

We were continuing to walk now. Both of us set our eyes out into the grey light around us, waiting to see anything of value.

"I've been summoned back," she stated, leaving no room for argument, but I wasn't afraid of prying.

"But it doesn't really seem like you fulfilled your mission," I pushed.

"I wouldn't be sure of that, Adam McLeon. I was sent here to find what could be the cause of the oncoming darkness my goddess and the oracles have foreseen."

"And you think you found it?"

Erika yanked her bow up, pulling the string back to her lip before letting the arrow fly. The projectile hit its mark with a snap and a painful yelp.

It had pierced the eye of a mooane; a long four legged creature, covered in a combination of dull green and white fur,

193

and vibrant green feathers that helped it to bend in with the forest floor. Its long legs were thin from the thigh down like a gazelle's so that it could run quickly. Its neck was long and flexible, and on top, its head was short with big eyes so that it could look around and see in nearly every direction. Around its face and neck, the feather's were thicker so that it could lay down behind the rolling mounds and lay its head on top, keeping watch for potential threats, but saving running for a last resort. Which is exactly what this one had been doing before Reika claimed it's life.

"I didn't even see him," I confessed.

"Neither did I," she said.

I turned to her, confused.

She raised her bare hand and wiggled her fingers.

"Radharc mushrooms, remember?" she smirked. "Their magick lets you sense things. I felt the mooane moving behind the hill."

"Well, shout out to God for making magick mushroom."

11

Reika

It was Adam who carried the mooane back to camp, but only after insisting on gathering wood as well to help the group. Even though I was a demi-goddess and therefore naturally stronger than his human body, he still packed several logs into his bag and slung the bloody kill over his shoulders.

He claimed that since I did the work of hunting our dinner, then he should put in the work of carrying it for me.

He mentioned the "sexism" again after stating that it was a "gentleman's duty," but after a short and rather confusing debate, we settled that his actions were nothing more than respectful.

They were all like that though. Respectful, honourable, all the way down to their cores.

When we made it back to camp, Darbie and Jack had retrieved a large pile of wood, and Ethan and Erika had laid out tarps over the moss to keep the sleeping bags they laid dry and away from little creatures. Protective runes were stitched into the borders of the tarps, and I recognized the language of the Egyptians declaring that no one with any ill-intent towards those on the inside would be able to enter. It was a broad enchantment, one that could backfire off of small things, like if someone in the group was bickering with another and tried to enter the space.

Still, I doubted this group ever possessed any ill-intent towards another, even during bouts of anger.

Ethan was the one to come and help Adam carry the mooane towards the edge of the clearing, away from our water source, in order to skin the large, beautiful beast. Then they hacked off chunks and approached the fire, where the rest of us lounged against rocks, enjoying the peaceful sounds of a fire crackling and a river trickling. I had expected them to start cooking over the fire, so when Ethan handed a raw chunk of white meat to Erika I furrowed my brows. She wrapped her fingers around it, fisting it tightly, before her hands slowly began to glow orange and the meat began ot sizzle.

"Are you cooking that with your hands?" Condan was clearly astonished.

She looked over at him and nodded.

"Cooks it more thoroughly and quicker than putting it over the fire," she explained. "No wait and no parasites."

She let go of the sizzling, perfectly crispy looking thigh meat. The bone still stuck out from the bottom, and I could tell just from looking at it that one bite into that meat and it would fall off that bone perfectly.

Ethan walked around Erika's back, behind Darbie and Jack, bringing the piece of cooked food to me.

He handed it down toward me, looking at me expectantly.

I shook my head, "A priestess should always eat last."

Ethan shook his head back. "Not here princess. You provided for us, we make sure you eat first."

I leaned away from it and looked to Erika for guidance. She put her hand closer to the fire, and I watched as air moved around her entire arm slowly, blowing into the embers, feeding it and making it grow hotter.

The red danced in her eyes. She smiled at me and I could feel myself grow warm and comfortable, like her magick was also able to cover me in a cozy blanket.

"Go on," she encouraged. "Take it. Or else Ethan might pin you down and force feed you. He's like an Italian mother."

"Okay…" I bowed and took the food from Ethan's hand.

"I'd offer you salt and pepper, but we travel light so you're on your own if you want flavour," Jack added as Ethan walked back to Adam.

I took a bite of the perfect moist thigh, not even needing to chew more than once before it had fallen into swallowable pieces.

"Hey Condan," Darbie called. "Can you create some salt and pepper for us?"

"That's not how the power of the dark dragon works," he replied.

Darbie hummed thoughtfully, "So you're limited on what you can create?"

Condan's jaw clenched. "Yes, but what I can create and manipulate I can do infinitely."

Ethan was next to Erika with two new pieces of meat now, placing them into each of Erika's hands. I noted the doubtful glance the two shared at Condan's words.

Near infinitely, Erika mouthed to Ethan, who turned to leave the congregation before allowing a smile to break on his face.

"I'm just saying," Darbie said. "I'm pretty sure God could create salt and pepper."

The group broke into mild laughter. Even I choked on the bite that was in my mouth a bit as humour shocked me.

197

Condan huffed and crossed his arms. He pushed his legs back, the rock and he both scooted back a few more inches.

When the laughter subsided, it was Ethan who reached out to make peace, presenting him with the next gift of food.

"We're just fucking with you," he said as Condan took the peace offering from his hands. "We do it to each other all the time. It keeps us humble."

Ethan started to walk away.

"I don't need humility," Condan spat towards the man's back. "Only weak men who think they're strong need to be humbled. My strength is beyond comprehension."

Ethan turned on his feet, continuing to walk backwards while pointing at Condan and saying, "And that's exactly what someone in need of humility would say."

Condan clenched his jaw. He removed his eyes from his challenger and stared into the fire. He held his food in his lap like a child trying to ignore the dessert that was laid out in front of them because it wasn't the colour they wanted.

Ethan handed the other piece to Darbie who ripped it in two and began sharing it with Jack.

Condan watched the perfectly cooked piece rip wonderfully and immediately looked down to the bit in his grasp. His jaw relaxed. Enough time passed for Ethan to make it back to Adam, where the two set back to cutting more sections of good meat out.

Noting that the man was distracted, Condan began to eat what was provided to him.

The eldest of us all, acting like the toddler of the family.

"So what happens once you're back with your goddess?" Darbie asked, leaning forward so that he could look at me around Jack. The latter noticed this and leaned back, letting his partner and I focus better on one another.

I licked my fingers clean of the juices left behind and tossed the bone into the flames. I had to hold up a finger as I fished the final bits of food out of my teeth.

"Artemis will debrief me," I started once I had finished. "She has been tracking my findings, but she will want to know my personal thoughts on the potential situation so that she can see it from my perspective instead of just what she's seen through her vision well."

"And what were your findings?" he asked, and followed the question up with a small, polite bite.

I looked to the ground and pondered the question.

Artemis and the oracles hadn't truly seen a clear image. They had only felt darkness and smelt blood in their visions. They could hear the clashing of metal and the shouts like that of the battlefield. But the images were nothing more than mud, mist and smoke flinging their way into the air, and one cracked and frozen welcome sign reading *Stornoway, Scotland.*

Even I could admit that these visions sounded like a force of darkness would bring about a new war, but with such an unclear message, it was hard to truly decide whether there was a near and present threat.

Adam approached Erika next, handing down two raw slabs. She fired up both, handing one back to him and tossing the other across the fire to Jack when she was done. Adam took the one she had given back to him and sat down on the rock next to her. Then Ethan squatted down next to her, leaning his elbow just next to Erika's thigh and handed the last two servings up to her.

"Artemis wanted to make sure there was no reason to worry about an oncoming threat that was somehow connected to your town," I told them honestly. "As far as I can tell, so long as the five of you are there, any threats that may develop will be handled and won't be of any concern for us. Especially not here in the Otherworld."

199

Ethan took his bit from Erika and rose.

"So your findings are that three humans, a pacifist wizard and an old dragon lady are capable of defeating a great evil?" he clarified.

"Yes." I said.

He shrugged and nodded at the same time. "Okay."

"What're you saying?" Jack quipped. "You think we can't?"

Ethan shook his head. "I didn't say that. I just think that we're kind of a questionable team to pit up against like the devil or something."

"She didn't say it was the devil," Adam pointed out.

"She didn't say it wasn't," Ethan argued.

Erika leaned forward and threw a few more logs onto the fire. She put her hand into the centre of the embers and I watched as her skin hardened like a diamond instead of melting off from the heat. She mixed the hot coals around and withdrew her perfectly unaffected arm from the heat.

"I think we could handle a lot more than we think, lads," Erika said, her eyes still looking into the flames.

She was completely unfazed by her own casual abilities. There were very few gods who could enter their unprotected bodies into flames. Even the ones who had dominion over fire were only capable of creating or manipulating it. While I knew a few existed, I had never met a being capable of being completely submerged in it like it was water and not come out melted down to bone.

Condan scoffed. "You're one of two beings whose power is as old as time and you're implying that you would need to rely on this group to help you win against anything?"

Erika flicked her eyes up to Condan.

200

"Let me put it this way," she said, and her voice commanded the silence around us to stand still. "You and I are evenly matched, yes?"

Condan nodded once.

"If you and I fight we won't beat one another. But the difference here is that you're alone. If this were a situation of scales, you on one side and I on the other, then this group on my side is needed to tip the balance. So yes, I rely on this group to make sure the scales are in our favour."

Condan summoned a bubble of water above his hands and ran them along the bottom of it to clean them off. When he was done, he flicked the sphere into the fire. It hissed and fizzed where it collided, threatening to go out - for a moment it did, but then Erika's eyes glowed red and it lit again with more force.

Condan leaned forward, resting his elbows onto his knees. The orange glow on his grey skin reminded me of the visions I had seen of volcanic ash falling from Pompeii.

"So then tell me," Condan said slowly. "What would your favour be? If darkness and evil are on one side of the scales, what do you stand for?"

Erika looked up into the night sky. Her shoulder upright, her body raised, but relaxed. Her forehead creased for a second. Then she blinked. Her eyes moved through the sky like she was reading the stars. When her face relaxed, her attention fell back to the firepit.

"Righteousness, I think I'd say," she said.

Condan laughed bitterly. "So everyone and everything needs to be morally correct and justified in order to be in your favour? Because that is what righteous means."

"No," she said softly. "I think the act of *trying* to be virtuous, of trying to be a good and kind and decent person is righteous. I didn't say perfect righteousness. I didn't say pure. I

201

didn't say innocent. Righteousness means being morally right, well it is morally right to just try and be good, even if you're failing, so long as you're still trying, that's moral."

"Trying and failing is still a failure."

"No, trying and failing is only a failure if you quit and let the failure be the final result."

"That's not-"

"If I try to kill you and fail and quit, never to try again, then sure that's a failure," Ethan argued as he stood up, almost looming over the elf like it was a genuine threat. "But if I come back round after you've been hospitalised and put some cyanide in your IV and kill you that way, then it wasn't a failure, it was just the long way around."

He began moving around the group, heading back towards the fresh filleted mooane in the corner.

"That's still a failure," Condan called.

"No, it's practice so you can have an even better kill the second time round," Ethan called back.

Erika and Adam chuckled to each other in the corner. I looked over at Jack and Darbie who were only looking at each other in silence, shaking their heads at the dubious conversation that was occurring.

"You can't be a failure at something and cover up your own short-comings as you practicing," Condan declared, his voice a few octaves lower and several volumes higher. "You're either good at something or you're not."

Ethan returned with two more handfuls of flesh that he handed to Erika again.

"I would disagree," he pushed. "For example, you were complete shit at talking to any of us like we were worthy of speaking to you. Now you're actually beginning to learn how to socialise like a somewhat functional human being."

"I'm not a human, I'm a-"

"Raging douchebag, yes we know," Ethan finished with a smile. "Would you like seconds my dear sire?"

There was the faintest outline of a smile tugging at Condan's lips, but he didn't let it pass. Instead he rose to his feet, brushing the ash of his pant legs as he did.

"No," he said. "Thank you though. But I think I'll be heading off to rest instead."

"Wow," Erika followed, faux mesmerised. "He even thanked you. They grow up so fast."

Erika handed the meal back up to Ethan, her gaze following it on the way up until they were looking at each other with enjoyable grins on their faces.

I looked between the pair, who's eyes and smiles matched wonderfully. Then over at Adam who had barely listened to the conversation beyond a few of the funnier bits. He had been looking out into the wilderness around us, a journal balanced in his lap. I could see the faint drawings of vegetation and notes scribbled beside them.

Ethan and Erika were more engaged, looking around and making eye contact and conversation with their counterparts. Even Ethan, who rarely spoke and tried to stay at the back of the pack, seemed deeply invested in the family they had built.

Eventually, Ethan's smile fell and he turned to give his attention to the other two members of the group.

Erika looked over at Adam. Noticing his lack of involvement, she slipped off her rock, nestling down into the space between his legs. He perked up then, shutting the book and watching her every move. She struggled to take one of her boots off, and the couple whispered and laughed amongst themselves while the other three talked and Condan settled himself against a tree in a dark corner.

When the shoe was off, Adam watched as she poked around the fire with her toes, stirring up the heat without needed to move. He watched and I could hear him commenting on how her skin changed shades and seemed to turn to glass.

Between points of conversation, Ethan was watching Erika. His smile rose and fell as her's did, even though he wasn't involved in the conversation.

I frowned. One was in love with the excitement, the other in love with the person.

I looked over at Condan in the corner, expecting to see him watching what I was seeing with amusement. In the darkness, it was hard to see him as his dark skin helped him to blend in with the world surrounding us. But even in the dark I couldn't miss his one lively eye flicking between the two lads. There was no amusement held in it though, merely contempt.

I understood then.

It's a square that has four points.

"I have a question for the magick users real quick," Adam announced.

I looked back to the group.

"Fire at will, captain," Darbie okayed him.

I watched Adam lean forward, wrapping his arms around Erika's shoulders.

"When we were visiting Venus, she mentioned that if her and her sister Athena were to work together they would *each* become twice as powerful," he explained. "How is that possible? Even if they could absorb magick like Reika can, wouldn't that leave one depleted."

Erika and Darbie both shook their heads.

"Witches are different," Darbie said. "There are individuals who choose to study and practice magick who call themselves witches and warlocks, but aren't genuinely *witches* or

204

warlocks. I'm technically one of those individuals who identifies as one because we have the same abilities, but I am not actually a true warlock because I wasn't born one."

"I don't mean to be a dick, but get to the point, Darbs," Ethan said softly, the smallest hint of worry in the back of his tone.

"Witches and warlocks are two subcategories for a race of people called the Indrarakta," Darbie said.

"The name is derived from san skrit, indra from indrajala meaning magic, and rakta which means red in reference to human tissue," Erika added.

"Which is blood," Darbie added.

Ethan sighed. "Still not getting why we need a history lesson."

"The Indrarakta's name is sanskrit," Condan called from the darkness. "Sanskrit is the origins for the language used in hinduism. The most powerful god, referred to as the king of all god-deities, is named Indra."

"There are thirty-three hindu gods that are dominantly mentioned, but none were ever actual *gods*," Erika explained.

"The more Indrarakta there are together, bound in what folklore now calls a coven, the more powerful each one becomes," Darbie said. "So long as they share blood, they can connect with each other on a legitimate spiritual level, and their powers multiply."

Erika chuckled. "Weird example, but think of it like how a baby is made. Two half cells come together and then suddenly millions of billions of cells begin to replicate themselves until a whole new human exists. Witches and warlocks with the same genes as the Indrarakta can do that, but with magick."

"So if Venus and Athena were to ever decide to work together they would multiply their potential magick energy without even needing to do anything?" Jack asked this time.

"Exactly," Darbie said.

Ethan pointed at me. "But Reika is half-human, half-greek god, she's not sanskrit and yet Venus made it seem like Reika should know about this and be able to do it too."

"Just because her magick comes from a greek goddess doesn't mean that she's not from a line of Indrarakta," Darbie remarked. "Indrarakta people existed before Greece was ever civilised and long before the Greek gods were born. Reika's mum could have been born of a god and an Indrarakta."

"So we find another one like Reika and put them together and they can super multiply magick?" Adam asked, now thoughtlessly stroking Erika's hair.

"Mhm," Erika mumbled, her eyes closed while she enjoyed the physical touch from her partner.

"That would require Reika deciding to stick with us instead of going back to the shadow realm," Ethan not-so-casually recommended.

I sighed. "I have a debt that needs to be paid. Artemis has protected me the last seventy years, I owe her my loyalty."

"We save the world on a yearly basis," Adam said. "If you join us you could argue you're paying her back by protecting her and everyone else."

I let out a short, sharp giggle, not expecting the sincerity of their offer.

"Thank you, but I'm comfortable being a priestess for now," I set my stance in stone.

"Well if you change your mind," Darbie leaned over to me and nudged my shoulder. "You know where to find us."

"I'm sure one day I'll come looking for you all," I promised. "Until then, I'll make sure to stay on top of my archery training. Since it look like your team already has it's designated warlock."

Darbie stood up, stretching.

"Ha! Very funny," he said, stifling a yawn. "Alright team, Jack and the resident warlock are turning in."

Erika leaned back, letting her head fall into Adam's lap so that she could look at him.

"What do you say?" she asked. "You want to turn in too?"

Adam nodded silently and kissed her forehead. I could see Ethan wince out of the corner of my eye. But he had clearly gotten good at hiding it over the years, because he moved right into finishing the last bite of his seconds, a motion so smooth that I almost thought I hadn't seen it.

"Who's on first watch?" Erika asked.

Ethan raised his hand, "I can take it."

I stood up.

"No," I rejected him. "I still have radharc mushrooms in my system. I'll be too sensitive to movement and sound to sleep for the next hour or more, so we might as well make it me."

Ethan looked down at Erika who shrugged, then over at Darbie.

"I trust her," Darbie said. "She fed us and hasn't killed us yet, both of those are two pretty important things."

Ethan tilted his head to the side in an accepting dip.

"Alright then," he said to me. "You can get first watch. We normally do hour rotations, but if you need to go for a bit longer to get the magick out of your system, I won't be mad getting a few extra minutes."

I gave him a smile. He was a strange character. Sometimes he was aggressive and rude. Other times he was funny and warm. I had never met anyone like that, and I was curious to know why he was.

"You can count on me," I said. "If literally anything is out there, I'll feel it half a kilometre away."

"Ehh, they've probably worn off a bit," Adam said as he followed behind Erika towards an unclaimed tarp. "Your range is probably closer to the length of a football pitch by now."

I cocked my head to the side. "What's a football pitch?"

"Oh Jesus, Lord, have mercy," Ethan mumbled. "We should have shown you what the world is like before sending you back to isolation, man."

I laughed. "Well if I ever receive a mission again, and I'm sent to earth, I'll make sure to stop by and you can tell me about the sexism and the football pitch."

"Sexism?" Jack asked from where he stood by Darbie who was already laying down in his sleeping bag.

Darbie reached up and pulled on the lads shirt. "Don't ask, I'm sure there's lots of things we're missing."

"But I need answers," he whined as he was dragged down to the ground.

"No," Darbie groaned. "You need sleep. We tapped out first so we got to pull watch next after Ethan. Shush up and maximise total sleep input."

Ethan cries in his sleep. His breathing picks up and he clenches and unclenches his fists while wet streams roll out of the corners of his eyes. I watched as one rolled over the tip of his nose before departing from his skin and splashing down onto his forearm, leaving small ricocheted droplets stained into the black fabric.

At first I had rushed over after hearing his breathing start to sound strained, only to find his cheeks wet and his face crumpled up like he was in pain. I had crouched down, planning on waking him up, but my curiosity got the better of me and instead I chose to stay there quietly and wait. I wanted to see if he would say anything that would give away the thoughts inside his head.

But he never uttered a word.

Eventually, my curiosity got the better of me. I still had the book I stole from venus tucked away in my boot, and I would bet that Athena Lupin was the kind of witch who would have created a spell that could reveal someone's inner thoughts.

I tugged the book out and quietly flipped through the aged, yellow pages. In the beginning, there were several spells in it regarding reanimating the dead for long enough to ask them questions or say goodbye. A few on how to locate dead people who were lost to time, including how to track souls. Then there were a few on transmutation so that one could temporarily travel to the land of the dead.

Lots of spells about the dead.

The second section was focused on Athena's innate ability: foresight. She wrote a detailed essay on how all beings are capable of seeing the future as well as others' pasts through our dreams, just that many aren't capable of realising what the meanings behind the images are.

The immediate following dozen or so pages were charts and logs of symbols she had seen in dreams and visions and what each of them meant.

After that, I found what I was looking for. A spell she called *Dream Walker* provided step by step instructions on how to enter into someone else's thoughts while they slept and see what they could see.

Noting that I needed nothing other than direct contact with magick ground and for my target to be asleep in front of me, I began to recite the incantation in the book.

"You can stop chanting," Ethan groaned as he rolled from his side, onto his back.

I looked over the lip of the book to see him laying with his head resting on his forearm, showing off how perfectly sculpted his biceps were even under the cover of his long-sleeve.

"The runes on the tarp won't let you cast spells on us either," he said. "Although, they didn't glow red so I'm assuming you bare me no ill will."

I shut the book and rested it in my lap.

"Sorry," I spoke. "You cry in your sleep and I wanted to know why. I thought it would be easier to access your dream and see what you saw rather than ask you about it."

He nodded slowly, then pursed his lips together and dragged his other arm up so that he could cradle the back of his head in both hands while staring up into the night sky. He didn't say anything, just looked off into the distance like there was something fascinating about the darkness around us.

I sighed, giving up hope and admitting that I would never know what consumed Ethan Lios's innermost thoughts.

"Well," I started. "It's your turn to pull night watch, so I guess I'll go-"

"I had an older brother," he said. "He died when I was seven. His name was Euan. My dad committed suicide when I was twelve because Euan being dead was more important than his wife and youngest son being alive. Then my mum decided one son wasn't enough to live for and crawled so deep into the bottle that she lost all sense of time or life. I've been rejected by everyone I love, left to be constantly surrounded by people who make me feel alone. And the one person who I feel sees me and survives in this lonely darkness with me has also rejected me to be with someone that I can't even hate because I love them."

I laughed awkwardly. "Well, looks like I didn't need that dream spell."

"No," he commented. "You did not need the dream spell."

"If it makes you feel better, I also only exist in a world of loneliness."

I let my head fall so that I could watch my fingernails dig at the worn leather of the spell book.

"I know," he sat up and reached out to take my hands into his. "It's why I trust you enough to tell you all this. I'm sorry you're alone."

"I'm sorry you've lost so many people," I replied.

I met his eyes and found them to be like diamonds.

"Your eyes look like Erika's skin when it's submerged in fire," I commented.

He furrowed his brows and cocked his head to the side.

"What does that even mean?" he asked.

"When she put her hands into the fire earlier, her skin turned into a diamond-like material. It reflected the light of the hotter blue flames at the centre of the fire, making her skin look like a light blue sapphire, sort of how your eyes look."

Ethan smiled. It was small, just enough to seem innocent and sincere. His skin seemed soft then too. The hardlines around his eyes and above his brows were gone. The dark circles faded away too, and a small bit of pink spread over his wonderfully carved sheek bones.

He rolled his eyes playfully.

"Go to sleep Reika," he whispered to me. "It's going to be a long hike tomorrow so you need some rest. I got watch from here."

12

Ethan

Dear diary, it's our first night in the forest and I get to watch Erika curl up and sleep with Adam. It's like an enchanted fairy tale. I'm so happy for my best friend ... And yet, I'm imagining what it would be like if he had never stumbled upon her that day in the forest.

I sighed and dropped my head against the trunk of the tree against my back. The fire was crackling softly, the wisp bugs were flashing blue in the darkness of the forest. Everyone and everything was either asleep or at peace.

Everyone except me.

Normally, it was easy to ignore the churning of my own thoughts. I could compartmentalise my thoughts and feelings together into a box so tight that it was like I could take them physically out of my body and light them on fire. But then Condan had to go and debate the potential success of a human having a relationship with Erika during our wander into the woods. All while the topic of his conversation was boldly leading the front like a lantern shining bright in front of a carriage on a dark night and it made it hard not to think about the what-ifs and the hows.

Dear diary, how does it feel to be loved by her?

I closed my eyes tightly, trying to blink out the thoughts that liked to linger just behind them. Then I reached into my coat pocket and dragged out the worn brown leather sketchbook. Its pages had rubbed against the inside of my coat pocket and my skin, helping to spread around the graphite and charcoal that polluted its paper. The edges had turned a sad grey instead of the gentle, creamy white they used to be.

I thumbed through the soft paper to the next clean page. Then I pulled out my pencil, about half the length it should have been from being so heavily sharpened.

I looked up and to my right, smiling as I observed the closest cluster of the wisp-bugs. Just like fireflies back home, they liked to flash and dance in the air, signalling to one another that they were there.

Their wings made them look like smokey jellyfish, and any time they flapped themselves up with their mushroom-like top, they lit up in their wonderful, fiery blue light. Their bodies, which dangled from the dome wings, were long and wet looking like a salamander's without a tail, but hard and see-through like a golden tortoise beetle.

I started to sketch the insect to the best of my abilities. I would never classify myself as a professional, but I was a fairly proficient artist and I would like to argue that any artist would find it difficult to draw a bug that you can only see for two seconds at a time and is constantly changing positions.

It was probably the fifth time I whispered "fuck" under my breath and erased one of my lines aggressively that woke Condan up. Or maybe it was the third and he had sat there watching me look around and scribble like a psychopath, I don't know for sure.

"Of course you're an artist," The Cunt's irritatingly and melodically deep voice practically hummed in my ear and I

214

jumped so far out of my skin that he could have caught my skeleton had he wanted to.

"Jeezus, fuck, man," I hissed as quietly as I could.

I looked around at our band of heathens. Erika stirred, her breath growing fast enough to let me know she was just on the cusp of being awake, but still not quite there.

I turned to my left to glare at the white haired asshole who was leaning over a rock, staring at me.

God, his dead eye creeps me out, I thought to myself. *It always looks like the damn thing is churning like witch's brew in his head.*

"Can I help you?" I asked.

He offered me a smile, and even though it looked like he was trying to be genuine, the perfect pearly white teeth against his ashy skin along with his one golden eye was nothing short of unsettling at best.

"What did you mean earlier when you said you had seen Death and were not afraid of him?" He practically purred the question out like a cat would have.

I sighed and shut my art book, setting my pencil and the pad onto my leg. This man didn't engage much with anyone, but for some fucking reason he was really obsessed with me and death, if I didn't give him my full attention, he'd probably freeze me to death.

"I've lost a lot of people," I said. "Killed a few more. I'm familiar with the idea of death."

"So you have never actually seen Death?" he asked.

I nodded slowly. "I just said I've killed people, so yeah, I've seen death."

He shook his head. "No. I don't mean death as in the act of losing life. I mean Death, the god, the being. The deity who tried to rival God and failed."

215

"As in the grim reaper?"

"If you wish to call him that, yes."

I let out a laugh of disbelief.

"Yeah, no," I told him. "Maybe in my dreams, I might have danced with him a few times. Fucked around and invited him over to my house for a game of fucking strip poker, but I don't think the bastard has ever shown."

"If you met him-" Condan began, but stopped.

I looked closely at his face. His jaw was tight, his eyes were sunken in like he was a heroin addict trying to get sober by going cold turkey.

He was looking at me with such intent, I realised I was his heroine at the moment. The only thing between him consuming me or letting me live was in self control.

"Can I give you a piece of advice?" I offered.

When he was silent, I took that as my opportunity to proceed. "I've never seen him, but Death has a particular smell and sound to him. When you're in his presence you can't really feel him at first, then suddenly it's like all your senses except sight go off like a fire alarm. I've seen people react to it just like I do. They can feel when Death is going to do something. The people who sense him like that are the ones who respect Death just as much as they respect Life. Personally, mate, I don't think you give a damn about anything other than yourself. So if you want to know what it's like to know Death personally, you better start pulling your head out of your arse."

Condan chuckled and settled down into his seated position, his shoulders falling as if he had just sat down into a comfortable sofa.

"Did you really *just* want to ask me about Death?" I snapped. "You scared the shit out of me for the dead?"

"No," he said. "I'm simply looking for a friend here. Reika will be returned soon and then we'll be an even numbered band, but everyone will have someone but you and I."

My eyebrows shot up and I nodded my head slowly.

"Yeah, buddy, I don't know how exactly to explain this to you, because clearly you're a little unhinged," I started, throwing caution to the wind. "But our pissing contest about God earlier was sort of me telling you I don't like you in more words. I'm not really interested in being friends and definitely not interested in cuddling with you by the fire like they do," I snarked, motioning out to my set of friends who were all cosy and dozing with their respected partners.

Condan chuckled. He lifted his body off the rock and strided towards me as if he felt no effect of gravity. It was so graceful, I was reminded that he was a prince at one point.

A prince of a people who brutally murdered entire races for power and wealth.

He crossed his legs and sunk down to the ground in front of me, tucking his heels underneath him like we were going to play duck-duck-goose. He rested his forearms on his knees and laced his fingers, paying his closest attention to me.

"I'm not romantically interested in you," he said. "You're not powerful enough to pique my interest."

I furrowed my eyebrows and looked down into the embers of the fire. I thought I had heard about every type of sexuality there was, but being sexually attracted to power was new.

I looked back to Condan and offered him a forced smile. "Thanks… question mark? Glad to know you don't follow behind me to stare at my ass. Not sure if I should be offended by the reasoning or not yet."

He waved his hand in the air. "Don't be mistaken, had you and I been born around the same time, and you were an elf or a demon - or even a fairy, to be truthful - who knew how to fight as you do now, I would have taken an interest in you. But since being gifted my powers, I have surpassed you in all regards. Even without the powers though, you may be impressive for a human but I've never found the whole dying thing particularly appealing."

"Mmm." I nodded facetiously. "I get that. I've never found the whole being a raging douchebag thing particularly appealing. Or dudes, actually, for that matter."

"Just masculine women who could kill you by thinking it?" he asked, his eyes as narrow as his question was.

There was nothing to miss in his tone or in his words. He might as well have said her name.

I stole a quick glance over to Erika and Adam. Her head was on his chest, his arms wrapped tight around her body, pulling her close like she was a weighted blanket. With how hot her body temperature was always running, she probably was a weighted blanket to him.

I rolled my eyes back to Condan. I was gritting my teeth to keep from saying something that would have earned me a painful case of frostbite.

"Admittedly," he began again and I thought I suddenly tasted tooth dust on my tongue. "Between the two of you, I would kill him, but only maim you. I like you much better."

"Thanks bud," I scoffed. "I love this little bonding session we've had about your sexual orientation and overall male preferences, but if you'd like to scooch back over to a random tree and go to sleep now, I'd appreciate it."

He dropped his hand down, digging his palms into the soft teal grass. His golden eyes roamed up my body, before he firmly pushed himself off the ground and draped his body closer to me.

218

In doing so, our shoulders became flush together, our backs against the tree, and I was suddenly painfully aware of how cold he was.

Having his arm against me was worse than sticking your tongue to a frozen pole. It almost burned how cold his touch was.

I flinched, but he just shifted closer until his leg was practically right on top of mine, our hips firmly shoved together.

"Fuck off!" I hissed and launched to my feet, my sketchbook and pencil flying off into the abyss somewhere.

I looked off to my right to see if I could spot where they went in the light of the fire and the glowing bugs. But Condan snatched at my leg, gripping me where my boot met my bloused pant. His middle finger slipped between the canvas of my shoe and the thick fabric of my combat trousers. The frigid touch of his grasp consumed me through the thinner fabric of my socks. The chill spread down to my toes and up to the top of my thigh, freezing me in place with pain until I lost all feeling of my leg.

I looked down to identify exactly where the touch was connecting in order to build my plan of attack, but spots were forming in my eyes until all I could see was a void where his hand and my leg were.

I pinched my eyes shut and shook my head, trying to get my vision to focus despite the pain, but I couldn't even get myself to breath, let alone see.

I forced my eyes open. The void had spread and clouded all of my vision.

I blinked once.

Then twice. Clearing my sight enough to see the blurriest smudge of Erika rising just beyond the campfire, like a phoenix rising.

I blinked again, trying to see her clearly, but this time I was too numb to open my eyes.

I could only feel myself enough to move, just enough to fall and feel my body slam down onto the hard forest floor.

The chill immediately stopped after that.

For what felt like hours there was nothing. Nothing but the ground beneath me. The world around me was black and weightless.

Warmth in the centre of my chest was the first feeling I had. Then another touch of heat on the side of my face, before it slid to the back of my head. It spread from both of those place, reaching back into my legs and the tips of my toes, and up to the back of my mind.

When my face felt warm again, I opened my eyes to find I was both above and below the world. I fisted the soft grass, making sure I wasn't dreaming. I felt the soft mounds of the Otherworld's moss, the dirt dug itself under my nail beds. It was real. I brought my hands up to touch the two patches of earth over me. She was warm, and soft; when I blinked the last bit of cold out of my vision I realised that her skin was actually golden like healthy wheat, her hair was brown like the richest soil, and her eyes were the colour of the softest forest floor.

"E?" I grunted.

Erika sighed and leaned down. Her hair draped around us like a curtain hiding us in the warmth between our chests. She dropped her forehead against mine, sending vibrations of energy into my mind, eyes and shoulders.

Then, she straightened her back up, sitting on her haunches so that I could push myself off the ground and onto my ass.

Adam was standing right behind Erika, watching intently and taking in the entirety of the spectacle. I could smell Darbie's strong cologne somewhere behind me, paired with the violent shuffling of someone's bag, but I didn't look back. My eyes were fixed on a target and I wasn't about to move them.

"Sorry," Condan said. "I forget sometimes how intense my touch can be for mortals."

I glared at him, my anger suddenly hotter than Erika's touch. I jumped at him, lunging up as quickly as my stiff body would allow, only to fall forward right into Erika's lap as my left leg remained stiff in each joint.

She gripped me across my chest, keeping my face from hitting the ground, while her other hand latched onto the back of my bad knee. More warmth bursted from underneath her touch.

She hauled me up and into her. I realised for the first time how light I I must have felt to the arms of a dragon. With Adam, she always acted like a normal girl her size, lifting things that weighed no more than herself. Yet here she was, dragging me around like I didn't weigh anything.

"Relax," she whispered down into my shoulder as she helped me to turn around onto my back once again. "We're gonna chop it up to an accident for now. Just cool off and save your strength."

"Trust me, I'm more than fucking *cool*," I snapped. "That's half the fucking problem. Mr.- fucking - White Christmas over there just turned me into a icicle."

Erika shoved her shoulder into mine and then rolled forward until she was scooping me up from my back and side and lifting us both to our feet.

"It was truly an accident," Condan rattled off sweetly while Adam came around to stabilise me.

"Shut up Mr. Snow," Erika snapped over her shoulder then locked eyes with me.

I flashed her a quick frustrated look, before turning and glancing at Darbie, who was pulling out a vile from his bag. It was filled with a thick brownish-green liquid that looked vaguely like the mucus one would cough up when they had pneumonia.

221

The lad proudly stuck it into the air shouting, "I found it!"

He dropped his bag and then stepped over it, making strides towards me. I leaned back into Erika's and Adam's arms, holding up my hands so as to push Darbie away if he got to close with that shit.

"Ah hell no," I said. "You are not getting me to swallow that ogre snot, or whatever it is. No. Not in a million damn years."

Darbie rolled his eyes at me.

"Oh quit being dumb," he tsked. "Ogre Snot would be useless, this is leftover amniotic fluid from a phoenix egg mixed with some forest nymph breast milk for flavour. It'll warm you up in seconds."

"I think he's good, mate." Adam outstretched his hand with me, waving him off.

Erika slapped both our hands away.

"It has excellent healing properties," she snapped. "He should take it."

I shook my head violently and pulled away from her. "I ain't taking shit."

"Say one more curse word, and I'm gonna slap you," she warned. "You're capable of more impressive language."

"You literally use 'fuck' in just about every other sentence," Jack called across the camp fire.

I stole a glance at him for the first time since coming back. He stood next to Reika, who was still deep within a sleeping bag, hair messy, and half asleep. She rubbed her eye and stumbled upwards out of the bag, which clung to her legs, nearly tripping her as she tried to shuffle it down.

"I can literally feel the cold still in your bones, Ethan." Erika said, dragging me closer to Darbie.

I looked down at her and shook my head. "Really, I'm fine. Your fire hands made me feel fine."

222

"Shut up, all of you," Reika groaned as she knelt down next to my leg.

Adam and Erika, who were still holding me upright, looked down at her, their grip twitching against my skin, waiting for a sign that they needed to yank me to safety.

Reika unrolled the tight lip of my trousers before pushing it up higher so that she could pull down my socks. Beneath the fabric, she was provided a perfect view of snow-white cold burns in the shape of fingertips wrapped around my ankle. She hesitantly placed her hand around the area, lining up her long, dainty fingers with the markings left on my skin.

Immediately, the bed of her nails glowed purple at the touch. Her eyes glowed as well. I could feel the leftover cold magick draining out of me. I could *see* the dead skin slowly growing from dead white to flush again.

Reika let go and rose up in front of me. She stifled a yawn while we all stared at her.

She offered us all a casual wave while she sleepily shuffled back off to her make-shift bed.

"Did you just suck Condan's magick out of his skin?" Jack asked as she passed him by.

"Mhm," she sounded as she stepped back into her sleeping bag.

She thumped down to her knees and then let her body plop over so that she was laying back down, her back turned to us.

"Goodnight!" Darbie called to her.

She stuck her hand into the air again and waved it once more, this time in a much less wakeful.

"Not to be inconsiderate towards your health and safety, my guy," Jack started. "But I'm gonna follow her example now that you're okay."

"Jack," Darbie hissed. "He just got frozen, we should just start our turn on watch so that he can rest."

"No, that's okay, Darbie," I said. "I'm fine. I can finish up the last half of my shift."

Erika gripped me by my jacket collar. She yanked me out of Adam's grip, spinning me around so that my back was to the centre of our camp. I latched onto her wrists so as to stabilise myself while she tossed me around. She hoisted me up, took two steps back, before plunking me down onto my back inside my sleeping bag. She stepped off to the side, and I started to rise, ready to argue, but she had already gripped the top flap of my bag and was flicking it down on top of me.

The silky fabric slapped me in the face, blocking my vision. Then a firm hand wacked against my forehead and shoved me back down to the ground.

"Sleep," Erika's voice commanded somewhere outside the darkness of my sleeping cave. "I'll take the rest of the night."

I flung the fabric off of me.

"Hell no," I snapped.

"Absolutely not," Adam said at the same time.

"You need sleep too," Darbie added to our unison.

Jack turned around, and crawled back into his bedroll. "Fine by me."

I rolled my eyes. "E, we have at least a fifteen hour day of just hiking ahead of us tomorrow. If you take the whole of the night watch you'll be up for close to twenty hours running off only an hour and a half of sleep at best."

"I've done worse," she said.

I sat up.

Reaching out, I grasped the hem of her shirt. It loosely hung around her hips, giving me enough fabric to fist if I had wanted. All I would have needed to do was bunch it up, and then

224

yank her down and she would be safely bundled up in the sleepsack, resting instead of bearing the weight of the whole world.

She had a nasty habit of sacrificing herself for the good of others. And just once I wanted to chip myself away to give to her.

I don't think anyone had ever broken off any bit of themselves to fill in the cracks of her soul she had given away.

But I would give her all of me if she just asked.

"I believe the point is, you don't have to do so now," Condan said, politely.

I watched Erika eye the dragon up and down. She was still standing over me. Where her body was, the air around rose in temperature. I felt like I had been moved closer to the still glowing fire pit, but I wasn't anywhere near it. My knuckles, which were still wrapped around her shirt, suddenly stung as the hair was singed off.

"Alright, alright, alright," Adam rattled off. "Accidents happened tonight. We're all uncomfortable because we're on a low budget camping trip. A lot of us are strangers so this is extra awkward."

He sighed, pitched the bridge of his nose for a second, then dropped his hands out in front of him.

"Let's just call it for tonight," he said. "If Erika wants to pul night guard tonight, we all know none of us can force her to do otherwise. And she's too stubborn to convince her, so we can cross that off. Ethan's fine and Condan already apologised so we can get rid of that one too. We still have four hours left to get some rest and then we're in for a long haul tomorrow, so we all can agree that getting rest now is important for the rest of us. Erika is going to be tired tomorrow so if we all sleep tonight then we will pick up the slack for her during the hike tomorrow, okay?"

225

I had forgotten that Adam had moments like these. He would suddenly come out of his day-dreaming shell and lead the pack like he was the strongest of all of us. And maybe he was. He was always so positive and hopeful that he could stand up in front of the rest of us pessimists and lead us down a path that didn't seem so freaking grey.

When he lost Erika three years ago, darkness enveloped him, but he fought it by diving headfirst into hope. Even when all of us had given up, he kept looking.

He was the better man.

"I don't agree with it," Darbie said. "But you're at least right that we can't make Eri do anything once she's decided on it." He looked Erika over with amused eyes. "And she seems pretty set to me."

Erika offered him a dramatic bow. "Thank you, Darbie. I appreciate your support."

He started walking forward, moving past her and I so that he could get back to Jack and his resting post.

"I don't really have much of a choice with you," he said and stopped when he was just a half step behind her. "I brought you home from a burning forest one day and then you spent the rest of our lives bossing me around. Which is why you were the last stray I brought home, because I learned my lesson."

"No you didn't," Jack rolled over to scold him. "You literally dragged three strangers home with you from the woods. It's why we're all here. Not to mention adopting a couple dozen dragons."

Darbie shook his head at his partner as he crawled into bed with him. "You three were different. Life or death situations don't count."

"Yes they do," Jack whispered, but rolled over to let his elf boyfriend spoon him.

I slapped Erika's thigh, gaining her attention. She looked down at me and raised a brow.

"I think you should at least wake me up for the last hour so you can get a nap in," I recommended.

She scowled at me for a second. I tried to give her my best concerned look, hoping that pathos would be a good mode of persuasion to use on her. When her eyes softened, I had to keep myself from smirking in triumph.

"I'll think about it," she said softly.

Then she looked up and pointed at both Condan and Adam.

"You two need to go to sleep," she commanded. "I don't want any more weird shit tonight, so I am banishing everyone to the sleep realm."

"Yes ma'am," Adam said and passed her by with a kiss on her cheek. "Wake me up if you need anything. If not, I'll wake up for the last hour to ride it out with you."

She shook her head. "You don't have to do that. Humans need more sleep than dragons do. I have a whole cash of magick I can use as energy, you don't."

He then leaned down to kiss her shoulder.

"I'm on an adventure with you," he said. "I'll have plenty of energy. And if not, then when this is over I'll take a nice, long nap."

She laughed. "You're naps are never naps, you always end up sleeping for eternity."

"I grow tired of the affectionate displays," Condan grumbled. "I'll retire now so I don't have to witness them any longer."

"Me too," I announced.

When Adam and Erika both made eye contact with me, I made sure to make a point of dramatically flinging the flap of my

227

bag over my head. The I flung my body down so that I could make a satisfying thud with the ground.

"You're so dramatic," Adam laughed and a foot nudged me in the butt.

I threw the flap back again to glare at him. I pulled a knife out and held it so it would just poke out of my bag.

"I'll cut off your toes, loverboy," I jokingly warned. "Don't make me get out of this bag."

"You two are impossible," Erika huffed.

She began pulling at Adam's shirt, gently pushing him towards his tarp. There was no hoisting into the air, no throwing him onto the ground so that he would do as he was told. So gentle and reserved.

I pulled the sack back over my head. Then I couldn't see anything.

13

Adam

We were up before the first sun was up, and the sun gods remained silent the entire time we packed up our camp. Erika had dried out the leftover mooane so that we would have plenty of jerky for the rest of the trip. She and Darbie were gathering the cinched sleeping rolls as well and storing it into Darbie's magickal storage realm.

"Are you sure you can handle all this extra stuff draining your magick?" Ethan whispered to the wizard when we brought him the last of the sleepwear.

Darbie nodded. "It's not much more. Besides, if we store it, we'll all be lighter and can move quicker."

"The quicker we get through the forest, the less time spent out in the open where we're at risks for attacks," Erika said back, our tones still remaining hushed. Her eyes flicked over to Condan, who was once again meditating, over by his pond. "Yesterday we were only out here for a few hours, today it's going to be a whole day. If nothing manages to happen then..."

She trailed off while her eyes wandered down in the direction we would be heading.

"Then, what?" I asked, reaching out to hold her hand.

She shook her head. "Forget it. Something is going to happen. Something always happens in this forest."

Ethan cleared his throat. "Anyone gonna explain the creepy statement E just made?"

"A lot of druids were slaughtered here thousands of years ago," Darbie said. "The dark elves and a few other groups wanted what the druids had and pushed them out of this area. It's what caused them to flee to earth. There's a lot of blood in this ground, and a lot of creatures who still roam it and consider outsiders a threat."

"Oh great," Ethan hummed. "Never knew that before. Probably wouldn't have come if I knew."

"Let's just hurry up and get moving," Erika grumbled. She stepped to the side to yell at Condan, "Hey, *Pantene*, you're in the front with me today."

Ethan turned to me and mouthed, "Pantene?"

I shrugged.

"Like the hair stuff?" he continued to mouth.

"I think so," I silently replied.

"Pantene?" Condan asked, closer behind me now.

I turned to look at him. I hadn't noticed he had risen or walked closer to us during my short exchange with Ethan.

"It's a conditioner," Erika said.

"Conditioner?" he asked.

Erika glanced at us, then back at him. "You know, like the stuff you put in your hair when you're washing it to make it soft?"

"I do not put anything my hair," he gasped as if we had insulted him. "The length and purity of a dark elf's hair is sacred. I would never cut it nor would I put anything in it."

230

"O-kay." Erika's eyebrows rose and she blinked the disbelief from her eyes. "Well, you and I are going to take the lead today. Ethan and Darbie are going to bring up the back while Jack and Ethan stick around in the middle."

Condan smiled in approval. "Strongest in the front to clear the way, second in command following in the back to maintain control and protection. And the weakest in the centre as a last resort line. A rather classic formation."

"No," Ethan voiced. "It's because I don't like you, so we want to keep you as far away from me as possible, Darbie want's to collect more plants and so he will be moving slower than the rest of the group, and Adam and Jack want to ask Reika questions before we return her for good."

Condan looked at Ethan with a scowl. "I'm beginning to think I would do more than maim you."

"Excuse me?" Erika snapped to attention and looked between my friend and the dragon.

"Nothing, E," Ethan said, his eyes still locked on Condan's. "Just an inside joke."

"Well save the inside jokes for home," she replied. "Let's move out!"

Reika and Jack finished bottling water for the group and jogged over. Jack tossed two extra jugs to Erika, who handed them off to Darbie. The plastic containers spun into teal smoke as soon as they were in his hands, before they evaporated into nothingness, disappearing to somewhere beyond the Otherworld. Two more jugs were split between Ethan and Erika. The rest of us were handed single litre bottles.

"Why do we need so much water?' Condan asked as he took the bottle with revolt.

"In case we can't find water again," I answered.

Condan laughed through his nose. "You are aware I can create water from nothing, right?"

"Well then, it's in case something happens to you," Ethan smirked.

He fished a roll of rope out from the large pocket on his leg. He unwrapped it so that it was only folded in half and dangled from his chest to his knees. Then he fed the curved side through the handle of the jug. When it was through, he threw it over his back, gripping the two ends of the folded rope so that the jug would hang on his back and ends would cross in front of him.

I tried to keep up as I watched him spin the ends around each other until a secure and semi-complex knot was in place right over his heart.

"When did you become good with knots?" Jack asked, his voice still groggy and his tone still permanently annoyed.

"It's a halter hitch," he said.

"What's a halter hitch?" I asked.

"A quick release knot normally used to tie up horses," Erika quickly interjected. "Speaking of quick release, let's quickly release ourselves onto the rest of our journey."

"That's cool," I said to Ethan, not paying Erika much mind. "How quick of a release?"

Ethan grinned and reached out to grab the rope. He tugged lightly just the one time and the noose came falling apart. The jug that was slung to his back fell to the ground with a satisfying thud.

I bent down to pick it up for him.

"That's freaking cool," I said in awe.

Ethan chuckled as he took the water back and started redoing the knot while we walked.

"I'll make sure to teach you when we get home," he said, his mouth still spread into a peaceful smile.

232

"I'll hold you to that," I enforced as we walked past the rest of our group. "Hey, did you ever take that one faery chick into the city to watch the football game?"

"No," he laughed. "She wasn't interested in the type of balls you kick, apparently."

"Just right back home with her then?" I slapped him on the chest.

He winced into a smile. "Yeah, something like that."

Erika

I watched Ethan and Adam bond for the majority of our walk. Ethan was meant to stay at the back of the group and keep an eye out for threats with Darbie, but Adam had a tendency of distracting even the most hardened of heroes.

Now Ethan and Adam whispered in hushed tones in the centre of our pack while Reika and the two lovebirds animatedly discussed magick in the back.

It wasn't according to plan, but it was alright. There weren't many times in life where quests would provide you with moments of happiness. I wasn't about to let this opportunity pass us.

"What is it that motivates you?" Condan asked me.

It was the first words we had spoken to one another in over two hours. The first hour of the venture involved him speaking about his glory as a prince and ended with me gently reminding him that I thought his people were murders and it was because of that that they went extinct before mine did.

I stared head on.

Our path should have been riddled with ups and downs as we hiked over annoying mounds of grassy ground and tree roots. Instead, Condan was flattening out the earth as we approached it, helping us progress quicker.

Redharc mushrooms glowed along our path, next to bright purple cucurbits with big, broad, wavy leaves that followed the light of the sun so aggressively that they would immediately drop when we passed by and casted our shadows over them.

"Pick that purple cucurbit," I instructed him and pointed to the large lilac, squash-looking fruit sitting a few paces ahead of us.

"No," Condan said. "Use your magick and bring it to us."

"No," I snapped back.

"Then I guess we shall not have it."

"Fine." I rolled my eyes

I adjusted my pack on my shoulders. It was empty other than the jug that was sloshing around in it. The movement of the water caused the bottle to shift, tugging the strings of my bag back and forth.

We took a few steps forward and I needed to adjust my pack again, the straps digging into my shoulders.

Two more and I was reaching up again.

Condan let out a loud groan after the third time.

"Fine," he snapped, and as we approached the cucurbit he reached down and yanked it off its baby blue vine.

He thrusted the fruit over to me without looking at me.

"Why thank you," I said.

I gripped either side of the fruit harshly until it split open, revealing a vibrant purple centre.

"This is a real cucurbit," I said. "It's not a poisonous one. We should stop here and collect a few from the connecting vines."

"Why?" Condan asked.

I slid my pack off of one arm so that I could put the two halves of the plant into my bag.

"Cucurbits are one of the only foods that replace magick after it's been depleted," I informed him. "Darbie could eat one of these right now and it will have made up for about a quarter of the magick drain we've put on him."

"You and I have no need for that," Condan called after me as I left him to walk back to the plant's bush.

I crouched down besides the collection of large leaves and began separating them to find more fruits. The leaves crinkled like paper as I pushed them aside. I reached down to grasp another smooth crop. I yanked it from its vine and put it into my bag with the other halved plant.

"This is unnecessary," Condan grumbled. "I'm going to carry on while you forage."

"Alright," I called over my shoulder. "Have fun walking alone."

I looked back from where we came. The group had fallen back in order for Adam to get a closer look at something on one of the trees. Ethan was standing watch over Darbie, who was crouched down on the side of our path gathering plants. They had fallen back so far that even though I could see Ethan laughing as something Darbie said, I couldn't hear it.

The redharc mushrooms at my feet began to hum. I looked down to see the pink rings around their edges glowing so fiercely that the light was almost shaking. I leaned over to poke the soft coral tops. They bounced against my finger tip and glowed even more.

235

I furrowed my brows. "Why are you glowing for me little buddies?" I whispered to them.

I looked around me. To my left, Condan was silently continuing on our path, flattening the ground as he went. I peered over my shoulder, but there was nothing but silent, peaceful woods behind me. I glanced back at my friends. Nothing was nearing them. In front of me, the forest rolled on into the distance until it faded into an unknown, blue and green abyss.

I looked back down at the mushrooms which continued to glow aggressively.

I sunk my hand into the dirt next to them and closed my eyes. I slipped my consciousness into the plants, first listening to what they were humming off, but fungi were difficult to listen to. They were an overly-connected organism, and all listening did was get me thousands of voices spouting a thousand different things in the same tone. I shook my head and tried to see what they were seeing.

There were tons of mushrooms spread over the entire forest, and so I was left catching flashes of several things. One patch was sensing some teenage nymphs harvesting the mushrooms to get high off. Another patch was getting swarmed by odin-crows. In between the visions from the other mushrooms connected to the ones in front of me, I could see brown scaled arms and legs striding over the hilly ground. Ragged and torn hair dangled from its knees and elbows. Claws instead of fingernails grew from its hands and feet, digging sharp lines into the soil as it walked. Blood was dried and crusted under the tips of the nails, and clumped together against the small patches of fur.

I caught an image of his face, grotesquely large on top of his mangled body. Jagged teeth, sharpened and layered like sharks, were left exposed - his lips had been ripped from his face centuries ago. Half of what used to be dangled from the bottom corner of his mouth. It was stained green and rust from the fluids of his victims running down it when he would bite into them.

In the final flash, I saw myself, and the creature standing over me.

I opened my eyes and looked up. His towering bloody loomed over me, blocking out the light from every sun in the sky.

I summoned my dragon's sword.

"Grendel," I tried to not whimper, but it was too late.

The mutilated body of something that was barely human even upon birth, was licking the torn patches of skin where lips used to be. His eyes were black as they look down at me, the whites of his eyes stained yellow from his unbalanced diet of eating people's flesh.

The sword formed in my hand, lightening careening up my hand in an excited crackle. I tried to stand, so that I could make a striking move, but Grendel had hunted me and caught me off guard. I didn't stand a chance. He raised him massive paw against me, pounding it into my chest, where in enveloped my entire torso and flung me backwards.

I flew through the air. Time seemed to slow down as I watched the bright green grass grow farther away. In my stomach-churning weightlessness and from the violence of his strike, my sword slipped from me. I watched it as it spiraled to my right and down. I wasn't able to see where it landed as my body fell backwards, my head and shoulder's beginning to descend toward the ground. My feet trailed behind me, higher in the air then my head, which tilted back until I could only see the sky and the upside down image of the forest.

My collision was not as slow. I slammed into the ground, my shoulders and the back of my head hitting first. My feet came down after, flipping me over once and with such a force that my entire body ricocheted off the soggy moss a few inches, just to drop back down.

I groaned. It was a struggle to try and get my arms underneath me. My shoulder screamed with every move I made. It popped as I pushed myself to my knees. At the sound of Grendel's feet pounding onto the ground, my adrenaline spewed into my bloodstream, and the ache in my limbs suddenly seemed like nothing.

I jumped to my feet. I dug my right foot into the dirt, hoping the weight and grip of my boots would be enough to keep me planted. He barreled over the bank in front of me, his black eyes beady and fixated on me. Without my sword, I let loose a honed ray of fire, glowing so bright it was almost a heavenly ray of light. It enveloped his entire body, but he kept rushing forward. I kept laying it on until the frame of his body appeared outside the confines of the light.

I dropped my hands to see a very smokey and angry, but otherwise uninjured, beast only a step away from me. He was moving at full speed and slammed right into me. I didn't travel nearly as far back as I did before. This time, I was projected into the air. But as my body was still ascending up, before it could arch down, my back slammed into a white baobab tree. Its small leafy top spun after me still intact, but it's thick trunk splintered into chunks the size of my forearm.

I fell down onto one of these chunks. It slid through my side, ripping a hole the size of my fist just under my rib cage, but not plunging deeper than my bones could stop.

Grendel kicked through the remaining tree so that he could swipe his clawed hand down towards me. I rolled to the side, narrowly missing the talons half the size of me as they tore through the forest floor.

I stumbled up to my feet, then side-stepped to avoid Grendel's other hand snatching for my tiny-by-comparison body. His claws slid into the soft ground like sharpened shovels, and he was stuck, giving me enough time to observe the density of his skin.

Grendel was the son of Cain and a demon. He carried the same curse that his father did, to live for eternity never being satisfied and never to be struck down by anything of the world so that he could continue to live in his suffering. From the looks of his thick, scaled skin, I was willing to bet the story wasn't an exaggeration.

In the poem *Beowulf,* the hero is able to defeat him and cut off his arm. But more than likely, this was just a story told to help magick-less humans sleep better at night in a world filled with magick.

A solid mass of frozen rock whistled past me, and slammed into Grendel's head. He fell to the ground, his claws ripping up through the ground as he crumpled over.

I used the opportunity to turn and run towards the forest bank, back to my group. Condan was standing there, just on the crest, his arms out to the sides, his hands facing into the air like he was once again meditating. Only this time, wisps of dark shadows tendrilled off his skin like steam, while earth rose around him, compressed into hardened balls of rock, and froze over, before being slung forwards toward the downed beast.

I stopped at the base of the hill and turned back.

Grendel was on his feet again. He slapped the projectiles away like they were gnats.

"Why is he not sustaining damage?" Condan asked, only irritation spread across his face.

"He's cursed," I yelled up to him. "No earthly weapons can hurt him."

"Your fire did nothing, and that's hardly earthly," he hissed.

Grendel lunged forward and both Condan and I immediately changed tactics. I channelled a current of wind towards his chest, just as Condan summon a dense ice spike to shoot up from the moist ground. The two collided at the same time, knocking the monster off his feet. He skidded back, his heavy body digging into the ground. When he stopped, he hardly moved, dazed from the strike.

"We can knock him off his feet all we want, none of this is going to break his skin," I said.

"You said that he can't be hurt by anything earthly, dragon magick isn't earthly, so clearly you're missing something," Condan snarled.

I slapped him across his face. "Don't ever speak down to me like that. Dragon magick is still elemental in its core. Anything that is created by us is earthy. Only our dragon armour is unearthly because it was created by a higher power."

I climbed to the top of the hill. Behind me, Grendel was just beginning to climb to his feet.

Condan stuck his hand into the air, and a block of ice formed above the demon's head. It propelled down, slamming him once again to the ground.

Down, in the centre of the flattened path, my sword lay abandoned.

"I already summoned my sword, I need to go get it," I told Condan. "Summon your weapon and your armour and get a head start, I'll be right back."

I lifted my foot, ready to run down and retrieve our saving grace. But Condan's harsh grip latched onto my forearm.

"I don't have dragon armour," he said through gritted teeth.

My blood ran cold. I looked behind me at Grendel who was struggling to get up again.

"What do you mean?" I asked, looking back at Condan.

"Muireann never had any need for a dragon rider," Condan said. "She never forged one of her scales into a weapon. Your armour and sword are the only thing divine here."

Grendel was back on his feet and descending upon us.

Condan and I moved together, opting to once again combine forces and both send different striked against him in order to push him back. But Grendel wasn't a dumb creature. He spun out of the way, continuing his advancement. He swung both hands together, trying to clamp Condan and I between his palms.

I ducked out of their way, rolling back to put distance between myself and the being. Condan leaped into the air, tucking his feet underneath him. He flipped backwards over Grendel's hands and landed on his feet.

I watched as Condan's hand grew until it was twice it's original size, covered in icy scales, and tipped with black talons. He thrusted it forward, penetrating through the thickness of Grendel's skin - who let out a bellowing cry.

Condan withdrew as Grendel swung at him with his good hand. But Condan was a prince of warriors, and he moved out of the way as if he was nothing more than a breeze. Grendel continued to advance, swinging at the elf aimlessly in a hopeless attempt to hit him. Condan spun around in graceful movements, almost like a dancer on a theatre stage.

Grendel screeched and swung his leg up. Condan, who had cockily grown comfortable watching the beast's hands, narrowly missed his foot, but in the process was spinning right towards Grendel's left hook.

I sprinted forward and sprung myself into the air.

I landed onto Grendel's back before Condan could be skewered. I wrapped my arms around the curves of his neck, my hands not even making it the full way around. He began to shake around violently, trying to fling me off of him. I dug my nails into his skin to try and stay on, and I felt my fingers break skin and push into the soft, wet tissue.

Blood ran over my fingers, but I didn't let go.

Grendel spun in twenty rapid circles, and I spun with him, but I didn't let go.

He slammed us backwards into a tree, colliding my body with the solid mass first, and together we broke through it. But still, I hung on with everything I had.

I couldn't see what was going on around due to the rapidly changing, jerky motions Grendel was putting me through. But I could only hope that Condan was smart enough to know to use this distraction as an opportunity to go get my sword so we could really hurt the son-of-a-bitch.

Grendel reached back and grabbed at me. I leaned away so that his palm could only squish down on my arm. Then he curled his hands and his nails pushed through the fabric of my shirt and the skin of my back.

I let out a blood-curdling scream as the wide, sharp knives were dragged across my body. When they caught on my shoulder blade, Grendel stopped, no doubt about to push them in, piercing my heart.

Shink.

The familiar ringing of celestial steel ringing through the air was my saving grace.

Grendel's hand fell away, and I let go of the best, plummeting four or more metres to the ground beneath me. I landed onto my feet, but my hips gave way from the force, and I plopped right onto my butt.

Immediately, strong, black legs stepped over me. Large hands held my sword out in front of them, with Grendel's thick, rust coloured blood slicked down the side.

242

The large arm of the creature was laying, twitching, on the other side of my saviour. It had been completely severed from its grotesque body from the elbow down.

I was scooped up from under my arms and dragged up to my feet. I looked behind me to see Jack and Adam pulling me up.

I looked Adam up and down, then turned around to the one holding my sword.

Ethan was advancing, the gleaming white blade practically singing in his grip. He sliced through Grendel's achilles tendon, and the beast collapsed to his knee. He swept his hand back toward Ethan, who smoothly stepped out of the way.

Once Grendel's face was turned, a glowing blue arrow hissed through the air, striking the beast in the eye with enough force to shock him. Grendel cried out and collapsed back, catching himself onto his arm. But Condan was there, and with his morphed limb, sliced into the monster's wrist. Grendel kept from collapsing this time, and rolled forward, slamming the bleeding nub of his former arm to the ground so that Condan was under him, trapped between his body and his wounded arms.

I ran forward, hoping to help the elf. Darbie made it first though, sliding under the giant body, right next to Condan. He jammed his staff upwards towards Grendel. A dome of blue-ish green magick came from the collision, and our adversary was shot several metres into the air.

While Grendel was flying upwards, Darbie grabbed ahold of Condan and in a swirling flourish, they vanished from under the beast. They reappeared next to Jack and Adam only for Darbie to collapse. His vibrant blue skin was pale and slick with sweat.

He had depleted his magick in order to rescue Condan. He was out of the fight for the foreseeable future.

I looked back just as Grendel fell to the floor. The ground shook violently enough that we all stumbled to our knees. Trees shook and rocks vibrated off of each other.

Crashing of wood drew my attention. I looked over to see a branch from an oak snapping off and falling towards Reika. She was still getting to her feet when it hit. It broke her bow and pinned her to the ground.

"Ah," she whimpered.

I looked to Adam who was already rising to his feet and pushing off in her direction. Jack moved to cradle Darbie's head, while he summoned a protecting circle over the pair of them. It was a smart move. Darbie wasn't going to be of much help, and Jack and Adam were mortal, so getting involved in this fight was nothing more than a death wish.

Condan was struggling to get to his feet. Blood stained his pants. A large patch of red pooled on his hip before running down to his knee. A puncture mark was torn through the fabric of his shirt, clinging to his skin from the wetness of blood. Nonetheless, the man looked ready for more.

I ran back into battle first. Ethan was already on his feet. Grendel rose to a knee and Ethan was swinging, cleanly cutting through the skin and bone of his knee. He quickly spun back and made another slice through the shin. Neither were enough to completely cut through the bone, but he had created a weak spot.

I spinted forward, passed Ethan, then jumped so that I could body slam into the section of weakness. Against the force of my blow, the partially cut bone broke in both places. I was bounced back from the force, and Grendel's leg folded in on itself and he fell face first towards us. With two weakened arms as well, he couldn't catch his unexpected tumble, and his jaw was left to slam harshly onto the ground.

Ethan didn't hesitate. He stepped forward, raising the sword above his head, and brought the blade down into Grendel's head, right between his eyes, all the way to the hilt. The blade of the sword wasn't even long enough to penetrate all the way through his head, but it was buried deep enough that the demon went limp before our eyes.

Ethan twisted the sword just for good measure, then pulled it out. Blood and brain matter clung to the blade and trickled off of its tip as it came out.

We were left with nothing but the deep huffing of our breaths. Both of us stood staring down at the dead creature.

"This is why you shouldn't put me in the back," Ethan grumbled facetiously.

At the mention of the back, I thought of Darbie, who had been with him.

I spun around, first seeing Condan, who was watching, his hand back to normal now and cradling his injury. Behind him, Jack had already dropped the defensive spell and was now just trying to keep his partner conscious. At the top of the hill, Adam was rubbing healing paste onto Reika's back and shoulder while speaking the activating incantation.

I turned and gripped Ethan's shoulder, forcing him to look at me.

Sweat had beaded on his forehead, making his shining black hair cling to his skin, outlining the blue of his eyes. Irregular beads of sweat were spotted across his nose as well, forcing me to realise that he had the palest of freckles hiding in his skin under his eyes.

"Reika and Darbie are down," I said. "You go check on Darbie, I'll go help with Reika."

I lifted my leg, and stepped towards Reika, but Ethan had other plans. His hand wrapped around my bicep firmly, but gently.

"Hey," he said. "You need to get checked out too. You have the most injuries here. Everyone else is covered, let me handle you before we go diving into anyone else."

I shook my head.

"I'm fine," I said, but my mouth was dry.

Ethan's eyes narrowed. "Bull-shit, E."

I shook my head again, and this time it began to spin.

"No really," I mumbled. Black dots formed in my vision. "Okay, maybe not…"

My sight started to fade out from the centre until I could see nothing. One ear rang and the other just heard Ethan's voice yelling at me.

14

Erika

I fell into a world that was blue.

I sat up to find my legs floating in deeply blue water. It stretched out as far as my eyes could see before it fell off into an abyss of indigo. It lapped against ground that was the colour of sapphires and rust.

I pushed to my feet, turning around so that the endless water was behind me.

I found myself in the middle of a blue desert. A white sun was in the sky, heating up the world so that it was hotter than earth, but the light itself was shrouded in thick, brown clouds. The minimal rays that pushed through to the ground casted shadows over the valley that I was in. Rocky mountains made-up of purple-ish rocks with large rust coloured veins running inside them lined the horizon

In front of me was nothingness. Only more sapphire and rust coloured dirt in a valley that followed the mountains as it ran out for miles before curving to the left of where I stood.

"This is a vision, right Fintan?" I called out, waiting to hear the dragon's voice.

But it never came.

I sighed.

"Great, so the orchestrator of this isn't my dragon friend, I love that for me. Means I can't just ask my way out of this," I said to myself. I looked behind me and glanced at the water. "Not really a water person so I won't be going that way," I turned back to face the path in front of me. "Guess barren blue desert that stretches on for miles is my only option."

I sighed again, then looked down at my feet which were luckily tied up in coyote brown military boots.

"Well, at least my dream-weaver was nice enough to give me comfortable shoes," I muttered as I started walking. "Couldn't have thought to give me a car or anything though, apparently. Kind of a bit rude, really.

"I mean, seriously? Who builds a dream world that stretches on for miles, just to have the dreamer have to walk the whole damn thing? That requires a lot of time! Time is precious even for-"

I blinked. In the flashing moment of darkness, my surroundings changed.

I came to a halt and looked behind me. The ocean of nothingness was miles back now. I had already reached the bend in the valley, where I could see the mountains lining the pathway up towards a kingdom of glass. It sparkled like a perfectly shaped protrusion of white crystal, growing out of the darkness of the earth.

"Damnit," I grumbled. "Why does it always have to be me? Why do I have to get the visions of creepy places, like castles of glass in dark deserts? Why can't I get a Penelope dream where an eagle comes and gets rid of geese? I'm always wandering through snowy woods, or witnessing bloody battle fields. This shit is getting old, just so you know."

I put my hands on my hips and glared up at the castle in the distance.

Then, in my moment of clarity, I realised, "Nobody can hear my complaints." I let out a loud groan. "Damn you unknown dream-weaver who isn't here to listen to me."

I dropped my hands from my hips and raised my middle fingers to the sun.

When I was done with my fit, I began walking ahead. The rough dirt beneath my feet didn't even kick up dust. It hardly crunched under my moving weight. If I hadn't been so adamant to hurry up and get out, I would have crouched down and felt it to see if it was soft.

I kept walking as I blinked, and this time when I opened my eyes, I was centimetres from a wall of ice.

"Ah, fuck!" I shouted and recoiled back.

I quickly took two steps back and looked up. The wall of ice grew towards the sky. I hurried to take more steps back so that I could see the whole structure.

It was the castle I had seen in the distance. The front wall went from mountain to mountain and rose what must have been three stories into the air. Behind me, there was a trench, steaming with hot magma, and over it, was a bridge made of one solid sapphire. Between the trench and where I stood, was a car length of earth that morphed from sapphire to rust to ice, until the walls next to me grew from it.

The bridge was laid out directly in front of what must have been the gate. I followed the ice wall forward until I was able to round the corner to where a broad archway opened up.

Inside, the castle walls protected open and well lit streets. Empty homes and market places were constructed from the same beautiful ice and dark blue gemstone. Dragon statues made out of the rust coloured stone sat in the centre of intersections and atop what looked like churches and gathering places. Plots of earth were circled around them, where green plants and ivy could grow up the feet or tails of the dragons.

The contrast of the colours made the space feel bright, lively and peaceful. The limited sunlight that was able to break through the planet's ozone bounced off the softly reflective ice, spreading it around until the kingdom was bright.

But I didn't have time to get caught up in the beauty either.

The widest road inside the walls continued to lead upwards to where a grand palace was nestled into the mountainside.

Two towers jutted out in front of one taller, domed structure. A circular landing lay lower, linking the two towers just under the grandness of the centre dome. Two rust-stone dragon heads, roughly the size of cars, were mounted on the towers. They were so large that I could clearly see their ruby eyes from down where I stood. Lava fell from their mouths, tumbling down until it disappeared into the abyss of the mountain.

The smaller ice structures leading up to the castle blocked my view of the entrance, but I could see the slightest hint of the top of another wall of ice.

I groaned. "I swear, if I take another step and I auto-transport into another freaking ice wall, I might fuck around and melt this castle down."

Nothing so much as a breeze sounded around me. It was like I was in a padded room. It was so quiet I could hear my own heartbeat in my ears. When I lifted my feet so that I could spin around and take in all the colours of the world around me, the scuffing of my shoes was painfully loud despite how lightly I was moving on my feet.

I turned back and looked up the wide, empty, white cobble-ice street. The royal blue gemstones outlined each brick of ice like grout. Strips of the seemingly iron rich dirt lined the street, only breaking to create what looked like crosswalks.

I began walking up the road.

Shops lined the street, and suddenly I felt like I was walking up a frozen version of the royal mile in Edinburgh. Ice and snow made up the walls, with frosted blocks for doors and crystal clear panes for windows. Inside the shops, I could see reddish-brown stones raised to make tables and countertops - each rock was perfectly formed like it had been handcrafted and sanded for days.

It was all beautiful, if it was populated it would have felt more like an enchanted fairytale and less like the final walk to the gallows.

I had walked past about four or five shops before concluding that my days of fast travelling were over. I did not want to stay in this dream forever either.

I pushed away my fascination with the wonder of this place and got down to business, picking myself up into a jog so that I could get up to the castle quicker. I could see the road bending and winding its way all the way up to the top in an attempt to lessen the steepness of the street.

Instead of the royal mile, the road could have been called the royal five mile with how long it looked.

I was getting through the first part of the shops, just crossing under an archway that supported another road, when I finally was zapped to a new location again.

As I passed under the arch, I found myself no longer running up the royal five mile and instead jogging across the terrifyingly open space of the platform between the two towers. A large bonfire at least a full story tall burned in the centre of the round platform. Behind the fire, the grand dome structure sat

251

completely open, revealing a throne room that looked decorated with red and blue stones.

I glanced behind me. I was only a few steps away from the ledge. The air moved up here. It whipped at my legs, practically grabbed at them, as if begging me to step off and let it carry me.

I hadn't flown before, but the tugging feeling I got in my chest had me considering that maybe I could. Especially as I looked over the kingdom and world below.

From the platform, you could see all the way out to the edge of the horizon. Back down the valley, following it back around to the right, there was the endless indigo ocean. A violent tempest, crackling with white lightning churned above it. The lightning would crack and reach out in all directions, like spider legs running across a tile floor. And then a single, clean bolt would shoot down to the ocean below, like the shot of a web towards a fly.

Diagonal from the ice kingdom and the tempest, across the barrenness of the desert, I could see a black mountain. Golden flames glowed from the top in pulses. I watched as it lit up and faded. In the silence of everything, it didn't take me long to deduce that the surges were in sync with my heart beat.

I turned away from it quickly. Even though it was a dream, it was probably best to avoid getting too mesmerised by it all.

I rushed over the to the throne room, reaching out to touch the fire as I went. I still felt nothing.

Inside the throne room, every inch of the walls and the top of the dome was a collection of sapphires and rubies. The stones were no bigger than the size of my thumb, resulting in what must have been millions of gemstones creating the most breathtaking skylight out of the entire room.

It was like looking at stars.

Like looking at stars while stranded in the middle of the ocean without a light. The rubies lit up as I got closer to them, sprinkling romantic red over my skin and the white floor.

In the centre of the awe inspiring dome, were two chairs.

"Chairs" was an understatement. These things were thrones. Thrones that put all other thrones to shame.

Silver sat over one solid blue gemstone chair and arm rests, making it look like the silver had shattered to reveal the dark, rich colour below. The back of the chair was smooth black iron, woven together with silver and ice until it reached the top where each material split, creating sharp, arched spikes, like the pillars of a king's crown.

The throne next to it was just as large, but could have been floating on a cloud for all I knew. A plume of white feathers and mist clung to the bottom and spread up to the seat of the throne where it became sparse, sharing space with silver platforms that had softly surging magma running between the sections. The arm rests and the back partially floated, with sections appearing solid and made from chunks of ruby covered in soft silver. Lightning rippled within the rubies. The light danced inside the gemstones, zapping from one side to another, causing the stones to sway inside the frame of the chair.

"Beautiful aren't they?" Condan's voice was behind me now.

I turned to see him approaching from a stairwell tucked away beside the landing. He was dressed in black and blue royal robes. Symbols of crystals were embroidered into the silky fabric, running down the flaps of the robe from his collar to his ankles. As he walked around the length of the wall behind the thrones, each decal caught the light of the sapphires in the walls and began to glow from white to baby blue.

"You can sit in it if you'd like," he said. "You'll find it fits you perfectly."

253

I watched him as he rounded the entirety of the grand room. Like a predator circling it's prey.

I balled my fists, ready for a fight.

"I'm alright, thanks," I said dryly.

He cut away from the wall now, making a beeline towards me, approaching from the side of the thrones.

"Suit yourself," he said as he reached the ice throne first. "But personally, I enjoy being a king in a comfortable chair."

He plopped down into the seat and it was like he hit the switch for a projector somewhere. Phantom images of people in silk gowns and suits walked around us. Some discussed in corners, whispering like close friends. Other's walked by looking like they were heatedly debating politics. There was a line of phantoms congregating in front of the thrones. They approached one by one, laid down baskets or envelopes or bags, said some things I couldn't hear, then they turned and disappeared into thin air.

The entire space was lively, visibly bustling despite the fact that it was all muted - nothing more than a silent, faded preview.

"What is this?" I asked condan.

"It's memories from a different life," he said. "One that has yet to come."

I looked away from the mirage of people, glaring down at the solid man in front of me.

"Only oracles and seers can see into the future like this," I said, scowling at him. "Are you suddenly a seer as well as a dragon, Condan?"

Condan chuckled. "I never said I was the dark dragon."

He rose out of his seat, and the images disappeared.

We were once again alone in the twinkling space. He stepped down from the landing of the thrones, moving away, towards the wall farthest from the stairwell he came from. Tucked in the corner, just off to the left and behind the thrones, was an altar. Two alcoves were built into the wall. One was tiled solely with sapphires and inside there was an ebony and blue black-opal dark dragon inside. The beast was hunched down, its tail curled up around its legs like it was protecting something underneath itself.

In the other alcove, only rubies decorated the space, reflecting off of a garnet and white opal light dragon. The serpent like being had his wings open wide and his head up towards the sky. It's mouth was open, revealing polished silver teeth, and an orange and aqua opal stone in the centre, like fire just igniting.

In front of both idols, a shared table of white marble held a silver bowl. A golden knife, that resembled a smaller version of my sword, laid drenched in blood next to it. The blood pooled off the blade like it was the thing bleeding. It ran down the side of the marble, until it stained the ice below.

"Who are you?" I snapped.

No words.

Blood dripped in thick globs from the edge of the table. The sound of the wetness slapping onto the solid ice echoed off the walls until it sounded like the second hand of a clock ticking by.

"*What* are you?" I changed my tactic.

Condan reached his hands into the bowl, dipped the tips of his pointer and middle finger into the blood, and then brought the digits to his forehead. He dragged them down to the centre of his chest, then across to both sides, leaving the bloody lined symbol of the cross over his face and heart.

I gritted my teeth. "What do you want?"

"What do *you* want?" he asked me back. "Haven't you grown tired of trying to save the world? Haven't you grown tired

255

of being the only one who has to sacrifice everything for everyone else? Don't you wish to be praised like the hero that you are? You deserve recognition for all the things you've done for others."

He looked at me. With both eyes. Both eyes were more orange than golden, as if the painter had lost their metallic paint and had to settle for mixing yellow with their own blood to make the paint thick enough.

I took a step away from him. "I don't want to be a hero," I said. "I don't want praise. I just want to live knowing I've done everything in my power to make this world a little better."

He filled in the gap I had made. His cold hand reached out and caressed my cheek. His touch didn't cool down my hot skin.

"But you could do so much more," he whispered. "If you were the ruler of it all, you could make sure nothing bad ever happened again. If you choose to take the throne with him, you can dispose of the imperfections. Create a heavenly world. This world doesn't need to be *better*. It can be the *best*."

I shook my head. I opened my mouth to speak, but Condan wasn't done.

"You will face it in the future," he declared. "You will have to choose between remaining weak in order to maintain what you claim to be the balance, or pursue an opportunity where you change the world into *this*."

He swept his hand out, and scenes of this planet flashed over the sapphire and ruby walls. The gorgeous but violent blackness of the mountain in the distance, danced with bubbling lava. The ocean I stared at churned and ripped its banks with hurricanes and tsunamis. And here in the earth kingdom, blizzards smashed against the frozen rocky mountains.

"This could be yours," he said. "The entire world would be yours to cultivate and journey through. As the father of the

256

world, you can raise and build what you please. And as the mother of the world, I will follow you, building up homes like this one where we can foster the growth of our power and our people."

I shook my head, but Condan kept talking.

"Even though this environment is hostile, dragons are the hardiest creatures to have ever existed. This is a world where your people can thrive. The dragons have access to their elements. And you can keep your precious humans around if you want. We can provide for them. They can be wonderful decorations to a world you get to form as you deem fit.

"You can rule over a world that bends to your every whim. A planet that takes its shape and its environment from the whispers of your lips. You won't be *a* god. We will *be* god. The one and only."

I shoved him away.

"We aren't gods," I hissed. "And humans? They're our equals!"

"Ha!" Condan shouted. "Don't insult me. Even your beloved dragon rider, with all your powers, isn't strong enough."

I stepped forward, pressing my chest against his. Steam rose between us.

"What the fuck are you talking about?" I shouted.

"Your soul in his body," Condan growled. "You were already weak when only your body was confining the light dragon, then you go and split it? Foolish. Weak."

"Once again," I bit out. "I don't know what you're talking about."

Condan's hand gripped my cheeks between his fingers.

"Not yet," he whispered down to me. "But you will. You will see that, despite what he says, I am right. He's not strong enough to see you succeed. You only win if you follow the true balanced path."

"If this is the world of a blanched path," I choked out between the forceful fingers clamping my mouth. "Then I will never become a queen, and my family and I will beat you, Condan or whoever you are."

"No, sweetness," he purred. "If your timeline plays out as mine has, if you choose *him* over me, then I will watch you claim each other's lives."

I spat at him. He wiped it away, then with the same hand backhanded me.

I was struck to the ground with enough force to crack the sapphire floor.

"*Your timeline*?" I hissed as I pushed to my feet. "You just said you're not really Condan, so who are you? And what timeline are you talking about?"

"You will lose when you fight me," he said again.

"You as in Condan or you as in whoever you are?!" I screamed.

He snatched me in his painful grasp again, tugging me towards his face.

"He. Isn't. Strong. Enough," he pronounced. "You lose. Or you gain this world. Those are the only two outcomes."

He threw me to the ground again. But I didn't collide this time.

Ethan

Erika awoke with a sharp inhale. She pushed up off the ground and looked around, looking like a lizard performing a mating ritual. Her shirt was still hanging only from her neck in the front, her bra still on, but unclasped so that the healing paste could do its thing.

I watched silently while she rolled onto her butt, one hand now clamped onto her chest, pinning her shirt down. She looked around frantically before settling on me.

"Where is everyone?" she asked.

I nodded in the direction behind her. "Condan, Reika and Darbie are all out collecting cucurbits. Jack and Adam are looking for more ambrosia bushes so they can either bring back berries or sap to make stronger healing paste."

She aggressively rubbed her face. Scrubbing the skin like she was buffing out muscle tension in her cheeks and forehead.

"You wanna tell me what's got you so tense?" I asked.

She stopped rubbing her face long enough to peek at me through the gaps in her fingers. She shook her head quickly and violently, before returning to her buffing.

When she was done, she looked over her shoulder. Then she turned and nudged her chin into the air in my direction. "How'd you get stuck on babysitting duty?"

"Condan insisted on going to get cucurbits for you and Darbie didn't want to let him run off on his own, so he brought Reika with him," I explained. "Adam and Jack know the plants better than I do, plus out of the three of us, I'm the only one who's been in this world on my own. I know how to fight off things out here alone if it comes to it."

Erika reached behind her back and fidgeted with her bra clasp.

259

"Survive and thrive apparently," she muttered. "You saved my life. I owe you for that."

I scoffed, but tried to cover it up into a chuckle. Unfortunately Erika knew me better than that.

"Don't dismiss it like that," she snapped. "I'm immortal, I've been doing this a longer time than you and I'm a hell of a lot more durable. You're human, your life is much more fragile. Not to mention short. You're twenty-five and you fight better than-"

"A two-thousand year old dragon lady?" I teased.

Erika rolled her eyes.

"Better than any knight I've ever known," she finished softly. "Speaking of your fighting skills, what happened to my sword after you were done with it?"

"It stuck around with me for a while, while we tried to get everyone sort of treated and away from the battlezone," I said. "Then I tried to hand it off to Adam, but as soon as he touched it it turned into a ball of lightning and went away."

Erika shifted uncomfortably. "The armour and sword sometimes have a mind of their own."

"It's nice knowing I'm their favourite."

We sat there staring at each other, neither one wanting to comment on what was being said.

A breath passed.

Then a second.

On the third, Erika was the one to break the gaze. She looked to the ground and began to struggle with her undergarment again.

"Fucking piece of shit," she hissed under her breath.

"Would you like help?" I asked, already getting up.

She shook her head as I slid down behind her.

"No," she said. "I just can't get it to catch."

260

I poked around her fingers, grasping each elastic strap. Her fingers let go, letting me take control. I twisted the fabric in my hands so that I could look at the metal hooks.

"One's bent," I said thoughtlessly and reached into my pocket. I pulled out my multi-tool and unfolded it so that the pliers would be out.

"I can just pinch it if you guide my fingers," Erika said.

I grasped her shoulder and pulled her back just enough so that she could look up and back at me.

"I might just be a fragile human," I vocalised. "But I can at least fix a bra hook."

"Clasp," she corrected.

"Whatever," I mumbled as I tugged her bra back into my grasp.

I slid the metal wire between the pliers teeth, grazing the steel against Erika's skin. The metal began to glowed red as it slid against her soft, pale back. I pulled the pliers away from her and they immediately began to cool down. Next I pulled my hand away, turned it over so that I could see if there were any burn marks, and when I found none, I clamped my palm down onto Erika's back.

When I felt no pain or heat, I picked my hand up and flipped it over so that I could press the back of it against her toned body.

I slapped my hand around like that a few more times before Erika finally pulled away from me. She leaned forward, then twisted so that she could look at me with pure confusion over her shoulder.

"You alright, buddy?" she asked.

"Uh-huh," I sounded and looked down at the pliers.

I pinched the top of them and waited to see if they would grow hot, but nothing happened.

I looked back up at Erika. "The pliers just heated up from touching your skin."

She looked at the pliers and frowned.

"That's weird," she said. "I'm not consciously heating up."

"I know," I said. "That's why I slapped my hand against your back. I was checking to see if you were hot to the touch, only for nothing to happen."

She raised her hand and scooped it forward, urging me on.

"Touch my arm," she instructed, and I followed.

I wrapped my entire hand around her forearm and sat there. After a second she looked up at me, expectantly.

"Nothing," I informed her.

She reached forward with her other arm, leaving her shirt to sway loosely on her torso, exposing the black and blue rose fabric of her bra. I squeezed my eyes together, reminding myself that I was a grown man and not a boy in set eight who'd be easily distracted by boobs. I opened them back up and focused on Erika's hand, which was dragging the pliers forward, poking them into her skin.

Upon contact, the metal started to grow hot. After a few seconds, the redness was growing up the teeth and spreading to the rest of the metal of the multitool. The centimetre of steel pressed directly against Erika's skin began to steam.

Erika and I looked up at each other at the same time.

"My skin detects possible threats,", "Your skin reacts to potential threats," she and I said at the exact same time.

We both grinned, laughing at both the fascination of discovering another one of her natural abilities as well as the amusement of our thoughts being in sync.

262

Then the pliers began to steam in my hand, burning the skin of my palm. I winced and dropped the tool, pulling away from Erika.

I shook my hand out, distracting myself from the mild ache. Erika reached into the air, gently wrapping her fingers around my wrist. She brought it into her lap, palm up. There, she laid her hand over mine and a cool breeze began rolling over my skin.

"This is fantastic," she said mindlessly, staring at my hand. "My injuries must have triggered it."

"Mmm," I grunted in agreement. "Fintan probably unlocked it for you."

She shook her head. "No, I think I always could with instinct alone, but my druid powers were just my first instinct for so long, I always immediately moved to use nature to heal and defend me when I was injured. I never tried out any of my new magick to see what I could do in desperate situations. And I never gave my body enough time to just let it react on it's own."

I leaned down, hoping to catch her eye. When I did, the excitement glowing in them was infectious and I found myself smiling.

"So you think you've always had skin with built in defence protocols?" I asked, only half joking.

"I think even when I'm not awake to actively make decisions with my magick, I'm powerful enough to have natural magickal reactions," she said and let go of my hand. "You weren't burned when you touched me because the subconscious can still sense familiarities. The pliers were metal, an unknown and potential threat so they got toasted. Oh, this is so cool. Adam is going to be psyched that we found another ability."

My smile cracked.

"Why don't we just get that bra fixed?" I offered, beginning to move back. "I'll just pitch it between my fingers this time."

"Are you sure?" she asked. "It may be stubborn."

I sighed. "I'm strong enough, trust me."

Erika's shoulders slumped. Her skin felt a little cooler beneath my finger tips.

I didn't say anything while I fixed her bra. As I strapped it closed, I cleared my throat.

"Now that you're not exposed," I said, standing up so I could go sit in front of her. "You want to tell me what you dreamt about?"

She threaded her arms through her shirt, pulling the cloth down over her body.

"Who said I dreamt of anything?" she asked, bitterly.

I crossed my arms over my chest. "You woke up with a start and immediately rolled into paranoid attack mode. Trust me, I recognize the symptoms of haunting dreams."

Erika's expression softened. She drew her knees up to her chest and rested her arms across them, hugging her legs close to herself.

"I think it was a vision, actually," she said. "Or maybe a prophecy. In any case, it was more than a dream. And I have the impression that no one weaved it for me to see. It felt too real for that."

"Oh-kay," I hesitated. "Wanna tell me what exactly you saw? Or what this *prophecy* told you we needed to do?"

She laughed bitterly. "It told me I needed to be the father of a world where I help kill off all the weak populations by - I don't know - forming a hostile planet, I think? And if I don't then bad things are going to happen anyway, so I might as well give myself the power to control every aspect of existence."

I laughed. I laughed so hard, I had to cover my face.

"Dude," she called in disbelief. "I'm telling you I had a gnarly dream about me needing to commit mass genocide in order to save the world, and you're just sitting there laughing at me?"

I laughed harder then. So hard that I needed to cough my lungs clear. I watched her bright, pale face watch me. She was perfectly outlined by the darkness of the green trees behind her. Her brown locks were pulled away from her soft features, up into a curly ponytail behind her head. She looked like she was about to dress into a football kit and run out onto the field with her hair like that.

She was brutal. But the colour of her eyes, the softness of her skin, the tumbling of her hair, it was all too soft to be warrioress.

Holy shit, I thought. *She is literally like a flame. Soft, beautiful and helpful when tame. But when she needed to, she could unleash herself and consume everything around her in an obliterating destructive display.*

"Can I be honest with you, E?" I started, then stopped to clear my throat again. "I don't think you should put much cents into dreams that aren't yours. Only invest into the life you want, okay? Not the life that others have been trying to force you to live."

She shook her head. "You're telling me to ignore a dream that warns me of imminent danger and, what? Find my spirit animal?"

I leaned forward and rested my hand on her wrist. "You have died twice, and come back and saved the world twice as many times, if not more. Whoever or whatever told you you have to turn to the darkside to win, hasn't met you."

265

"What if my death isn't enough this time, Ethan?" she asked darkly, and I was floored. "What if whatever is coming requires more than one sacrifice?"

I shrugged. "Then you have four friends willing to lay down their lives beside you."

"I can't let you die."

"You don't get to decide that for us," I gently argued. "We all chose each other. If we choose to follow you to the crypt, you need to know that we're all okay with that."

Erika cracked a smile. "Well Jack would probably have something to say about it, but..."

I chuckled and let go over her arm.

"Jack always has something to say about anything that is a mild inconvenience to him," I said with a grin still plastered on my face.

"Eh?" Jack's voice called from over the forest bank somewhere. "I can hear ya, ya dickhead!"

"Oh I'm sorry!" I called back. "Does my honesty inconvenience you?!"

His head rose over the top of the grass. He had a large branch of ambrosia bush propped onto his shoulder. He brought it down to point it at me accusingly.

"Be careful, Lios," he warned, but there was humour laced in his words. "I will turn you into a pig and spit roast you."

Adam rose up over the hill next to Jack.

Erika laughed next to me so loudly that all of us were immediately drawn to her.

"If Adam joins in, you don't need to find a stick to spit-roast him," she laughed loudly.

"Alrighty, then," I cringed and got up, moving as far away from Erika as possible after her horrible innuendo.

"Erika," Adam sighed disappointedly. "This is why you can't make friends of your own."

I moved closer to him and looked back at Erika. Her mouth fell open in disbelief. She took a second look at Jack and I but we were already enjoying the show.

"Oooh," Jack and I cooed together.

"We should have brought some popcorn to pop off that burn," Jack said and then raised his hand for a high five from me.

I scrunched my nose at him. "You've had better ones."

"Can I still get a high five?" Jack looked at me sadly, his hand still in the air.

I looked up at the hand and shrugged. "Sure. For pity's sake."

I reached up and met Jack's hand with mine.

"All of you are on your own for a fire tonight," Erika warned.

I let go of Jack's hand to reach into my front pocket. Just underneath a bandana I keep on hand for wiping snot or blood from my nose, was my pack of cigarettes and my lighter. I pulled out the box and fished out one of the slender white sticks. I put the paper between my teeth and shoved my hand back into my pocket where I abandoned the cardboard box for the metal tin lighter.

I made sure to make eye contact with her as I flipped the top open in a satisfying *shink* sound, then lit up the cotton wick in a small, low roar of flames. I held the flame to the cigarette and took a small, smokey drag once just to show it was lit.

"Congratulations," she said. "You can have a fire and a side of lung cancer tonight."

I inhaled a larger amount from the cigarette before pulling the thing out of my mouth. I held it for a second before blowing it out, half slipping past my lips, and the other half running out my nose.

I pointed my cigarette pinching fingers at her. "You're just mad that I can do everything you can do now."

"As, fucking, if," she yelled.

Adam crossed his arms too, a larger bit of ambrosia bush dangling from his belt. "I'm with Erika on this too. She's sort of an indestructible badass who can also make fire."

I took another drag.

"I killed Glendale," I said.

"Grendel," Jack corrected.

"Same thing," I waved him off. "I wasn't armoured. Didn't have any powers. That's pretty badass and indestructible. Plus, I also resisted the siren's call-"

"Wait, you what?" Erika asked, jumping up to her feet.

"Honey!" Darbie called, running forward as the banks of the forest lowered into flat land for him. "I'm home!"

Jack dropped his branch and all but skipped to him.

"Eri!" Darbie exclaimed as Jack slid into his side. "You're awake!"

Condan was right behind Darbie. He had healed within seconds once the fight was over and now he was just looking at all of us smugly. He and I were the only ones who weren't presently injured. Erika may have been good to go now, but she was out for an hour or two before she was even conscious.

I wanted to slap the smug look off of Condan's face. He probably would have been dead had it not been for Darbie, who was depleted only because of him helping the dark elf. Erika was the same, she could have left Condan as a distraction and gone to get her sword, instead she stayed behind for him.

I rolled my eyes at the sight of him.

268

"Anything exciting happen while I was out?" Erika asked the group.

Reika silently slipped into the spot next to our dragon lady. The two ladies smiled at each other. For a second I almost thought they were going to hug like girl-friends would.

"I sucked the magick from a painting orchid and now everyone is talking in colours," Reika said.

Erika sucked her lips in between her teeth and looked to Darbie for further guidance. Darbie stared at the pair grinning from ear to ear. Erika pointed at the demi-goddess for clarification sake.

"Is she high?" she asked.

Darbie nodded. "Higher than a giant's asshole. It's amazing."

"Why is she high?" Adam laughed uncomfortably.

"They're taking my virginities," Reika said confidently and I choked on my cigarette smoke.

"Aye-yo?" I coughed out. "You wanna rephrase that, chief?"

"Everything that she won't be able to do once she gets back to the priestesses, but can do now and not get kicked out, we're doing," Darbie explained. "I. E. taking her experience virginities."

"In that case," Erika said and looked over to Condan. "Build our camp friend. I'll get a solid fire going. Darbie, summon your best alcohol and let's eat ambrosia and anything else we can find around camp, and get cross faded."

I licked my fingers before rolling them over the tip of my cigarette, putting the heat out.

While everyone else celebrated, I muttered; "Guess that puts me on night duty."

15
Erika

The campsite was much less sophisticated tonight. The group had been much more excited about getting drunk and high together after a tiring battle than setting up a place with perfectly placed sitting stones and a running waterfall.

Instead, as soon as the ground was flat and a divot in the ground was big enough for us to light a fire, we all focused on gathering wood so we could hurry along and get to the fun part.

I laid staring at the sky. It was clouded with stormy air tonight, casting pink and green wisps of clouds across the starless heavens.

Adam was in a deep sleep next to me. His skin still had the faintest hint of a magick flowers and berries.

I wasn't one for drugs. A good beer for sure, but mostly because it was literally burnt out of my system within a few minutes. The idea of chewing on painting orchids or eating sinsyn berries and seeing colours or hearing wisps of each other's thoughts just sounded like a bad time to me.

I spent my days seeing the colours and lengths of people's souls, I didn't need more colour in my vision, and I definitely didn't need to know what my friends worried about.

I looked over at Adam. A peaceful, sweet smile was on his lips. They were so soft. So pink. His skin was like that too. Not a scar in sight. I reached out and ran my fingers over his cheek bones. There were no bumps or blemishes that pushed up against my touch.

I pulled my fingers away.

On the far side of camp, just on the outskirts where the light barely touched him, Ethan had leaned against a black rock jutting out on the grass covered mound. He was turned and looking away from the camp. He had one leg propped up, with an arm resting across the knee. His head was down towards the ground and his hands seemed to both be in his lap, but I couldn't see them.

He was perfectly still.

Quietly, I slipped out from the sleeping bag. Being extra careful not to wake up Adam with my movement, nor anyone else with the noise I made.

I moved around the fire, carefully making sure to step over Jack and Darbie. I casted a glance back to see Reika sleeping soundly on her mat. Adam was curled up on our tarp over the soft grass a few metres behind her.

Condan was leaning against a tree, eyes closed and in a peaceful sleep. With his soft features he could almost appear attractive.

I slid up next to Ethan in order to relieve him of watch duty, expecting to find him half asleep after the day he had, but instead I found him wide awake and writing in a pocket journal. He was drawing a very gorgeous and detailed sketch of the white corinthian flower just off to his right.

272

"That flower has the power to restore someone's ability to feel love," I whispered as I settled down next to him. "It's one of the few magickal plants that is naturally stronger than the curses it cures. No potion brewing required."

He must have heard me coming because he didn't flinch. In fact he didn't even look up from his drawing. I waited, expecting him to say something, but he didn't.

We were both leaning against a black rock, warm despite the chilling air that was beginning to settle in between us.

I leaned over and bumped him with my shoulder.

"Hey," I whispered, "Are you mad at me?"

He sighed and shook his head.

"No," he said, casting me a sideways glance. "There's just nothing to discuss right now. Respectfully, you and I seem better fit for strategy and pep talks only."

I pulled my knees up to my chest, wrapping my arms around them and resting my chin on top.

"I know you didn't really like me three years ago when this started," I said. "But I had figured we had gotten over that. I thought you and I had become good friends?"

I watched the side of his face as he stared over at the flower. Never once did he take his eyes off it. From where I sat, and with how his head was turned, I could see the muscles flex in his jaw as he ground down on his teeth.

"We are friends, E," he said. "Sometimes it's just... I don't really know what exactly it's like. It's just always so heavy or deep and emotional, then other people show up and it's nothing. The whole thing becomes, awkward, I guess?"

I shook my head, confused.

"Why is it awkward?" I asked

"Because Adam is my best friend," he answered, but it didn't really clarify anything.

273

I looked over my shoulder at Darbie and Jack who were asleep in each other's arms.

"Is it because you feel like a third wheel?" I tried again.

He groaned and let his head fall back against the rock. His blue opal eyes looked up at the stars. The bright teals and pinks of the sky and the phoenix birds that flew in it, danced in the darkness of his deep blue sight. He let his head fall ever so slightly so that his gaze could tumble onto mine. His sharp features looked so sweet in the light of the Otherworld's night sky. Small strands of his soft black hair cascaded down across his eyes and he looked at me through them like they were curtains and he was a cast member of a play taking a peak at the audience.

He looked at me like he could see all of me and I was suddenly very aware of how little I knew about Ethan.

He had always understood my past; my fears and my trauma that I carried with me from a life that no one should ever have to live. He understood what it was like to have so much pain that you don't want to be alive anymore, but also loving life enough to not want to die.

He knew me without having to ask or write it down. Just from watching and listening he knew. And what kind of friend was I? I didn't know anything about his life.

"I'm sorry," I said so quietly that it was almost drowned out by the sound of the grass swaying.

He drew his knees up enough to lean forward on them with his elbows, his face dipped closer to mine watching me closely.

"What are you sorry for?" he asked equally as hushed as my voice had been.

"You're right, we only talk when bad shit is happening. I've been a terrible friend to you, haven't I?" I voiced my fears.

274

He reached out and pushed stray hair out of my face, leaving me pleasantly surprised.

"If you've been a terrible friend then so have I," he declared.

I disagreed, "No, you notice me and pay attention. You remember things that even Adam sometimes forgets or doesn't notice to begin with."

"I've always done that," he mumbled and pulled away, looking back to the flower like it was more important than life.

"I know," I agreed, but cautiously. "But you've never made it apparent."

"Like I said, that's because Adam's my best friend," he snapped, his eyes turning back to me like daggers. "He fell in love with you in one day and eventually, you did the same. So no shit, I wasn't going to make anything apparent."

I tilted my head sideways, showing my lack of understanding.

Ethan looked out into the wilderness. His eyes were shadowed with the darkness of the unknown around us. His features were hard again, the curtains were down and I couldn't see what he was withholding behind them.

"E…" he started, then stopped, eyes still staring out.

I watched him as he watched the world. His eyes looked over everything but me. I almost felt guilty as I sat there, not moving, waiting to hear what he had to say. I figured if I just didn't leave, if I pressured him enough, he would finally open up and show me just a little of what he had hidden inside.

"You beat the crap out of me in primary school," he said so simply. "I was a little bully to you because I didn't know how else to talk to you, and you wouldn't take my shit, so you beat the crap out of me with a stick after school, do you remember that?"

He offered me his eyes, softer now, and I took them. Smiling at him and shaking my head gently.

"No," I said honestly. "But it sounds like something I'd do. Why'd you want to talk to me in primary? Was it because I was the new kid?"

He leaned his head back against the rock and looked at me like it was so easy.

"My brother had just died," he said. "You were an orphan. We had loss in common. I couldn't talk to anyone back then, no one understood. I was a lost seven year old so I couldn't talk to adults, and none of the other kids had ever experienced a blow like that. I guess I just assumed you and I could have been friends. Like we could have... I don't know..."

"Understood each other?" I finished for him

His features were sweet again.

"Yeah," he said. "I felt like you and I could have understood each other."

I smiled down at my hands crossed over my legs. My fingers, palms, even my knuckles, were calloused. I looked over at his, draped down with his notebook and pencil just hanging in them. His hands were calloused too, maybe even rougher than mine.

"I think we do understand each other. Right from the start, I think we understood each other," I said and met his gaze. "I think you're probably one of the only people who has always understood me without me needing to explain it."

"Adam?" He asked.

"He understands, but because everyday is full of questions that I answer," I explained honestly. "He's interested in me, and in life, and the world around him - all that is something I need from a life partner, but he doesn't look at me and know my heart's contents without it being spoken."

Ethan was silent as he stared at me. Out of the corner of my eye I could see his fist balling around his pen and unballing. His skin went white as he gripped it tight and then would flush back to his sun kissed ivory colour. I saw the skin of his knuckles fade back and forth at least twelve times before he spoke again.

"I've always seen you, E," he said like it was painfully matter-of-fact. "Just so we're clear. Before Adam fell in love with you in the woods, I saw you." He paused to breathe and I felt his hot breath fan across my cheeks, making me blissfully aware of how close his face was to mine. "Even after, I still saw you. But Adam is my best friend and he claimed you first, so I'll keep what I *see* to myself."

I shifted uncomfortably, and, of course, he immediately noticed.

He pulled back, putting as much space between us as he could without getting up and moving. My shoulder and side were suddenly cold as he took his body away from it. I hadn't realised we had been sitting with every inch of our sides pressed together until there was nothing but cool air where he had been.

"Sorry," he hissed like I had just struck him in the face. "I didn't mean to make you uncomfortable."

"I made myself uncomfortable by not being uncomfortable with what you said, and then I felt guilty because your words don't make me uncomfortable," I countered. "So then, it's not you who makes me uncomfortable, but my guilt that makes me uncomfortable."

"That's a lot of discomfort," he chuckled.

He leaned back, our shoulder's brushing against each other again and the heat coming back to me. We sat in silent warmth for a few moments, and I listened closely to the sound of both of us breathing the same air.

"Why do you feel guilty?" His voice was low and tight, like he was waiting for something to jump out of the darkness and attack us right then.

I leaned in like I had no control over what I was doing. I could smell him; he smelt like smoke and warm scotch straight from the barrel, with a strong note of cedar wood. I liked it. I liked it alot, so I drank it in and settled down into his shoulder. My forehead pressed into the crook of his neck, his hair tickling my forehead and the crease by my eye.

"I feel guilty for the same reason that you have always kept silent," I whispered into his warm body. "Adam is your best friend."

Ethan

Erika dozed off leaning into me. She was blissfully warm and smelt like warm vanilla and jasmine. I turned my head to gently nestled my face into her hair. I pressed a kiss onto her crown.

"I'll always be here for you, okay?" I whispered down to her, knowing she couldn't hear me, but wishing she could. "I'll be whatever you need me to be."

I leaned my head back against the rock behind me and accidentally dozed off.

In my dream, I woke up in a snow covered forest. Off to my right, just beyond a snow bank, I could see the orange glow and rising smoke of a fire. I began walking towards it, not ignoring the fact that I was only in a pair of basketball shorts and a t-shirt, no shoes, and yet I still felt warm.

As my bare feet shuffled through the snow and I crested over the snow bank, I looked down at a small clearing. In the

278

centre there was a man with white hair. He had a well trimmed beard and golden eyes. He was wrapped in a white and gold cloak, sitting on a log by the fire.

Behind him, there was a small pitched tent made up of a white cloth with golden suns on it, and two sticks to hold it up. A long, metal spear had been set upon two tall stick so that it could reach across the fire in front of him. An iron cauldron had been hung from the spear and a heavenly smelling stew was steaming from it.

"Would it be rude if I asked 'who the fuck are you?'" I called down to the man.

"Yes!" he shouted back.

He leaned forward and stirred the pot, not sparing me a second glance.

I chuckled and made my way down. As the man settled back down onto his log, I took up the one next to him.

He eyed me closely and I drew one foot up onto the wood, hugging my thigh to my chest as a bit of cold began to settle into my bones.

"Hmm," the man started. "You are not who I expected."

I looked at him with my eyebrows raised. "I didn't expect anyone, so you're at least doing better than me."

His face drew into a scowl. "My soul is hers now. Between you and the other human, you were not the one I expected to be allowed in."

I looked around, waiting for something or someone to come over one of the snow banks and tell me what the hell was going on. But instead, the only thing I heard was the crackling of the fire, and the only thing I saw was this white haired, wise looking old man with a stick.

"I'm asleep aren't I?" I asked him.

He nodded slowly once.

279

"This is your first time touching her?" he asked.

I shook my head. "No?"

"Then this is your first time falling asleep beside her?"

I sighed and crossed my arms.

"Yeah. That one's true. She's in love with my best friend."

"There are different forms of love, you know?" he peered over at me then, and I caught the true glow of his eyes. "There's love that's all feeling and passion. It makes you feel alive and young. Then there's the opposite end of the spectrum, a love that's practical. It exchanges what the parties need in order to satisfy them long-term and help them grow. Both are excellent types of love, but they lack what the other can offer. A true life-partner, a true-love if you will, should be able to possess both of those key features," he explained. "I won't deny that she loves him. I will simply say that the love she holds for him is only on one end of the spectrum. They have the passion and he makes her feel alive, but he cannot empathise with her, he cannot protect her, he cannot stand next to her and look as strong as she does when she leads armies into battle."

He stoked the fire some more before he threw the stick in completely. Then he settled one hand into his lap, and the other onto his small white beard. He stroked it thoughtfully.

"Son," he cleared his throat and looked at me directly. "You are here, and he is not. I can feel how much you don't believe me. But hopefully that reminder will be enough for you to realise that your lifetime of waiting is not going to last much longer."

The dream didn't fade out, but rather ended in an abrupt rush of darkness, followed enjoyably by the scent of jasmine.

I rolled my head back up and blinked the tired out of my gaze. When my vision cleared, Condan was standing at my feet, staring down at me with his creepy eye.

I jumped to my feet, shocking Erika awake as I went.

"Fuck no," I snapped. "I'm not doing this shit again. One night of frostbite is enough."

Erika stood up next to me. She softly reached around me, putting her hand on my core and nudging my back so that she could stand between me and the icey prick.

The rest of the camp shifted in their sleeping bags until, slowly but surely, we had four pairs of eyes looking over at us with sleep crust still gathering in their hung-over gazes.

"What's up Condan?" Erika asked, her voice hoarse from sleep.

Condan cocked his head at me like my reaction was anything less than expected.

"I need to relieve myself in a manner than is not fitting close proximity to the camp," he said.

"You woke us up to announce you have to shit?" Jack groaned. "You can literally form earth with your mind. Summon a hole, let it go, then send it down into the depths."

"I don't believe in desecrating nature like that," Condan said, then looked back at me. "Plus, after our experience with Grendel, I would appreciate someone looking out for me in such a vulnerable time."

Adam sat up. "Battle buddy pairs does seem like a pretty good idea to me. Erika and I are on next watch, we can start it now while you two go handle things."

Erika looked back at me, turning her head so quickly that her hair nearly flicked me in the face. We locked eyes and she didn't even have to say anything; she didn't want me alone with

Condan. I wasn't about to argue either, *I* didn't want to be alone with Condan.

She looked over at Darbie, but he was already slumping back down into bed, no doubt still a little tired after going full depletion.

When Darbie was no help, she looked back at me. I could see the tension in her shoulders. We were being diplomatic, Condan seemed like the type of character who would seek petty revenge on those who insulted him, and we were walking a fine line to avoid disrespecting him by revealing the level of distrust we harboured.

"Alright," I said, hardening myself in order to put Erika at ease. "We'll be back soon."

Erika's lips parted. Her eyes were fixed on mine while I gathered up my axe and travel pack.

"Surely you won't need all your belongings for a quick visit into the woods?" Condan asked.

He was looking at me, cocking his head to the side and furrowing his eyebrows like he was confused. But the relaxed line on his lips mixed with the lack of curiosity in his eyes let me know that he had already gauged my hesitation.

All the warning signals in my body were going off. Condan was acting coy and I didn't know why. He was playing some sort of game with me, trying to get me away from the pack.

"Just your weapon should be more than enough," he insisted. "You can watch my back while I do what I need and then if you're in need of the same favour, I can return it."

Erika shifted forward. "Maybe I should go with you both as well. It took all three of us to take on Grendel. There are worse things than him in these woods, you two could use another person."

282

Condan reached out and put a soft hand on Erika's shoulder.

"We'll be fine, Erika," he assured her, his voice friendlier than ever. "We won't be gone long at all, I assure you. I'll watch his back as he will watch mine."

"But-" she started.

"No buts," he shushed her, then turned to me. "Come, the quicker we leave and are done, the quicker we can come back and rest."

He turned and began walking into the darkness of the woods.

I looked over at Erika who was looking at me with pursed lips and distress lines all over her scrunched forehead.

I dropped my pack to the ground. I shifted the heavy axe in my hand. It had been about a week since I had last used it, and after using Erika's sword earlier, I was very aware of the density of the weapon. Her dragon sword was light, almost like grasping a feather. And it could cut through air, it was so sharp. Now, I just felt like I was holding a bat, or some other bludgeoning weapon.

"I'll be back in a few minutes," I promised her. "Keep the fire warm for me."

Her jaw clenched and I could see the muscle just underneath her ears flexing as she clenched her jaw.

"Be careful," she said. "There are a lot of unpredictable monsters out there."

I didn't say anything. There was another pit in my stomach, similar to the one I had before in the trolly cars. Only this time, it churned up acid in my belly and sent ice across my shoulders.

Condan was already several paces ahead of me, and I had to take quick strides in order to catch up.

"Hey!" I called. "Wait up."

He didn't glance back at me as he continued to wander off.

"I want to get away from the light of the fire," he said.

I was a step or two behind him, walking quickly, but still not catching up. Despite seeming like he was walking at a leisurely pace, he was moving quickly over the rolling terrain.

"I really don't think that's necessarily," I said. "They're not going to be looking out into the darkness trying to catch a glimpse of your ass."

He chuckled. "I'm not worried about that. I don't doubt that they're not looking. I more so worry about the smell and the sound."

I looked over my shoulder, hoping to still be able to see the light of the fire, but I couldn't. I couldn't even hear the fire or the voices of my friends.

In fact, I couldn't hear anything. And everything around us was different and... moving? Even though I was walking, it seemed like the trees behind us were receding at a much faster rate than the speed of my stride.

I stopped walking to see if my eyes deceived me. They weren't. The patch of land around us was moving away from our camp at a rapid rate.

"How far away have you sent us?" I snapped, turning back to look at Condan.

As I spun, a sharp pain erupted in my neck, it was enough to knock me on my back. Ice enveloped my throat as I fell to the ground. I tried to yell for my friend, but my airway felt like it was frozen solid.

"I hope you know I won't apologise for this," Condan said, his voice like velvet and the satisfied grin on his mouth like a string of pearls. "I needed someone they would blindly chase

284

after. From what I can tell, you're the only one they'd throw caution to the wind for."

I started to rise to my feet, my grip tight on my axe and ready to take a few of his limbs.

An ice bolt formed out of thin air by his head. He didn't even need to flinch to send it flying down at me. I watched it, expecting it to strike me in the chest, but instead it struck through my leg. It punched its way right through the bone and out the back of my upper calf. I dropped to my side. Letting go of the axe, I reached out to grasp my leg. The skin on the sides of my it was the only thing holding the bottom half to my knee. All tendons and bone had been obliterated by the spear of ice.

I tried to scream out in pain, but my throat was still frozen shut.

My vision started blurring like it did before as freezing cold pain shot through my entire body. I began to shiver as a cold sweat broke out over my entire body.

Between the black spots clouding my eyes, I could see Condan leisurely moving towards me. I struggled to look up so that I could glare at his face.

"I tried to tell you," he said. "I wouldn't kill you, I respect you too much for that. I'd just maim you instead."

Behind him, I watched an icy portal open up. The gateway glowed bright white, filling the world around us with light. The magickal holler of it's churning transportative power was as loud as a hurricane. Wherever he was going, the weather was horrible.

I could hear my friends shouting in the distance then. An arrow whistled by Condan's head and he looked over the horizon, annoyed.

"Time to go," he said, then crouched down and hoisted me over his shoulder.

285

I raised my arm and pounded on his back, but it might as well have been a pat. All of my joints were tightening up with pain.

He spun around, and for a split second, I faced towards my friend, who I could see like specs in the distance, running over the rising and falling of the earth's floor. Then he stepped through the frigid portal and they were gone.

We stepped through into the basement of Darbie house. Following our safe entry, the portal behind us closed

The portal-painting, still encased in glass sat to our right - the door leading up into the house to our left.

Condan turned towards the left and walked up the stairwell.

"We need to get some new recruits," he explained. Whoever is left can burn with the rest of this house."

I grunted, my vision nearly gone, but my hearing still clinging on.

"After we're done with your home, my friend," he continued to speak. "I'll show you my old one. I think it would make a great setting to trick the light dragon and her friends into chasing after you. Oh, I'm so excited. You and I can have some wonderful bonding time while we wait for them."

16

Erika

The portal was gone long before I got there, but the ice it left behind *smelled*. I rubbed the thin, long, crystalline flakes between my fingers. They smelt like salt water, and froze in choppy sheets like the wind was slicing through the air as they formed.

I let the droplets fall to my feet as the rest of my friends caught up to me.

"He took him somewhere near the ocean," I said, turning back to look at them.

"Can you gather anything else?" Jack asked, half out of breath.

His eyes were scanning around the area. Darbie already had his staff out and was roaming it over the ground around us to see if there was anything magickal we couldn't see that he could pick up. Adam walked past me, my sword in his hand, and started looking around the area beyond us. Reika stood at the edge of the area, watching.

"I can only smell the saltiness in the ice crystals," I explained further. "And the shape of each one of them gives me the impression that it's somewhere humid and windy."

"Well that leaves a lot of potential places," Jack snapped.

"Do you think he would have taken him back home?" Adam asked before I could snap at Jack for his tone of voice.

I looked back at my boyfriend. "Maybe, I get the feeling that Condan has other places he holds closer to his heart than Scotland though. And I really don't want to dedicate all our time getting back to the portal just to be wrong. If we can figure out where he went then we can find a closer portal to travel with and save more time and magick."

"We can summon a gate right to him if we can figure out where he went," Darbie said, finishing his sweep and standing his staff up next to him. "It'll take a lot of magick, but it will also give us a potential advantage. I don't think he would expect us to drop in right on top of him."

I nodded. "I agree. I think if we portal home, it's gonna tire you out and you won't be able to summon another one if we figure out where he went after the fact."

"We should get to Artemis then," Reika said.

We all stopped moving.

She was standing still, not helping in diagnosing where our friend went. Instead, she was looking off in the direction of her temple. Her bow was still drawn, and it was pulsing with light like a tracker getting close to its mark.

I looked behind me at Adam. He was still knelt on the ground, my sword now laying next to him. His fingernails had dirt underneath them, letting me know he had been poking around in hopes of finding something.

He looked up at me and shrugged.

We had already established a sense of trust with the demi-goddess by this point. Now it was just a matter of if we had enough faith in her to waste time galavanting into the forest to find her goddess.

288

"Why?" Jack was the one to question it, his tone still as bitchy as it was with me.

Reika glared at him, clearly not appreciating his tone either. "She's the goddess of the hunt. If anyone can track our friend, it will be her."

"Even through a portal?" Darbie asked.

Reika nodded. "I assume so. I've never seen Artemis use her power to track a man, only animals here in the forest, but she is the best, I promise."

Darbie looked between Adam and I. He glanced over at Jack who let out an exasperated sigh, and turned away. Then his gaze returned to us.

"Okay," I said. "You lead the way. Go as fast as you can, we'll keep up."

Reika didn't hesitate to step off. She jogged through the forest, moving around the rises and falls of the horribly uneven ground. Jack was the second one after her, then, after he had banished his staff, Darbie was on their trail.

I turned to Adam. "I'll take up the rear."

He nodded and ran after them. Watching him from behind, I couldn't help but notice how heavy my weapon looked in his hand, and suddenly I felt bad. I was always the one who pushed him to take on the dragon armour and the sword. It was the strongest material he could ever wield, making me think he would be safe. But it was also heavy weaponry. Adam was more of an adventure, an observer, or a historian. A bow would probably have been better for him, like Reika.

I shook my head.

I could deal with that later. Figuring out what Adam fought best with was never going to be a priority so long as one of our own was missing.

The temple was not what I had expected. As we approached it, I could only see the faintest hint of a gate overgrown with the surrounding forest, giving the impression that the temple itself would be mostly nature and less manmade structure. But as we went through the marble columns, we found ourselves overlooking a city rather than a temple.

The forest ended at a cliff that surrounded a round trench filled with a network of dirt roadways and several small marble temples each of ancient Greek design. In the centre, a circular colosseum rose up in distracting grandeur, and just behind it, raised so as to look over everything, there was a rectangular temple just as tall, but not as large as the colosseum. It was built up against the cliff behind it, and roots from the tree system above had grown out of the cliff and begun wrapping around the roof of the temple, until new smaller trees were rising off the top of the temple like green steeples.

"Holy shit," Adam whispered under his breath.

Reika was already beginning to descend down stairs built into the cliff face.

"Come on!" she called as she descended. "Artemis is going to be in her altar on the other side of the colosseum, we have to hurry to get across the entire temple."

"This isn't a temple," Darbie said. "It's a whole city."

I stepped to the edge and looked down, making a mental note that we were going down about fifty or so stories without any railings to keep us on the stairwell.

I looked across to the temple again.

It also meant that a temple twenty or so stories tall was built in the otherworld… Away from humans… In the middle of the forest away from civilization… By a goddess who hated men and preferred animals over people…

I watched my three male friends as they quickly but carefully followed our new friend down the questionable staircase.

I had a horrible feeling that we were not going to like what we found here. But just like with Adam and my sword, I had other priorities to worry about.

I followed down the cliff-face. In front of me, everyone was huffing, trying to catch their breath after the miles we ran to get here and now the uneven shuffling down a rock stairwell cut into a sheer drop off.

If the running wasn't enough to get our heart rates up, the imminent threat of death to our right was.

At the base of the stairs, Jack and Adam stopped to catch their breath.

Reika stopped to look back at them.

"We don't have time to stop and breathe," Reika snapped.

"Yeah, well some of us have to, lady," Jack snapped.

Darbie moved closer to Reika, both of whom looked at me.

"The more time we waste, the more evidence fades away, the less Artemis can use to find Ethan," Reika said. "We need to move."

I nodded. I didn't disagree, but Jack and Adam were human and they had just finished running a half-marathon - part of which were terrifying stairs. They needed a break, and I needed to get Ethan back.

"Alright," I said, finally settling on a plan. "Reika, take me the rest of the way to see Artemis. We'll come back for them."

"Hell no." Darbie stepped forward, blocking me from Reika. "Did we not learn anything from this? We're not splitting up again."

"We need to move, now," I emphasised.

Darbie gritted his teeth, but waved his staff in the air regardless, summoning his bag, which fell a foot or so in the air before he caught it in his hand. He began to shuffle through it, as he walked towards the two panting boys.

He withdrew a bright red bottle and handed it down to them.

"Drink half each," he said. "Don't ask too many questions, just know we'll have to deal with some consequences later."

Adam took it from him and downed half. No hesitation. He then handed it over to Jack who shook his head adamantly.

"I'm not taking it until I know what these consequences are," Jack snapped.

"The consequences are, our friend potentially dies if we don't toughen up," Adam was nearly shouting at him. "Now shut up and drink it, or else we'll leave you here and go save Ethan without you. If I have to choose between abandoning a friend who had no choice and one who does, I'll be going after the one without the choice, thanks."

Jack shut his mouth hard enough that I heard his teeth clap together. He looked around at all of us and, realising he had no allies in this matter, took the bottle from Adam. He finished it, and without letting him dispose of it, we all turned and headed off.

The sound of glass shattering behind me didn't even cause me to look behind. We were all too focused on Reika and her rapid movements into the city.

Once we were past the first ring of smaller, domed temples, we began to see priestesses. Many of them were only wrapped in white tunics that fell at their calves, pinned together with silver crescent moons. A few others had bows and quivers just like Reika, their tunis falling mid-thigh, showing off buskin shoes - their toes out, but their shins and the top of their feet covered with hardened leather.

Reika kept us amongst the shadows, causing my concern to rise. None of the other priestesses had seen us yet as we ran along the outer rings, slowly looping in towards the temple at the back.

As we came about halfway to the large altar, the outer rings opened up into a small flat courtyard. A fountain well was pouring out ambrosia and water and several priestesses in the longer tunics were gathered there, filling up tall ceramic vases.

We slowed to a walk as we came into the courtyard. We had already caught their attention by the sounds of our feet, and now their eyes were growing so large as they realised three men were present, I feared their eyes were going to fall from their heads.

I took a breath.

I could hear my heart beating firmly in my chest.

Badum.

Badum.

Badum.

It took longer than I expected. But then again, the priestesses had probably never had men come into their temple before, and even though they knew males weren't allowed, they likely had never had to react to it.

"Men!!" One shrieked and then the others followed suit, screaming and dropping their pitchers, leaving them to shatter on the ground.

293

They ran off, yelling amongst the streets.

"Run!" Reika shouted back at us and suddenly we were sprinting.

I hung back, letting the guys move in front of me so that they could be protected from the front and the back. As soon as they were ahead, I fell in, glancing over my shoulder constantly.

It didn't take long before priestesses in short tunics were moving in behind us and beside us, firing arrows towards the lads in the middle.

I took great care not to hit any of them, only lighting their arrows on fire midair so that they could never find their mark.

A larger, silver arrow arched through the sky from an unknown origin. It cascaded downwards, billowing through the smoke and flames of my fire and the surrounding ashen arrows of the other priestesses. Nonetheless, it still came down.

Instead of fire, I pulled both arms back, then pushed them forward, sending a sheet of air through the sky, pushing it off course and into a cliff to the left of us.

Three more silver arrows flew into the air in quick succession and I repeated the same movement. When another volley came through, backed by fifty or so normal arrows, I snapped.

"Fuck this," I hissed and summoned a gust of wind to pitch me into the air.

As I flew, I sprayed fire and air, sending the attacks into oblivion. I rose through the line of smoke left behind, and looked down into the city to see two lines of archers, with Artemis standing behind them.

She almost seemed larger than the rest of the women, standing there in her glowing silver robes and armour. She looked like she was wearing the moon, with stars trapped inside the glowing metal of her chest plate. Her bow was made of white wood, the silver string hummed back and forth with magick, and as she drew it back, a silver arrow formed. It started off as a ball of white light in the centre, like a star, then stretched out until it was hooked into the draw string, with its tip pointed straight at me.

I changed my direction so that I was flying straight towards her. She let her arrow fly. As it sprung towards me, I had just enough time to roll my eyes and grind my teeth together in annoyance before stretching my arm and fingers out in order to catch the heavy thing in my grasp.

I brought myself down right in front of the line of priestesses, all who had their arrows trained on me. As soon as my feet hit the ground, I was marching towards them. I melted the magick star arrow in my hand and splattered the liquid metal off to the side.

Artemis eyes grew at the sight of this. Her bow faltered in her hands, and she let them fall just enough to leave her centre exposed. I could see the sudden hitch in her breath as she watched me.

Now that I was up close, she was beginning to recognize who I was.

"Enough, Artemis," I bellowed across her ranks. "We need your help. And you can either give it to us or not, but either way we don't give a shit about your petty rules."

Her nostrils flared and her face was overcome with anger.

"Petty rules?" she screeched and notched another arrow.

She let it fly, and this time I both wanted to test Ethan's theory as well as prove a point to the goddess. So I stood there, not moving, and let her weapon make contact with my chest.

It slammed into my body, causing pain to advance through me, but it didn't penetrate. Instead, the tip shattered as the end of it tried to push its way through, and as more of the metal came into contact with my skin, it rapidly grew red from heat before melting down over me.

The hot, melted metal dripped off my clothes with steam and smoke billowing up as it fell in large goops by my feet.

Now, every priestess was faltering. Bows were no longer raised out in front of them ready to fire at will, instead they were hesitantly cradled at sides or in front of them. Nervous whispers were exchanged amongst their rows.

"Go on," I commanded confidently, without feeling the need to raise my voice. "Fire another shot at me. See how far my patience runs."

"You're supposed to be dead, Erika of the Druids," Artemis all but spat at me.

I chuckled. "Well it's not the first time."

"Just because you aren't dead now, doesn't mean you won't be soon," she hissed. "Bringing men into my temple is punishable by death."

I rolled my eyes.

Behind me, I could hear the scuffling of feet. I turned around to see my friend bounding and being dragged in by a squad of women. Knives held to their throats, and thick cords around their wrists.

I wasn't rolling my eyes any more. Now I was trying not to cringe at my stupidity.

In my cockiness, I had left my friends, assuming that showcasing my power would end this quickly and get us to the next step. I hadn't thought about the fact that I would be abandoning my friends - my weakness - leaving them exposed for Artemis to capture.

I looked back at her, keeping my confidence - now a facade - at it's high.

"Let them go," I said. "Like I said, you're either going to help us and then we'll leave, or you're not and then we'll leave even quicker. Either way, I don't give a shit about your sexism."

"Sexism?" she scoffed.

"Still don't know what that is," Reika called quietly behind me.

If there hadn't been so much tension in the air, I would have laughed.

Artemis pushed through the ranks in front of her. "You accuse me of being sexist? I'm not sexist, I merely know how men are."

She was in front of me now. Close enough that I could have punched her in the face if I wanted to... Well I did want to, but I knew I shouldn't, so I didn't.

Instead, I stepped out wide so that she could see the men behind me. I motioned my arm over them, taking a quick glance to take in their appearances. None of them looked injured, which was good, because if they were, I definitely would have punched her.

"You say all men are horrible, all men are sex-greedy pigs, but these three are prime examples of how you're wrong," I said. "For one thing, two of them don't even find women sexually appealing and therefore have no interest in you or your priestesses. And the other was a virgin before he dated me and has only been with me since, so, sorry, but you're wrong. Making you kinda sexist."

Artemis summoned an arrow and pointed it at Adam. "I'll kill him nonetheless."

I snapped my fingers and my sword animated into my hand. I pressed the blade against Artemis's neck until it poked through her skin, drawing the smallest stream of blood.

"Kill him and I kill you," I seethed.

"Kill me and my priestesses kill all your friends, including my ward," she said back.

I squeezed the hilt of my sword. We were glaring each other down through the sides of our gaze, neither one of us willing to back down.

"Trial by combat!!" Reika shouted. "A threat against life has been made. We request a trial by combat to see who fate favours more."

Artemis chuckled. "You propose that she fight me in exchange for, what? Your lives?"

"And your help," I added. Artemis looked at me with disgust, but I continued nonetheless, figuring she'd still make a deal she found disgusting if the pot was sweet enough. "If I beat you, you help us track our friend across worlds *and* let us go. If you beat me, you can kill who you want or keep who you want as lifelong slaves."

Artemis's eyes crinkled in the corner and a satisfied smile curled on her lips.

Artemis was a lot like Condan. She blamed others for her issues and felt that if everything went according to how she wanted, things could be perfect. In her world, women would rule over everything, and men would be decimated to a handful of whom would be kept alive for breeding purposes only.

She thought that men were the source of destruction and oppression, which I found very ironic considering she wanted to destroy and oppress them more than they even gave a single damn about her.

Nonetheless, if she won in trial by combat and had Reika and I as slaves to carry out her bidding, she would have enough fire power behind her to potentially carry out that dream of hers.

"Fine," she said and dropped her bow. "Trial by combat. If you win I will help you and you all go free. When I win, the men die and you and Reika become mine to command as I deem fit."

"Deal," I let my sword disappear so that I could outstretch my hand to her.

She took it, and with the motion, binding rings burned into our backs and shoulders.

We both winced as they singed under our clothes. And once they were done, we let go.

Artemis stepped back, a smirk still plastered on her face.

Fucking gods, I thought. *They're always so cocky, even when they've already been beat.*

"Take the prisoners to the holding cell in the stand," Artemis called over my shoulder to her minions. "I want them to see this fight." She focused her attention back to me. "And I'll let Reika show you our armoury. No outside weapons are allowed, no magick, and we fight until the other is disarmed and dominated." She spun around, happily about to walk off.

"Define dominated," I yelled at her back.

She turned around, even more annoyed now than she was before.

"As is you, flat on your back, with my spear pointed at your throat."

The massive colosseum was just that, a *massive* colosseum. The Greeks were always a big fan of amphitheatres, but the grandeur of this one was definitely much more on the level of the Romans had the Romans had access to magick like the priestesses here did.

The ground was rough dirt, well compacted from the lack of use. Archways around the stage floor had iron gates built into them that were rusted. Even the one that led out from the armoury required Reika and I to combine our strength in order to shoulder our way through.

Above, the stands consumed at least a whole story of height. On the same side of the colosseum that Artemis's altar stood behind, was a decorated and covered patio with a white marble throne that sat empty. Just to the side of it, Adam, Darbie and Jack sat in a thick, rusted iron cage.

Darbie and Adam leaned into the bars, looking down at me, while Jack leaned against the side, his arms crossed over his chest as he pouted.

In the back of my mind, I was worried about them. Not just because they were locked in a cage, but because of what Darbie had fed them. If I had to guess, it was liquid sun, a drink from egyptian warlocks. It was blood from the god Ra, and would temporarily give the consumers more power and strength, but eventually that part would begin wearing off and they would begin to feel like they were burning from the inside out.

If I had to guess, we had twenty-four hours before they were going to need magickal medical attention that we couldn't provide here. We'd need to be home, surrounded by Darbie's equipment for that.

I sighed.

Yet another thing that had to be written onto the to-do list underneath the problem at hand.

Artemis was finally coming out into the amphitheatre. Her ladies cheered in excitement. Reika, who was standing in the shadow of the throne, just next to the cage, shifted uncomfortably, but waved down to me and offered an awkward thumbs up nonetheless.

I turned away and watched my opponent.

300

Artemis had chosen a spear as her weapon, just as she had indicated earlier. She was still in her moon armour, which was clearly magickal, but I wasn't about to say anything.

This was her kingdom, she made the rules. And even if I called her out for unfair attire, it really wasn't that unfair. I had figured out that metal didn't stand a chance against my skin. It still hurt like a bitch to get hit, but I took no piercing damage. I wasn't going to be bleeding out any time soon, and I healed quickly enough that I wasn't really concerned with internal bleeding.

I had opted for a sword. My parents taught me how to use one, and I honed the craft during my time as a soldier. Even though it wasn't my personal blade, it still felt comfortable in my grasp.

"Today we witness the beginning of a change for our temple," Artemis began a speech. She went in on how for centuries men had oppressed them - she was about to say something about when she won there'd be a new era, but I didn't listen. Reika had told me the rules, and showed me the commandments that were etched into the walls of the armoury as well as into the walls around the amphitheatre.

There were several rules, but the only one I cared about: once both opponents were in the fighting stage, the fight was on.

I had strided forward, and planted a solid front kick into Artemis's side. She was flung down to her side with such a force that she dug into the ground and slid back, breaking up the compacted dirt into a patch of sand.

She shot to her knee and scoffed. "How dare you?"

"Thought you followed your rules," I chidded. "Once both fighters are here, the game's on."

She shook her head, now rising to her feet. "You're foolish to anger me. Even more so to opt out of armour."

I arched the sword down, flicking my wrist at the bottom so that it would roll up over my finger, making a full rotation before slipping back into my grasp, a small display of proficiency.

"Armour would just slow me down," I said.

She lunged, her spear thrusting forward towards my belly. I scooped my blade around in front of me, catching the spear and forcing it away. I spun into the now open space between Artemis and myself. I held my sword above my head, locking the spear up and over me so that Artemis couldn't bring it down to try to strike me. Once I was tucked safely into Artemis's blind spot, I pulled my sword back, slicing it downwards so that I could cut across Artemis's lower half.

My blade met first with the bottom of her chest plate, before it slid out, cutting through the side of her tunic, and leaving a large, deep gash from her hip to the back of her thigh.

Her lunge then turned into a stumble and she fell forward onto a knee.

Had I not been short on time, I would have been respectful and waited until she was standing and facing me again. But I didn't have the time. I advanced as she was struggling to her feet.

She noticed this, and quickly tried to swing the spear like a bat, hoping, no doubt, to catch me by surprise and knock me off my feet. But she was merely underestimating my experience.

I brought my sword up and stepped aside so that I could catch her metal against mine. I finished my last step as our weapons collided. I was within striking distance now. I let go of my sword with my right hand so that I could grab her spear and hold it there. With my left hand still gripping my weapon, I swept it down with enough force to cleave through her magick chest place.

Splinters of silver metal twinkled down from her body in a whimsical magickal spray. Blue blood from where the tip of my blade had dragged over her chest blossomed against the purity of her white tunic.

In a fit of pain, she let go of her spear to grab her chest. She fell back, blood running down her leg and now down her entire torso.

I flung my sword down at her so that the hilt would hit her in the face. It collided with the satisfying crunch of nose cartilage breaking. The sword bounced off her from the force, landing off to her side while she fell onto her back. Instead of reaching for it and fighting through the pain like a soldier would have, she held one hand against her chest, and gripped her nose with the other.

I flipped her spear over so that I could point it down at her.

I leisurely stepped forward until I was standing over her. She tried to begin to sit up, but I moved in, pressing the spear again.

"How did you define being dominated?" I asked facetiously. " 'You, flat on your back, with my spear pointed at your throat?' Does that sound about right?"

Artemis glared up at me as she leaned over to spit blood out of her mouth.

"Fine," she said, and I could see blood staining her teeth. "You win. You'll all go free."

I pressed the blade against her, drawing more blue blood.

"And I'll help you!" she added quickly and I withdrew the blade from her neck.

"I can't tell you where your friend has been taken to as he was pulled through a portal," Artemis said as we followed her into her altar. "But we have an oracle who can."

"She's lucky there was a but in that sentence," Jack whispered to Darbie behind me. "Because if there wasn't I was gonna vote we kill her for the fun of it."

I snapped around to look at him, completely shocked by the statement that came from his mouth.

Jack looked at me with an insulted scrunch of his nose. "She's bitchy and useless. Might as well get rid of her."

"I can hear you," Artemis called back.

Her voice echoed off the tall, dark walls of the temple. The entire structure was one long, spacious room. Three massive columns were spaced out on each side of the temple for no reason other than to frame in the four statues that made up the only thing inside the room. On each side, between the three pillars there were two marble carved animals. On the left, there was a doe and a lioness. On the right, there was a mother wolf and sheep.

"At the end of this sanctuary you'll find a stairwell that leads down into the depths underneath," Artemis explained. "At the bottom, you'll find our oracle. She'll tell you where and how to find your friend. She'll also likely tell you more things about yourself and your life that you don't wish to know, so enter under your own accord."

"You're not coming with us?" Adam asked from beside me.

Artemis stopped walking as we reached the first statues. We stood with the doe and the mother wolf both looking down on us.

Artemis handed Adam the torch in her hand and shook her head.

"Every time I visit the Oracle, she tells me things which I don't want to hear about myself as well," she said. "I don't make it a habit of going and visiting her unless I absolutely must. I'll wait up here, and when you're done, I'll make sure to have my chariot outfitted for you."

"The one that carries the moon across the sky?" Adam asked.

Artemis nodded at him then looked at me. "It will take you to whichever portal you wish, so you can get to your friend quicker. Then it will return to me. I will help you, but I refuse to let any more of my priestesses be at risk for you."

Reika pushed forward from the back of the group. "My lady," she spoke softly. "After they meet with the oracle, I would still like to go with them. They could use my help."

Artemis sighed. She looked between Reika and I. Then she closed her eyes, and nodded.

"Very well," she said when she had opened them again. "You are not a prisoner here. You can leave if you wish. But once you have, you will not be welcome again, just remember that."

I watched Reika. Sadness flashed across her eyes. Then fear. Before resolve settled into her shoulders and inside her gaze.

"I understand," she said, and looked at me.

I suppressed the proud smile that was tugging at my lips.

I turned and kept walking. Adam moved behind me, the light in his hands lapping at my feet. The sounds of the rest of us moving echoed back at us.

"If I could offer some advice," Artemis called. "Leave the men at the top of the stairs. The oracle is more *sexist* than I am."

I tossed a glance and a "thank you" back at the goddess before moving on.

At the other side of the altar, the white walls - washed grey in the darkness - revealed one small speck of golden open doorway. Inside, a set of stairs spiralled down into an unknown. Sconces casted warm light around as they followed the walls down.

At the doorway, Reika headed in while I stopped and looked back at my three remaining friends.

"Wait here," I said. "I know we shouldn't split up anymore, but we also need information."

"We know Erika," Darbie said, his voice serious. "Just hurry and come back."

I descended down after Reika. With each step we went, the air around us became filled with less golden glow and more smoke. It smelt like sage and burnt olive oil. As we neared the bottom, we were consumed in a thick blanket of smoke.

Reika recoiled back into me, and I caught her, encouraging her to move forward.

"It's making my eyes water," she hissed.

I nodded. "I know, but a few more steps and we'll be in another room and it'll mostly be above us. C'mon."

I didn't understand, smoke no longer bothered me. But she needed to be comforted just enough to keep going.

She waved her hand through the air. She clutched her eyes after and sunk to the ground next to my feet.

"No," she said. "You go ahead. Come get me when you're done. I need to head back up."

I let go and stepped over her. We didn't have time to argue.

A few more steps and I entered into a cavern around the same size as an olympic pool.

Several brass bowls ran down the centre of the space, each with a different type of flower or herb burning inside of it. A thin woman, barely wrapped in worn and torn blue robes, danced between the bowls, reaching into a sack on her hip and pulling out more plants to throw into the flames as she moved. She sung as she swept around the room, but her words were in ancient Greek and completed rhymes and I was quickly lost in their meaning.

A cloth, the same colour as her robes, was wrapped around her eyes, but she still managed to float around the room. She arched and spun between each standing bowl of flames until she eventually reached me.

I had been standing in the doorway. I hadn't said anything. I hadn't touched anything. I hadn't even moved. But she knew I was there.

She caught my hand in hers as she swooped by and she pulled me into her dance. I followed along stiffly as we curled around the room, spinning and twirling while she sung cheerfully and tossed things onto brass bowls.

On the fourth one, she pulled out a rose littered with thorns and slapped me with it, cutting my cheekbone and down across my lips. Then she threw it into the fire. Red smoke rose then, and she leaned in and pulled us around the bowl in circles while she inhaled the vapours deeply.

Then she pulled me along, moving the the next one. She pulled out a scorpion from her bag, and I immediately leaned away from her, but she brought him close to my hand that was still tightly in hers and he pinched me. She then chucked him, and the small piece of my flesh that was in his claws, into the fire. The flames turned purple and let off green smoke which she opened her mouth to swallow.

"Can I know-" I started, but she shushed me and pulled me on to the next bowl.

She pulled a diamond out of her bag next. She yanked my hand forward so that she could turn it over and placed the large gem against my palm. It consumed nearly all the space of my hand, but she managed to hold it in place, pointed end against my skin, with one hand. The other she drew back, and then slammed forward, slapping the back of the gem so that it would puncture my skin. Only it didn't, the unbreakable precious stone shattered to pieces.

The oracle smiled, catching some of the rough bits in her hand. Her teeth were brown and caked with layers of God-knows-what. I shivered in my skin at the sight of it.

She chuckled the dust and chunks of the diamond into the fire, which roared even higher. Everything turned white, from the flames, which grew to lick the ceiling above us, to the smoke, which covered the entirety of the top of the room, it all ran whiter than the tunics of the women outside.

"Hmm," the oracle hummed pleasantly. "Your friend will live, but at a cost. One life kept, for one life lost."

"Oh, not a fucking riddle," I muttered.

"A complex bond of love and brutality made," she continued. "And from its breaking with blood, all be saved."

"Okay, great," I huffed. "Where is he?"

"First in your home, to leave carnage and ash, then, in his own where ice and flesh shall clash. Deep in the forest, as black as him, you'll find the man already stained with sin. What will be worse is what you will bring, some things that die do not come back in spring."

She began to laugh deeply. I tried to ignore the shiver running down my spine.

"In the forest, as black as night," I noted to myself. "In his own home. Okay, so we'll need to figure out his history. Any other information on where to find Condan?"

"Two souls lost, and a body and a leg. You can't avoid it even if you beg." She continued rambling on. "Will it be worth it, this man that you save? Eventually, anyway, he will be your grave."

I shook the fear that was creeping in at her words.

"Alright," I said, turning to walk away. "We're done here."

But she snatched my hand, holding me in place with painful force.

"The book of life and the book of death, you'll find one engraved in his chest," she whispered, inches from my face. "One night in darkness as you two lie, you'll see your names declaring you die. You'll go beyond this mortal plane, as a sacrifice carrying out our blame. Kill the man you love and you'll be done. Break the outcome that he has spun."

She took a deep breath and straightened up. Then she breathed out smoke that was green, red and white. Letting go of my wrist, she stumbled backwards before falling to the ground, convulsing and singing the same song she was singing beforehand, one that I was beginning to realise was the rhyme she had just spoken to me, but in greek.

I back peddled out of the room quickly, bumping into a basin as I went and knocking it over, spilling the burnt rose and embers across the floor.

I sprinted up the stairwell, reaching Reika half way up. She looked down at me with concern as I ran.

"You okay?" she asked. "You seem distressed."

I swallowed the lump in my throat. "Yeah, I'm fine. She just had a lot to say and was super creepy."

"What did she say?"

I shook my head. "It was a riddle. Give me a few more seconds to commit it all to memory so I can make sure to get it right."

Reika looked above us, then back down to me. "We're almost at the top. Will thirty seconds be enough for you to remember before you have to tell the men? Because they'll be demanding."

I nodded. "Yeah, I'll be fine by then."

"Okay…" Reika hesitated, but carried on nonetheless.

At the top of the stairs, she was proved right. The lads saw us and immediately flocked to the doorway.

"What happened?" "What'd she say?" "Where are we going?" "Are you okay?"

It felt like a thousand questions being hurled at me. The world was spinning. Reika reached out and grabbed my forearms, helping me to the floor.

"Back off guys," Reika snapped. "It wasn't ideal conditions down there. Let her catch her breath."

"You seem okay," Jack pushed right back.

Reika glared over at him. "I couldn't even make it down the last flight of stairs through the door, that's how bad the air was. I have no idea what the oracle said."

I let my head fall in between my legs.

"It was a riddle," I said, head still down.

"Well then let's hear it," Jack said. "We'll need time to decipher it."

"Hey," Darbie hushed. "Back off. We won't get anything done taking our anger out on each other."

Adam knelt down next to me and began rubbing my back. I leaned into his hand and looked up.

"There's a lot more to what she said than just his location, there's also situational information, so I'm gonna say it all so that we can decide what to do, okay?" I asked.

Everyone mumbled in agreement.

"Okay," I breathed in, hardening my heart against the words I was about to recite. "'Your friend will live, but at a cost. One life kept for one life lost. A bond of love and brutality made. And from it breaking with blood, all be saved.' That's the preceding part, when I asked where he was she said 'In your home, to leave chaos and ash. Then in his own, for ice and flesh to clash. Deep in the forest as black as him, you'll find this man already stained in sin.'"

"Deep in the forest as black as him," Darbie echoed and immediately set to pacing.

"She also said 'what will be worse if what you bring. Some things that don't live in spring,' or something like that," I added. "'Two souls lost, and a body and a leg, you can't avoid it even if you beg.'"

"Oh joy, two of us are gonna die and someone's losing a leg," Jack laughed bitterly.

Reika held her hands up. "Calm down, not necessarily. These things are always way more complicated than they sound. Condan has an elf and dragon soul in him, maybe it's his soul and his body that die."

"That line doesn't say anything about dying," Adam argued. "All it says is 'somethings that die don't live in spring,' might be referring to a plant, or something about the foliage where we're going."

"Or it means one of us is dying and not coming back," Jack snapped.

"The black forest!" Darbie shouted and we all looked over at him. "I would lay money that he's in the black forest."

311

"Like Germany?" Adam asked.

Darbie nodded. "Yes, there are several castles and ruins in there that would have existed around when the dark elves were still alive and living on earth. He likely has a castle out there somewhere, at the very least it's the perfect place to hide because there's so many magick types amongst the woods."

"Okay, so we find a portal that dumps us out into the dark forest?" Adam started to plan. "We have some artefacts at home that can point us in the direction of the strong magickal pull in the area. we should stop there beforehand."

"We need to go home anyway," Darbie said. "I need to get some liquid moon to counteract the liquid sun you and Jack drank earlier."

"Can't that wait?" Reika asked.

Darbie shook his head. "No. They have less than half a day before they're consumed in debilitating burning pain."

Jack looked at his partner and blinked, face flat. Darbie raiseed his hand in surrender.

"I was just trying to keep you both moving," the elf defended himself.

Jack said nothing, and just turned back to me. "Let's get a move on back home then, shall we?"

"Only hiccup," Adam stopped us. "When we get home, how do we get to the black forest without having to take a plane? We don't exactly have the time for public transportation?"

"I can portal us to my old house there," Darbie offered. "We'll pick up some dried cucurbits from my stash at home so I can have enough energy for a fight."

"So we have a plan and we have our heading," Jack said. "Now can we go?"

"You all still want to go even when the oracle made it sound like someone's gonna die?" I asked.

The three men all shrugged.

"Someone always dies," Darbie said casually.

"Yeah," Adam agreed. "We're kinda used to it by now. Normally it's not one of us."

"And if it is, normally it's you," Jack added.

"And normally you come back," Darbie said.

Adam nodded along.

17

Ethan

I have officially decided I don't like the cold. Or the dark. From now on I will sleep with a heater and a night light.

My hands were drawn up above me. Thick chains, beaten and formed into lopsided ovals, were clamped onto my wrists. Frigid water ran down them, catching the rust that caked the old metal, and running down my forearms. Cool liquid ran over my arms, to my shoulders and down my back causing my body to wrack with cold shivers. Annoying droplets fell onto my head in inconsistent patterns. I tried to look and see where the water was flowing from, only to have more splash into my vision - the rust burning my eyes and forcing me to look away.

There was no longer any pain in my leg. Instead, I couldn't feel it.

If I looked down, I could see the mutilated tissue. My bone was exposed, and the fleshy part of my muscle was hanging off my skin in some places. The area around it was black and purple, and small crystals of ice gathered along the edges of the open hole in my limb.

I threw up the first time I saw it.

Then I passed out.

When I came-to for the second time, and stared down at it once more, I dry heaved, but with nothing on my stomach, nothing but spit came.

The lower half of my calf and foot dangled uselessly from my knee. My other leg flexed painfully to try to keep me from having all my weight pull on the chains. I had been hoisted just high enough that only the very tip of my toes could reach the floor beneath me.

I risked a glance up to my hands.

The rough edges of the cuffs had already rubbed through my skin, and water-washed streams of blood were beginning to roll across my body from my wrists.

I sighed and let my head fall. I struggled to hold myself up on the edge of my foot. The room around me was nothing more than a cold, wet, rock-walled cavern, like a dungeon in a castle except with no cages.

There was a stairway in the far left corner from me. Next to it, along the opposite wall, Condan had a desk, with an ancient, dilapidated chest and what looked like thousands of notes stabbed to the stone wall behind it. Other notes in languages I couldn't read were scratched into the walls themselves around me. There were even words on the floor and the ceiling, like someone had been trapped in here before and left alone for years.

In the back corner, where I was, the single set of chains ran through loops mounted to the wall, secured with a hook at the end of the line which was mounted just next to the desk, on the opposite side of the stairway.

Beneath me, the floor had been rubbed smooth, as if hundreds of people had been in my exact position; barely dangling enough to scrape the floor with their foot - sanding it down in the process.

Besides the water falling onto me, there was another consistent sound of water trickling somewhere else in the room.

315

I looked down only to find a small canal cut out of the ground around the edges of the room. It ran until it met with an iron grate at the end, just a few feet to the right of where the chain's hook was fastened. Had I been here for enjoyable reasons, like a historical tour or some shit, I would have liked to know where the water running through the grate was going.

Somewhere high above me, up the stairs, a heavy door opened then slammed shut. The clicking of heels or some sort of loud shoe, clip-clopped down the stairway. They were quiet at first, leading me to believe that the stairs must have been incredibly long. Then they grew louder as the feet rounded the last corner.

Condan wandered into the room in a button down and grey slacks. A black belt secured the perfectly pressed and starched shirt into the clean looking trousers. With black, shining cap toe oxfords. He looked like he was walking in to give a job interview, only his hands were deep in his pockets like a regional manager who already had job security.

Behind him, a younger child followed. She was barefoot and in nothing but a white winter nightgown. Lacy frills accented the edges of the long, thick sleeves, and reached up around her neck like an eighteenth century gothic vampire. Her skin was pale like one too, even from across the room I could see the tiny streams of her blue veins in her face and fingers.

"Condan and Bella Swan," I called satirically. "My two favourite expressionless immortals."

Condan and the vampire child finished their waltz over to me. They stopped a few feet short and stood there, watching me struggle.

"Condan, clearly you don't understand basic hospitality," I struggled to get out as I tried to focus on keeping myself on one foot and not wincing from the pain in my wrists at the same time.

316

"But, normally, you introduce your houseguests to your prisoners. It's only polite."

Half of Condan's mouth curled up in an amused smile. He then turned and leaned down to the girl so that he could whisper in her ear.

When he pulled away, she looked up at him and nodded excitedly. She turned and skipped off to the chest behind the desk.

"Wait, Marie Antoinette," I called after her. "Come back, I didn't get your name yet."

Condan looked down at my leg and immediately ice moved up from the floor and into the open wound. I could feel sharp daggers of ice push through the frozen, dead skin, into healthy masses of muscle. Pain bursted up my leg, consuming the entire area before moving up to my hip in rapid throbs.

The pulsing of pain and panic started there, in my knee, up to my hip, then moved through me until it hit my chest. My heart pounded rapidly, like I was running a marathon with something heavy pressing my chest down.

I tried to firm it at first, keep my pain to myself so that he wouldn't know it was getting to me, but the pain was too much.

I let out a scream so loud that it rang around in the room until it was so high pitched that it sounded as if it wasn't there. My vision filled with spots, until I decided it was better to just close them anyway.

After a few minutes, the pain subsided, or more so my nerve endings gave up, and I was able to open my eyes without seeing black dots.

Now, vampire child was kneeling in front of me with what looked like a dozen torture devices laid out in front of her. She organised and re-organised them, moving them around like a child laying out their toys for a stranger to see.

Behind her, Condan was at the table, sorting through papers and writing onto new and old sheets alike. He glanced up at me and let his head fall to the side. His gaze was almost lustfull, like I was the prettiest girl at the party and he was watching me smile and have fun while he hid behind the punch bowl.

"Clementine," he called out and the little girl looked back at him, her ringlet blond curls bouncing around her face as she did. "I think you should introduce yourself to our guest, dearest," he said and she smiled excitedly.

The little girl popped up to her feet. She rounded around her line of fun-tools so that she could stand in front of me and stick her hand out.

"It's nice to meet you, good sir," she said so sweetly, I almost remembered how cute she could have been in other circumstances. "My name is Clementine Maltby."

"Clementine is the first evidence of my ability to split the dragon soul into a new body and keep the same consciousness," Condan explained as he rose from his desk's chair and approached me.

Clementine let her hand fall to the sides of her dress. She scampered towards Condan, wrapping her small arms around his cold body, like a young daughter to a father.

"This lovely creature was born in 620 BC," Condan continued, hoisting the child into his arms and brushing her curls away from her face. "She would have died of what you now know to be the hepatitis had it not been for a vampire who found her to be rather attractive."

She was maybe eleven at best, but in that moment I wasn't about to focus on the undertones of pedophilia when he was explaining to me that this girl was in fact nearly three thousand years old.

"I found her a few years later," Condan said, looking at the girl sweetly. "She was rather feral, and running from humans

318

who wanted to kill her for consuming them. So I took her in. And I killed her, but kept her body around because I knew I could use it."

I watched as Condan caressed her cheek in a less than fatherly way, before he leaned down and kissed the child. The child who responded back by sticking her tongue into his mouth.

I jerked away. My hands felt slick with disgusted sweat. Bile built up in the back of my throat, and had I not been completely empty of food and water, I would have projectile vomited onto the floor again.

"That's fucking sick," I hissed under my breath.

"Don't worry," Condan laughed. "Years later I split one of the dragon's souls and put part of it into the body you see now. For a few dozen years she was able to control both her old human body, as well as this one. This body isn't Celemtine's original body, her first was human, and weak, and so after proving we could split the soul and put it into another one, we did it again, moving more of it into this immortal host before killing off her old one."

"I'm the only dragon soul in an immortal body besides Condan and your whore," Clementine finished for him, her small hand stroking up and down Condan's chest. "Of course, as a vampire, I stayed under the radar of the rest of the Otherworld, so I was never with the rest in haven."

Condan set Clementine on the ground. She moved back to her assortment of tools, picking up a set of needle-nose pliers. The teeth were long, narrow, and rusty, like little brown claws.

"Clementine had been following you all around, waiting for the right moment to steal the ring and let me out," he said. "But that disgusting rodent the light dragon gave the ring to rarely took it off. It wasn't until Reika came that Clementine saw her opportunity."

319

She pushed the desk chair across the floor, the wooden legs scraping against the solid ground in random bouts, until it was propped next to me. She crawled onto it while Condan gave his speech.

She was small. Even with the extra two feet the chair gave her, she still had to reach up and stand on her tiptoes to snag the lip of my fingernail with the pliers. She yanked hard once, ripping part of my nail out of the bed before the metal lost their bite and slipped free.

I hissed. "Child cunt," I whispered.

She giggled. "Oopsies, sorry. It's been a while. Here, let me get that for you," she said then gripped the hanging nail again and tugged, ripping it from my flesh completely.

I ground my teeth down against each other and glared at her.

Her face was inches from mine, and I could see the bright green of her eyes now. They were horribly abnormal. They were light and brighter than the shades of an actual jade gemstone. Her hair was richer too, like strands of spun gold instead of straw. Her skin was perfectly clear and dewy looking.

She was an absolutely adorable little girl, one that could have worn angel wings and been the star of a christmas play... had it not been for her serial killer smile and the blood from my finger dripping down to her lips as she turned her head to catch it in her mouth.

"Reika was the weak link," Condan went on. "Clementine just had to wait until she was sure you would all take Reika in. Then she waited to be alone with the witch, which wasn't difficult since you imbeciles insisted on treating her like a friend and let her roam freely. With a little bit of magick and charm, Clementine was able to twist Reika's desires into getting my ring off that rancid human and getting me out."

Clementine pulled out another nail. This time she enveloped the bleeding finger in her mouth. I felt her cold tongue swirl around my skin while she swallowed down every drop of blood that came out.

My stomach twisted into sour knots as she sucked to her heart's content.

"It's uncomfortable for you, isn't it?" Condan grinned as he asked.

I glared up at him.

He pulled a hand out of his pocket and reached forward. He touched my cheek and I yanked away. His hand stopped for a moment, until I had settled into one place, then he moved forward again until he could cup my face in his palm.

"The torture is easy, you're not a stranger to pain," he whispered. "It's the destruction of your humanly idea of innocence happening right next to you that's uncomfortable."

My nose twitched as anger washed over me. Everything about him was vile. Repulsive. Sickening.

A sadistic serial killer. A psychotic paedophile.

He cocked his head to the side. No doubt noticing my discomfort.

His smile grew, amusement dancing in his eyes. "Would it break you if I picked up Clementine, raised her skirt and procreated with her right here in front of you?"

I pinched my eyes closed and threw up again.

Condan's roaring laughter filled the room. I could hear his shoes clapping on the ground again as he moved away from me, but I kept my eyes as tightly together as I could.

"Keep going Clementine," Condan said. "His screaming will make for great background music."

I couldn't feel my leg or my arms now. The blood and water running down felt like nothing until it hit between my shoulder blades, then I could feel the cold again. But I couldn't shiver anymore.

I had been here for days before the torture started. Now I found myself floating through more long bouts, half conscious and half not.

The world was only dark to me now. I hadn't opened my eyes since I met Clementine, hoping that time would pass quicker if I wasn't awake for most of it. Unfortunately, given the snippets of conversations and events happening around me, I found myself aware and living through most of it.

Everyday, Condan would be here, writing on the walls or talking with voices I found familiar but couldn't place.

Today, Condan arrived at what felt later than usual, and had still yet to leave. Someone had only brought him a meal once, leading me to think I was now somewhere between lunch and dinner time.

Clementine was here before he arrived, letting me know that this was two days after the last time.

They were at least kind enough to give me forty-eight hours to recover, it seemed.

The vampire child had been dismissed just after he had finished his meal, after she had taken all my fingernails and deduced where the dead skin and the live skin began on my leg by sawing up my exposed bone.

As usual, after her brutal inspection, she had taken the time to try to feed me bone broth with carrot so that I wouldn't die in her absence.

If it wasn't for the cold slowing my blood circulation, and Condan who froze each exposed wound, I probably would have bled out.

"We'll build our forces there," Condan said to a group of unknowns. I could hear their feet scuffing around his desk with him, mumbling in agreement as he spoke. By the sounds of their voices, I had a feeling they were dragons. Their voices sounded young.

"When we're ready, and have found enough of us, we can take this world and the otherworld and shape them into an empire designed for us," he declared proudly. "A palace where we're finally allowed to prosper instead of living under the constant attack and repression of others.

"Dragons are the strongest creatures alive, yet we've allowed ourselves to be killed and enslaved all in the name of peace and balance. We can have balance, without peace. There is equality in brutality as well. An evenness in suppression. And I intend to preside over it."

"And what of Erika?" One of the dragon's, who's voice I recognized but couldn't place, asked. "She supports freedom. She doesn't believe that dragons should rule over all creation."

"The light dragon will do what needs to be done to protect those she loves," Condan snapped. "I have no quarrel with killing humans."

A dragon cleared his youthful throat. "We were humans at one point too."

I heard the sharp scrapping of wooden legs scraping the floor. Somewhere on the other side of the room, furniture collided with rock. It may have been Condan's chair being flung back, or maybe it was his desk being pushed into the wall as he shoved one of his followers' bodies into it. I didn't have the energy to look.

"And now you have been blessed with power," Condan snarled. "Don't ever speak of humans again, unless you are discussing their expulsion. Any ties you had to those temporary bugs are torn. You have no families, no homes, and no place amongst the mortals. Let them die in both your hearts and in this world."

"I don't think humanity deserves to be slaughtered off," the same voice said weakly. His words were forced, like he was choking back tears.

"Then you shall join them," Condan whispered, but his velvet words echoed off the walls like a thousand sensual whispers.

Then a horrible sound of liquid and wet, squishy objects splattered to the floor. Like he had drawn a shirt out of a bucket of water, just to lift it up and chuck it onto the floor.

I could have convinced myself that a wet shirt was all it was, but the putrid smell of iron filled the air and I knew…

"I need you awake," Condan spat in my face whilst slapping me.

Sometime during my unconsciousness, I had been taken down from my strung up position and moved to the floor. The chain had been adjusted so that each cuff was strung at different loops in the wall, pulling my arms apart and leaving me to drape between them. I was now spread open at a height where I was too low to kneel, but too high to sit. My shoulders, wrists, ribs, hips, legs, even my fucking armpits were sore. I felt pain everywhere and nowhere at all.

"How long has it been?" I mumbled, trying to grasp onto the little consciousness I had left in my body.

Condan chuckled. "This place is like Haven. I've charmed it so that time can move differently here."

I heard his stiff button down and ironed pants shuffle as he straightened up. Then his fine shoes click once, like he was turning to stare out a window.

"Really, it's only been a few hours," he said. "But for us it's been seven days. Which is why I need you awake. I need you alive. So, you need to actually eat this time."

I forced my eyes open, angry at the thought of my friends who had only been without me for a few hours. Knowing them, they were already running themselves into the ground trying to find me.

And it was all because of an old-as-fuck, sadistic cunt.

Excuse my language, ladies.

"Erika is a rather stubborn bitch," he said. "I need leverage in order to convince her to join me, and you're the only one of her friends I'm willing to let live. Well, maybe besides that elf, but he would have been harder to capture."

"She'll never fucking join you," I coughed out. "She'll always choose the needs of the many over the needs of the few. She's a soldier, you won't break her by breaking me."

"Then I'll simply put her into an eternal freeze," he declared. "She would be easy to defeat."

With my one leg, I struggled to push myself up. I was weak, so I leaned forward against the chain to help hold myself up, and so that I could be closer to the grey prick in front of me. Even in my half-stood state, he was still miles over me, and he made sure I knew it, as he stood with his hands in his pockets and an amused smirk on his face.

So I looked down on him too.

325

And I spat on his fucking shoes.

He didn't yank his feet back like I expected, but when I looked up into his eyes again, violent anger practically glowed on his face.

"She's going to break you," I said.

Condan snapped.

He lunged forward, snatching my throat in one hand. He hoisted me up, crushing my windpipe and cutting off the air to my lungs and the blood to my brain. He slammed me into the wall behind us, pinning me above him so that the chains pulled tightly into my skin, cutting me deeply as they tried to look for any relief from the tension he was causing. My legs both dangled beneath me. Even if one wasn't completely dead, it still wouldn't have changed the lack of movement from either. I was simply too exhausted. And now, with Condan cutting off all blood and oxygen to my mind, I couldn't even think to move.

"Your strength is respectable," Condan said. "Your resiliency is impressive even if you had been an immortal. The fact that you've survived this long as a human is the singular reason you will be the *only* human I keep alive when I form this world into what it should be."

"Piss… off…," I choked out. "Sadistic… cunt."

He tugged me forward, away from the wall. Then slammed back. Then he let go, and I crumpled down. The chains caught me, and ripped at my skin as I fell down past where they would allow.

I gritted my teeth, and sucked in a sharp breath between them as a raging throb emanated from my rib cage.

Condan took several steps back. We watched each other as he moved. As he grew away from me, ice spread across the wall, slowly moving towards me. It inched closer and closer, and I could feel the air around me getting colder. Small collections of spiky ice birthed on the chains, jumping from link to link as the cold crept in.

"I'll have Clementine come feed you," he said. "But first, I think you need to *cool off*. You should never eat with an angry mind."

"I'm gon' shit on your fucking grave."

I was so cold, my body was flexing and unflexing every muscle for me, rocking me back and forth like I was dry heaving, only I wasn't. My breaths came out raged, and every time I did breathe, it hurt. The air was so cold, that breathing it froze inside my nostrils, down my throat, and into the depth of my lungs. My diaphragm was probably covered in ice.

Clementine brought me bone broth with carrots in it again.

I ate about two bites before she licked my fingers. Then I threw it all back up.

"You need to wake up," warmth spoke to me. "You need to listen to everything he's saying and note what he's doing."

I wasn't cold anymore. I felt like the sun itself was shining on me. And when I opened my eyes, it was.

The world around me was lush and green, the sun was out and shining from a perfectly blue sky, gently speckled with crisp white, puffy clouds. The leaves in the oak trees above me caught the sun and scattered it, raining it down around us.

Us being me and the elder man from my previous dream kneeling beside me. He patted my leg, drawing my attention down to the two healthy and uninjured limbs stretched out in front of me.

"You have to wake up," he said.

I rubbed the groggy from my eyes. I leaned forward and looked back to find I was lounging against a towering yew tree. Its roots ran partially out of the ground around us, jumping over each other and lacing in a way that mirrored the branches above.

I struggled to my feet, rubbing my face some more to wake me up.

The elder followed me, rising up to stand shoulder to shoulder with me, staring up at the perfectly symmetrical tree.

I marvelled, "It looks like-"

"The tree of life?" he proposed before I could say it.

"Uh-huh," I mumbled, still staring up at the massive plant. It must have been five stories tall.

"That's because it is."

I looked over at the man. He looked over at me, a gentle smile on his face.

"Strange isn't it?" he asked. "That the tree of life is one that is so potently poisonous to all living creatures. There's a lesson to be learned somewhere in that."

He looked back to the tree.

"You're Fintan, Erika's dragon, right?" I asked, finally.

"Hmm," he hummed peacefully. "Erika's. Your's. Condan's. The entire world's, really. Dragons were always meant to share themselves with all of creation. We were meant to protect and nurture everything. Somewhere along the way, some of us forgot what we were meant for."

328

"Like fallen angels?" I said under my breath.

He turned and offered me a sad smile. "Something like that." He looked back to the tree. "You need to wake up. I can't hear or see what Condan has planned for the future, that's not in my power. You have to provide that information for Erika when she comes for you."

I shook my head. "No. No, you can't let her come rescue me," I argued. "You have to stop her. Let me die, it's not worth rushing into a fight with Condan. He has too much power and too many stronger beings in his arsenal."

Fintan closed his eyes, and I watched as silent tears rolled down his cheeks.

"It's not my will," he whispered. "And I wish this cup would pass from you, but you will need to drink it."

I blinked and he was gone.

I turned around in circles, looking to find him. But the gold and white of his cloak was nowhere amongst the lush greens of the forest.

I looked up at the tree of life and blinked again. Then the world was suddenly on fire. The tree was engulfed in raging flames. Without thinking, I ran towards it. Surely the tree of life couldn't be burned to the ground.

I ran up the roots, littered sparingly with flames, to the trunk which was roaring with full bodied fire. I shoved my palms deep into the heat without thinking, and gripped the solid wood inside with my finger tips.

The fire ceased, and instead the burning went to me. It rolled up my arms without any flames, and spread in my chest. It tore at my lungs and ripped at my oesophagus. I threw my head back and tried to scream, but only smoke came out.

I watched as the burning leaves of the canopy billowed black, my grey smoke breath standing out in front of the

329

backdrop of darkness. Then the ash in the sky began to form together, growing denser. Blooms of smoke hardened into blocks of rock. And my breath grew less thick. The smooth tendrils of grey broke apart into wet huffs of white.

I was still chained in the wet hole Condan held me in. The rocks were still grey above me, below me, behind me. My breathing still came out as frigid white vapour.

I looked over to the desk where Condan was standing by. He had his back turned to me, and he was writing with chalk on the wall in an ancient language. I couldn't make sense of the words, but I recognized a battle diagram when I saw one. Years of only being interested in history class and being on sports teams had given me that skill.

A map of the Otherworld was sketched onto the wall. Felicity and purgatory were drawn underneath it as well, shaping the map like a sideways diamond. Triangles and half circles littered the purgatory side, with one large rectangle standing just on the edge of it. Words were written to the right of the rectangle, then a drawing of a collection of triangles with an arrow curving up to the centre, where the divide between purgatory and felicity met the under belly of the otherworld, just underneath the council of magick's headquarters.

In another diagram, the half circles were left in purgatory and felicity, while the triangles were scattered above in the Otherworld, which was now separate from the two after realms.

"What language is that?" I croaked.

Condan stopped writing. He turned back slowly, lightly tossing the chalk onto his desk. He wiped his hands off by clapping them together several times. He rounded the wood corner of the table and began to approach me.

"It's my native language," he said, slipping his hands into his pockets. "So old that no one speaks it, and no evidence of it exists for others to learn how to read it."

330

I nodded. "Does it make you feel homesick?" I asked.

Condan's forehead creased. He slipped his hands out of his pockets so that he could cross them.

"What could you possibly mean?" he asked.

"Everyone you knew, every*thing* you knew, is gone," I said, struggling. "You are completely and utterly alone, without a home, without a family, without any comfort to return to to rest. Even if you slept in the same building, in the same bed, with the same people, for the rest of your life, you will always be homesick for what you had before and can never have again. The fact that only you can speak and read that language, doesn't it remind you of how homesick you are."

I watched the muscles in the back of his face, just under his ears, as they flexed. Then he shook his jaw slack and licked his lips.

"Writing in my language gives me peace of mind," he said with a wicked smile.

"How's that?" I shot back.

He leaned forward so he and I were eye to eye. "It means that no one except me can know with absolute certainty what I'm thinking. I know that if, by some miracle, you get out of here alive, you will never be able to tell anyone what I am moving to do."

He stood up straight again, before letting his hands drop from his chest and walking back to his stone chalkboard.

"I imagine your friends shall be coming soon," he enunciated into the air. "I sent all of my pets away in preparation for their arrival."

"That was stupid," I called back. "Now it will be five against one. Not great odds."

"Exactly," he said, his white writing utensil striking against the stone with a satisfying tick. "No need to keep the other dragons here as potential collateral damage when your friends will be such easy ants to squash."

"We have a celestial dragon too," I argued.

"You have a girl suppressing her power because she has control issues," he laughed. "I couldn't call her a druid let alone a dragon. The only reason she's still alive is because she needs to be."

"Why?" I shouted. "Why does she need to be alive?"

Condan let his head fall as he chuckled. He slid his right hand into his pocket. Holding the chalk in his left, he raised it up to one line of unknown language across the top. He tapped the chalk underneath it.

"This is why," he said.

I licked the blood that had started popping up from my dry, cracked lips. "I can't read it, remember?"

He looked over his shoulder at me. "Exactly."

18

Adam

"The portal is just up ahead," Erika called over the roaring wind.

Artemis's chariot was quick, but it was open to the world around us as well. The air whipped by, sending bugs and noise into our faces. Jack and I had to crouch down behind the gleaming pearl walls to save our skin from the harsh blasts. Even Darbie and Reika weren't immune as they turned their faces away, facing towards the back of the vehicle so the air wouldn't slash at them from the front.

Erika faced forward into the gusts, leaning against the chariot walls like she was lounging against a wall in a quiet alley.

I tried to raise my eyes to look at hers, only for the wind to steal away the moisture from them, forcing me to close them and look down. The brief glances that I was able to snatch were filled with harsh lines and dark gazes. Her sight was set only on what was in front of us.

The chariot careened down. The feeling in my stomach went up, then down, then to either side, and back up before following us.

The wheels slammed down individually on either side, first the right, which bounced back up, thus forcing the left down.

Then the left rose up again, before finally, together, the two wheels met the solid sounding floor and stayed down together. They rolled across textured ground before rushing to a stop, throwing Jack and I forward into Erika's legs, who - without looking down - grabbed my shoulder and Jack's collar in order to keep us from pushing past her into the front of the chariot.

With a jerk, she pulled us both to our feet, but didn't stay to check and see how we were. Instead, she spun on one foot so that she could slip around me.

Despite being in the front throughout our journey, she was the first to jump off. Her boots sounded heavier when they hit the ground, but her steps were quiet as she headed towards the mouth of the alleyway.

"Come on," it was Darbie who flicked his wrist against our skin, drawing our attention back to the task at hand. "We can't waste any more time."

He herded us all with his arms, forcing us off and towards the path to our way home.

Erika was waiting for us at the start of the alley. Her expression was grim. When we caught up to her, Darbie and Jack carried on down the street towards the gateway in the wall, but I stopped beside her. Reika stopped to look between us, hesitating. She looked at me, then over at Erika. Her eyes roamed over the expression of her face, before she looked back at me. She stared at me for only a few seconds before turning and walking off down towards the other two.

I reached out and gently grasped Erika's elbows, forcing her to look at me.

"Erika-" I started, but her frustrated furrowed brows and tight jaw stopped me.

"We don't have time to stop Adam," she spoke lowly.

I swallowed the lump that was forming in my throat. "It's all going to turn out alright. These last few years have taught me that-"

"These last few years have been easy," she said, her voice harsher than before. "The actions that have occurred today may be the starting events of a war. In war, people die. Has it not occurred to you that your best friend could be the first?"

I snapped my jaw shut tight. Turning on my toes, I headed away from her, rushing along towards our pathway home with Erika planting strong steps behind me.

Erika Gavina, the girl- no- the woman I had loved and longed after for years, was complex. On the surface, she looked young, no more than twenty-one or two, and she had mastered how to carry herself at such an age as well, even keeping up the facade in private so as to ensure she would never break character around others. But in situations that broke her concentration and turned her focus and concern away from her presentation, I found she spoke like a noblewoman or a high knight from an ancient time.

And I was just a young man.

Literally a *young* man.

My life experiences were few and small in comparison to someone who had lived a life like Erika. Or even Ethan, if I thought about it. Ethan had been carrying his family since he was no more than eight years old and his brother died - his parents had never raised him and he was forced to hold them together for five years. But then his father committed suicide and his mum spiraled from a functionally numb alcoholic to a full-blown drunk.

Did my friend ever question if he was a failure? Did he ever wonder if he hadn't done enough to save them?

Erika's words made me feel like I hadn't done so. I was failing my friends by assuming that all would be well in the world just because I had them. Knowing about the Otherworld and magick had pulled me into a daze where I thought everyone I loved was unkillable. But Ethan, my best friend, who had fought by my side even before we knew about this world, was human and he could die at any moment.

Darbie had opened the portal just moments before we caught up, and it was Jack who was the first to dive in. I followed immediately after him, leaving Darbie, Reika and Erika behind to hold the portal open before eventually crossing through.

Pushing through the magick, my lungs were once again bogged down with the feeling of being filled. Inflating each organ to capacity required what was likely the equivalent of compressed air through the bottom of a murky lake. Not to mention, on the other side of the magick, the portal was still locked behind a glass case, one that Jack had partially broken through on his way out. As I followed after, I took out the rest of the jagged bundle of glass.

A sharp edge pushed into the top of my cheek bone and the crease of my eyes, cutting through the skin as I fell through. I tumbled down to the ground, clutching my eyes closed in a wince, and holding the corner of my face in the palm of my hand.

In my blind state, I saw nothing, but heard the roar of an unknown world, and felt heat around me. Next, my friend's hands were grabbing at my shirt and pushing me down to the ground. I gazed over at him out of shock, and found his face washed in blinding red and black.

Behind him, spreading down from the stairwell into the basement, fire licked its way in. It had spread over the ceiling and around the walls, slowing clawing towards us like the sharp and mangled hand of a demon. Smoke filled the roam, reaching down at us.

Jack was yelling at me, pressing us both to the ground and pulling us back towards the portal at the same time. I couldn't hear what he was saying over the roaring of the flames.

Even though the flames were some feet from us, the heat was enough to catch our hair on fire. Jack's was the first to go, and he let go of me so that he could grasp at his head with his hands. I followed soon after. The pain was horrible, but the shock was worse - and grabbing at my scalp and forehead with my bare hands wasn't any better. The flames scorched not only my head, but my hands.

Jack and I both collapse on the ground in pain.

But then Erika came through.

I could barely see the shape of her boots, but they were unmistakably there. I watched one of her knees drop next to her feet, then a hand was reaching out, grabbing me at the base of my skull. Under the warm touch of her hand, the pain ceded.

I tried to follow the line of her arm to her face, but she was engulfed in flames and I couldn't see past her elbow. I looked back down to her feet, watching to see if she was going to change her movements. Just on the other side of her, I could see the faint mass of Jack, lying motionless on the ground. The outline of Erika's other arm was there as well.

Then Darbie's staff came down onto the ground behind Erika. The slamming of the wood against the hard floor was louder than the numbing roar of the fire.

Then it was silent.

We were lying on the floor of a dirty, dark, dingy, and dated wood floor. It was so worn with mud, that the wood panels were nearly black.

I grunted as I tried to roll over so that I could look up with Erika. She was glowing white and orange. No, never mind, not glowing. She was still on fire. Her eyes were white, flicking back and forth between Jack and I. Her arms were white too, covered in armour that curled around her fingers, then up towards her shoulders. Each sleeve looked like a thousand diamonds bejewelled together, then linked with gold chainmail. Her chest was covered in one solid mass of reflective gem as a chestplate, with smaller scale shaped diamonds once again linked together in gold along her sides and shoulders.

Her shirt was smouldering and falling off in pieces to the floor to reveal this.

I followed the embers to the ground with my gaze.

Then I let my eyes close.

Darbie

When we had come through the portal into the house, I was shocked to see flames, but only for a second as my hair caught fire. Then I summoned a protective shell so that I could focus on teleporting myself and my friends out of there.

Erika had gone through before me, and she had already knelt down over the boys. I could see the flames trying to strike them, only to be reflected off of her back, like she had created a hard wall out of herself to cover our lovers.

I grabbed her as she held on to them, and waited one more second for Reika to come through, slamming into my back. I teleported us out of there as soon as she came into contact with me, and sent us to the only place I could think of that would both get us close to Condan and provide us shelter; my old cabin in the black forest.

I had studied the creatures here for decades after the Otherworld and earth were shut off from one another. I had wanted to see if there would be an effect on magick creatures when this world was severed from the free flow of magick that the otherworld had.

Now, the cabin was nothing more than a dilapidated shack. The entire structure was brown with mildewed wood, rather than the golden walls of fresh pine logs I had once cut. Every window had never held a glass pane, but now, they didn't even have borders or sills, and the door had fallen outwards, laying down like a welcome mat in front of the frame.

The structure didn't matter in that moment though. My love was laying on the ground beside Erika, his skin beginning to shrivel up, tearing itself away from his muscle.

In a panic I took a step closer to him. But the heat was too much. Instinctively, I took a step back from my best friend, who was radiating heat worse than the flames.

"Eri!" I yelled at her.

I looked at her for the first time since we arrived, only to find an angel knelt over in her place.

I took another step back. Then a third. A fourth. Then I was in the doorframe. I could see the entirety of the one room cabin from where I stood.

Reika had been behind me, and still was, her hands on my back and bicep, holding on to me as if she was going to toss me aside should the angel turn out to be a threat.

It was pitch night outside, but inside, the space was lit enough that I could have seen the details of each fallen and run-down part of the place.

The gold and glass armour wrapped around the archangel's body sprayed the tiniest rays around the room by the thousands, like a hundred diamonds splitting one single light into millions.

In its hands, it cradled Jack and Adam. I watched as their burns went back in time, unravelling and slowly moving back to lay smoothing on their bodies. Their hair grew back in soft tufts until they were back to their respective places.

Then the angel rose to its feet and turned to look at me. Facing me, I could take in the whole of it. Its gorgeous breastplate was intricately carved, resembling scales made up of crystals. Even the golden chain wasn't linked in normal circular links, but rather scale-shaped twists of metal, overlapping on another like the skin of a lizard. More gold and crystal armour layered itself on its legs.

I looked up from its legs to its face and watched as its illuminated eyes stopped shining, allowing me to see its face.

Erika looked back at me, blinking what looked to be a mixture of both exhaustion and confusion out of her eyes. She fell to her hands and knees as the heavenly armour fell away in little flashes of light.

"Erika?" I hesitated, but stepped towards her now nude body, nonetheless. "Are you okay?"

She nodded, her face and body hunched towards the ground while she huffed heavy breaths.

"What was that?" I whispered.

She coughed, then craned her head to look up at me, her chest still pressed down into herself.

"I don't know," she said. "I saw Adam and Jack and I could feel Fintan and I both panic. Next thing I knew, I was grabbing them and telling the fire that had burned them to take it back."

I shook my head. "No, I mean what was that armour you were wearing?"

She furrowed her brows and looked down at herself. "Darbie, I'm naked," she said as she looked back up at me.

I knelt down next to her, shaking my head even more now. I could feel the remaining curls on half of my head bouncing around. The other half of my head had caught flames upon entry and was likely singed down to nearly nothing.

"No, no, Erika," Reika said breathlessly, still hiding in the doorway. "You were wearing, like, crystal and gold scale armour. You were so bright, I couldn't see you at first."

She pursed her lips at us, frustration creasing on her forehead.

"Guys," she said sternly. "I. Am. Naked. No armour."

I leaned back onto my heels so that I could give her my best annoyed gaze.

"Your lack of imagination is why we never dated," I deadpanned.

"No," she scoffed. "My lack of a dick is why we never dated."

I nodded. "That too."

She looked over her shoulder at out men, then back at me.

"Do you have a change of clothes I can have, so we can get a move on?" she asked.

I sighed. The back of my head buzzed as I thought about the clothes I had stored away within my magick. I was magick-fatigued after the last teleport, to the point where even just summoning a change of clothes for Eri was like someone was pounding on the back of my skull with a closed fist.

I winced as a pair of sweats, a hoodie and some running shoes dropped out of my churning world of goodies. They fell into the small space between Erika and I, and she didn't hesitate to snatch them up.

I tried to hide my small collapse as I sent my storage world away. But Eri and I had known each other too long for that.

341

"We don't have any more cucurbits left do we?" she asked as she pulled the hoodie on first.

"Bitch," I snapped, annoyed both because I was tired and because she knew damn well we were out of supplies. "We don't even have fucking coffee."

She stood up so that she could slip into the black sweatpants. They were mine, and very baggy on myself, but they fitted Eri's muscled thighs and barely left enough space to slide over to her hips. Luckily, they were then baggy around her hips, letting her move somewhat comfortably. She only tied the draw strings off tightly to keep them from sliding down in the back.

"Thanks for teleporting us here," she said. "Sorry it's left you tired."

I stood up and moved around her to check on our friends. While their burns were gone, the cuts and bruises they had from bashing through the glass were still there. Luckily, those were nothing but flesh wounds. They would probably leave scars, but they'd be so faint that it wouldn't even matter.

"I'm more worried about what this means for us," I said as I knelt down to inspect the gash by Adam's eye.

"Explain," Eri demanded.

I looked over at her as she tied the laces of the running shoes. She and I weren't very far in height, so our shoe size wasn't too far off, but still, the one size up that difference meant she had a lot of loose space to move around in. I hadn't thought to summon socks. Worse, in my current state, I doubted I could have summoned some for her without needing to lay down for several minutes.

"I'm down for the count, Eri," I said and her attention snapped to me. "Give me a good hour of rest and I can teleport us back home or maybe complete a healing spell, but that's it. I couldn't even summon you socks right now."

"It's alright," she said.

"I got us out of the house and closer to Condan," I continued. "But that also means I sent us to him without supplies and completely depleted."

"It's alright," she said again.

"I'm not going to be any help." I was panicking now. "I'll just be dead weight."

"Darbithar Praecantiodomini!" Reika shouted from the doorway.

Immediately I was floored. I hadn't heard my full name in centuries. I hadn't heard it pronounced correctly in a millennium.

"Shut up!" she screamed as well. "If you think negatively, negative things will happen. We're travelling with two humans, surely you can't be more useless than them."

"Oof," Jack grunted as he slowly shifted on the floor. "Used your full name and called us useless."

"Jack," I gasped and swooped down beside him, practically pulling him into my lap. "You're okay."

He patted my arms, urging me to let him go, but I ignored him.

"Yeah, hun," he said. "I'm alright, and I don't wanna know how."

"Erika turned into an angel," I said.

"What?" Adam groaned now, looking at Erika.

She raised her hands into the air in surrender. "Don't look at me," she said. "I have fuck all idea what he's talking about."

"She glowed like a star and healed you both of your burns," Reika interjected.

"Oh, like a Jesus," Jack said.

"No," Erika shook her head.

343

Adam sat up. "But he healed the sick."

"Let's not compare me to-"

"More like just an angel," I said. "She was all ball-of-lighty and stuff."

"Can we just-" Erika tried.

"Oh that's really cool," Adam gapped. "Can she heal all wounds?"

He reached up and ran his finger along the corner of his eye.

"No," Reika said as he examined the blood. "Just burns it look like."

"Enough!!" Erika bellowed and all movement halted.

She stood in the middle of us. Her hands were balled into fists, and she looked over each of us like we were the enemy.

"One of us is missing," she declared. "Taken by someone of unknown ability and *stability*. Ethan could be dead right now. Or worse, alive and being tortured. While we stand here, discussing casually amongst ourselves. We are alive, conscious, functional and otherwise healthy. We should be regrouping to decide where he most likely is, then mobilising towards his location." She glared around the room, taking the time to settle her eyes on each one of us, singling us out and drawing our focus onto only her. "Cut the fucking chit-chat. Get up. Get thinking. Get prepared. This isn't a game."

Jack stood up, staring her down as if he stood a chance.

"Increasing the tension and stress in the room isn't going to help," he snapped before I could stop him.

Erika only needed one step to cover the space between them. Then she was in his face. Even with his height, he couldn't tower over her. Her forehead was at his nose line, but her aura was staring down at him.

344

"Have you ever held a mangled, bloodied, cold body in your hands, Jack?" she asked. "You can smell the blood even when it's cold and thick, or dry. It smells like metal, and the skin smells like bad meat mixed with loch water that's been trapped in a harbour for too long, left to go stagnant and pungent with bacteria. And the rigidness of the skin and bones? It's like handling a frozen stuffed doll, only it smells like that pungent, rotting blood, and looks like the twisted and shredded version of someone you love."

Jack shivered. I stood up, and he leaned a millimetre back, into me.

"That's how you'll find Ethan if we keep going at this rate," she finished. "So you tell me, what's not helping? The tension? Or the time you're fucking wasting?"

I stuck my arm between the two, pushing back my friend and pulling back my lover.

"Okay," I lulled the space between the two. "Let's calm down so we can think. There may be some animal skin maps of the area I left behind here. We can use that to figure out where Condan and Ethan may be."

"If you have a map and something precious to Ethan on hand, we can use both to find him," Reika offered.

I shook my head. "I don't have any magick, remember?"

Reika crossed her arms and stared at me indignantly.

"Right…" I changed. "You're a demi-goddess witch. You can do the spell. My bad."

"Where would the maps be, Darbie?" Erika asked, stepping away from Jack and turning her attention towards me.

I spun around the room. In the far corner, there was a window with my old workbench still tucked under it. The chair I used to sit on had collapsed, leaving only the seat itself and part of the back underneath the table. A series of shelves were built into the right hand side of the bench, and a few scraps of leather paper-sheets remained tucked within them.

To the left of the workbench, was the fireplace. The entire wall was made up of stacked stone so that there was no risk of the heat alighting the logs. As the wall went farther away from the empty hearth, notches of shelves were cut into the rocks. All of them appeared to be empty in the darkness, but the moonlight shining through the barely-existent ceiling provided enough sight to see a box remaining on the middle shelf.

I pointed to the sheets on the workbench and the box on the shelves. "There may be something useful there," I said. "But we should also pull up the floorboards underneath the bed, over there," I pointed to the wooden square laying in the far corner from the door frame. "I used to hide things under my bed for extra storage."

Erika headed towards the bed.

"Darbie and Jack, take the box," she called over her shoulder. "Reika and Adam, see if you can make sense of the sheets on the desk."

"We can't see shit in this lighting," Jack spat.

Erika spun, flinging her hand out as she went. A bundle of flames flew beside us, before splashing in the dry fireplace. Upon impact, the fire stuck there and began to roar to life as if it had just engulfed a massive stack of logs rather than dust.

She pulled her hand back and flicked it out again, sending two more smaller streaks of orange out. They met their targets - one inside the cracked and bent husk of a lantern, and the other onto the tip of a torch still resting in its iron clasp against the wall by the door. Both of the dead lights took to the flames like starving children. They held onto the fire and flickered brighter than I ever saw in the past.

The room was filled with orange light within seconds.

Erika caught Jack's eye, but let it go without saying anything. She turned back towards the bed and carried on. She wasn't gentle as she lifted the skeleton of the frame up and chucked it out the window above her head. Then she squatted down and dug her nails into the ledges of the wood flooring. I turned around and headed towards the box with Jack, but I could hear her nail scraping and chiselling at the wood behind me. Then the sharp and sudden tearing of dry wood from itself.

I turned and watched as she used the newly made opening as a hole to reach her entire arms up into. She hooked them in at the elbows, then yanked them up, ripping up four or five panels in one go. She then began to claw around at the dirt below, digging down a few inches before giving up and moving on. She repeated the motion of slipping her arms under and pulling up sections. I could see splinters pushing against her skin, but they broke off and fell away like crumbs rather than penetrating.

I turned back to my appointed task. Jack had already made it to the box and had pulled it down from the shelf. He now was sitting with it on the floor by the fireplace spinning it around in his hands trying to figure out how to get it open.

"It's a puzzle box, hun," I said and moved down to assist him.

I pushed the bottom of the box back, exposing a loose panel, which I slid open. An old brass key, not bigger than my pinky, tumbled out into my lap.

"Cool," Jack laughed sarcastically. "Now we have a key to go into a wood box that has no key hole."

I took the key and thumped it against his nose. He scrunched it up and rubbed the skin with his fingers.

"Your bitterness is only cute in less stressful situations," I critiqued him softly. "Now hush-up and watch."

I wrapped the tips of my finger around one of the decorative flowers on the top, then I spun it. The centre circle,

347

inside the petals, rose up, and I reached out and unscrewed it the rest of the way. When I pulled it out, a key hole was revealed, prompting me to look at my love with a smug grin.

I held the key out to him. "Wanna put the key in the key hole now? Or do you wanna keep sitting there throwing your little temper tantrum?"

He scowled at me, but said nothing as he took the key from my hands and slid it into the hole.

"You're lucky you're cute," he mumbled under his breath as he turned the key.

I leaned over and whispered into his ear, "Thank you. I get it from my mom's side."

He popped the lid open, then turned to smirk down at me. I gave him a peck on the cheek. When I pulled away, his eyes flickered behind me for a moment before he focused back, reached out, grasped my head, then pulled me in and kissed me hard on the lips.

He only held me for a second, before he released me and looked down on the box. He shuffled through the top layer of random nick-nacks of dead bugs and random rocks I at one point may have deemed important. Underneath the dusty junk, a ball of sheep skin was rolled up, faded paint littered the limited skin I could see.

"Hey I think that's it," I said loud enough for the group to hear.

Jack rushed to turn the box over, throwing all the contents out onto the floor. Both of us then moved to our knees, leaning over so that we could draw out each corner of the balled fabric. At first, we opened it blank side up, and struggled against one another to decide which way to flip it in order to get it over. I let it go, giving up and letting Jack take over.

He flopped the thing over, and faded colours marking landmarks of the black forest stared back at us.

"We got it," I whispered in disbelief to Jack, then I looked up and shouted to Erika, "We got a map-" I stopped, just watching, unsure if my eyes were deceiving me or not.

Erika was knelt down in the dirt. A few sticks and rocks were littered around her, but nothing of importance. She had stopped digging to look over at me while I yelled. When I stopped and looked past her at the gaping hole in the roof above her, she cocked her head to the side.

"Darbie?" she asked, then followed my gaze.

A hand with fingers inhumanly long, as if each one had been dislocated at every knuckle, was reaching over the jagged edges of the wood panelled wall. Its nails were long and black and sharp. The arm that was inching over the tear in the structure, had fingers, misshapenly long, and seemingly disjointed.

When its head creeped over, smiling down with a permanent grin cut into its face, it was almost enough to make one vomit from nervous discomfort.

I was so frozen in place at the very thought of it existing, that I didn't even think to yell out what it was.

I had studied its victims when I lived in these woods. The cold bodies of the children and adults alike who wandered too deep into the forest and stayed out too long past the setting of the sun. They never had any marks on them. They never showed signs of dying from the cold, or an illness, and most certainly not from blood loss. The villagers created a horror-story about it.

An elf-king, capable of killing anyone with just a touch. The erlking.

He crawled up the wall until he was perched at the top. His legs tucked under his hips with an inhuman kind of flexibility.

349

Erika, no doubt growing tired of it's black beading eyes staring down at her, jumped to her feet as she reached out to grab it. As usual, her instinct was combat. Close handed, violent, bloody combat. She would beat, stab or burn this thing to death so she could get on with the task at hand.

But she couldn't touch it.

"Don't touch it!!" I shrieked so loud, that birds sleeping off inside the woods began screaming into the night and flapping into the moonlit sky.

Erika snatched her hand back. The erlking, realising my knowledge, changed approaches. Instead of waiting for us, the prey, to go to him, he lunged down at Erika, long, clawed hands and feet pointed forward at her.

She tucked and rolled forward into the wall whilst it landed behind her. She stood up, her back flat against the boards behind her. It spun around on the ground like a dancing spider, then leaped through the air once again, hands stiff and facing forward like ten tiny spears.

Erika jumped to the side just in time for it to barrel into the wall where she had been standing. Its nails jammed into the weak wood and stuck there. So, she rushed over towards us while it pulled itself out.

Reika dove to the ground beside us, her hands running over the map. Without hesitating she closed her eyes, palms flat against the painted skin, and began to chant.

Erika eyed the purple witch and spun on her heel in front of us, facing down the erlking again. He had released himself from his stuck position, but remained against the wall, watching.

How could a human kill it without getting close enough to touch it? They couldn't, not without a gun or several archers with bows at the ready. Even then, I'm not sure how much damage either of those would do against it. I had never even seen him in real life, only heard stories from other creatures in the forest and dozens of scared villagers who claimed he snuck into their houses to steal their babies.

Now, in front of me, I was faced with the painful fact that I, a scholar of everything magickal, had no idea what I was looking at. I had no idea how to fight it. I had no idea what it did with its victims after it killed them. I had no response beyond:

"He's the erlking," I shouted. "He's a cursed elf king. The slightest brush against your skin and you die."

"No problem!" Erika shouted back, then rained down a wall of fire.

In likely both shock and pain, the erlking skittered out the door, taking his creepy grin and discomforting long joints with him.

"He'll be back," I said. "I don't know how or why, but he needs to kill to live."

Erika looked back at me and nodded once. She looked over at Adam who was standing next to the three of us on the floor. She turned on her heel. In a crackle of blue electricity, her sword materialised in her hand. She flicked it through the air at Adam, who caught it with ease.

"Jack, Adam," Erika said, pulling both of their attention. "Triangle around the two wizards."

"On it," Adam swung the sword a bit, re-familiarizing with the weapon he was gifted while he turned to watch the window and open roof off to our left.

Jack responded by standing up without a sigh. He stepped over me, bending over only to pick up my staff. He positioned himself to my right, his head on a swivel as he also assisted Erika in watching the door.

Erika faced away from us, back towards where the erlking had last been standing. On that side of the structure, there was nothing more than the single centre post of the roof leaving it completely exposed. That, along with the two corner windows over the bed and the open door frame, made for a lot of entry points.

Meanwhile, the rock wall behind us was not only completely intact, but also growing hotter and hotter with the raging fire inside it, acting as a literal firewall. The roof was also much more complete, with each strip of wood secured deep within the rocks and therefore able to withstand the elements much better than what would have been an exposed pine corner on the other side.

"I need something that is sentimental to Ethan," Reika announced.

Jack looked down at us in a mild panic. "We- we don't have, like, anything," he sputtered. "We left it all behind when we rushed after him and Condan."

Reika pinched the bridge of her nose.

"It doesn't have to be directly related or belonging to him," I stated, trying to throw out options so the group wouldn't lose morale. "It could just be something that symbolises what matters most to him."

"Oh! Oh!" Adam called as he released the sword with one hand in order to dig through the depth of his pocket. He pulled out a small box of shortbread. "Here," he said happily and tossed them back to me. "They have the thistle on them. He's proud to be Scottish."

Jack looked at the shortbread, then up at Adam, his body still facing out.

"That's not going to fucking work," Jack snapped.

Adam turned to look at him. "Then you offer something better," he shouted.

"We have movement," Erika called. "Front door, I hear rustling and spotted the passing of a large shadow, twice."

"Large shadow?" Jack clarified. "Elf-king was long and slender, but no taller than you."

Erika knelt down and drew out her knife, positioning it in her grasp so that she could throw it as soon as something passed through the door.

"This shadow is different," she said. "I think we have two enemies circling us. Reika, hurry up with that spell."

"The cookies aren't working," Reika snapped back. "I need something closer to his heart."

The flapping of heavy wings made all our heads turn up. Black, massive raven wings popped into view in the small opening by Adam.

"Eyes down," Erika yelled.

I was beginning to look down when I saw a raven beak a foot long, forcing its way in through the small hole.

"Nachtkrapp!" Erika was shouting, her boots slapping down hard against the floor.

Nachtkrap: *noun.*

Origins: *Southern German and Austrian.*

Definition: *A massive, human-like raven often mentioned in cautionary tales used to get children to go to bed.*

A nachtkrapp is described as being eyeless in norse mythology. Regardless, in every type of mythology, one glance into its eyes meant instant death.

Adam flung himself down, over Reika and I. I looked up to watch him, keeping my eyes locked with his so that I could see what was happening in my peripheral without having to look. Adam's eyes were wide, breaking the crust of the cut by his eye open. Drops of blood fell down between Reika and I, splatting on the map.

The nachtkrapp opened its massive mouth, ready to take a chunk out of Adam's back, but Erika was there, slamming into

353

its feathery body. It snapped its beak as it was flung back, nipping Adam just enough to tear at his shirt, ripping it from the back to his side.

He winced and moved to look up at it, but I reached out and pinched his face. I yanked him down so that he was looking at me.

"Don't look at it!" I screamed at him so that Jack could also hear. "Eye contact will kill you."

Adam nodded.

"The blood works!" Reika called out.

Adam and I both looked down, watching as the blood from Adam's cut was moving across the map.

The sound of thudding and cawing erupted in the background. Erika shouting obscenities while her and the nachtkrapp tumbled around us.

Out of the corner of my eye, I could see the black bodied mass of feathers slamming to the ground. Then a pale skinned Erika rolled over it, her head buried into its torso so she couldn't look at its eyes.

"New problem," Jack called. "Handsy's back."

I looked up at him, then followed his gaze to the door. The erlking was slowly crawling back in with delayed, jerky movements.

"Just to clarify, we can't look at the bird and we can't touch the crawling demon?" Adam asked rapidly.

"Exactly," I said to him then immediately looked at Reika, "How much longer?!"

"This is a complicated enough spell in calm conditions," she hissed. "Do you really wanna rush me in stressful ones?"

"Yes!" all four of us shouted from our various positions.

Adam hoisted himself away from the two of us. He craned his arm back, hoisting Erika's sword into the air.

"Jack!" he shouted. Then he threw the sword and added, "Thor's hammer!"

Jack raised my staff into the air, shouted the elvish word for lightning, and swung the large stick down towards the erlking. Electricity zapped through the air, latching onto the green stone embossed into the top of my staff as Jack swung it down from the heavens.

Adam's sword stuck into the ground right in front of the erlking, who had to snatch its hand back in order to keep from being stabbed, while Jack summoned his lightning. The erlking didn't have time to react as the lightning flung itself off of the tip of the staff, towards the sword, only a few inches from the erlkings body.

The energy ran down the blade, looking for more conduit to travel down. When it found the wood floor instead, it made one last leap, zapping into the erlking's body, which flew back into the wall it had once hung from.

"Yes," I celebrated under my breath. But it was all too soon.

The erlking hit the wall, then landed face down on the ground beneath, only laying flat for a second before popping back up into it's pointy limbs.

Future note for my journal: *The erlking is immune to lightning ... ?*

"Uh..." Adam looked back at us. "Reika? About that location..."

"Oh for fucks sake," she hissed and popped to her feet, leaving the spell behind.

She marched over to Erika and the nachtkrapp, who were currently between the workbench and the bed. Erika had her arms around its fat neck and was repeatedly slamming it into the wall, while it pecked rather large holes into her shoulders and back.

Reika literally ripped her glove off, casting the frayed fabric aside, before she shoved the bare fingers into the feathered body of the deadly bird. I watched her eyes as they glowed brighter and brighter purple.

"Erika!" Adam shouted, and I looked over at him.

The erlking had wiggled down like a cat ready to pounce, and I watched in horror as he pushed off the wall, directly towards Adam. Its long nails were mere centimetres from his face when Erika's blast of air sent the long body into the wall beside the door so hard that it broke through.

"Reika!" Erika shouted.

"One second!!" The witch was bellowing now.

Her eyes were shut tight and casted towards the ground whilst she resumed Erika's slamming of the bird. Her veins were glowing underneath her skin.

The erlking scuttled over the rubble, grin frothing with rage.

"Reika!!" Erika shouted, this time sounding angry.

With one final slam, the nachtkrapp broke through the wall. Reika turned on her heel and shouted, "Don't look!!"

I turned back to the erlking, who looked at her with his black eyes and hissed. Then he choked and fell flat to the ground. His body began twitching and seizing, each long body part curling up into him until he was on his back, twisted inward like a dead spider.

Then it was silent. Only the sounds of our heavy breaths.

"Did you just take the nachtkrapp's death vision?" Jack asked, from beside me, eyes still trained down.

Reika was huffing, but managed to puff out, "Yeah. Yeah, I did."

"How lon-g will the k-killer vision last?" Erika asked through wet coughs.

Reika sighed. "No idea. A few hours maybe? I sucked him dry so maybe a whole day. It depends on how much magick I use on this spell."

I looked up at Erika, who was nodding her blood covered head.

"Don't look at the purple," she said. "Got it."

Erika reached up to poke at her shoulder, littered with open chunks of flesh.

Reika turned and walked towards me. She reached up and grasped the soft edges of her hood, pulling it up over her head so that the fabric could fall down and cover the top half of her face.

She knelt down beside me, and pressed her hand on the outskirts of the map once again.

"If you imagine details of him in you head, it'll cause you to have a deeper connection with him spiritually," I explained as she began chanting again. "The closer you feel to him, the stronger your magickal focus on him will be as well. Your magic works a lot like your subconscious with dreams, it will create whatever you think, but if you're thinking it on the deepest level, it will create it for you without you having to exert too much energy."

She remained in her chanting state, but I knew she could hear me. The melodic rhythm of her words began to thump on at a slower pace, while Adam's blood on the map began to roll over the paintings quicker. The red liquid ran over the small brown square which marked the cabin we were in, and rolled along the river beside it until it reached the small depiction of the ruins of an ancient fort. It stopped there before allowing itself to soak into the fabric, staining the grey paint of the ruined tower, but ultimately allowing us to still see what and where the dot was.

I looked up at Erika. "It's in the ruins ten or so kilometres from here."

Erika crossed her arms over her chest. "Define ruins. How old are we talking?"

"Several millennia," I said. "They were ruins even before the otherworld and this world were separated. And when I was studying here, I never went near that place, you could feel the dark magick polluting the air around that place."

"So you don't know what it's like inside?" Adam asked.

I shook my head. "I don't think there is an inside beyond the single standing tower. If that's even still there. The whole structure is in a worse state than this cabin."

"Well if that's where Ethan is, we'll just have to assume Condan is keeping him at the top of the tower," Erika interjected.

Jack chuckled in the corner. "It's like the ending to sleeping beauty."

Adam cracked a smile. "Yeah, but who's Prince Phillip and who're the fairies."

"I mean..." Jack motioned between us three men. "There's three of us. Three fairies..."

"Guys," Erika said calmly.

"Yes?" Jack responded.

"Focus," she said with a stiff, "please."

"Aye aye, Captain," Jack said as he saluted her.

She rolled her eyes.

Reika scooped the map up so she could cradle it into her forearms. She rose, her head still down so that her hood could continue to shroud her eyes.

"I'll keep the map out," she said. "If Ethan moves, the blood should become wet again and go where he does."

"Let's head out before Condan can get the chance to leave," Erika said, her arms falling to her side.

I watched as she strode over to her sword. The blade had struck the ground hard, burying itself a good book's length into the floor. Even Reika or I, two immortals naturally stronger than any human, would have struggled to withdraw a blade that deep into the ground from its sheath. Erika, on the other hand, wrapped her fingers around the hilt. Stepped out so that her stand was wide. And pulled the blade out smoothly, as if it had only been buried into butter.

She tossed the weapon up so that the hilt would rise up, allowing her to grab it by its blade. Then she held it out to Adam, so that he could grab the pommel of it. When he had taken it, she turned to me.

"Darbie, you lead the way," she instructed. "Move us along quickly, but also try to give yourself enough time to regain some strength, can you do that?"

"Of course, Eri," I promised, but it was hollow.

In truth, we could be there in an hour if we moved rapidly. Two if we were planning to conserve our energy. I could feel my magick chugging back, but it was slow. Bitterly slow. Like making tea in ice water.

"Here, Darbie," Reika said, shuffling sideways towards me so she didn't have to face me. "Take the map." She pushed it out towards me and I gently lifted it from the cradle she had made for it in her arms.

Reika reached over her shoulder, pulling her bow off and notching an arrow, leaving it to rest at the ready. Adam rolled the weight of the sword between each hand, checking the balance of it after Jack struck it with lightning. The latter was walking past me now, heading towards the door with my staff still in hand. He eyed me as he passed, raking in my appearance. He offered me a smile, and then a nod towards the door.

19

Adam

Darbie was giving the directions, but it was Erika who took up the lead. Like always when she was tense, she was putting as much distance between us and her. As well as speaking out as if she was the only one with a brutal past on the team.

I winced at the thought.

She was the only one with a brutal past, comparatively.

"How many wars was she in again, Darbs?" I asked the elf who was striding beside me.

He looked over at me, then up at Erika who was marching along towards the rising sun ahead.

"Three," Darbie said. "We both lived through the first. It killed our families and was the reason we met. She fought in the second one, conscripted by what would become the magick council to fight against magick-born who wanted total control over earth. The third one was the war between the gods after free movement between the two worlds had been cut off."

"Brought in by the magick council again, right?" I asked.

He nodded. "Yeah. The Morrigan is the head of the war seat. She advises how the magick council should approach battles. Being a celtic goddess, she was partial to having a celtic champion. Erika was easy prey. She didn't know what she was or what she was capable of, so it was easy for them to spin some web of lies that she was saved by the grace of the gods so that she could save the rest of the world.

"She was their good little soldier for hundreds of years while the war between gods waged." Darbie laughed bitterly. "All because two groups of gods disagreed on whether the otherworld should be a hierarchy or a democracy."

"Was it a brutal battle?"

"Mmhm," Darbie hummed sadly. "You know how civil wars are always the deadliest battles in countries' histories because citizens are just killing each other?"

I nodded.

"Well," Darbie stopped to swallow hard. "Imagine a civil war that lasts over two hundred years. The total casualties still out-number the amount of living magick-born today. And Erika was at the front line of that."

I looked towards the soldier at our head. With the pink sun rising behind her, she looked beautiful. Like a stereotypical romance sweetheart about to run off into the colour to find her happiness. Then she would glance back to make sure the group was still together, and I'd see the darkness of her face against the brightness of the day.

"I think that's why she gets like this when things go bad," I said.

"Like what?" Darbie asked.

"So aggressive. It's like her autopilot from the wars kicks in and the only instinct she has is to charge towards the front line until she drowns in blood."

Darbie winced. "Can I tell you a story, quickly?"

I nodded silently.

361

Darbie's eyes turned glassy, and I watched as he blinked the wetness away before speaking.

"My parents died when I was around the age of fifty," he said. "Elves age differently, so this was young for my people. I didn't know everything about magick that I was supposed to, and with the war between magick and man going on, with the slaying of dragons also happening as a terrifying undertone, there wasn't exactly anyone who could teach me about magick.

"I met Erika when another fight between a dragon and a DeathMarker spilled over into the forest by my house. I was collecting plants to try to study on my own when the flames started. I should have ran out, but I had nothing to live for and knew there were tons of others in the woods. So I ran to the fire. And I found an unconscious human. A real beefy guy, probably a black smith or something.

"I couldn't pick him up, and the fire was getting closer. I kept struggling before eventually just giving up and sitting down next to him. I closed my eyes, ready to go out next to this stranger. Then Erika ran up, a little nymph baby in her arms. She slapped the shit out of me. Told me to stop being a weakling in some harsher druidic words as she shoved the baby into my hands and literally threw the human over her shoulder."

Darbie stopped talking so that he could look down around the map and kick a pebble that was on the dirt path ahead of us. The brown rock skidded across the forest floor losing chunks of itself as it went. We both watched as it continued to roll on its self-destructive path until it finally collided with a larger block of stone and broke into smaller pieces.

"That was how we became friends," he summarised. "Before she went off to war. She was actually the first person who ever let me study their powers, because she was just as curious as I was."

"So then," I hesitated with every word. "Nothing much has changed about her in all this time."

Darbie shook his head. "No. She was always this brutal. Always intense. Any other state is the one that's temporary."

Up ahead, Erika dropped to her belly, laying low on the lip of a risen hill. She shimmied up, slowly shifting her hips side to side as she went. Dust rose up around her as she moved, then curled back down towards her back like a wide bottomed heart of dirt wrapping around her.

Darbie and I dropped into a crouch as we rushed up the dry hill beside her. As we crested, we fell onto our stomachs as well, crawling up with our forearms to get on line with her. Over the ridge, down across a valleyed clearing, was the rubble of a castle.

One wide, thick-walled looking tower remained standing on the right most side. To the left of it, massive blocks of yellowish stone were strewn about, some worn down with rounded edges and broken corners, others still almost perfectly intact so that one could rebuild the structure of the caste had they wanted to.

At the top of the tower, the structure ended in a set of flared battlements. Then, built on top of the tower, a smaller structure that looked like a hut stood low and fat, with a steepled roof. Arched windows were cut into the short walls of the pinnacle structure, and through them we could see chains hanging from the ceiling. Ice sprawled out from within it, wrapping up to the top of the roof.

I heard the sounds of dirt shifting behind me. I leaned onto my side to look down at Jack and Reika who were crawling up behind us.

Reika shuffled up to my right, and Jack to my left - using Darbie's staff to split the elf and I up so he could squeeze in between.

363

We took a moment to lay there, taking in the scene in the cold and light of the rising sun. I could hear my heartbeat in my ears, blending in with the sound of my friends' hushed breaths.

"There's no wildlife here," Reika whispered.

It fell silent again while each of us waited, listening to see if there was a hint of a bird in the distance, or bugs buzzing through the air. But not even the breeze blew.

I looked back behind us. Even the ground changed as we got closer to this place. A bus length away, the ground was still speckled with dense grass and foliage. The trees were full and dark. But here, on this hill we laid on, the grass had died and only dirt remained. The trees were also twisted down into strange angles, like giants had pulled and bent them as they liked.

Darbie shuttered. "I told you, you can feel the darkness here."

"Mmm." Reika shifted beside me. "Yeah, it makes me feel sick."

I looked over to Jack and Darbie, then past them, to Erika, who was beginning to shuffle down off the hill.

"Erika," I called after her in a sharp whisper.

She turned around, her butt so low in her crouch that it nearly dusted the ground.

"Where are you going?" I continued to whisper harshly.

She nudged her chin in the direction of the castle. "We need to get a better look at what we're going into. I'm going to find another vantage point."

"We shouldn't go alone," Darbie said. "That's how we got into this mess in the first place."

Erika rolled her eyes. "Condan and I are evenly matched-
"

"I would argue otherwise," Darbie snapped. "You may have the same amount of magick potential, but he's had ten times as long to master his."

"He's threatening my family, time means shit in this situation," she replied, and then it was Darbie's turn to roll his eyes. Nonetheless, Erika continued, "Darbie, you and Jack move around to the right, see if you can get a better look at the top of the tower. Adam and Reika, stay here and keep an eye out. Jack can you cast rays of light?"

"You mean can I perform one of the simplest illusions possible?" he scoffed. "Yeah."

Erika let out an exasperated sigh. "Okay, cool," she snipped out. "Reika, Jack, if you see Ethan and can move in on him, send up a blue ray. If you see Condan send up a black one. And if you're in danger go for red. Otherwise, meet back here in less than an hour so we can come up with a game plan, okay?"

"We're actually making a plan for once?" Jack gasped. "It's a fucking miracle."

Erika shook her head and moved on, rounding deeping into the woods while keeping her eyes fixed on the ruins.

"If you're in danger," Darbie said and he and Jack began moving away. "You can also just scream really loud."

I chuckled a bit. "Thanks Darbie," I said. "You two stay safe. We'll see you in a bit."

And just like that, only Reika and I were laying in the dirt, with no sound beyond our own breathing and heartbeats to fill the air.

"We should be charging in with you in the front," I finally muttered after several minutes of silence had passed. "Just let you glare down anything that crosses our path."

"And what happens if I accidentally glare at Ethan?" she replied coolly.

"You know what Ethan looks like, just don't look at him," I argued.

Reika laughed bitterly. "That's not how a nachtkrapp's curse works."

I looked over at her expectantly. Her head twitched towards me, but stopped, halting her in her tracks so that her gaze stayed locked onto the castle.

"The nachtkrapp is a parent who's been cursed because they failed to look after their children, resulting in their deaths," she explained. "They're cursed to always want to take care of children, but always kill them by simply being near them. Children can't help but look at a massive raven-like monster, but as soon as they see its eyes, they die."

"In conclusion," I sighed. "You don't have to look into Ethan's eyes to accidentally kill him, he just has to look into yours."

She nodded. "Besides, we don't know how long this magick will last, nor do we know what else is in the castle. This is the safest approach."

"So you agree with how Erika is running this?"

"I didn't say that," she said. "I think Erika is acting as if she's surrounded by hardened soldiers, which is causing a lot of disconnect amongst the group. She needs to learn to communicate. But besides that, yes, I do think that her strategy is the best course of action."

"I just wish-"

"Stop," Reika warned. "You're in a relationship with a woman who's whole life has been built around war. Accept her as she is, or face the fact that you may need to be with someone softer."

I pressed my lips together.

366

The rest of the time passed in silence and polluted thoughts. Darbie and Jack were the first to return.

"There's nothing along the backside," Jack whispered. "The wall is still intact, as well as the moat that surrounds it."

Darbie and Jack crawled back up the hill beside us.

"The moat connects to a river along there," Darbie added. "It cut us off from reaching the other side. We tried to get around it, but it too deep into the forest."

"The water is too deep and way to strong to swim across, too," Jack said. "It's like its been charmed to push a thousand times harder so that no one can swim up to the wall."

"There's probably a weakness Condan is trying to cover up there," Erika whispered as she snuck back up behind us.

We all jumped at the first sound of her voice, but settled quickly as she drew herself up to meet us. Her face was covered in soot, and her already ill-fitting clothes looked even more tattered as she got closer.

"Why do you look like you've been crawling down a chimney?" Jack asked, disgusted.

"Because I have," she said, looking back at him. "There's an old vent on the south side of the ruins that drops down into the underbelly of the castle. It looks like an old furnace room or something. There's a stairway that leads into a hall. One way goes up toward the ground level where we can get to the tower, and the other way goes down deeper."

"Did you go deeper?" Darbie gasped, completely bewildered.

Erika shook her head. "No, I do, to some degree, value my life. I don't need to descend into hell without at least someone backing me up."

"So you do possess at least one brain cell then?" Darbie joked.

367

Erika cracked a smile. "Be careful. Keep talking shit like that and I'll hit you hard enough you'll go down to one as well."

"Not possible," he scoffed in return. "I possess too many."

Erika rolled her eyes, but stayed with a relaxed expression.

"I can smell Ethan, I think," she said. "His aftershave wafted up the stairs, so I he may be up in the tower. Given how quiet it is, Condan must have left him up there to freeze."

"The dark dragon is probably in the earth below," Reika said. "His elements are water and earth. The deeper down, the more at home he feels."

"The air coming up from down that hall was bitter fucking cold too," Erika said. "If it were up to me, I'd say purple is right."

"So whats the game plan?" Jack asked.

Erika sighed. "We can all fit in the chimney, so we should stick together. We get in, move to Ethan, get out. Stay out of sight as best as we can. We don't know where Condan is or who he has with him. If we get out in the open, especially on earth, we're sitting ducks."

"Stealth mission," Darbie muttered. "Shouldn't be too hard."

Erika pursed her lips and looked back over at the ruins. Marred with soot, she looked darker. A dark cut of black coal lined her cheek, making her cheek bone look raised and sharp. She could have cut me with the way it looked.

I smiled to myself.

I would have let her cut me if she wanted to.

She was beautiful even in her brutality. I wasn't going to forget that ever again.

She looked back at us, and her eyes met mine. Immediately, they softened. She blinked slowly, her thick blanket of black eye lashes batting down against the debris painted skin. She offered me a smile.

"We're almost done," she said to me. "We'll have him back soon. Then we can go home and rest." She looked over the rest of the group now, her features stiffening again as she regathered her authority. "Alright, let's move. Stay low, stay quiet."

She moved off the hill first, followed close behind by Jack and Darbie. Then Reika tapped my shoulder, letting me know she was ready, and I moved off, the purple goddess close on my heels.

I didn't look back at her, but I listened out for her footsteps as we moved. She was lighter on her feet than I was, making it hard to hear her over the sounds of myself, but the silence in the world around us helped.

Through the dark woods, we moved quickly. If I looked to my right, I could see the layout of the ruins change. The tower was slowly moving to the background, and the sprinkled rubble of walls and corners of stone were laid out in front. The closer parts of the ruined castle were in much smaller pieces, but the back portion, the one protected by the tall trees directly behind it, was still made up of completed sections.

In a few places, I could see where the floor of a second story jutted out of walls, leaving the half destroyed rooms open. Some of them had wood rods running through the stone walls that still stuck out even after the rocks had fallen away, making the walls look like a half decayed skeleton with the rib cage protruding from thick, grey tissue.

The ruins eventually met with the tree line, casting shadows into the forest so that the darkness enveloped everything.

369

We moved along the chipped and broken wall of the castle, still tucked away under the canopy of malformed trees, until we reached a wall with a square window cut out of it. Black stains ran up the rock from the square, hinting to the pillars of smoke that once had consumed the air we were standing in now.

"This is it," Erika whispered, stopping to kneel down in front of the opening.

Jack, on the other hand, didn't stop. He dove past Erika, head and staff first into the chimney. If it hadn't been for her quick hands and fast reaction, he would have gone all the way down. But instead, her hand gripped his ankle as the rest of his body went down, and she was able to tug him to a stop.

She hoisted him out, and he came out with the staff stretched out above him, leaving him looking like a dust-feather spray-painted in black as he flopped onto his knees.

Erika sighed. "Jack, going down head first means you land head first. Into a stone building. Where the floor is stone. Stone isn't really good for the head."

"Right…" Through the black dust, I could see Jack's eyes tint red with embarrassment.

"You wanna try again?" Erika asked. "You're more than welcome to go first."

Jack nodded and stood up. This time, he lifted his legs up one at a time and fed them into the window. He sat with his butt hanging over the ledge so he could hold himself up while he turned to look back at Darbie.

He nodded down the hole. "You come in after me, okay?"

Darbie moved closer, and Jack pushed himself down. Then Darbie was following in my friend's footsteps, lifting himself in and pushing himself down.

Erika looked over to Reika. "You want to go next?" she asked.

Reika shook her head.

"My hood is likely going to fly up as I go down," Reika explained. "Better I go last so all of you can get down there and look away."

Erika nodded, then looked at me.

"Then I guess you're up," she said.

"Age before beauty," I snarked with a playful smile.

Erika rolled her eyes, but moved towards the chimney nonetheless. "Every time," she muttered as she crawled in.

I moved over to it next.

"I'll wait a few seconds before I follow," Reika said. "Give you all enough time to turn around.

I looked back at her. Her head was low, and her black hood was so far down I could barely see her chin.

"With your hood up like that, you almost look like the grim reaper," I commented off-hand.

She shifted her head to the side. "I pretty much am right now."

"Well, if something happens in those two seconds you're up here," I said as I crawled in. "You use those powers of death on them first and ask questions later, okay?"

She scoffed, then lunged forward and shoved my back, pushing me down the dark and dusty ventilation shaft.

The shaft wasn't long. Maybe two metres at most. But it was at just the right angle, and long enough, that for the last foot or so, my heart started to crawl into my throat.

Then my friends were around me, grabbing my body mid air so that I wouldn't slam into the ground. The three sets of hands gently set me onto the solid floor before stepping away.

I walked forward with Erika beside me, her finger pressed to her lips in a silencing motion. On my other side, Darbie and

371

Jack were backing away from the vent with their eyes sealed tightly shut.

A few moments later, a soft set of two taps plunked onto the ground behind me. They were followed by the muffled sound of fabric moving, before Reika whispered, "Okay, I'm good."

Erika was the first one to look back at the demi-goddess. I looked over at the two sorcerers first, then rounded back to check on Reika. She was the only one who seemed completely unaffected by the chimney. She had already been dressed head to toe in black, now she just looked matte.

"Everyone okay?" Erika whispered.

Darbie and Jack gave each other short, quick pat downs, while Erika reached out to put one hand over my shoulder to the back of my neck, and the other on my chest.

"You always have such a strong heartbeat," she whispered up at me.

I leaned down and kissed her quickly.

"Only because I have you," I said in return, resting my forehead against hers. "You can fall asleep listening to it when we get home."

She let go of me and began stepping away.

"I'll hold you to that," she said.

She moved around me, walking towards the stairs leading up to the rest of the room.

The shaft had dropped us down into a pit set into the space. The basin was stained completely black and had small metal vents cut into the base corners, hinting that this pit was likely a massive fire poole at one point.

On the far side of the pit, opposite the vent, there was a set of three stairs, raising us into the main chamber. Iron shelves were built into the wall to the left, and to the right there was an iron door open wide.

Erika approached the open door. Darbie and Jack followed next, and Reika and I followed suit at the back of the pack.

Darbie and Erika were the closest to the door to actually look out. From my vantage point, I could see a hallway, blue from the rock and darkness. Going up the hallway to the right, there was the faintest hint of light. But the other way, I could feel the chill blowing in, even from where I was standing.

"Condan's down there," Erika nodded down towards the cold.

"And Ethan's up the other way," I clarified. "Let's go get him then."

But no one moved. Erika grimaced.

"Condan is down there," she said again and looked over at us. She met Darbie's eyes first, and he seemed to reciprocate what her's were saying. Then she looked at me and I furrowed my brows, not understanding.

"We could end this," she insinuated. "He doesn't know we're here. Jack and I could go down there and take him by surprise."

I shook my head and opened my mouth to speak.

"Jack doesn't go without me," Darbie said before I could. "Reika can go with Adam. She has her magick and the death rays, they can protect each other."

"No-" I tried to say.

"This could all be over before it begins," Erika muttered.

Darbie was nodding. "It's not a bad idea."

Jack tightened his grip on Darbie's staff. "I have a few things I'd like to teach that elf."

Reika sighed behind me, but said nothing.

I looked back at her, hoping to find some kind of support in my stance that this was a bad idea. But Reika was just shaking her head, not saying anything.

"Let's do this, then," Erika whispered, her voice sure. "Adam and Reika go get Ethan and get him to the cabin. The three of us go and eliminate the threat."

"What about not splitting up?" I hissed.

Erika looked at me. "It's three against one. Those odds are good."

"What happened to getting Ethan, then going home to rest?" I snapped.

She shook her head. "We'll be right behind you."

"But-"

"Adam," she said. "If he stays as a player on the table, he could hurt a lot more people. There are two birds here, saving our friend and taking out a threat. We can't do both with one stone this time, we have to become two."

Reika's hand was tapping my shoulder again, letting me know she was ready.

Ready for what? I wondered.

We were going into the assumed, which was just another term for the unknown. We assumed we knew where Ethan was. We assumed that Condan didn't know we were here. We were assuming this was going to go off without a hitch.

ASSUME = ASS out of U and Me

"Fine," I agreed nonetheless.

Erika stepped into the hallway then, and moved down just enough for the rest of us to move out. Darbie and Jacky passed her, then they stopped and waited. I went into the hall and stopped beside Erika while Reika went up the hall behind me.

"I love you," she said. "When we get home, I'll set up the entire house while you sleep."

374

I reached out and held her hand.

"I don't think I can ever fall asleep again without you laying next to me," I said.

She squeezed my hand. "Then I'll nap with you."

"Okay," I said and we both let go. "Be safe, I'll see you when this is done."

She nodded and backed down the hall, holding my eyes long enough for me to take a breath. Then she turned around, rounded the curve of the hall, and was gone.

Behind me, Reika had gone up the walkway to a set of stairs. A series of three steps rose, followed by a slightly inclined piece of hallway, which connected another series of three steps, followed by another strip, and so on, all the way up until I couldn't see any farther.

She was waiting at the top of the second set of stairs, her cowl down, the darkness in front of her and the light bleeding in behind. I didn't spend another second waiting to go.

Darbie

The farther down we got, the colder it became until, eventually, breathing hurt.

Jack's grip tightened on my staff and the gem began to glow, hinting to me that he was summoning warmth without meaning to.

"Erika," I whispered and she stopped. She looked back at us, concern on her face. I shook my head. "It's too cold down here for us."

I wrapped my arms around Jack's shoulders. She took one look at him and stepped closer. Heat radiated off of her body until we were surrounded in it.

"Better?" she whispered back.

I nodded.

She turned around, but before carrying on, called quietly over her shoulder, "Stay close, I'm going to keep the warm bubble small so we can still feel where to go."

We all moved quicker after that, but it was still taking too much time. There were too many doors and hallways. We were using the cold as our guide, so we had to take each direction and head down it for a while before it started warming up. Then we would turn around and start again down another direction.

Once wrapped in the heat, we started running off the hints of ice, which made us travel even longer. Frost ran much farther on the frigid rock than the cold air did, and we couldn't feel it now.

"We've been going for hours," Jack said. "Do you think Adam and Reika got Ethan out?"

"The fact that it's been so quiet means there wasn't a battle or anything," I replied. "They probably snuck in, snatched him, and snuck out without making a sound."

"These tunnels run so far down that even if they weren't totally silent they probably weren't heard," Jack replied.

We reached a four way intersection in the hall. The route in front of us continued to descend downwards, while the two off to our left seemed to curve back up. We walked straight ahead, carrying on into the depth.

A few steps past the intersection, Erika suddenly stopped. Jack slammed into her back before bouncing back into my arms. The girl didn't budge.

"What the hell," Jack hissed.

Erika turned half way, and smelt the air. She squinted, confused by her own sense of smell. She took a second deep breath and let it out before looking at me.

"I think I smell Ethan's aftershave," she said, her forehead wrinkled.

I took a step back, Jack still in my arms, and looked down either hallway.

Then I looked back at her. "Do you think we moved round in a circle?"

She turned fully now and walked around me, pulling in deep breaths as she moved. She followed her nose as it led her down the corridor to the right.

I brought Jack to his feet and we quickly followed after.

Not even a metre down the new path, I could smell Ethan's aftershave too, as well as the faintest scent of stagnant water and-

"Blood," Jack said as he started to take harsh sniffs of the air too. "It smells like blood down here."

Erika stopped again.

We all did.

We turned to look at one another. A silent understanding of what the situation likely was passed between us. We each took a deep breath at once, an unintentional group strengthening exercise so that no matter what it was we found, we wouldn't break.

Erika swallowed hard, then turned and carried on.

At the end of the hall, there was only one way to go. Another hall turned off and continued to head down until it ended with a massive iron door several metres ahead.

We stopped and stared down the hall.

"Maybe the smell of blood is coming from that old rusty door," Jack said, hopefully.

Erika took in a shaky breath and closed her eyes. At the end of it, she opened them.

"Come on," she said. "We can't waste time."

She led us down the cold, stone passageway. The only light came from the blue of my staff in Jack's hands, and even that flickered under the pressure of fear and the air. This hall was the darkest and the coldest we had been down, and as Erika reached the door and began to pull it open, even the heat from her body wasn't enough.

It was so cold that every muscle in my back immediately tensed and no amount of trying to breath or relax was helping it. My immortal skin couldn't handle the frigid air. Jack, meanwhile, immediately crouched down into the foetal position, pressing his body into itself and then into my legs.

Erika struggled to push the loud, heavy, metal door open. She shoved her shoulder into, and leaned so far over that I feared she was going to slide face first into the ground. But it inched open.

When she had pressed it flat against the wall beside it, she moved back over to us and grew warmer. Her skin began to glow orange, and bits of gold popped up along her skin like pretty little heat blisters. The hall around us was lit up in the colour and warmth of flames that weren't visible or audible.

Jack relaxed against me and straightened up to stand.

"Fuck," he hissed. "There's no fucking way Ethan is down there. If he is, he's frozen to death."

Erika looked at him solemnly, then gazed down through the open doorway.

A long set of spiral stairs descended into icy darkness. There wasn't a speck of light that came up from them, but we could hear the faintest sound of metal clinking together gently somewhere far beyond our eyesight.

"Something or someone *is* moving down there," I commented.

Jack snapped his head around to look at me. "Yeah, it's probably Condan, preparing to kill us."

"You two can stay up here if you want," Erika said, her tone already sounding defeated. "But I need to know for sure who's down there. I need this to end, one way or another. I can't take another war. I can't take more death."

I watched her back as it rose and fell.

She was broken when I found her. Without a house. Without a family. Without a home. I thought that had changed when she gained all of us. But hearing how she spoke, watching how she looked down into that darkness…

"I'm not letting you go alone," I said. "Go ahead, we're behind you."

Jack and I followed the heat as she headed down. My staff was no longer our main source of light, but rather the golden hues shining off of Erika in metre lengths. She might as well have been a human sized lightbulb.

The lower we got, the louder the clinking got until I could make out the familiar sound of chains dancing together, rolling off one another.

Eventually, we reached the bottom. Erika entered the room and sweeped her eyes over the entire space, giving Jack enough time to see Ethan first.

"Ethan!" he shouted and ran across the room to where Ethan was chained up, beaten, bloodied and blue from the ice.

Erika finished her sweep and, finding the space empty and safe, she was the next to rush over to the chained, injured man.

I looked around the room as well. The entire space was black like a starless night sky and covered in etchings. Words,

379

diagrams and various images were carved into the rock walls. There wasn't a single space that was left unmarred. Considering the size of the room and the font of the writing - which wasn't much bigger than a centimetre or two tall per letter - it must have taken the artist years to fill all the space.

Behind the desk, just off to the side of the door, the wall was especially detailed. Diagrams with shapes and arrows were also littered with single words and paragraphs combined, like someone had spent days trying to depict the complexities of their darkest thoughts.

I recognized the language, but couldn't read more than a few words.

"Erika," I called out to her.

She had reached Ethan and Jack now, and while Jack held the unconscious man up, she had set to trying to figure out how to undo his binds. Now, she stopped to give me her attention.

"This is ancient elvish," I told her.

She shook her head and shrugged. "He's an old fucking elf, makes sense. Just remember what you can and let's go find Adam and Reika."

I rushed over to her, spouting out, "No, Erika. *Ancient* elvish. Like elvish from before there were different races of elves. Before this castle would have ever been here. Before this *forest* would have ever been here even. This is a language from the original royal line of the elves."

Erika looked at me, trying to wear her best poker face, but her eyes - slightly wider than normal - gave her away.

"He's not just a prince of the dark elves," I said in a mild panic. "He's like, *the* prince of *all* elves."

"He said he was around when they pushed the druids out of the otherworld," Erika argued. "The prince involved in that wasn't even significant enough for me to remember his name

380

from the history books. If he was the elf prince from all the legends and he had been involved in the slaughtering of my people, more people would know about it."

Jack shifted Ethan so that he could look over at us.

"Explain," he grunted. "Please."

"There's a myth amongst the elves that a ruthless prince is the reason why there's different races of them," Erika explained while she began melting one of the chains. "He was a prince hell-bent on creating the perfect race, capable of with-standing all kinds of environments. He performed... *experiments*, we'll call them, split people's souls and tour apart their magick trying to find ways to make elves resilient to things like needing oxygen underwater, or feeling the heat of fire. The experiments resulted in elves like Darbie, a deep sea elf, who can naturally breathe underwater in the ocean, and other elves like volcanic elves, who's skin is resilient to heat and who can breath ash."

"He was a psychopath who wanted to make the strongest being possible so that he could take over the world and rule it how he deemed fit," I practically shouted. "Our psychopath sounds a lot like that doesn't he?"

The chains fell apart, running through the hoop that held it to the wall in thundering clangs.

Erika focused on Ethan's body now, tucking herself under the opposite arm as Jack.

"We don't know what his plan is, let's not jump to conclusions," she said with ease despite hoisting up pretty much all of Ethan's body weight. "Let's especially not speculate that Condan, the elf with the power of the dark celestial dragon inside him, is a hundreds-of-thousands year old elf king who wants to create the perfect race."

"Shit," Jack muttered. "It'd be like a super-charged Hitler."

I flung my arms out, shouting, "Exactly! And he was a human who still managed to kill millions. This could be an ancient, intelligent, ruthless, beyond powerful, *immortal* Hitler trying to cleanse the world."

"Darbie!" Erika snapped and I hopped to attention. "I understand the situation. I understand the risks. I understand what we may be up against. But right now we can't do anything about it. We need to save our friend. Potentially friend*s*, plural, since we don't know what happened to Adam and Reika. Then we need to regroup, gather our information together, and come up with another plan for the future. Can you pull your shit together until then?"

"Yes," I said without hesitation. I had known Erika for two thousand years, she had protected and led me through some of the worst situations in my life. The very tone of her voice was enough to remind me of that. "Tell me what to do."

She nodded over to the diagrams behind the desk.

"Memorise as much of that as you can," she ordered. "I have a feeling it's important."

I marched over to it, and began to memorise as many shapes as I could and tried to decipher as many words as I knew based on the little information that was available in the world for me to have studied in the past.

Erika and Jack laid Ethan down onto the ground behind me and I could hear in hushed tones their plans of approach regarding how they were going to temporarily stabilise his wounds for the move. I wanted to turn around and help them, to offer the minimal medical intelligence that I had. I wasn't a healer by any means, but I knew more about patient care than either of them from the little involvement I had with the wars. I hated everything about conflict, so helping to save lives with medicine and magick had been the only thing I was willing to do.

But my brain was more important in the long run, here. Neither Jack nor Erika had the same mind I did. I had trained myself over the years to capture information so that I could be a successful scholar. Between the three of us, I was the only one who had any hopes of retaining any of the information from the chicken scratch in front of me.

I started from the bottom and read upwards in lines from left to right, just as ancient elvish had been written.

Words like "ascend" or "rise," and "battle" or "killing" were repeated frequently, but because several words in ancient elvish were interchangeable, I couldn't tell exactly what was being said without the context of the statement around it.

At the very top of it all was one sentence, laid out completely alone, surrounded in untouched rock.

"If it dies, I die," I read the sentence aloud.

I looked back over at my friends. Erika stopped to look back.

"What does that mean?" she asked.

I shrugged. "Might not even mean that. It could also be 'if it fights, I fight,' or 'if it kills, I kill,' or even 'if it lives, I live.' There are so many words in the elvish language that all say the same shit, but mean something else."

Jack looked at me and glared.

"Okay, but," he began to argue. "'If it dies, I die,' and 'if I live, it lives,' are literally polar opposite, how does that make any fucking sense?"

"Elves were warrior people," Erika explained calmly as she leaned down to gently wrap Ethan's mangled leg, even taking the time to fold in the dangling flaps of useless skin and muscle. "To kill and be killed were both reasons to live and to die."

Jack drew in a deep, shaky breath. Then he let it out, his eyes glossing over.

"Great," his voice cracked. "Super-charged, murderous, killing-machine Hitler."

He took another breath in, then pursed his lips and tried to breath it out slowly, but it was uneven as tears began to fall down his cheeks.

Erika froze, looking over at the love of my life who was beginning to cry while he looked down at his possibly dead friend.

"Hey," she said and Jack looked up at her. "His race and his power may make him a super-charged, murderous, killing-machine Hitler, but I'm a druid with the light dragon in me. He's gonna have to face off with a super-charged, ultra-protective, saving-machine Mother Theresa, okay?"

Jack let out a short, sob choked laugh. He wiped his cheeks with the back of his wrists and nodded.

His hands were covered in the blood of his friend.

She looked over at me.

"You good to go?" she asked.

I nodded. "As good as I'll ever be."

She tucked her arms under Ethan, then rolled to her feet, holding him against her without any help. Jack rose up as well, shifting my staff in both of his hands while he chewed on his bottom lip.

The two of them started heading towards the door, and I used that opportunity to take one last look at the writing on the wall. When they made it to the doorway, I looked away and went after them.

Erika

Hours. It took hours to get to Ethan. Then hours to get out. But as we came out of the castle underground into the light of the ruins, there was no denying that the sun had barely moved from its place in the sky.

Did a whole day pass by that we were under there? I wondered.

But that couldn't have been it. Half a day maybe. Even that seemed far fetched. It couldn't have been more than five or six hours.

I had prepared myself for the sun to be high in the sky, marking the shifting of morning to afternoon, but instead, there was still early morning haze clinging to the top of the tree line, and the sun had just passed the tips of the forest.

I looked around curiously, waiting to hear or see any signs that the world outside had changed.

To my left, through the winding ruins of the castle's ground level, was the archway leading into the tower. Through the doorway, I could see the stairs which were covered in freshly gleaming ice.

I drew my attention to the top of the tower, where a bright red beam of light was shooting up into the sky. It mixed with flashes of blue and black and the clanging of metal.

"Adam and Reika!" Darbie shouted.

He was next to me suddenly, along with Jack, and both of them were wrapping their arms around Ethan's torso, pulling the lifeless body away from me. I didn't argue, I released the man into their grasp and ran towards the door. I jumped over barriers that were short enough to volley, and rushed to move around corners that were taller.

I don't think I have ever run that fast in my life.

Jack's words were running on repeat in my mind.

Super-charged, murderous, killing-machine.

A super-charged, murderous, killing machine who hated humans and craved power above everything else. That was up at the top of an ancient tower, fighting my human boyfriend and my magick-sucking ally.

I slid across the dusty cobblestone of the tower floor, slipping so that I was crashing down on my hip by the stairs. In less than a second I was back to my feet, clawing at the hard ground and using it to drag myself up quicker.

Three large stories to the top. I think even the most toned athlete would be out of breath when they got there. But I was fueled with fear and rage.

At the top, the stairs let out into an open landing. Built into the backside of the tower was an added structure, like a stone tent with triangular-ish archways for doors around the entire thing. Inside the structure, on the bottom level, was a massive brass basin. Behind the basin, a single stairway led up to one long catwalk that ran the length of the wall.

Everything was covered in a layer of snow.

Reika and Adam were backed into the end of the catwalk. Reika was in front of Adam, a circular mass of purple energy in front of them. Adam had armed himself with Reika's bow somehow. As Condan volleyed his magick at them, the purple mass would break, and Adam would use the gap as an opportunity to fire a shot.

Each arrow failed to meet its mark, but the quiver remained filled. As the arrows flew away, they would break apart into stardust, only to reform into solid projectiles with the rest of their kin back in the quiver.

My sword had been lost on the stairwell, where it lay waiting on the third stair up. The snow it laid on was melted and dripping down the ledge of the rock step.

386

I went to the sword and took it up. It was light in my hand. Against my skin, the steel began to crackle with the blue lightning it displayed when manifested.

The sound of the crackling weapon drew Condan's attention to me.

He looked over his shoulder and we met my eyes, holding there long enough to make our decisions. When sent blasts each other's way. Him with ice and I with fire. When the two elements met in the middle, the trails of them corrupted into colour. My flames became riddled with black, filling the air over my head. While his ice turned a blinding white, spraying over the catwalk before fading into nothingness.

He turned back to the two next to him with enough time to parry a silver arrow, sending it down towards me. The tip spiralled right towards my eyes, but it disintegrated before it could reach me, and instead sprayed soft tingling dust onto my cheek.

I moved up a step, watching our assailant as I went, but he was skilled in combat and knew how to handle multiple adversaries.

He moved like it was a dance.

One blast to my friends, then one to me, then parry before sending another attack my way.

When I thought I had memorised his pattern, I sent a double his way, throwing my sword then following the movement immediately with a shower of hot embers. He formed one solid wall of ice to block both, then hoisted it up with one hand, spinning it around and down so that the block of ice came down on Reika's shield of magick, all while he was able to turn and fling a castle brick the size of a mini coop at me.

I was caught off guard by the flawless choreography and took the square boulder head on. It smashed me straight into the wall by the stairwell, shattering to dust and pebbles against my

387

body. I crumpled to the floor on top of the stones, only to have another hit me from the side, flinging me off, down the stairs.

That time I was prepared, and after a few seconds in the air, I had the bright idea to tell the wind to catch me. Fire and air were my natural elements, despite the fact that I always forgot about the latter.

I settled softly onto the ground by the basin.

Condan had turned his attention back to Reika and Adam now that I was out of proximity. What remained of the ice block still held my sword, plunged deep inside like it was excalibur in the stone. The ice had slid past Reika and Adam, and sat in the corner behind them, waiting to be drawn.

I bared my teeth.

Adam and Reika were going to have better luck if they stayed away from Condan, so using ranged weapons like a bow and arrow or magick was a much safer bet for the two of them. The sword, in this situation, would only be useful to myself who could risk getting close enough to Condan to try and land a strike.

I focused on the sword, telling it to banish itself so that I could resummon it. The electricity started to running up and down the blade, but then the ice surrounding it would crack, as if it was tightening around the weapon, and the lightning would fizzle out.

Condan simply looked at the rock ceiling above Reika and Adam and the structure began to come down on them.

Giving up on my sword, I focused my attention on creating a great enough force of wind to blow car sized boulders up and away so that they wouldn't crush my family.

With great effort, I succeeded, which pissed Condan off. He snapped his attention over to me, and just like that, I was struck with another wall of ice. This time I was knocked through the wall, finding myself rolling out from inside the structure and into the open air of the tower roof.

I looked up and watched just in time as Reika used his distracted state to bitch slap the elf with her shield of energy. He stumbled around, catching myself on his hands and knees. Adam let go of the arrow he had already drawn back. It struck Condan in the right shoulder, pushing clear through until it was slicked in blood as black as night.

I let out a small yelp as my right arm went limp. Blood began to trickle down my arm from my shoulder. I struggled to get to my knees so that I could tug my shirt down and see where the wound was. A pinky sized hole gaped through my rotator cuff, just where the arrow had gone through Condan. Only he had a hole in his shirt to prove it, and I had nothing besides the sharp pain of penetrated tissues and the rolling of blood.

"If it dies, I die," I muttered as I got to my feet and jogged back in. "It can also be they. If they die, I die." I grumbled as I moved under the archway. "Getting really sick of all the play on words."

I conducted a stream of wind, picking up the basin and sending it flying towards Condan's head. He held his hand out, and as the metal touched the tip of his finger, it covered itself with ice and shattered to sharp bits.

His hand still out to me, I watched what felt like slow motion as a spear of ice slowly began forming in front of it.

Adam was grabbing my sword now. It came out like butter in his angry hands. He only needed to step once, then lunge, and he was bringing the blade down. The tip pushed against the ribcage, just under where the arrow had struck, cutting through Condan's shirt first. Then the skin began to break, pulling open under the weight and edge of the steel. Bone broke against it, slowing it down, but not stopping it.

I fell to a knee in pain. I struggled to try to pull my right hand back and reach where the wound was forming, but with the pain from the arrow, I could barely move my arm, let alone lift it and reach behind me.

Condan, on the other hand, must have been tougher than I was. Before the sword could get all the way through him, he was throwing his left hand back harshly enough that his entire body flung with it. He backhanded Adam so hard that he was swept completely off his feet and into Reika's arms. Reika dropped her shield to catch him, and Condan used this as his moment to strike.

I held my breath, fearing the end, but Reika was quick. She dropped Adam and pounced. Condan, who was midway through forming a terrifying looking ice spike once again, got punched by a girl. He stumbled a half step back, and looked back at the demi-goddess who wigged him again, this time spinning him so that he was turning towards me.

I was still trying to get to my feet when his ball of ice hit me square in the face. Then I was airborne.

Then I wasn't.

20

Erika

I heard the sword be pulled from its sheath, that's what woke me up. Then, when I opened my eyes, I saw the sky above me was nothing but black smoke. My own sword came down in front of my face, below the black.

I rolled out of the way, tucking to my feet and rising to face my opponent.

Fintan stood in front of me with our sword in his hands, armour on his body, and the flames of a massive tree around us.

The canopy of the tree hung low, closing us into an inferno of flaming leaves, smokey ash, and crackling roots.

I looked down at my feet, which were bare on top of the smouldering base of the tree. Each of the veins of wood embedded in the earth were pulsating like a weak heart beat and the top structure began to break apart.

"It's going to die anyway," Fintan shouted over the screaming of the world around us. "Everything is supposed to die eventually."

"What?" I yelled.

He shook his head, clearly frustrated. He brought the sword up crossing his body, then he brought it back across, slashing me across my face.

"Fuck!" I shouted and grabbed my face. I pulled my wet hands away to look at the blood, but there was nothing. I glared up at him. "Why are you doing this?"

"Why are you fighting to live?" he shot back.

"Because-"

"Why do you deserve to live?!" he screamed into my face.

"I'm trying to save his life!" I stood up straighter, pushing my face into his.

His eyes narrowed. "Which one?"

My mouth gaped, as I searched for an answer, but nothing came.

"Do you know how to save him?" he asked. "I promise you, he will die if you don't save him."

"Show me," I begged.

He flipped the sword around, offering me the hilt. "Make the bond."

"The dragon rider bond?" I scoffed. "How will that help?"

He spun the sword back around and pushed it into my stomach. I grunted and waited for the feeling of being stabbed too well through me. Instead, all I felt was a punch to the gut, followed by the sound of metal snapping.

I looked down to see only the hilt in his hand, a jagged fragment of the blade left attached. The rest of it was broken and lying on the floor between us. My skin, which I now realised was exposed as I stood naked amongst the flames, was riddled with diamond-like scales with gold flesh beneath each one, like a billion dollar lizard.

"Condan forced the dragon to submit to him," Fintan said. "You give in to the dragon, and it will be your strength. He mocks you for your control issues, but his will be his weakness. Submit to our nature, so you can share it with him. Our hardness will be the only thing to keep him from breaking."

I swallowed.

Then I met his eye. "How do I make it?"

"It will leave you exposed, vulnerable. They will become your only weakness so you must leave yourself raw to that," he began. "Because of this, it can only be made with someone you've already given your soul to - someone you love more than anything else in existence - or to someone as they lose their soul to death. Someone equally as raw with you as you will be to them. Find a way to focus only on them and the colour of their soul. Reach for it. Touch it. And I promise their's will do the same to you. The dragonrider bond is more desirable to the mind, body and soul than the very desire to breathe. You just need to create the right opportunity."

I nodded. "And you promise this will save Adam from Condan."

Fintan stared down at me with hardened eyes. I looked back and forth between them, looking for the words that were going unspoken.

"Fintan?!" I shouted at him as if he hadn't heard me.

The branches of the burning tree cracked above me. I looked up to inspect the damage. The flames were running deep inside the wood, peaking through only by cracks in the weakening structure. I watched as a crack grew larger and larger until the orange glow of the fire was raging through it. It severed the branch from the rest of the tree and the heavy, flaming limb fell down onto me.

Before it struck, I woke with a start.

393

The world around me was enveloped in a storm of ice and snow. The faintest sight of Darbie kneeling next to me, holding me against him was slowly registering.

Behind him, Jack was struggling to hold up a lifeless looking Ethan.

In front of me, Adam still had my sword and was backed against the end of the catwalk by Condan, who was trapped between Reika and Adam.

I needed to get to them. I needed to make the bond. I had to save him.

To my right, Jack dropped Ethan onto the icy ground. He flopped down next to the frozen body and scrambled to pull it back up into his chest. I wasn't sure if it was the fact that the swirling ice was restricting my already dazed vision, or if I was truly seeing that Ethan's chest was no longer rising and falling. He could have already been dead and we were just lugging around a dead body.

I looked back over to Adam and Reika who were fighting valiantly, but losing. Reika's magick was coming out in short small bursts, and Adam was struggling to swing my sword around any more. Meanwhile, Condan seemed like he was bored by this point.

"No," I whispered to myself. "I need to get there. I submit. I need to give him the strength."

My strength was slowly returning, but not fast enough.

I wasn't going to make it.

21

Adam

I held Erika's sword and lunged forward into Condan. He moved to the side to dodge it, and in my exhaustion I was too slow to retract quick enough. He reached forward and grabbed the blade with ease.

He tugged on it, yanking me forward with him.

"Don't kill him!!" Darbie shouted suddenly from below.

I looked down, barely making him out through the snow storm. Amongst all the white of the blizzard, I could see he was cradling Erika who was bleeding into his arms and the floor beneath.

"It'll kill Erika too!!" Jack screamed up at me. An unconscious Ethan was draped across his shoulder, weighing him down.

After Erika had been knocked unconscious, Reika and I had set to keeping Condan going long enough with hopes that she would come too, or Darbie and Jack would come recharged enough to help.

Now, even with the thickness of the snow around us, I could see the exhaustion on all their faces. Reika looked it too, and I was sure that any second now she would have to tap out.

I looked back to Condan, who was still holding my sword in place, but had turned, focused on Reika, who was glowing purple and pelting small fragments of bone from an unknown location at the evil elf.

I pulled the sword back from him. In his distracted state he let the blade slip from his grasp. The sharp edges cut deep gashes in his hands.

From below, I heard Erika calling out in pain. I looked down to make sure she was alright.

"Fucking kill him!" she screamed up at me, struggling to push to her feet as blood stained her entire right side and her hands.

I turned to do as she commanded. Even if it killed her, none of us had any fight left. It was now or never. We didn't have time to figure out another way. At the end of the day, saving the world was more important than saving the love of my life.

When I looked back, Condan was already staring at me. His blasts of killer ice were aimed at Reika, who shielded herself with a waning wall of magick, but his eyes were set on me.

I should have just swung at his throat.

No thoughts.

No aim.

Just harsh, sure footed movements so that we could end the threat.

Instead I hesitated to listen to my orders.

Hesitation, my friends, is the true killer in life.

I hesitated to make a move on Erika when I first met her at fifteen. It was now eight years later,and while I was blessed to say I had been dating her for the last three, if I hadn't hesitated, we could have had more years together.

Now, because of hesitation, it was only ever going to be three years.

Condan moved his power to me. With no magick to shield myself, and no armour to protect me from his volleys, his ice struck square in my chest. At first, it was painfully cold, like falling onto hard ice with no gloves on.

Then everything was numb, and I fell backwards, stiff and too cold to move.

Immediately after, I suddenly felt warm. Like I was back laying in bed with Erika.

I could see it actually, the heater running in the corner and all her blankets kicked off so they were piled onto me. She slept curled up in a ball with only a small sheet on any more, even if it was cold.

I snuggled in next to her, wrapping my arms around her constantly hot body. Nestling my face into her sweet smelling neck; jasmine and something else I could never quite figure out. Tangerine, maybe? But it wasn't so citrusy, maybe pineapple.

Wrapped in her warmth and her scent, I let myself drift off into a long, perfect sleep.

22

Erika

I watched as the ice pike went through Adam.

It was so white it almost looked blue around Condan's hand.

Then, as it went out through Adam's back, it was slicked red.

I watched as Reika dropped her defensive shield and ran forward, panic painted on her face. But Condan was an experienced fighter, and he didn't need to turn and look at her in order to reach out and strike. His fist hit her hard, right against her temple, and she went down.

I summoned a spear of fire and volleyed it towards Condan, summoning a stream of tight air to follow after it. His glowing eye looked at the flames and batted it away with a rush of snow, but then the wind came hard after it. He was knocked back. The ice around his hand, impaling through Adam, cracked just above his fingers and broke off. Condan went slamming into the wall behind him, and Adam collapsed onto the ground.

I sent more more flames, but he wasn't down more than a second before he was standing, arms outstretched, and commanding the rocks and ice in the walls around us to collapse in.

"We have to go!" Darbie yelled at me, but between the snow whipping around us, the shaking of the Earth, my flames and the sadness that pounded in my chest, I could hardly hear him.

I couldn't see what my friends were doing behind me, but I felt Darbie's staff slam down onto my shoulder as I continued to try and advance. Then I felt nothing. Just the spinning emptiness of portal travel. When I came out, my feet were stumbling on uneven soil. I tried to catch myself by stepping back, only to trip more and land on my side.

I looked up. Jack was outstretching Darbie's staff to me, while Darie held onto it tight. Jack rested his other palm on Ethan, who laid unconscious on the green grass, his body completely blue besides the small cuts, the bruises, and the ice burns.

Darbie collapsed, his body pale and slick with sweat. He was panting, but at least he was alive. Teleporting us hadn't killed him.

"Erika," Jack begged, tears streaming down his eyes. "Ethan's dying, please. Do something."

My attention flicked behind me. The castle was only a hundred or so metres away. It was collapsing, but was still there. If I sprinted, I could get there, maybe get to Adam, bond with him. Give him his life back.

I took a step towards the crumbling rock. Then stopped.

I could hear the heartbeat. I could hear it growing weak, like a watch running out of battery. I could feel the pain, sense the cold that was running through him. He felt alone, abandoned. His mind was running in a dark place with no light to lead him. I was feeling his soul.

I looked down to Ethan and saw his soul's light flickering.

I was feeling *him*.

He was there, on the verge of death, his soul open and perfect for the dragon bond. And if I didn't make it, he was going to die.

I turned and dropped to my knees in front of him. I leaned over, aligning our faces so that I was staring down into the sharp lines of his broken face.

I hesitated, trying to feel for another soul, but I found none.

I cupped my hands under his head and brought his face up to mine. Forcing his mouth open, I pressed my lips to his and breathed in just enough of my essence to fall into that dark place with him. Inside, he couldn't make out anything at first. My light was the first thing he could see, appearing before him as nothing more than a bright light.

"Ethan," I called out to him.

He looked at the light unwavering, unsure of what was going on or where he was. But after a moment and the echoes of my voice, recognition washed over his face. He stepped forward and reached out to me. His fingertips graced the light and we were both ejected from the darkness.

He took in a great, deep breath. Gasping for any energy he could suck into his lungs. His eyes snapped open just long enough to meet mine. His arms shot up to grip my biceps hard.

"There you go, Ethan!" I yelled down at him, seeing the pain and the struggle to cling to life in his eyes. "You have to want to live! You have to fight for it!"

He breathed in deeply a few more times. With each breath his grip grew tighter and tighter on my arms.

He coughed once, closed his eyes, wincing, and I could see the desire to give up on his brow. I shook him and he looked at me, his eyes soft and sad.

400

He wanted to go. He didn't want the bond.

"You son of a bitch," I snarled at him. "I lost him, I'm not gonna lose you too!"

I dropped him and he slammed back on the ground hard. I then cocked my hand back and brought it down across his face, slapping him so hard that the desire for death momentarily left his expression and instead he was looking up at me in shock. Then, just to hammer the nail in, I grabbed him by the collars of his shirt and yanked him up until his lips met mine.

I held him there, in a kiss, until the ground around us began to steam and his hands became tight on my arms again.

When I pulled him away, and we both opened our eyes, his were glowing orange. Fire churned in them and smoke curled up from his mouth. I leaned down, setting him down gently. As he rested back onto the ground, his body relaxed, and he fell into a healing sleep, an expression of peace on his face.

I leaned back onto my haunches. The sound of rocks settling caused me to turn and look over my shoulder. The ancient structure of the tower was reduced to rubble. Not a single heartbeat left. The traces of magick that curled in the air were faint, leading me to believe that Condan had done what Darbie did and teleported out before the building collapsed.

The dark dragon was lost to the wind, both his dragon and elf soul still intact, giving him two magick sources to tap into. He also had Reika with him, a demi-goddess and a priestess of Artemis who could suck magick out of a person. If she chose to help him, those two would be a formidable force.

I, on the other hand, had just bound myself to Ethan, making him my weakness.

I had also lost Adam. The person who had made me want to live again.

I turned back around and looked up at Jack and Darbie. Jack had moved to cradle Ethan's head in his lap, and Darbie was laying on his side, breathing hard down by the poor kid's leg, which had been completely frozen by Condan. The skin was completely black and brittle from the knee down. The bone and tissue were already dead.

But the dragonrider bond was working its magick. I could see golden lines twisting under the skin, just above where the black started. The healing process had begun to remove the dead parts and heal what could be salvaged.

"Will it save his leg?" Darbie asked me.

I shook my head. "I can't bring back the dead. The bond can only stop something that's about to die. True resurrection is something only God is capable of."

"So he won't have a leg?" Jack struggled to ask between sobs.

I reached out and held Ethan's hand. I could feel his pulse in his palm. It was strong now, like the shakes of a volcano when it's erupting.

"No," I confessed. "But he'll be alive."

Jack and I both looked back towards the wreckage behind me.

"I'm sorry, Erika," Darbie whispered.

I looked over at him. He was crying too. He was on his knees now, his hands on the ground. His body was shaking and tears were plummeting to the ground.

"I'm so sorry," he wailed. "I shouldn't have teleported us here. I should have teleported us up to him."

I gritted my teeth, forcing all the emotions down.

"No," I forced out. "Even if you had, you wouldn't've had enough energy to take all five of us. And we don't know if Condan would've used the opportunity to kill someone else."

"But if I had just-" he whispered.

I reached out and grabbed his shoulder. He looked up at me, his face completely wet with tears and sweat.

"Stop," I hushed him. "Your actions saved the four of us. Even if you only saved one person, I still would never ask for more from you." I looked at Jack. "None of us saw this coming. We weren't prepared. We took a loss, but-"

My voice broke and tears started coming now.

In war, I never broke. I never stopped fighting, I always headed straight into the centre where I could die because I didn't care if I lived. There was no one for me to go home to, no one whom I loved enough to want the battles to end.

Unlike before, there was a loss that could break me now. And I let the feeling of pain win. I doubled over and let it rock my body down to the core.

I didn't cry, I screamed. I screamed so loud that birds in the distance took off into flight. So loud that wildlife scattered, trying to get as far away from the glass-shattering sound.

My body steamed, the ground around me singed and shrivelled from the heat. Darbie and Jack jumped back trying to escape the unsafe temperature radiating from my body.

I looked at Ethan's body and watched him glow, like the hotness was nothing but an enjoyable summer's day. He was immune to me now. Incapable of getting burned by my touch.

I reached out and touched him. Unlike Adam, who had always felt cool under my fingers the last few years, Ethan's body felt warm, just like a body should be. I leaned forward and rested my head on his chest, listening to his heartbeat and feeling his heat on my cheek.

It was enough to calm me, and so the heat rolling off of me in waves subsided.

I let my tears stain his shirt.

403

In the distance, just hidden in the treeline, leaves rustled.

I sat up, sniffling and wiping away tears. Darbie and Jack turned around, ready to fight. I summoned fire to my hands, ready to just envelope everything and everyone around me in flames.

A white hue peaked out from behind the tree before Karael did. As she stepped around the trunk, barefoot and glowing, I let her presence rush over me like grace. I extinguished the flames and slumped down.

She walked towards our group and stood between Darbie and Jack.

She gazed down at Ethan, then over at the rubble before, settling her eyes on me.

"What do you want?" I asked her.

She frowned. "I'm here to do my job. To escort an innocent soul to the afterlife."

Jack looked behind me, Darbie looked down at the ground. I looked at Ethan, his features slowly becoming more golden and less blue.

"I'm not supposed to, but I'll salvage the body for you when I collect his soul," Karael said. "That way you can give him a proper druid burial."

She walked on towards the castle, her form slowly growing less solid and fading to an ethereal form so that she could touch his soul when she found it.

Only a few moments later, a shadow fell over my shoulder and onto Ethan's face. I looked over to see Karael holding Adam's bloodied body in her arms as if he weighed nothing. She laid him down at Ethan's feet and rose to look down at the other living, but unconscious man.

"I'm so sorry," Karael whispered. "You have been cursed to live a life where you are constantly forced to choose doing the right thing over saving the lives you love."

I looked away from her soft face and over to Adam. His lips were already blue, but as was most of his body. His skin was almost purple in some areas, where rubble had crushed him. A few thin and splintered bones stuck out from where his collarbones had once been solid, as well as from his right bicep and left forearm. His wrists were crooked and his hands bent in unnatural positions. A leg was bent outwards from the knee, and the other was riddled with blood stains just like his chest.

"Could I have saved him if I chose him instead?" I whispered back. "Please tell me honestly, even if it goes against the rules of spirits."

I was begging with a woman who never broke rules even in life, but I was hoping that for once she would see my desperation and bend for me.

"Erika…" she hesitated.

"Please," I whimpered. "I just need to know."

Darbie stepped forward. "We can't go back, Eri. We can't afford to think in what ifs."

Karael knelt beside me, her white touch rested on my shoulder where she rubbed her delicate fingers over the tension there.

"I won't answer your question," she said. "It won't do you any good to know it. But please trust that saving Ethan was the right thing to do."

23

Erika

We brought Ethan and Adam back through a portal Karael helped us summon.

None of us were surprised to find half of the house collapsed into coal. Half of the dragons were gone, but Xavier and a few remained. They had begun to put the pieces together before we got there.

Darbie and Jack emerged first, dragging Ethan between them. Xavier saw them first and started running. He halted when he saw me behind them carrying Adam's body.

"The east wing of the house is destroyed," Xavier said when we reached him. "Darbie's bedroom and the mastery classroom are gone, but the west wing is still intact. The stairs and a few of the guest rooms are useable."

"Okay," Darbie said, but it was hollow. There was no direction or weight to it. None of us knew where we were going.

"I'll organise a room for him to rest and recover in," Xavier informed us before trotting off to the other side of the house.

Darbie looked back at me. We held each other's eyes. We had been here before.

When you return home from war, you bring back the dirt and the grime from the battlefields. Even after you shower, it's like that muck doesn't come off. There's not enough water in this world that could wash away all the dirt that covered us, it was equivalent to all the soil piled up over the bodies we had buried. Now we had another.

I walked towards the barn where I could lay Adam's body away from the house and the weather for a few days. I needed to prepare a pyre for a druid funeral.

I would need to dig down into the earth a few feet before building up a stack of wood tall enough to be worthy of the status he would have had in my lifetime. It would take at least two days to gather enough trees and dig a big enough basin to catch the ashes. I would need Darbie to trap his body in a protective bubble to keep him from decaying before I could lay him to rest.

But asking for the favour could wait.

I laid Adam down on a workbench in the corner of the barn. The sun squeezed in through the wood slats of the building, painting their warm rays over Adam's now wretched face.

In the safety and silence of the space, I dropped to my knees. I held onto his wounded hand and pressed my forehead against it.

I wanted to cry.

The pain was there.

But it didn't come. Just dry, choke out breaths that struggled to go out or in, as if I had been punched in the gut.

"Please, don't be gone," I mumbled. "I'm back to the place where I don't want to breathe anymore. I don't want to exist without you. Please. Fucking please, Adam. You took my soul and you can't return it and I don't know what to do without it.

"What have I inherited from your death? Not wanting to live? An inability to feel anything more than hollow? I'm impossible to love Adam, you know this. So how dare you leave me to be unloved for eternity? How dare you leave me with a battle to be won? You know that, without you, I won't even be able to win the fight going on inside me.

"Adam, how could you leave me? I just needed a little more time."

The wooden floorboards creaked as someone approached. I turned to see who would dare interrupt my mourning.

Jack stopped next to me, his hands in his pockets. He had grey dirt smeared under his eye and across his cream coloured jumper.

"I'll handle his family," Jack said, not looking at me. "We'll tell them he was caught in ruins that collapsed while we were excavating or something like that. Ethan too, in case he wants to disappear."

I nodded, but didn't say anything. Jack wasn't paying attention to me anyway though. He was looking at Adam. Talking to Adam. He was just speaking as if it were to me so he didn't have to admit it.

If Adam were here, he'd be worried about how we were going to cover up the truth, fabricating some solid cover for us. But he wasn't here to come up with the story. So Jack was doing it for him, and now he was here to keep his friend in the loop. Because that's what we would have done if he was still breathing.

"I was going to give him a druid funeral," I confessed.

"I think he'd prefer that to a normal one," Jack agreed. "Darbie is helping the dragons with the house. I can try to create a solid enough illusion to mimic his body and give it to the coroner's office for his family."

"I should be the one to tell his family."

"You're still wanted for murder," he pointed out. "And sending the spell-covered version of you to lie to his family even more just feels like an insult. I'm sorry, but I think you should use this as an opportunity to let yourself die to the public too. There's no reason for anyone outside of this house to know you exist. You don't need to pretend like you're going to have a normal life anymore, he's dead."

I swallowed down the painful hard truth. Jack's timing was shitty as usual, but he was being real. The only reason I interacted with society was because Adam asked me to. He wanted the best of both this world and the other. That was done now, and it was best to leave it behind sooner rather than drag it out.

I rose to my feet, offering Jack a comforting, but impersonal grip to the shoulder before moving on.

Stepping outside, I walked away from the barn and wandered into the woods.

Nearly a decade ago, Adam had found me here, reading poems to a horse because memories and magick I shouldn't have had haunted me and kept me from being normal. Now, Adam's body would rest here while his soul moved on to somewhere else.

If you believed in what my people believed, you'd burn the body so the soul could float up into the heavens with the rising embers of the fire, and there it would circle as one of the stars, waiting to be reincarnated when the earth called it back down to live again resulting in a shooting star.

Living the life I've lived and seeing the things I've seen, I knew this isn't the case, but it was a nice melancholy dream to think that I would see him again.

In a clearing no more than a half kilometre away from the house, I began to dig out a hole for the base of the pyre. The space was the shape of the moon and the sun colliding; two spheres meeting together, one slightly smaller than the other.

I dug my hole in the centre of the larger circle. Then, I cleared another in the centre of the smaller one. When I was done, the sun had set so long ago the sky had turned to purple from blue in the realm above the trees.

I followed my foot path back to the house and silently crawled up the stairs to the front door. On this side, inside the house, you couldn't tell that half of the structure was missing. The stairs *still* stood in front of the door and rose up to the second story. The hallway was *still* beside them led back into the sage coloured kitchen. And inside the kitchen, Darbie's blackberry brandy *still* sat in the cabinet above the fridge.

I took it and brought it with me up those steps.

Just to the left of the top stair, the door leading into the guest room was wide open, revealing Ethan laying under the ugliest orange sheets I'd ever seen. I could almost laugh at how hideous they were, but I held onto that for a happier day.

Two doors down, the third guestroom's door was shut, leading me to assume Darbie and Jack were fast asleep inside.

In between the couple and Ethan was the door leading to where Adam and I had lived before we moved into our cottage. I winced at the thought of our newly bought home.

Darbie had been listed as our heir when we bought it. That way he could clean out the damn thing before his family could get inside and find things they shouldn't if we died. Now that Adam was gone and the world was going to think I was too, I'd either have to have Darbie sell it, or keep it so I could live in a place that would constantly remind me I was alone.

I shuffled into Ethan's room. They had changed him into loose clothing and bandaged up the rapidly healing ice burns that were still present on his skin. They had laid a thick layer of

410

blankets over him, tucking them up under his armpits so that only his chest, arms and face were showing.

In the corner, a heater hummed, and I rolled my eyes.

He had experienced frostbite in an extreme fashion, but he now had Fintan's magick pumping through him like an antibiotic for all things cold.

I walked over to the heater and turned it off.

There was a chest-of-drawers painted the ugliest green and off white. I opened each drawer, not surprised when I found it empty, save for a book on witchcraft and wizardry, and an itchy looking blanket. I shut both back in and left the chest behind me, having half a mind to turn around and burn it for being both hideous and useless.

Across from the chest, and in the far corner of the room, there was an orange armchair facing Ethan's bed. I dragged my feet as I made my way over to it. I was exhausted, physically and mentally, and after coming so close with death, Ethan wasn't going to wake up from his slumber just because my boots were scraping across the hardwood floor.

I let myself collapse back into the overly soft cushions of the chair.

I watched Ethan rest while I sipped on the blackberry brandy.

"One life kept for one life lost," I muttered the oracle's prophecy between sips that were growing into swigs. "Two souls lost, and a body and a leg. Couldn't avoid it even if I begged."

I laughed bitterly as angry tears stained my face. I didn't wipe them away. I let them fall down onto my dirty sweatpants, and watched as the salty water fell brown instead of clear. If I could see my reflection, I probably wouldn't have recognized the person staring back.

411

"Will it be worth it, this man that you save?" I choked out, faltering with each syllable.

If Darbie and Jack weren't asleep just down the hall I would have screamed. I would have shouted at the top of my fucking lungs into the air, cursing out a being I wasn't sure existed.

I set the bottle of brandy down on the floor beside me and let my head fall into my hands.

Tomorrow, I would cut the wood and build the pyres.

But tonight I would let myself be broken. Tomorrow would be the day I built.

And if Ethan rose on the third day, then we would hold the funeral and say goodbye to the one we loved.

But tonight, it was okay to be broken.

24

Ethan

"So it was more than a week for you?" Jack asked, sitting next me at the dining table.

Darbie walked out of the kitchen, two mugs in his hand, both of which let off so much steam that at first I thought it was smoke. He set one down in front of Jack, who sat with his back to the kitchen, facing me. Then, he rounded behind me so that he could take up the seat to my right.

The soup in front of me had gone cold by comparison. Darbie had prepped it specifically for me, boiling down lamb bones into a broth to supply me nutrients and "help my connective tissues," he claimed. He had added squash, spinach and carrots so I could have some softer, but solid food on my stomach.

All it did was remind me of Clementine. Instead of feeling comforted, it just made me feel like I wanted to vomit all over again.

"Condan said that time moved differently there, like how he had done with Haven," I explained. "I had been there three days by the time he was starting on the diagrams you said you saw. Another three days and they were drawn, but not filled in with as much detail as you say."

Darbie nodded along. "So then probably another two or three days for him to finish. You were probably down there for nine or ten days. Did they feed you? How did they keep you alive?"

I grimaced and pulled my hands into my lap under the table. I didn't want him or Jack to see them shaking.

"There was a vampire child," I said. "She would... feed me. If you could call it that."

Jack shifted beside me. I watched as he casted a brief glance over to Darbie who returned it. Then he looked back at me.

"What did she feed you?" he asked. "It wasn't like her blood, was it?"

I shook my head. "No. Bone broth with carrots."

Darbie, who was holding his warm mug to his lips, looked over the rim of the cup and gave my soup a sideways glance. His eyes went wide and he immediately set his mug down, taking up the bowl instead.

"Let me just," he started awkwardly, then stopped to wave his hand in shy and uncertain motions. "You know, find you something else to eat."

He got up from the table and headed around to the kitchen.

I let out a relieved chuckle.

Jack sighed. I followed suit, letting out one of my own.

The front door, just behind the wall of the dining room, beyond my vision, opened quickly, then slammed shut. Heavy footsteps moved across the floor in a succession of three before Erika was walking into my line of sight.

414

This was my first time seeing her since I had first woken up. She was messier on the outside now, but seemed less so in her mind. When she was in the room with me, she seemed half drunk and spouting angry nonsense. Now, she moved in controlled tightness.

"So you're up?" she announced. "Good. We can limp you out to the woods so you can join us for Adam's funeral."

I winced. I let my eyes drop to my hands, still resting in my lap, and I watched as I ran my own fingers over my knuckles, trying to convince myself to stop shaking.

"Did Darbie and Jack catch you up to speed?" she asked.

I raised my head and shook it.

"No, I was just telling them about what I experienced," I explained. "Apparently you guys had the briefest experience of the time warp Condan concocted."

She was standing beside Jack now, and I waited, expecting her to pull out the seat beside him and take it up. Instead, she remained standing, crossing her dirt covered arms over her chest.

"Time warp?" she asked.

I nodded. "Condan charmed the lower sanctuary so that time moved quicker down there. The day it took for you guys to find me was over a week for myself and Condan."

Erika uncrossed her arms slowly. The angry crease that seemed permanently set on her brow softened too.

"You endured torture for a week?" she asked under her breath. I could feel both the remorse and the disbelief weaving together as her words met my ears.

I swallowed the guilty lump in my throat. "More like ten days or so."

Erika closed her eyes and looked away from me. She breathed in deeply, like sucking in air would pull her together

415

too. Then, with a sigh, she opened her eyes and crossed her arms again, turning her once more hardened stare to me.

"I'm sorry we didn't get there sooner," she apologised, but it was rough and flat, filled with walls that I couldn't climb over.

She looked down at Jack who quickly looked back at me.

Um," he started. "Right, we told everyone that Erika, er, Michelle? I think that's what we were calling her? Well never mind. Erika and Adam. We told everyone they died. Erika was cremated and sent to her distant cousin in France to be buried in some ancient and distant related family crypt. An illusion body was given to Adam's family. They cremated him and are holding a service in a few days. We also said that you were badly injured and in a hospital in Germany because the wounds were so bad they couldn't transport you."

Jack paused to suck in a big breath after spouting off his speech in almost one breath.

Erika cleared her throat. "It's up to you if you want to die or not," she said. "We can tell your mum you died of your wounds. Give her a fake body to bury too."

My mum had lost her eldest son and her husband already in this life. It had pushed her to drink until she no longer existed to the world around her. Even though I was still alive, she had abandoned me to drink. But now, the thought of convincing the world I was dead felt like *I* was abandoning *her*.

"Can I get back to you?" I asked.

Jack looked back at Erika. She offered a small nod.

Darbie came back with honey tea, saltine crackers and steamed zucchini.

"Try this," he offered. "It's all soft food so hopefully your body won't reject it. You have a bad case of malnutrition though. We'll need to keep your protein and fat intake down, but your

416

carb intake up. Unfortunately you'll be eating a lot of small portions the next few days."

"Are we sure?" Jack asked. "I mean, besides the bruises and the missing leg, he actually looks really good. I think the bond thing pretty much did the job."

Erika hummed behind him.

"Let's play it safe the next couple days, just in case," she said. "At the very least it'll give us all something to focus on."

I sighed.

"I really do feel okay," I spoke. "Just a little defeated is all."

Jack laughed bitterly. "Don't worry, that's going around these days."

Erika turned around and began walking out of the dining room. I watched as her small but solid frame receded from me. At the doorway she stopped. She rested her hand against the wall and leaned back to look at us.

"I'm going to bring Adam's body to the pyre," she announced softly. "When you're finished eating, Darbie and Jack will show you the way. It's time he rested."

The fire wasn't hot to Erika and I. We sat close to it, watching it consume his linen cloth wrapped body and take it up to the heavens in smoke and embers.

I was closer to flames than I had ever been in my life, and I could see the fine details of hot coals like never before. If I lifted my leg up and reached out just an inch, I could have poked them with my bare toe.

Behind us, Darbie and Jack were walking back to the house. They had stayed until the body was enveloped, then Jack's tears drew them away.

I looked over my shoulder and watched as they passed by the other built pyre, heading towards the narrow footpath etched through the woods from hard rounds of travel.

"Who's the other Pyre for?" I asked.

"You," Erika said simply.

I let out a short, disappointed laugh. "Gee, thanks. Glad to see you had faith in me."

Erika shook her head.

"It's symbolic, dumbass," she said. "You're bound to me now. From this day on, so long as I'm alive, you will never age. You will never be sick. You will never be cold. You will never be human. I'm sorry, but if you choose to not fake your death, it will only be temporary. Eventually, you will have to leave it all behind you."

"So you're saying I should just ignore my pain and guilt at the thought of abandoning my mom?" I snapped.

She looked over at me. Facing her head on, I could see the streaks on her face where tears had washed away the dirt.

"I'm saying you shouldn't make it worse by drawing it out," she answered. "And I *am* sorry for that."

I didn't say anything. She looked back to the body as the smell of burning flesh began to reek through the air. I grimaced, and she raised her hand out. Just like that, the wind blew it away, and instead, the sweet smell of jasmine permeated through.

I watched her while she held her hand in the air. She spun it around smoothing, like a ballerina would move theirs during a beautiful performance.

"You look like you're dancing," I commented thoughtlessly.

A faint smile graced her lips.

"I'd need music to do that," she replied. "This is just me moving the air up."

I nudged her with my shoulder. "Give me about six hours to crawl to the house and back to get my figure-eight banjo thingy and I could figure out how to play us a song."

She genuinely smiled for a second then.

"That reminds me of a poem," she said. *"A damsel with a dulcimer in a vision I once saw."* She paused to let her eyes and hand fall into her lap. *"Could I revive within me her symphony and song, to such a deep delight 'twould win me."*

She looked up to the sky. "And a waning moon to top it all off." She chuckled. *"A savage place as holy and enchanted as ever, beneath a waning moon, was haunted by woman wailing for her demon-lover."*

"Oh," I gasped breathlessly as recognition graced me. "Wait, I know that one. It's a drug induced dream, isn't it?"

Erika looked over at me and nodded peacefully. "S.T. Coleridge. A vision in a dream. He told me about it after he had it."

I pulled back, a bit surprised. "You knew the poet from hundreds of years ago."

She laughed a bit. "I not only knew him, but I also slept with him."

I shook my head. "What would Adam say?" I mocked her, still trying desperately to lighten the mood.

She looked into the fire. "He knew," she choked. The tears began to come again. "He knew all the worst parts of me. He deserved better."

She was sobbing now, and I reached out to pull her into my chest, not quite sure what else to do.

419

She cried and clung to me, balling my shirt up into her firsts. I ran my hand over her hair, brushing out the bits of dirt and the stray strands, calming down her curls just as much as her nerves. I shushed her and rocked us both back and forth like an infant who had woken itself up from it's nap.

"I'm so sorry, Ethan," she said, her voice wet and ragged. "I know you were prepared to die. I took that from you. I forced you to stay here when you didn't want to."

I shushed her some more. "Don't say. It's not true." I laid back down onto the dirt so that she could lay on me and I could stare up at the dark sky.

"I want to live now," I said honestly. "At the very least I want to live to see the day where I take Condan's leg and you take his life. And if I live past then, which now I hope I do, I want to live to see you finally be happy, Erika."

She shook her head against me.

"You and I," I started, but stopped to fight the tears that were pushing back. "Adam was the one who made us feel like we weren't alone. He's gone, and I'm not. So I gotta do that for him now, okay?"

I started to sob then. To wail.

The loss. That hurt way more than losing my leg. It wasn't a hole in my limb, it was a cavern in my chest, consuming my very ability to breathe. I felt hollow in the space between my ribs. Erika shifted, burying her face just there.

I heard her breath me in, then she moved her head back so her heart was pressed against me. I ran my fingers through her hair and pulled her in until it felt as if she herself was filling the void.

We laid there like that until the fire was nothing but hot embers, quietly popping by our feet.

"My mum will inherit a lot of money and a house," I said into the silence when our crying had stopped. "She'll probably think I was a drug dealer and not some excavator."

Erika laughed in broken bits. "Well, you'll be dead so you won't have to explain it."

I laughed then too. The sadness was still there, holding the laughter back a bit, but it came through nonetheless.

"I guess that's one plus side," I said. "Downside, she gets my house so now I'm homeless."

Erika shrugged, pressing her shoulder into my side. "Darbie and Jack always have rooms available."

"Mmm," I moaned uncomfortably. "I really don't need to live with my practically married couple, overly doting friends. Especially not with the fact that I'm mono-legged now."

Erika finally created a genuine, wholehearted laugh. One that vibrated into my body through our connected chests and spread through me.

"They will definitely be constantly bugging you," she said. "'Ethan, do you need some more soup?' or 'Ethan, do you need me to help you to the bathroom?'" She mocked and we laughed the faintest bit harder.

"Oh geez," I cringed at the mere thought of it before I even spoke it into existence. "Those two would one hundred percent offer to shower with me."

And then we were both cringing. Then laughing. Then nothing. Just our breaths, and the stars and the pain that was still there but lessened.

"Does it scare you that we handle death too well?" She asked.

I scoffed at the notion. "No we don't, E. We just bury it and ignore the fact that we're burying ourselves along with it."

The quiet fell in again. I took the time to breathe in the world around me. It still smelt of jasmine, but I couldn't tell any more if it was from the world, or from the girl laying on top of me.

"You can live with me," she whispered.

For the first time since we had laid down, I drew my head up and looked down at her. She raised her head so that she could look at me too.

Her whole face was swollen and red. Her bottom lip was raw from where she had probably been chewing it in an attempt to stop the weeping.

"The cottage has plenty of space for two people," she said, struggling to meet my eye. "It'll go to Darbie so we can still live there without needing to buy it back from the family. The furniture is there, just waiting to be built."

I shook my head, trying not to feel guilty at the idea of filling the space that was meant to be filled by Adam.

"Ethan," she shook me and I couldn't help but feel torn at the sound of her begging. "I can't live with Darbie and Jack who will walk around and treat us like we're made of glass. But I also can't survive living in that place alone."

I sat up straight, nearly throwing Erika off me.

I was frustrated.

'Then sell it," I snapped. "Listen, it's one thing for me to comfort you since Adam was my best friend and he's not here to do it. But I'm not sure I can take living in a place that was meant to be his home either. So just sell it. And we'll get another."

She shook her head. "No, I can't sell it!"

"Why the fuck not?!"

"Because it was meant to be his home!" she screamed my own words back at me

422

I closed my eyes, not able to look into hers. They were so green in the contrast of the red that the tears had caused. It was like they were lit with pain and I was being forced to look directly into the light of suffering.

"Okay, E," I submitted, opening my eyes again. "Since I think it's a good idea for us to live together, and since you can't let that place go, I will live there with you. But only until you get to a place where you can let it go. Then we sell it. Or donate it to his brother. Anything other than live in it. Okay."

"Okay," she agreed, then asked, "My roommate and my general?"

I looked at the pyre, then at her.

"Show me those worst parts of you," I demanded. "Then, show me how to burn it."

She recoiled, leaning back with uncertainty.

"If I'm going to be your general," I clarified. "I need to know your weaknesses. You need to know mine. Then we need to help burn them out of each other."

She shifted back, looking at me with confidence. Then she stood up. She brushed the dirt off her pants before reaching down to help me up.

I held on tight to the walking stick Darbie had given me for the time being.

"You want to burn out my weakness?" she asked. "Okay. Then get on that pyre and burn to death. Then my only weaknesses will lay here as ashes, completely burned out of existence."

"I don't understand," I whispered and reached out to cup her cheek instinctually.

She wrapped her hand around it, while the other reached out to tap the centre of my chest.

"If I die, you will keep living as a normal human," she said. "But if you die, you take my soul with you now. That's what the dragonrider bound does. It shares our strength by giving you the power over our very life." Her nail beat against me. "You are my rawest, most vulnerable weakness now."

I brought my hand in to rest over her's, only managing to touch her with my fingertips as the walking stick got in the way.

"If I die, you die," I echoed and she nodded.

"But if I die, you get to go back to being normal."

I shook my head.

"No, E. If you die, I'm dying too."

Read the Poem That Inspired the Book
"Kubla Khan" or "A Vision in a Dream: A Fragment"
by S.T. Coleridge

425

Erika, Ethan, and all their problems will return in Book Three: Part One of the Friends of Dragons Trilogy: *Of Marble Men and Maidens*

Other Upcoming Works from Feather Publishing:

<u>Upcoming works:</u>

To the Boy I Loved when I was Twenty by K.R. Feather

He's a Knockout by Clara Coast

A Collection of Poems: On Joy and Other Miseries by K.R. Feather

<u>Works Currently Available on Amazon and Kindle:</u>

Blessèd Creatures: Book One of the Friends of Dragons Trilogy By K.R.Feather

A Collection of Poems: On Death and Life by K.R. Feather

Epilogue

Erika

The wizard flipped through his massive spell book. He was muttering under his breath while his little satyr minion struggled to finish etching runes into the ground in a circle around us. The ground was grey, thick rock and it took him scrubbing the ground with a sharpened stone to get the symbols to stay.

Each rune was about a foot in diameter, and spaced out so that one lay in front of each of the eight pillars representing the eight phases of the moon.

A demon was two pillars to my left, and an angel was two to my right. The demon was gagged and chained to the new moon pillar, his black blood running into the circular trench at his feet like the outline of a hollow moon. The angel was unconscious and bleeding gold down into a full size basin, glowing like the full moon who's pillar she was tied to.

Across from me was Ethan, who was just beginning to show signs of awakening after I knocked him out and dragged him to this mad man's front door.

In the pillars between the demon, angel, and us, were four other minor magick creatures. A half-satyr half-nymph with fiery red hair and adorable freckles across her entire green body; a demi-demi-god on Ethan's left who was trying to summon some sort of deity in ancient egyptian, but he didn't have enough juice to get his voice out to anyone; and two bound sirens, who were hanging from the pillar by their feet so that their heads could dangle into buckets of water, were beginning to shed their scales around their bare legs from how hot it was inside the summoning chamber we were in.

While the magick altar we were all currently on was solid rock, just fifty feet below and completely surrounding us, was raging hot magma.

We were chained to a summoning altar built into the depths of an active volcano.

Why?

Well, two reasons really. One, evil villains like to look cool, so they choose unnecessarily dramatic locations to do spooky shit, and, two, because we needed answers and there was a chance this spooky villain had some.

"Mortality…" the wizard mumbled as he ran his finger down the index of the red, skin bound book. "See also Death, the Inevitable: Oblivion."

"Do we wish to make them oblivious, sir?" the satyr asked.

The wizard, who was old, thin, frail, and completely unstable both physically and mentally, swung his arm around, cascading lightning through the air until it zapped the ground next to where the poor young satyr was standing.

"Shut up, imbecile," the old wizard screeched. "Oblivion as in endlessness, not as in stupid such as you! We're looking for a spell to take their life spans and give them to me."

I cleared my throat and jiggled the chains holding my hands above my head so that I could give the old man a wave.

"Excuse me," I called. "Yoohoo. Over here."

The old man let his head fall back before he turned to face me. He was shaking as he walked closer, his hands not stable enough without the other to hold the book within their grasp. He had a gnarly case of Parkinson's, and judging by his age, I bet crippling Dementia was just around the corner.

He was looking for the fountain of youth to reverse the effects.

"What do you want, *thing*?" he grumbled and he hobbled closer.

His eyes were a very dark blue, and I could see the grey of wet macular degeneration around his irises. He was also going blind.

"First of all," I started. "I'm not a thing. Just because you don't know what I am, doesn't mean I don't have feelings too. Secondly, the spell you're looking for isn't under *Life*, or *Death*, or *Immortality*. It's under *Absorption*. Because, you know, you're going to absorb our years of life in order to add to yours. I feel like that should've been obvious."

"You're telling him what spell to use?" the demi-demi-god screamed from his pillar. "Are you crazy?"

He was a well built man. Very golden in skin. Ebony in hair and silver in the eyes. Very attractive all around. But let me tell you, he sounded like a girl.

"My guy," I shouted back at him. "I don't know about you, but my arms are sorta getting tired from being chained above my head for the last two hours while we watched these guys flip through pages and draw on the floor."

"That's two more hours of us getting to live!" he shrieked some more.

"Silence!" the old man yelled.

He may have had some shaky hands but boy definitely didn't have a shaky set of pipes.

"Yeah, silence," I echoed. "After all, you're not gonna die, so don't worry about it."

The wizard's head snapped back to look at me. "What do you mean you're not going to die? I have-"

"Like I said," I interrupted. "Don't worry about it. By the way, what's your's and the satyr's names? I'd feel bad just calling you old wizard and satyr for the rest of my days."

The old wizard furrowed his brows, his long, thin beard shaking with him as he looked back and forth between the satyr and me.

"His name is Sir Charles and I'm Imbecile," the satyr stated proudly.

"Wait," I paused. "Your name is actually imbecile?"

"Yup," Imbecile announced proudly. "Sir gave it to me when he first found me."

"Oh, that's so fucked up," I whispered to myself, before then raising my voice and asking; "Do me a favour Imbee, chuck a rock over at the human's head will you?"

"And why should he do that?" Sir Charles the Wizard snapped.

I blinked three times in rapid succession.

"It'd be funny?" I said with so much uncertainty that it came out more as a question.

Imbecile shrugged before chucking a rock full force at Ethan. He completely missed his head and hit him right in the crotch instead...

On second thought...

I guess that means he didn't miss his head...

But I digress.

Ethan's eyes shot open as he cringed forward. He struggled to breath in normally and he cradled his own crotch with his legs as his hands were chained above him.

"E," he grunted out. "I don't know how, but I know this is your fault."

430

I started to laugh, but stifled it.

"Hey, Ethan," I called over to him.

"What?" he snapped.

"Ask this guy the questions for me."

"I'm kind of busy mourning my lost progeny, over here."

I rolled my eyes.

"Shut up," I called back. "You're fine."

"I'm going to slap you when we get home," he snapped back.

"You don't believe in hitting women."

He straightened his back, the pain finally passing. "For you I'll make an exception."

"Are you two together?" Sir Charles the Wizard asked, motioning back and forth between us. "A human and a... whatever she is?"

"Would it be weird if we were?" I shot back.

"Well us humans are sort of powerless, weak, and destined for short lives," Sir Charles the Wizard-of-Racism, commented.

"Damn," Ethan winced. "My own species letting me down."

"Technically he's just your own race," I argued. "Species is defined as a class of organisms that can have kids together, so *technically* everyone in this circle is your species, just a different race."

"I'm not really interested in an angel or a satyr," Ethan argued.

I sighed. "Just because you're not interested doesn't mean that you couldn't have half human babies, just means you won't."

"Can you two get to the fucking point?" The demi-demi-god yelled in his panicked tone. "What are you going to ask him and how can you promise we won't die?"

"Right," I agreed with him then turned back to Ethan. "Ask the man if you will."

Ethan rolled his neon blue eyes between his thick blanket of black lashes, shaking his head in annoyance.

He pursed his lips.

Looked at me.

Sighed.

Looked at Sir Charles the Wizard-of-Racism-and-Shit-Merlin-Beards.

Sighed again.

"Alright, dude," Ethan started. "Has a creepy looking grey elf with a dead eye and super lushious white hair stopped by to ask you for that book in exchange for anything?"

The wizard looked back at me with raised eyebrows. When I just smiled at him, he turned back to Ethan.

"No," he said without hesitation.

Ethan's shoulders fell. "Are you sure? He's got the dead eye that's super eerie, but also a gold one that's just as unsettling. Does that sound familiar?"

"Nope, never met him," the elder reaffirmed.

"Absolutely positi-"

"Oh for fucks sake," demi-demi-god shouted. "He said no, now get us out of here!"

"Jeezuz, dude," I said back calmly. "Are you trying to stall to save a few minutes of life or speed us up to get it over with? Makeup your mind."

"You said we aren't going to die," he argued. "So whatever you two are planning, just get it over with."

432

I shrugged. "Well. I guess since this was a dead end, might as well wrap it up."

I looked up to the iron chains with enchanted runes etched into them, making them repellent to magick.

Fintan's fire was a thousand times older and stronger than the runes. His heat was nothing short of celestial rays.

Ethan and I both melted through our chains like they were chocolate. When I was done, I wiped the wet metal off my wrists and flicked it to the ground as I strolled up to Charles.

He shuffled back, fear burning in his eyes as he tried desperately to search through the book for some sort of spell to protect him from me. I let my eyes burn like embers just to entice him into more fear.

"Tell me, Charles," my voice came out in waves mixed with Fintan's and the wizard peed himself as I looked over his age-shrunken body. "If I heal you, make you young again, when the age comes back, will you take your death peacefully, or will you try once again to consume the lives of others."

"Oh he'll definitely do it again," Imbecile chirped happily. "This is the fifth spell we've done. Each one helped him to grow younger and live long enough for us to find stronger ones."

I looked from Imbecile to Ethan who silently summoned his dragon armour, covering his body head to toe in ebony so dark that it absorbed him like a void. In between each body of thick plate armour was chains of molten red, linking each piece together like streams of lava. His white and silver sword reflect the black volcanic-rock-like gloss of his armour in the sheen of the blade. The head of a molten red dragon came down over his face leaving only his chin below, like his mouth was half dragon's teeth and half human lips. His eyes glow against the light of the red, turning the beautiful clear blue into liquid fire, swirling within his skull.

433

Had he been the one standing in front of Charles instead of me, the elderly man's heart would have stopped beating.

Ethan wore my armour in such a fashion, that even I would sometimes mistake him for Death himself.

I looked back to Charles.

"How old are you?" I asked.

He hesitated, but inevitably, his own narcissism was his demise. He thought he was worth more than other's lives and he was clearly desperate for power. Someone so in love with themselves can't help it, they feel the need to brag about the power they possess.

"I'm two hundred and seventy two," he smiled and I could see the decay beginning to eat away at his teeth.

"And how many have you killed?" I balled my hands into fists so tight I broke the skin of my palms.

"My first spell required me to kill my entire town of fifty," he boasted. "The second was more, maybe a hundred. Then another twenty. And then ten, and now these eight."

"That's nearly two hundred lives," I counted in disbelief. "One soul is only worth one year for you. You disgust me."

Ethan stepped forward, impaling his sword through the man until his hilt was pressed flush against his spine and the blade rose into the air in front of him. He raised the bleeding murderer into the air as the elder curled into himself in pain, blood spewing from his core as his weight caused him to shift downwards, ripping him open against the blade.

Ethan swung the blade one direction gently before rapidly and forcefully swinging it the opposite, chucking the frail body over the sides of the altar and plummeting towards the lava.

When that was done, Ethan banished the armour and sword, revealing his solid and dark natural body. Tattoos now

434

danced up and down his arms making his skin more black than cream.

But even the darkness of the colour in his skin became bright when bonded with the clarity of his turquoise eyes or the softness of his coral lips. He was like a black opal. There was no distinct place where his darkness ended and his light began. He simply was both, wrapped in precious gemstone, made only brighter after being scored in fire.

"Well that was another dead end," he said, settling his gaze on me.

"Not without its benefits though," I pointed out. "Saved some lives today."

"And brought about some justice," he added. "I guess you knocking me out to offer me as a sacrifice and then lobbing something at my balls paid off."

"I did not lob anything at anyone," I argued. "The satyr did that."

I pointed over at the satyr who was wandering over to the edge where his master was flung over just moments ago.

"Speaking of," Ethan wondered. "We should probably get the rest of the victims down and figure out what to do with the supporting role over there."

"And then after we can get adobada tacos?" I asked.

Ethan shook his head and gave me a chuckle. "Sure. We can portal to Mexico for a taco trip."

I balled my fist and jerked my arm down towards me in an excited pump.

"Means I don't have to clean dishes tonight," I celebrated.

Ethan rolled his eyes. "Living with you and going Condan hunting has really opened my eyes to how lazy you are."

"I'm just saving my energy," I said.

"For what?"

"For when I rip Condan's skeleton out of his frigid fucking body."

Made in the USA
Columbia, SC
06 June 2024

36523960R00262